D0974335

"John Lutz knows how to make you shiver."
—Harlan Coben

"Lutz offers up a heart-pounding roller coaster
of a tale."
—Jeffery Deaver

"John Lutz is one of the masters of the police novel."
—Ridley Pearson

"John Lutz is a major talent."
—John Lescroart

"I've been a fan for years."
—T. Jefferson Parker

"John Lutz just keeps getting better and better."
—Tony Hillerman

"Lutz ranks with such vintage masters
of big-city murder
as Lawrence Block and Ed McBain."
—*St. Louis Post-Dispatch*

"Lutz is among the best."
—*San Diego Union*

"Lutz knows how to seize and hold the
reader's imagination."
—*Cleveland Plain Dealer*

"It's easy to see why he's won an Edgar
and two Shamuses."
—*Publishers Weekly*

Pulse

"One of the ten best books of the year."
—*Strand* magazine

"Grisly murders seen through the eyes of killer and victim; crime scenes from which clues slowly accumulate; a determined killer . . . compelling."
—*Booklist*

Serial

"Wow, oh wow, oh wow . . . that's as simple as I can put it. You gotta read this one."
—*True Crime Book Reviews*

Mister X

"A page-turner to the nail-biting end . . . twisty, creepy whodunit."
—*Publishers Weekly* (starred review)

Urge to Kill

"A solid and compelling winner . . . sharp characterization, compelling dialogue and graphic depictions of evil. . . . Lutz knows how to keep the pages turning."
—*BookReporter.com*

Darker Than Night

"Readers will believe that they just stepped off a Tilt-A-Whirl after reading this action-packed police procedural."
—*The Midwest Book Review*

Night Victims

"John Lutz knows how to ratchet up the terror. . . . He propels the story with effective twists and a fast pace."
—*Sun-Sentinel*

The Night Watcher

"Compelling . . . a gritty psychological thriller. . . . Lutz draws the reader deep into the killer's troubled psyche."
—*Publishers Weekly*

Final Seconds

"Lutz always delivers the goods, and this is no exception."
—*Booklist*

ALSO BY JOHN LUTZ

Pulse

Switch (e-short)

Serial

Mister X

Urge to Kill

Night Kills

In for the Kill

Chill of Night

Fear the Night

Darker Than Night

Night Victims

The Night Watcher

The Night Caller

Final Seconds (with David August)

The Ex

Single White Female

*featuring Frank Quinn

Available from Kensington Publishing Corp. and
Pinnacle Books

JOHN LUTZ

TWIST

PINNACLE BOOKS
Kensington Publishing Corp.
www.kensingtonbooks.com

PINNACLE BOOKS are published by

Kensington Publishing Corp.
119 West 40th Street
New York, NY 10018

All Kensington titles, imprints, and distributed lines are available at special quantity discounts for bulk purchases for sales promotions, premiums, fund-raising, educational, or institutional use. Special book excerpts or customized printings can also be created to fit specific needs. For details, write or phone the office of the Kensington special sales manager: Kensington Publishing Corp., 119 West 40th Street, New York, NY 10018, attn: Special Sales Department; phone 1-800-221-2647.

ISBN-13: 978-0-7860-2829-0
ISBN-10: 0-7860-2829-7

First printing: October 2013

10 9 8 7 6 5 4 3 2 1

Printed in the United States of America

First electronic edition: October 2013

ISBN-13: 978-0-7860-3311-9
ISBN-10: 0-7860-3311-8

For James Richard Pope

Too soon gone

PART ONE

Who is this woman with us in the dawn?
Whose is the flesh our feet have
  moved upon?

—HART CRANE, *The Harbor Dawn*

1

Medford County, Kansas, 1984

Abbey Taylor trusted to God and Ford to get her into Medford so she could buy some groceries. She was driving the family's old pickup truck. It was harder and harder for her to get around, much less into town, so she figured she should take advantage of feeling good on a nice sunny day and load up on whatever she could afford.

Billy had stayed home from work again today and was sleeping off another night out with his buddies. That involved plenty of meth, which was why he was in no condition to go in to work as an auto mechanic in Medford. All he wanted was to lie on the old vinyl couch and listen to some natter-head on the radio railing about how crooked the government was. Hell, everybody knew that already.

So Abbey, in her ninth month of pregnancy, left Billy to his anarchist dreams and waddled out to the old truck parked in the shade.

The truck was black, so it soaked up the sun, and as soon as she managed to climb inside, Abbey cranked down the windows. That let a nice breeze in, scented by the nearby stand of pine trees.

She turned the ignition key one bump, and needles moved on the gauges. The gas gauge, which was usually accurate, indicated over a quarter of a tank. Abbey knew from experience that would carry her into town and back.

The engine stuttered once and then turned over and ran smoothly enough, though it did clatter some. She released the emergency brake, shoved the gear-shift lever into first. The truck bucked some when she turned onto the dirt road, but she got it going smoothly in second and kept it in that gear so she could navigate around the worst of the ruts and holes. One particular bump was so jarring that she feared for the baby.

Soon she was on blacktop, and she put the truck in gear and drove smoothly along. The ride into town was pretty, the road lined with conifers and old sycamore trees and cottonwoods. The warm breeze coming through the open windows whisked away most of the oil and gas odor seeping up through the floorboards.

About halfway to town, on a slight hill, the motor began to run rough and seemed to lose power.

Abbey stomped down on the clutch and jammed the truck into a lower gear. That got her more power, but only briefly.

Then the engine chattered and died, and she steered the truck to the slanted road shoulder.

Abbey cursed herself for trusting the old truck. And she was worried about how Billy was going to react when he found out she'd run out of gas on the little traveled county road to Medford.

She heard a hissing sound and saw steam rising from beneath the hood. A closer look at the gauges showed that she hadn't run out of gas at all. The truck had simply overheated. She thought of Billy at home on the couch.

Where's a mechanic when you need one?

At least it had happened where she'd been able to steer the balky vehicle into the shade.

Abbey tried to judge just where she was stranded. It was almost the halfway point, and a far walk for anyone, much less a woman in her ninth month of pregnancy.

What if . . .

But Abbey didn't want to think about that.

She opened the door and kicked it wide with her left foot, then wrestled herself sideways out from behind the steering wheel. It was less trouble than it might have been because the truck was on a slant to the left, and her real problem was to catch herself when her feet contacted the ground and keep her balance so she wouldn't go rolling down the grade. Despite her problems, thinking of what that might look like made her almost smile.

Abbey stood with her hand against the sun-heated metal of the front fender for a moment, gaining her balance, then waddled around to the front of the truck.

Steam was still rolling out from underneath, but the hissing had stopped. She knew then that she'd screwed up. She wanted to see what the problem might be, but she'd forgotten to release the hood latch in the truck's cab. Keeping both hands on the truck to help keep her balance, she made her way back to the open door on the driver's side.

She was halfway there when she heard the sound of a motor.

So there was another vehicle on the county road!

Abbey felt like singing with relief.

Then she realized she might have a problem. There was no guarantee the driver of whatever was coming would notice the truck pulled well off the shoulder like it was.

She tried to make her way back to the road side of the truck, all the while listening to the approaching car or truck motor getting louder.

Damn! It went past her. A dusty white van with tinted windows, rocking along faster than was lawful. Its radio or cassette player had been on. Abbey had heard a snatch of music as it passed.

Wait! She heard music now. A rock band. Sounded like the Stones' "(I Can't Get No) Satisfaction."

Abbey thought, *Ain't that the truth?*

Then she heard the motor, growing louder.

She *had* been seen! The van was backing up.

She glimpsed it between the trees, then it rolled backward around the shallow bend and slowed.

It parked only a few feet from the truck. Mick Jagger shouted, *"I cain't get no—I cain't get no—"* as the van's door opened and a heavyset, smiling woman awkwardly got down from behind the steering wheel and slammed the door shut behind her.

She was tall as well as bulky, and stood with her thick arms crossed, looking at Abbey, then the truck and the puddle beneath its front bumper, then back at Abbey. Her smile widened, showing bad teeth with wide spaces between them. Though badly in need of dental work, it was a kind smile and Abbey was glad to return it.

"Hell," the woman said, "you got yourself a problem, sweetheart. But it ain't hopeless." Her voice was highly pitched but authoritative, each word abrupt.

"The engine just stopped on me," Abbey said. "Overheated."

"I'll say. I'm familiar with these things." She strode over to the truck, the soles of her faded gray tennis shoes crunching on the gravel. "You know where the hood latch is?"

Abbey shrugged.

The woman went around to the driver's-side door and opened it, reached inside and did something. The hood jumped upward a few inches. She slammed the truck door shut then walked around and raised the hood all the way, exposing the engine and the steaming radiator.

"Don't s'pose you carry any water," she said.

Abbey shook her head no. "Maybe we oughta take the cap off the radiator. It might make it cool down faster."

"Burn your hand, sweetheart. Maybe your whole damn arm. Gotta let these things run their course." She propped her fists on her hips and glanced up and down the road. "Ain't what you'd call heavily traveled."

"Never is."

"And you, in your delicate condition, oughta be someplace outta the sun."

"Couldn't argue that."

"My name's Mildred," the woman said.

"Abigail Taylor. Or just Abbey."

"You was headed for Medford?"

"Was."

"I'm goin' that direction, Just Abbey. How about I drive you there, you do whatever it is you gotta do, then we can come back this way with a jug or two of water. That might be all you need to get back home. You got a husband?"

Abbey was taken slightly aback by the question. "Sure do. He's home sleepin' now. Had hisself a rough night."

"Men!" Mildred said. "Still tryin' to get at you, I bet."

"Uh, no," Abbey said. "It's close enough now, that's stopped till after the baby."

"Baby good an' healthy?"

Abbey had to smile. "Doctor says so."

Mildred held her arm to balance her as they walked over to the van; then she helped Abbey up onto the passenger seat, next to the driver's.

Abbey settled into the seat while Mildred climbed up behind the steering wheel and got the van started. It rode kind of bumpy, but Abbey was glad to be moving.

"Gotta stop by my place and pick up somethin' on the way into town," Mildred said. "You mind?"

"Not at all," Abbey said.

Mildred turned the air conditioner on high and aimed one of the dashboard vents directly at Abbey.

"Too much?"

"Just right," Abbey said.

The day wasn't turning out to be such a disaster, after all. And she'd made a new friend.

She couldn't have been more wrong.

2

Some people thought it would never rain again in New York. It had been almost a month since a drop of moisture had made it to the ground. The sky remained almost cloudless. The brick and stone buildings, the concrete streets and sidewalks, were heating up like the walls and floor of a kiln that didn't cool all the way down at night.

Quinn was fully dressed except for his shoes. He was asleep on the sofa in the brownstone on West Seventy-fifth Street, lying on his back with an arm flung across his eyes to keep out the sunbeam that seemed to be tracking him no matter which way he turned.

The sun had sent a beam in beneath a crookedly closed drape, and an elongated rectangle of sunlight lay with geometric precision in the middle of the carpet. The brownstone didn't have central air, and the powerful window units were running almost constantly, barely holding the summer heat at bay.

Quinn was a big man, and solid. He took up most of the sofa. Ordinarily he'd be working this afternoon, but business was slow at Quinn and Associates Investigative Agency.

Quinn knew Pearl was holding down the office. Fedderman was talking to a man in Queens whose car kept being stolen again and again. Sal Vitali and Harold Mishkin were down in New Jersey, keeping close watch on a wayward wife, whose husband had hired Q&A to see if she was cheating on him, and was himself cheating on her. Quinn knew the parties were, most likely, more in need of a marriage counselor than a detective agency.

He'd seen this before. Harold Mishkin would probably wind up consoling and counseling. He was a friend and mediator to all humankind, and probably should never have been a cop. The NYPD, the violent streets of New York, hadn't seemed to coarsen him or wise him up over the years. It was a good thing his partner, Sal Vitali, looked out for him.

Maybe because of the heat and drought, crime seemed to be taking a break in New York City. Legal chicanery was no doubt still going strong, but only a small percentage of the illegal was finding its way to Q&A. The cheating married couple, the guy with the stolen and stolen car. That was about it for now.

Quinn stirred. He knew someone had entered the living room. Jody Jason, Pearl's daughter, and Quinn's ersatz daughter, who lived upstairs. He didn't move his arm or open his eyes. " 'Lo, Jody."

"How'd you know it was me?"

"Your perfume."

"I'm not wearing any."

"The distinctive sound of your shoes on the stairs."

"I'm in my stocking feet."

"Okay," Quinn said, opening his eyes and scooting up to a sitting position. "You and I are the only ones in the house, so it had to be you."

"Not exactly a Sherlock moment," she said.

Jody, skinny, large-breasted like her mother, with springy red hair *un*like her mother's raven black hair, grinned at him. Pearl was in the grin, all right. "Occam's razor," she said. She was kind of a smart-ass.

That attitude could help her in her work. She was an associate attorney with a small law firm, Prather and Pierce, that fought the good fight against big business, big government, big anything that had deep pockets. The average age of the attorneys at Prather and Pierce was about twenty-five.

"I didn't know Occam needed a shave."

"Always." She headed for the kitchen. "Want some coffee?"

"No, it might make me vibrate."

"Something cool?"

"Makes more sense."

He heard her fidget around in the kitchen, then she reappeared with a mug in each hand. "Don't worry," she said. "Yours is orange juice."

If it moves, sue it, was lettered on the mugs. She handed him his orange juice and then settled down across from him in a chair, tucking her jeans-clad legs beneath her slender body. "Business will pick up," she said.

"Not if some guy's car stops getting stolen."

"Huh?"

Quinn tilted back his head and downed half his orange juice. It was cold and tasted great. "This case Fedderman's on. Guy's a graffiti artist, uses spray paint, dolled up his car so good it keeps getting stolen."

"He should take some color photos of the car, leave them stuck under a wiper blade. Maybe the thieves will be satisfied with a picture and leave the real thing at the curb."

"I'll suggest that to Fedderman."

"Feds will understand."

"Like Occam."

Jody looked off to the side and thought for a moment. "No," she said, "like Feds."

"Sometimes," Quinn said, "you are eerily like your mother."

"That a compliment?"

"A warning."

She took a long sip of her coffee. "Business will pick up," she assured Quinn. "In this city, with all the dealing and stealing that has to be set right, Q&A will get its share. Maybe something by way of your friend Renz."

"I'd rather Renz not be involved. He complicates things."

"Still," Jody said, "he's the police commissioner."

"Occam with a beard," Quinn said. "And unshaven scruples."

"Yeah," Jody replied. "That's more like normal life."

"If there is such a thing," Quinn said, finishing off his orange juice. He licked his lips. "Any more of this in the fridge?"

"Nope. Nothing cold except beer and bottled water."

"Let me think," Quinn said.

3

Medford County, 1984

Umph! That couldn't have been good for the baby. Abbey held onto the armrest and console so she wouldn't bump around so much.

Mildred turned the dusty white van onto a narrow dirt road, then hard left onto a gravel driveway that wound uphill through the trees. Clumps of dirt and stones clunked off the insides of the wheel wells.

The driveway leveled off, and the van jounced over a yard that was mostly weeds and bare earth. Mildred parked in the shade near a ramshackle house with sagging gutters and a plank front porch. It needed paint so badly it was impossible to know what color it had been. Nearby, at the end of a curved walkway set with uneven stepping stones, was a wooden outhouse.

"Don't believe what ya see," Mildred said. "We've had indoor plumbing a good while."

Abbey could only nod.

"I'll leave the motor running and the AC on so you'll be comfortable," Mildred said. She struggled down out of the van and slammed the door behind her.

Abbey saw her go into the house, then emerge a few minutes later with a large cardboard box. The van's rear doors opened. One of them squeaked loudly. Abbey craned her neck to glance back and see what was going on, only to find that the back of the van was sealed off by unpainted plywood, blocking her view. She could hear Mildred moving around back there, loading the box, or whatever it held, into the vehicle.

After about fifteen minutes, gravel and leaves crunched and Mildred appeared outside the door on Abbey's side. She opened the door.

"C'mon down outta there, sweetheart. I wanna show you something."

"Is it important?" Abbey asked, remembering how difficult it had been to climb into the van.

"I would sure say so." Mildred smiled.

Abbey didn't have her seat belt fastened, because of the baby, so she swiveled her body awkwardly and controlled her breathing while Mildred's strong hands helped her to back down out of the van.

When she gained her balance, Mildred held her by the elbow and supported her while they walked to the back of the van. Both doors were hanging wide open.

Mildred turned her so she could see into the back of the van.

Abbey didn't know quite what to think. The rear seats had been removed and there was black plastic covering the van's floor. Clouded white plastic was stuck with duct tape to the sides of the van and to the plywood panel separating the rear of the vehicle from the driver and passenger seats. There was nothing else in the van except for a medium-sized cardboard box up front by the plastic and plywood.

"Get in," Mildred said.

Abbey thought she must have misheard. "I beg your—"

"In!"

Mildred shoved Abbey forward so her knees were against the edge of the van floor, then placed a hand on the back of her neck and bent her forward so Abbey's palms were on the black plastic.

"Now listen here—"Abbey began. Her words were cut short by a hard blow to the back of her head.

"Crawl on up there!" Mildred said. "And mind you don't harm the baby."

"I don't—"

Another slap to the back of the head. "Get goin', you fat sow, and make sure your belly don't drag."

When Abbey had crawled painfully up into the back of the van, Mildred scrambled in beside her, looming over her, smelling of stale sweat.

"Wanna scream and get it over with?" Mildred asked. "Ain't nobody out here to hear you."

"I wanna know what the hell—"

A wide rectangle of duct tape was slapped across Abbey's mouth. She was pushed forward so all her weight was on her stomach. "Can't be helped, sweetheart," Mildred said by way of apology. There were ripping sounds—more tape being stripped from the roll. Mildred bent Abbey's arms behind her and taped her wrists together. "Now let's turn you over."

With practiced ease, Mildred crossed Abbey's ankles and wrestled her onto her back. The pain in Abbey's arms bound behind her was severe as the weight of her pregnancy settled. Mildred forced Abbey's left leg over and taped her ankle to a steel loop screwed into the van floor. Did the same with her right leg.

Abbey was lying with her legs spread now, unable to move, with Mildred between her knees. She had never felt so vulnerable.

Mildred, breathing hard from her effort, reached forward beyond Abbey, grunting as part of her weight came down on the bound woman. Abbey caught a whiff of her foul breath as Mildred strained to drag the cardboard box across the plastic on the floor, closer so she could reach inside.

Abbey was almost bursting with rage. If she could only get her hands around Mildred's fat throat she'd kill her!

She really felt that she could kill this woman!

More fetid breath as Mildred forced words through clenched teeth. "Careless bitch like you, in your delicate condition, take off in a rattletrap truck that overheats, don't deserve no baby. Oughta be a law."

Abbey stared at her. *What the hell does all that mean?*

Fear began to edge through Abbey's rage. Real fear. It had been in the background of her mind, waiting, as if primping to play its biggest role ever. Now it came to occupy every molecule of her bound body. Abbey understood that kind of fear. It meant she was aware of something she didn't yet fully comprehend, that she couldn't yet face.

But that she *must* face.

Mildred lifted a small folded white blanket from the box and laid it against the side of the van. She arranged it gently. Then she drew from the box a knife with a sharp point and a long, serrated blade.

Abbey thought her lungs might rupture as she screamed into the duct tape so hard that the muffled sound almost made it out of the van.

Mildred held up the knife so Abbey could see it.

"Know what happens now?"

Abbey knew.

4

He was real.

There he was again. He must know she got off work at Gowns 'n' Gifts at five o'clock, because shortly thereafter she would see him.

Though he kept his distance, he didn't seem to mind that she saw him.

Bonnie Anderson was sure she was being stalked. It had been going on for over a week. Each time she saw him she'd be more afraid. She *wasn't* imagining him. Though in truth she'd never gotten a clear look at him. Often his head was bowed so the bill of the cap he usually wore blocked or shadowed his face. But there was something about him, in his movements. A resoluteness. A man with something on his mind.

With me on his mind.

Bonnie shuddered and crossed the street.

He followed, of course.

She stopped.

He stopped.

Bonnie was a beauty, with long blond hair, a slender,

shapely body, and a face whose planes and angles had intrigued a college art class almost as much as the rest of her. That was all too apparent with the male students, which always amused Bonnie.

No doubt the man following her was similarly aroused, but he didn't amuse her. He scared her in a subtle way that made her body seem drugged.

She was sure he wanted her to see him, wanted her fear to grow. For some reason, he was nurturing her dread.

She glanced back over her shoulder, and there he was.

He stood now about a hundred feet behind her on the crowded sidewalk, statue still, and stared from beneath the shadowed arc of his ball-cap bill. It was odd how she couldn't see his eyes but *felt* them on her.

Her fear expanded, and with it her anger.

You want me to be afraid, you bastard!

She spun on her heel and walked directly toward him. *Cope with your fears by facing them.* He seemed to smile—she couldn't be sure—as he leisurely entered a nearby deli.

Without hesitation she followed him into the deli.

It wasn't much cooler in there than outside.

A gondola with steel trays of heated food ran down the middle of the deli. Shelves of packaged food were along one side wall. A series of glass-door coolers ran along the opposite wall, stacked with bottled and canned drinks and dairy products. Beyond the coolers, more shelves of groceries. People were milling about at the counter and among the shelves and coolers. A few of them were carrying wire baskets.

Bonnie looked around for the blue ball cap and didn't

see it. Didn't see the bastard. She went to the back of the deli and walked along the heads of the aisles, pausing to stare down each one.

He was gone. Somehow he was gone.

Had he been the product of her imagination? A mirage, maybe, from the heat.

Probably he wanted her to think that. Actually, he might have slipped back outside when she had her back momentarily turned and she was striding along the cooler aisle. He'd had time to manage that. Just.

Charging back out onto the sidewalk, Bonnie bumped into a woman hard enough to make her stagger.

"I'm sorry, too," the woman snarled

Everybody was irritable. The weather.

A male voice behind Bonnie said, "Bump into me, sweetheart."

She turned and saw a boy about sixteen leering at her. He wilted and backed away as she glared at him; then he walked past her and over by the curb without glancing back at her.

If only they were all so easy to discourage.

A dry breeze was blowing, turning the city into a convection oven. Bonnie wished to hell it would rain at least enough to cool down all the damned steel and concrete in the city. She looked up at the sky, not expecting to see a cloud. There were two small ones. They looked as dry as cotton.

Bonnie was only a few blocks from her apartment. She walked them uneasily, unable to keep her head still, trying to catch another glimpse of the man who'd been dogging her.

But she knew she wouldn't see him. He was through with her for now. She hoped.

* * *

Sal Vitali and Harold Mishkin sat in Sal's car and watched for Joan Plunket to emerge with her not-so-secret lover, Foster Oaks, from their room at the Blue Sparrow Motel in New Jersey. They both knew the couple would emerge soon. They must.

The detectives knew that Bob Plunket, Joan's husband, was right now in a Manhattan hotel room with his own not-so-secret lover, his fellow accountant Laura Loodner. Laura Loodner's husband, a jeweler named Marty, knew nothing and loved only his cat.

It was Bob Plunket who'd hired Q&A to get the goods on his wife, Joan.

It was Sal and Harold's job to keep track of this marital mess. The case involved a lot of staking out, spending time in the car as they were doing now, watching and waiting. Sal hated this part of detective work. He usually drove the car. Harold usually drove him crazy.

Like this evening, as the two men sat in Sal's old Taurus in the Blue Sparrow parking lot and watched and watched the door to room 256. It was a maroon door, like all the others, on a catwalk that looked down on a swimming pool where four or five teenagers were frolicking. Sal had only a quarter tank of gas, so they didn't want to roll the windows up and idle the engine so they could use the air conditioner. They sat with the windows down and were grateful for a slight, hot breeze moving through the car.

A short man but powerfully built, Sal had been Harold's partner in the NYPD for twelve years, where he'd fallen into the habit of looking out for the weak-stomached, sensitive Harold. The other thing about Harold was that he could be obtuse as well as brilliant,

and damned aggravating. But the two men were close,
like dogs that had for years gotten each other's backs in
a kennel full of biters. They were stuck with each other.
Harold didn't mind. Sal did, but he was resigned.

The teenagers, along with Harold, were making the
bored and jumpy Sal nervous with their noise. That
was why Sal had parked the Taurus here, under a shade
tree, still with an unbroken view of room 256, but with
greatly reduced noise from the pool area. Now Sal had
only Harold to endure. That was enough.

They'd both gotten tired of listening to music on the
radio, and besides, that was running down the battery,
so Sal switched off the radio and they simply sat and
watched and prayed for the door to 256 to open.

"Whaddya suppose they're doing in there?" Harold
asked.

Sal sighed. "Scrabble, most likely." He had a voice
like stones rattling around in a drum.

"I think our client's nuts," Harold said. "His wife is
twice the looker of that accountant chick."

"They work together," Sal said. "Office romance."

"Both accountants."

"Go figure."

"Figure what?

"Never mind."

Sal thought that might be the end of conversation
for a while, but he heard a loud ripping sound.

"Thought I might show you this," Harold said. "My
cousin Sedge, the one in advertising, gave me a tip,
and I'm passing it on to you."

Sal looked over to see that Harold was wearing what
looked like a black Velcro glove.

"New product," Harold said. "Sticky Hand. Sedge

has the advertising account, and they're going to do the stigma act on this and sell millions of them."

Sal said, "What in the hell is it? And what's the stigma act?" He looked hopefully at 256. It didn't move.

"Sticky hand is for people with HSS."

Sal yawned. "Which is?"

"Hair-shedding syndrome."

"Never heard of it."

"You will soon. After the stigma campaign."

Sal had to admit this sort of interested him. "There's going to be an HSS campaign?"

"Certainly is. TV, radio, newspapers. Attractive women won't get dates because men will notice the hair on their shoulders or arms. Hair from their own heads. They're shedding. The guy says to his guy friend, 'I like her, but she doesn't turn me on. Not with that HSS.' "

"Then what?"

"Then somebody tells her about Sticky Hand and her troubles are over."

"My God," Sal said.

"But Sticky Hand has other uses. Like with Larry."

"Who is?"

"Sedge's dog. He's a collie. Now, Larry sheds—"

"They're out," Sal said. He handed the camera to Harold, who had the better angle. Joan Plunket was standing on the catwalk outside 256, which was still open. Joan made sure her blouse was tucked in, smoothed her slacks. "Get that shot," Sal said, "when she's rearranging her clothes."

"That dog sheds all over everything—"

Foster Oaks appeared and closed the door to 256 behind him. His suit coat was tossed over his shoulder, like he was Frank Sinatra. He impulsively leaned down and kissed Joan Plunket on the lips. Used his free hand to caress her breast.

"Get that!" Sal said. "Get that one, Harold!"

"The average person sheds eighty hairs per day," Harold said. "Everyone will be ashamed to have HSS. Everyone will shed approximately eighty hairs per day. Approximately everyone will buy a Sticky Hand."

Joan and Foster Oaks were walking along the catwalk now, holding hands.

"Where's the shutter button on this thing?" Harold asked.

"Goddamn it, Harold!"

But Harold was smiling.

He passed the digital camera to Sal, who went to SLIDESHOW and clicked on it.

Harold had managed to get photographs of Joan Plunket and Foster Oaks that were almost pornographic.

Harold for you.

5

Bonnie realized she was walking too fast in this heat. Perspiration had soaked into her clothes and lay as a sheen on her arms.

I must not smell so good. Hope he doesn't notice.

She slowed down and relaxed somewhat, thinking about Rob Masters. She'd met him two weeks ago at Grounds for Everything, a neighborhood coffee shop. They'd fallen into easy conversation. He was a sales rep for a line of furniture. Bonnie was a sales clerk in a bridal shop. Gowns 'n' Gifts. Small world, both of them being in sales.

"I didn't think that many people still went in for large traditional weddings," he'd said, over his vanilla latte.

"You'd be surprised. There's a big demand for gowns and bridesmaid dresses."

"Not to mention gifts." He smiled. That was one of the things she liked most about him, his smile. It held nothing back, and was like a glimpse of something beautiful inside him. He was just . . . normal in the looks department, but you could trust a man who smiled like that.

Or did it mean he was a terrific con man?

After all, he was a salesman.

He'd made a sale with Bonnie, because she suddenly wanted to see him, to be with him. A whim. She followed whims a lot. They seemed to work out for her.

She entered Grounds, pleased to find that the coffee shop was coolly air conditioned. Maybe her clothes, her arms, would dry in the cooler air that wafted like a blessing across the floor and eddied about her ankles.

And there he was, sitting at a booth near the window. He didn't see her right away, and she found herself reassessing him. His looks grew on you. Sure, he wasn't classically handsome, but he was a pleasant-featured man, seemingly at ease with himself and the world. Not a head-turner, but worth a second look. He was leaning back in the padded booth, his legs extended and crossed at the ankles.

"The bridal gown beauty," he said, noticing her approach.

She nodded to him, smiling, and ordered a chocolate latte.

Don't throw yourself at him.

She didn't look his way again until she'd gotten her latte and moved toward the booth.

"You keep marrying them," he said, "and I'll sell them furniture." He sipped his latte and moved his legs out of the way so she could sit opposite him. "I often wondered, once the wedding and all the hoopla is over, what do women do with those bridal gowns?"

Bonnie shrugged. "Mostly they put them in a box with white tissue paper and seldom look at them again.

Sometimes they give them to their daughters to wear at *their* weddings."

Rob smiled. "Kinda nice."

"I think so."

"None of my business, but were you ever . . ."

She knew what he meant and was pleased. She'd wanted him to wonder. Wanted to get it out in the open.

"Married?" she said.

The smile.

"Once," she said. "When I was nineteen. It lasted four months. It was—"

"You don't have to tell me. I didn't mean to pry."

"No, no, it's okay. It was a mistake, is all. For both of us. We knew it and parted before any more damage was done."

"Damage being?"

"Kids. Neither one of us would have made a good parent."

"Really?" He was looking directly at her, into her. "I admire your honesty."

"I have a temper," she said.

Now he *was* interested. "No kidding?"

"Yeah. But it passes quickly. Like a summer storm. Still, I know I hurt people. I'd especially hurt a sensitive kid."

"Hurt physically, you mean?"

"No, I didn't mean that. But, to be honest, I guess it might be possible." She revolved her ceramic mug on its coaster. "Not everyone's made for the homey, domestic life."

"Yeah, that's true. So what *are* you made for?"

"I'm still looking, I guess. Right now, I just want to keep my job, pay my bills, and enjoy life." She gave him what she thought was her sultry look. "I'm still working on that last part."

He took a slow sip of coffee and regarded her carefully. They both knew the game. She'd given him his opening.

But all he said was, "This is damned good coffee."

She had other cards to play.

"I've got to admit I'm worried about something." She glanced around her.

"Getting in the way of the fun part?"

"I'll say. There's this guy who's been . . . well, stalking me."

He looked at her as if trying to bring her into focus. "You mean like he wants to do you harm?"

"I think so. I mean, I don't know what I think. But I look behind me, and there he is."

"You're a beautiful woman. You must be used to men following you."

"Stalking."

"Okay, that too. Aren't those guys usually harmless?"

"Usually, I'm sure. But I know he's giving me the willies."

"Maybe it's the drought and all this heat, making people behave in weird ways."

"This guy isn't a product of the drought."

"You could call the cops."

"Let's not kid ourselves."

"Yeah, they've got other things to do, supported by more evidence."

"What you said about the heat . . . maybe it makes sense. I read in the paper that crimes-against-persons statistics are higher. People do get crazy ideas in the heat. Tempers flare. Imaginations run wild."

He looked into his latte, looked up at her, back into his coffee. "Listen, if it'd make you feel any safer, I could walk you home, go in and look over your apartment, make sure the boogie man isn't there."

"Oh, that's too much trouble!"

"Not at all. You mentioned you live in the neighborhood."

"Four blocks away."

He shrugged. "Not much of a hike, even in this weather."

"No," she said, smiling at him in relief she didn't have to feign, "I guess it isn't." She shivered. Now her arms had goose bumps.

"Hey, you really *are* scared."

He thought they'd been playing a game. Well, they had been. Still were. Only the stakes might be higher than she imagined. The man in the blue cap *wasn't* her imagination.

Rob finished his latte and set the tall mug aside. "You ready to go?"

"As I'll ever be," she said.

Not quite, he thought. This would be a simple reconnaissance visit, then a good-night *trust me* kiss and a date for tomorrow night. There were preparations to make. A future and an end to plan.

Considerations as he stroked himself.

Matters to ponder.

No rush.

6

Two weeks later

After a good dinner with wine at an Italian restaurant.

Drinks.

Comfortable conversation, commiserations, confidences.

Drinks.

The now familiar walk to her apartment.

"There's some wine in the fridge," Bonnie said. "You wanna get it while I change?"

"White or red?" Rob asked. He placed his scuffed leather briefcase alongside the sofa and loosened his tie.

"Whatever's in there."

Bonnie walked into the bedroom and shut the door, then crossed the hall to the bathroom nude, glancing into the living room to see Rob's stocking feet. *Glad he's making himself comfortable.*

"With you soon," she said, and went into the bathroom.

She took a quick shower, not waiting for the water to

get warm enough. Shivering, she dried herself off. She'd kept her hair relatively dry, so it still looked good.

Standing before the full-length mirror that was mounted on the back of the bathroom door, she tried to decide: Nothing? Or something?

Something was always sexier, she decided. Besides, it was something to remove. She opened the bedroom door a crack, still could see the black socks in the living room, and darted nude across the hall into the bedroom.

Bonnie slipped her diaphanous pink negligee over her head, fluffed up her hair, then put on her slippers with the built up heels that made her calves look sexy.

Rob was on the sofa, fully dressed except for his shoes. He was sipping a glass of white wine. Another, full glass was before him on the coffee table. When he saw her, he appeared shocked, then he smiled.

"I guess there's no point in wasting time," he said. He stood up. "You have some wine. I'll take a quick shower, too, and then I'll be back."

"Gotta turn the hot water on high," she said after him, as he went down the hall toward the bedroom and bath.

He mumbled something indecipherable to let her know he'd heard.

Bonnie sipped some Chablis, noting that it didn't taste bad, considering how long it had lived in the refrigerator.

When the shower stopped hissing, she had to wait only a few minutes before Rob came back into the living room. He was completely nude, still with droplets from the shower on his shoulders. She was surprised by his physique, which appeared much more muscular without his clothes. Muscle and tendon played whenever he moved.

She remarked that he, too, didn't believe in wasting time.

Only it didn't come out that way. Instead she'd uttered a string of slurred, incomprehensible words.

Alarmed, she tried again.

Same result.

Beneath her puzzlement, fear took root. There was something in a far part of her mind she didn't want to think about, didn't want to face.

Rob seemed unsurprised by her inability to communicate.

She tried again and *could not* make sense.

The bastard! The sneaky bastard!

"You put something in my wine," she said, though it didn't sound like that at all.

He paid no attention to her. Wouldn't have understood her, anyway. He was bending over, picking up his brown leather briefcase. Inanely, she wondered if he was going to try to talk her into buying furniture. If he even sold furniture. There was no reason to think he hadn't lied to her about that, too.

My God! Like a rag doll!

She tried to move but could only wriggle enough so that she slumped down farther into the sofa cushions.

Rob opened the briefcase and withdrew a roll of gray duct tape. He held it up and smiled down at her. "Good for so many things," he said.

She tried to tell him to go to hell but made only a gurgling sound.

Damn him!

If she couldn't speak, maybe she could scream.

She opened her mouth to try, and he ripped off a rectangle of tape and slapped it over her half-open mouth.

"You almost figured that out in time," he said. Then he shrugged. "It wouldn't have been very loud, anyway. Be a good girl and maybe later I'll let you try again."

Bonnie attempted to rise from the sofa. Rob reached for her as if to help her stand. Instead he forced her upper body downward so she was in a seated position with her bent legs splayed out. Gripping the back of her neck and pushing her upper body down as far as it would go, he sat on her back to keep her down. She heard more tape being ripped off the roll, then felt it being wound around her wrists and ankles, fastening them together so she remained in her awkward, splay-legged, bent position, her bare back exposed.

He stood up, stretched, then looked around. Walking from window to window, he made sure again that all the blinds were closed.

Obsessive-compulsive, Bonnie thought through her agony and terror. Surely, while she was in the shower, he'd already made sure everything was sealed off from the outside world. She told herself she should have tried to understand him before now. If she'd applied her pop psychology to him instead of looking for what she so desperately wanted to see, she might have noticed something unusual about him.

Or not. He was so damned *usual*. He worked so hard at it. She could see that now, how difficult it must be for him to make normal look so effortless when he harbored such monstrous thoughts.

He lifted her from the sofa and placed her gently on the floor on her back so she was bound in her curled-forward position in the middle of the living room. The harsh carpet fibers made her back itch terribly.

She strained her neck to look to the side rather than at the limited view between her hands and bare feet. He was reaching again into his briefcase.

Bag of tricks . . .

He removed from the briefcase a plain yellow envelope, opened it, and slid out some eight-by-ten photographs.

He squatted low so he wouldn't have to bend over to show them to her.

They were vivid. They were in color. They were photos of a nude woman on her back, bound with tape the same way Bonnie was bound. Her stomach had been laid open in a wide U-shaped cut beneath her naval, arcing down low toward the pubis. Some of the woman's internal organs had been removed and were lying on the floor near her. Jutting from her exposed intestines was what looked like a plastic statuette of the Statue of Liberty.

Bonnie did everything she could to keep from vomiting, knowing she'd choke to death behind the firmly fastened rectangle of duct tape.

One by one he displayed the photos in front of her so she could see them. He didn't bother looking at them closely himself. He was interested in *her*.

"I want you to know what's happening," he said. "So we'll wait a while longer while the sedative wears off before we get truly serious. In the meantime . . ."

He reached into the briefcase and withdrew a coiled leather whip.

The pain began.

7

"Worked at a place called Gowns 'n' Gifts, over near Broadway," Renz said. "She was the ideal employee, never late even a minute. But she didn't show up for work this morning, so they sent somebody around, and this is what they found."

"This" was Bonnie Anderson, nude and lying on her back with her legs splayed, her abdomen laid open with a single curving slash. The wound was ragged, and the large flap of skin peeled back to reveal internal organs. A lot of blood had soaked into the living room carpet. There were footprints in the blood, but obscure ones.

Dr. Julius Nift, the obnoxious little ME, looked up at Quinn and said, "Where's Pearl?"

"Doing other things," Quinn said. "She'll be along later. I'll tell her you missed her."

Nift smiled. "I do wish you would." He loved to get under Pearl's skin and seemed sincere in lamenting her absence.

There were half a dozen radio cars parked outside, and CSU techs were in the other rooms, already finished in this one.

"Why did you call me?" Quinn asked Renz.

Renz was wearing his full police commissioner's uniform today. There must be a ceremony scheduled. A bead of sweat escaped from his hat and tracked down his forehead. Renz noticed Quinn studying him.

"Funeral today," Renz explained. "Detective Norman Land."

Land had been killed while pursuing a burglar in the Garment District last week. "One of the good ones," Quinn said.

He looked again at the dead woman. She'd been young, in her twenties. There was the usual duct tape plastered over her mouth, distorted by her attempts to scream.

Her eyelids had been removed, giving her a startled expression that Quinn knew he would never forget.

"Why did you call me?" he asked again.

"Because it's obvious we've got a serial killer here. This is not a good time for that to be happening. My special review and reappointment are coming up next month."

Renz had gotten into trouble over some missing drug raid money. Quinn thought he probably was innocent. Not that Harley Renz had any principles; there simply hadn't been enough money involved to interest him. The shameless, conniving Renz was an expert when it came to calculating the risk-to-gain ratio.

"She bleed to death?" he asked Nift.

Nift, still squatting next to the corpse and his black bag of instruments, managed a slight shrug. "Maybe. My guess is she died of shock. She was alive when he cut off her eyelids. Probably when he gutted her."

"Any sign of sexual activity?"

"Doubt it, but I'll know more when I get her to the morgue."

"So what do you know for sure?"

"That's an unfair question."

"I don't care."

"She was cut with a serrated blade," Nift said. "Sawed. It also had a sharp point with which to make the initial opening. Looks like the killer wore something over his feet, maybe surgical slip-ons, judging by the footprints. He was prepared for the large amount of blood."

"From experience," Renz said, looking meaningfully at Quinn. He knew Quinn wasn't yet committed to the serial killer assumption. There were no such previous murders in New York, but the manner and ritual of this one strongly suggested there would be more.

"Same knife used to remove her eyelids?" Quinn asked Nift.

"Looks that way. It's not a neat job. But the eviscerating job *is* fairly neat."

"Like he's a medical doctor?"

"No. Like he's done it before."

"Killer clean up in the bathroom?" Quinn asked.

Nift nodded.

Quinn walked down a short hall to the small bathroom. There were signs of blood there, but all of it was smeared and he'd bet it all belonged to the victim. He had run the shower, but it didn't look as if he'd taken a full shower. Too smart to leave hair in the drain. This killer was careful.

Quinn returned to the living room.

"What's that?" he asked, looking at a blood-smeared object protruding from the victim's laid open abdomen.

Nift had obviously seen the object before. He deftly used a large tweezers to lift it from the gore of Bonnie Anderson's body cavity.

"Statue of Liberty," he said, grinning. "We're dealing with a patriotic killer."

"It's a cheap plastic souvenir," Renz said. "Sold all over town. His calling card."

Quinn knew what Renz meant. Serial killers often left something behind so their crimes would be connected. They were interested in their grisly body count, yearning for the anonymous sort of fame that would eventually destroy them.

Quinn was convinced now. There was ritual and compulsion here. And a certain kind of structured madness. In all likelihood, they had a serial killer on their hands.

"Usual arrangements?" he asked.

Renz nodded. Q&A often did work for hire for the NYPD and had a standing agreement as to terms. This worked because Renz had the public fooled into thinking he was brilliant and honest, and because Quinn had a well-founded reputation as the best there was in tracking and apprehending serial killers.

"Let me know about the postmortem," Quinn said to Nift, who was standing now and giving paramedics room to wrestle the corpse into a body bag. "And fax me photos."

"Will do," Nift said.

Pearl walked in, and he seemed to brighten. He was standing rigidly to his full height of under five-foot-five, his chest expanded and his expensively tailored suit coat buttoned. Pearl had opined that he had a Napoleon complex. In fact, she'd mentioned it to the little bastard to get back at him for insulting her. Nift had seemed pleased by the comparison, which had served to increase Pearl's anger.

Obviously for Pearl's benefit, Nift absently inserted his open hand inside his suit coat lapel in the iconic Napoleon portrait pose.

He noticed Quinn watching, and quickly removed the hand.

With a last glance around, Quinn moved toward the door. Renz detoured around a lot of blood to join him. Pearl followed, saying nothing. She knew Quinn would fill her in later.

As for the murder scene, she'd seen all of it that she wanted, and didn't want to see any more of it than was necessary.

They stepped around the uniform posted in the hall and walked toward the elevator.

"You two had breakfast?" Renz asked Quinn. "I got some papers for you to sign, Quinn. And there'll be more info coming in on the victim."

Quinn glanced at Pearl, who nodded.

"We can stop for some doughnuts," he said.

"That how you keep in such good shape?" asked the rotund Renz.

"Doughnuts are brain food."

"This meal is on the city."

"Not doughnuts, then."

8

The morning rush was over, so the diner wasn't crowded. The scents from the grill behind the counter were still heavy in the air, along with the aroma of freshly brewed coffee. The atmosphere was almost a meal in itself.

They were settled in a booth in the White Star Diner on Amsterdam. What they had all recently seen in Bonnie Anderson's apartment they could set aside so they still had appetites. In their business, compartmentalization meant survival.

Quinn ordered eggs over hard and hash. Renz asked for scrambled and sausages. Pearl had an everything bagel. They all had coffee. Cop pop.

Quinn and Renz got contractual business out of the way before the food arrived. They'd just finished eating and ordered more coffee when Renz's cell phone jangled.

He dug the phone from his pocket as he stood and pivoted, graceful for such a fat man. He walked a few feet away for privacy. Quinn and Pearl looked at each other and knew that neither could overhear.

Renz returned to the booth and sat down in front of the fresh cup of coffee the waiter had put on the table during the phone conversation.

"Nift," he said.

"Fast worker," Quinn said.

"I told him to get right on it, then give me the preliminaries. Also what the techs have come up with so far."

"So what'd Nift do?" Pearl asked. "Confirm the victim's dead?"

Renz dabbed at his lips with a white paper napkin and grinned at her. Looked at Quinn. "She's still a smart-ass," he said.

"Never outgrown it," Quinn said.

Renz had been taking notes on a folded envelope during his phone conversation. He consulted them, then sat back, keeping his voice down so they had to strain to hear him.

"Victim's full name," he said, "was Bonnie Maria Anderson. Twenty-nine years old. Originally from Chicago, been in New York two years. Last year and a half, she was a sales clerk at Gowns 'n' Gifts. On West Eighty-first Street. I figured Pearl might wanna check that out. Woman who found the body owns the place."

Pearl wondered if she'd just heard a sexist remark. She decided to let it pass.

Quinn didn't know what she'd decided. "We'll both go," he said. "What else did you learn from Nift?"

"The blood all over the carpet was the victim's. Same blood that was smeared in the bathroom when the sicko cleaned up after the murder."

"She wouldn't have had much opportunity to put up

a fight," Pearl said. "The creep probably wasn't even scratched."

"True. That's why there's nothing we can use under her fingernails." Renz squinted down again at his notes, causing the fat to bulge out above his collar. "Footprints at the scene look like they came from surgical slip-ons or oversized socks. Our killer appears to wear a ten-and-a-half or eleven shoe. The lab people are just getting started. Anything pertinent comes up, I'll let you know."

"The eyelids . . ." Pearl said.

"Oh. Looks like he cut them and tossed them aside," Renz said. "They were in all that blood and nobody noticed them at first."

"Why do you suppose he'd cut off her eyelids?" Pearl asked.

"He wanted her to look at him," Quinn said. "He wanted them to be looking at each other when she died, so it was a shared experience."

Renz grinned. "Man knows his psychos."

"In and out of the NYPD," Quinn said, and sipped his coffee. "They find her computer or pad?"

"No sign of a computer in the apartment, though there was a printer near a desk."

"So he probably took her computer, either to be on the safe side because he might be mentioned or shown on it, or simply as a precaution."

"Or simply to steal a computer," Pearl said.

"There's always that," Renz said. "But I think we can all agree that what happened to Bonnie Anderson wasn't the result of a screwed-up burglary."

Quinn and Pearl agreed with him. The killer had come prepared.

"Last meal material," Renz said.

Pearl said, "We gotta catch him first."

"It's good that you can still joke, after what we saw this morning," Renz said. "You got a strong tummy for a woman."

"I hear that all the time," Pearl said.

Quinn picked up in her voice that she might be getting irritated with Renz. He wanted to head that off.

"Speaking of last meals," Quinn said. "What was Bonnie Anderson's before she was killed?"

"Fish," Pearl said.

The two men looked at her.

"I saw it," Pearl reminded them.

"True," Renz said. "Cod, to be exact, with some kind of sauce on it. Also some kind of pasta with white sauce. Looks like she had that instead of a salad. White wine. Traces of Ambien. Nift said that along with the wine it'd be enough to knock her for a loop, but only for a little while."

"Long enough to get her bound and gagged," Pearl said.

"So he could control her," Quinn said, "but he didn't want her to miss what he was doing to her."

"Thoughtful of him."

"The eyelids again," Pearl said.

The waiter returned and poured fresh coffee. No one spoke until he was gone.

"So she had Italian food," Quinn said.

"Probably. It was ingested about nine-thirty."

"Late dinner," Quinn said.

"Maybe they were at a play," Pearl suggested. "There wouldn't be a playbill or ticket stubs if they were. The killer would have been smart enough to take them with him."

"Have to be a short play."

"There are some."

"Maybe there'll be something on a charge card account," Renz said.

"More likely on her killer's account. Even more likely he paid cash for their tickets—if they even attended a play."

"What about Lady Liberty?" Pearl asked. "The plastic statuette stuck in the carnage where her stomach was laid open."

"Cost approximately seven dollars. You can buy them all over New York wherever people are screwed out of their money by cheap merchandise."

Pearl shook her head. "I mean, why would he leave a souvenir in his victim's fatal wound?"

"His signature," Quinn said. "Or one of them. The smart ones sometimes use various ways to obscure what they *must* leave at the scene. It means something, but probably only to him. Same way with the eyelids."

"So how do we know his real signature hang-up?"

"We'll know."

They all knew how. It would require more victims in order to discern the consistent calling card.

Renz finished his coffee and leaned back. The bulk of his stomach inched the booth's table over toward Quinn and Pearl.

With a glance at Renz's ample abdomen, Pearl said, "Any notion as to why he'd open a woman's midsection?"

"That's the kinda thing you're paid to find out," Renz said, not liking it that Pearl had asked her question while staring at his stomach. Or maybe any thinly veiled insult was only in his mind. It was hard to know with Pearl; she could find so many ways to aggravate the hell out of people.

He stood up from the booth and buttoned his dark uniform coat over his white shirt. The coat was way too small for him. Pearl hoped the buttons wouldn't fly off like bullets and wing her.

"Stay in touch," he said to Quinn. "I gotta get some work done. So do you guys. I'm gonna stop on the way in and get some doughnuts."

"I wouldn't do that," Pearl said.

"It's tradition," Renz said, and swaggered away in full regalia. "Tradition . . . !" they heard him sing loudly as he headed for the door.

"His version of *Fiddler on the Roof*," Quinn said.

Pearl sneered. "I wish the fiddler would fall *through* the roof."

"Mess up a great musical," Quinn said.

"That's what tradition gets you."

Quinn remembered that was what the musical was about, tradition and what it could do, but he didn't share his thoughts with Pearl.

9

They were in Gowns 'n' Gifts, a small shop on West Eighty-first Street. The place was full of white this and white that. Most everything was cute. Sal could abide cute only so long.

The Plunket case was now inactive. Bob Plunket's wife, Joan, had confessed her affair with Foster Oaks, though Bob hadn't confessed his with Laura Loodner. The Plunkets were going to start seeing a marriage counselor.

Of course, Bob wanted to drop the Q&A investigation. He did want the photographs, though, of his wife and Oaks at the motel. He made mention of posting them on the Internet. Harold said he couldn't harbor much hope for that marriage. Sal said he couldn't much care.

The thing was, they were off the Plunket case now, and full time on the Bonnie Anderson murder.

Harold Mishkin glanced around the bridal shop and sniffed and smiled. "More than one sachet, I bet."

Sal grunted. He thought the shop smelled like a cheap hotel room immediately after sex.

"You're standing on a train," Melanie Tudor said.

Harold, a slender man, slightly bent, slightly gray, and with a completely gray drooping mustache, looked around in alarm, as if expecting the wail of a locomotive whistle.

"She means wedding-gown train," Harold's partner, Sal Vitali, grated at him. It was Sal who flashed ID and introduced himself and Harold to Melanie Tudor, a short woman with an intricately wrought orange hairdo.

"I suppose you're here about poor Bonnie," Melanie said.

"We are, ma'am," Sal grated.

A man with a dry cleaner's plastic bag slung over his shoulder stopped and put his hand on the shop's doorknob, then walked on.

"He lost his nerve," Melanie said, "but he'll be back."

"What marriage is all about," Harold said.

Melanie glared at him.

"We understand you found the body," Sal said.

Melanie bowed her head. "Yes, yes. It was awful." A tear glistened at the edge of her right eye, but maybe she could cry on cue, owning and operating a wedding shop.

"Do a lot of people return things here?" Harold asked.

Sal pretended his partner hadn't spoken. "Could you describe that morning, Miss Tudor?"

"Misses," she corrected.

Sal smiled. "Good."

"Only for business purposes, Detective. I live quite happily alone."

"Were you ever married?"

"Why do you ask?"

"I'm prying."

"Once. For a short time." He glanced over to make sure Harold was taking notes.

"What prompted you to go to the victim's apartment?"

"Bonnie was half an hour late for work, and not answering her phone. That wasn't at all like her. And I needed her that afternoon so I could attend a showing of the latest bridesmaids styles."

"You sell those, too," Harold muttered. "Their dresses, I mean."

"Oh, yes." Melanie pointed to a rack of dresses off in a corner.

"They're kind of drab," Harold said.

Melanie Tudor smiled. "They also don't fit well."

"So you went to Bonnie Anderson's apartment," Sal said, nudging her along, wishing Harold would shut up and take notes.

"Yes. I got no answer on the intercom, of course. So I rang for the building's super and explained that it was extremely important that I see Bonnie. When we went upstairs and he knocked on her door, there was no answer, and no sound from inside."

"And that's when you called the police?" Harold said. It was his role to prod and keep the subject talking, a routine he and Sal had used for years. It had never occurred to Sal that maybe that was how Harold had developed his annoying manner.

Melanie was looking only at Sal. "We didn't call the police just then. I told the super Bonnie was diabetic and might need immediate attention, and kept orange juice in the refrigerator just for that purpose of reviving her if she went into a coma."

"You were lying about that?" Harold asked.

"Of course. Bonnie was in perfect health. But the super had little choice but to use his key." Melanie moved back a few steps, surrounding herself with diaphanous white material. "A woman's life might have depended on it."

"Lies and marriage," Harold muttered, "go together like a horse and—"

"Harold!" Sal interrupted him.

Melanie Tudor was staring at him from her nest of virgin white material with contempt. She seemed to be concentrating on mere insult, which people usually didn't do if they were lying like crazy to save their lives. Or somebody else's life. Melanie and the super slid lower on Sal and Harold's suspect list.

"When you first entered Bonnie's apartment," Sal asked, "what did you notice?"

"The smell," Melanie said immediately. "It was so odd. Like burnished copper. It was almost like taste."

Sal knew she was describing the smell of copious amounts of blood. It was something that stayed with a person, which maybe explained all the sachets smelling up the shop. The odor was better than what Melanie's memory might keep conjuring up.

"And the first thing you saw . . . ?"

"Bonnie. What was left of her. She was lying nude on her back with her eyes . . . her eyelids were gone. She looked as if she'd been flayed. And her stomach was . . ."

Melanie's own eyelids fluttered and she fainted dead away into the surrounding folds of nuptials material.

Sal and Harold both moved quickly to break her fall, though she would have landed softly in all that white.

She was conscious but weak, and they led her over to a chair for men, uncomfortable and little so they'd soon become restless and pay almost anything to get out of the shop.

"I'm so sorry," Melanie said, sipping from a glass of water Harold brought her from a small half bath near the changing rooms.

With trembling hands, she guided the glass's rim to her lips. Harold's hands were trembling, too. He and Melanie looked like a couple of startled deer.

Melanie gazed up at Harold. "Are you married?"

"Not anymore," Harold said. "No one can abide me."

"No one can," Sal reiterated.

He waited until Melanie seemed her usual self.

"We won't get into what you saw," he told her. "Did Bonnie have any plans for marriage?"

"Oh, lots of them. Everything was worked out except for the groom."

"Did she date a lot of men?"

"In the hopeless search for a good one, yes. She used T4Two.net, a genteel online dating service."

"Did she mention any of the men she met that way?"

"No, she kept that part of her life private. Other than that the men she met online were almost always duds, she was not talkative about her experiences. But I should say . . ."

"What?"

"That Bonnie was particular. Some of the men she met through T4Two.net, other women might have thought they were just fine."

Sal wondered if Melanie had inherited any of the rejects.

"Did you know any of Bonnie's friends or acquaintances?"

"Not really. Ours was a business relationship. I've found it's never wise to become too friendly with my employees. It's only inside these walls that we're the best of friends. It's important that we project good cheer and optimism."

"One big happy family," Harold said.

"So's the Mafia," Sal remarked.

"With the head of the family firmly in charge," Melanie said, not at all miffed by Sal's comparison. Sal mused that she wouldn't make someone a good wife.

"Is there no man you might point to as being special in Bonnie's life?" Sal asked. "Anyone she might have mentioned more than once?"

"Not really. She seemed to pick them up, examine them, then put them back. As far as I know she had no dearest friend—of either sex."

"She seems to have led a lonely life, working in the marriage shop," Harold said.

"True," Melanie said. "However, what she did outside the shop, I have no idea. If I did, maybe I could be of help to you." She began fidgeting with some sort of tiara fitted with jewels, signaling that she was busy and the conversation was over.

"Nice crown," Harold said.

Sal got a card from his wallet and handed it to Melanie. "In case you think of something else . . ."

Melanie gave Harold a look. "Oh, I assure you I'll think of something else as soon as you walk out of here."

10

Quinn parked his aging black Lincoln in front of a fire hydrant and stuck his NYPD placard on the dash. Such a miracle, parking free in Manhattan.

Fedderman, seated next to him, said, "Ever see that photo of a car parked in front of a hydrant and the fire department rolled down two of the windows and ran the hose right through it?"

"*Through* the car?"

"In one side and out the other," Fedderman said.

"Isn't that illegal?"

"You wouldn't worry much about that if your house was on fire."

"Two wrongs making a right," Quinn said. "So what's the problem?"

Fedderman understood Quinn's point of view, but was glad the old Lincoln was Quinn's car and Quinn was driving.

Both men got out of the car and stood in front of the fire hydrant in the hot sunlight. Directly across the street was the apartment building where Bonnie Anderson had been murdered. It was a redbrick structure with bulging iron grillwork over the street level windows that kept air conditioners in and B&E practitioners out. There was a skeletal iron framework for an awning above the entrance, but no awning.

"You check the businesses close by," Quinn told Fedderman. "I'll talk to Bonnie's neighbors. We can stay in touch by cell phone."

Fedderman gave a casual mock salute and walked away. Quinn watched him, a tall, lanky man with a basketball-sized belly and a suit that didn't fit. Something about the way Fedderman wrote with a pen or pencil caused his right shirt cuff button to come undone. It had happened early today, and the white cuff was flying like a signal flag from the sleeve of his suit coat, flapping as he walked.

Quinn turned away from the sartorial disaster and crossed the street toward Bonnie Anderson's apartment.

It wasn't the sort of place to have a doorman, so he entered the small tiled foyer and checked the mailboxes. B. ANDERSON was still there. And the white showing in the slot of the brass box indicated that her mail was still being delivered. Quinn was making a mental note to get a mail key copy from Renz when he noticed that half the tarnished brass mailboxes had keys in their slots. Either they were left there for convenience, or they were stuck and no one had gotten around to repairing them.

He tried the key in Bonnie's mailbox. It went in halfway then and no farther. Quinn tried to rotate it one way or the other. It didn't budge. He tried to remove it and try another of the keys, but it jammed in the box.

"Help you?" a suspicious voice asked from behind Quinn.

Quinn turned to see a stocky blond man in a green work outfit that looked two sizes too large even though he was well over six feet tall. "You the super?"

The man nodded.

Quinn showed his ID.

"Yeah, I recognize you now. Seen you now and then on the TV or in the papers. You look bigger than your photos."

"I actually am," Quinn said.

"I'm Fred Daily. I guess you wanna talk to me about Mizz Anderson."

"I will in a little while, if you're going to be around."

"I will be. Right down those steps in my apartment and office. Just buzz, and if I ain't right there I'll pick it up on my iPhone. Got a special App."

"Right now," Quinn said, "I'm trying to get into the victim's mailbox. You have a master key?"

"Sure don't. Doesn't matter much. Only a few of those old locks work. Building owner ain't quick about authorizing repairs, and nobody much complains 'cause they know the tricks of how to get their box open." He stepped closer to the bank of mailboxes. "Like with Mizz Anderson's." He gripped the stuck key and leaned heavily against the box with his free hand. Slapped the box once, twice, and the brass door popped open.

Quinn smiled. "I'll remember that."

"Takes technique."

"I'll practice," Quinn said, removing the mail from the box. "Any secret about closing it?"

"Nope." Daily reached around Quinn and gently closed the brass door. It clicked neatly into place. "I'm gonna figure out how these things work and then take out a patent," Daily said.

"Do it on the Net. Saves time," Quinn said.

"You serious?"

"Always."

"I can believe it."

Quinn moved toward the elevator.

"Ain't workin'," Fred Daily said behind him.

"Was it working yesterday morning?"

"Oh, yeah. It went on the fritz just about an hour ago."

"Must have known I was coming,"

"Some people are like that."

"Some elevators," Quinn said.

He got the key to Bonnie Anderson's apartment from Fred Daily and started to climb. His right leg began to ache from when, as a cop, he had been shot in the line of duty. The bullet had entered his thigh and been removed from where it had lodged in the bone. Sometimes the leg ached when rain was about to fall, but he doubted if that was the case this time.

The apartment was stifling and silent and still smelled of death. Quinn walked over and switched the window air conditioner in the living room on high. The unit hummed and the compressor kicked in and started a vibration that rattled the vents. Cool air spilled into the room, but it would take a while to overcome the oppressive heat.

Quinn stepped around the bloodstains on the carpet and made his way into the bedroom. The CSU unit had gone through drawers and the closet, but he thought that sometimes in their search for stray hairs and nit-sized clues, they could overlook the obvious. Quinn gave it all a closer look.

The dresser drawers held panties, nylon hose, a folded nightgown. Another drawer was stuffed with balled tube socks of various colors, sweatpants, pullovers, and T-shirts. The bottom drawers held dressier blouses, folded Levi's, black and flesh-colored tights, odds and ends like a flashlight, ballpoint pen, and sunglasses, a clip-on reading lamp that looked as if it had never been used, and elastic headbands tangled together. There was a black winter sweater with a Filene's Basement price tag still affixed.

On top of the dresser were a comb and brush and a can of hair spray. A red plastic pig with a slot in its back to catch loose change—felt about half full of coins. There was also a framed photo of two elderly people standing in front of a modest house with a front yard that needed cutting. Bonnie's parents in Chicago. Pearl had phoned them, broken their hearts, and found out that they knew practically nothing of their daughter's life in New York. Nothing pertinent to the investigation, anyway. Also in Chicago, an old boyfriend, now a father and involved with another woman, expressed surprise and great sadness at the news of Bonnie's death.

A bedside table had a drawer containing an old Sara Paretsky paperback novel, some loose batteries, a spiral notebook, and a blunt number-two pencil.

Quinn looked at the notebook and found nothing written in it. There were no paper fragments caught in the spiral, indicating that the notebook contained all its pages. It was there for nighttime notes Bonnie had never written.

And there was something else, way in the back of

the drawer—a computer mouse with a wire and USB plug.

Quinn went back to the living room, over to the desk that had yielded nothing useful. He bent over for an angled view of the wooden desktop. There was a slight rectangular discoloration the size of a laptop computer.

So Bonnie *had* owned a computer. Probably she'd converted to a wireless mouse and put the old mouse in the bedside table. Almost surely the killer had taken the computer. That was no surprise, but it did suggest that the computer might have held a clue to the killer's identity, something incriminating. Something as traceable as a computer, you didn't steal it and risk tying yourself to a murder unless you had a good reason.

Of course, all of this assumed that Bonnie Anderson hadn't been killed by a stranger. A certain hairstyle, smile, a mere tilt of the head, could be enough to trigger an attack by a psychotic serial killer.

That was something most women knew, but could do nothing to guard against without joining a nunnery. Even then, the terrible truth pursued them.

Death was as random as life.

11

"I read about that in the paper," a busy Hispanic bartender said to Fedderman. She seemed fascinated but shaken, staring at the postmortem photo of Bonnie Anderson after she'd been cleaned up and her features rearranged. Something clever had been done to make it appear that she had closed eyelids. False lashes had even been applied. But there was no doubt that she wasn't asleep.

Fedderman was in the Lap Dog Lounge in the West Seventies. It was cool and dim, and not a bad place to be during a hot day in Manhattan. On richly paneled walls were framed photographs of various Westminster Dog Show winners, posing proudly. All breeds seemed to be represented. There were messy paw prints on some of the photos. Autographs, Fedderman assumed.

Along the wall of photos were two rows of wooden tables and chairs. Across from them, facing the wall of canine royalty, was a long mahogany bar, where Fedderman slouched on a stool.

It was too early for most drinkers, which was okay with Fedderman. He wanted to talk without being interrupted, and here he was alone with a fetching bartender. Though she didn't look like a breed that would fetch.

He was in the Lap Dog only because a coaster from the place had been in Bonnie Anderson's purse. It was a circular vinyl or plastic coaster with the likeness of a little long-haired dog with its tongue hanging out. It was cute, all right. Fedderman could understand why Bonnie would steal the coaster.

The bartender, whose name was Rose, looked up from the morgue photo and gave him a sickly smile. "You a cop?"

"Yeah," Fedderman said, figuring that technically he was telling the truth, what with Q&A's contract with the NYPD.

"You here to ask me questions?"

"Sure am."

"You gonna put handcuffs on me?"

Hoo boy! "Do you want me to?"

"I should think about that." She leaned on the bar, causing her blouse to part and reveal considerable cleavage. Fedderman was having second thoughts about being alone with her. "Ask away," Rose said.

"You obviously knew the dead woman."

"Yeah. Bonnie, the papers said her name was. Some guys in here called her Bon Bon because she was such eye candy."

"Was she that attractive? I mean, I only saw her . . . afterward."

"A beautiful woman, I'm not so sure. But she was a cutie who knew how to make the most of herself. And kind of a semi-regular here."

"And that would be . . . ?"

"She'd be in here maybe twice a week, different nights. She tried to hook up with the right guy now and then, but pickings are scarce, maybe because of the economy. Anyway, nothing seemed to work for her until the last one."

Huh?

"Who was the last one?" Fedderman asked, keeping his expression neutral.

"I don't know. Didn't know Bonnie all that well, tell you the truth. We talked some when business was slow, is all."

They talked together. Rose, you're a treasure trove of information.

"What did you two talk about?" Fedderman asked in an offhand way.

Rose lifted a shoulder. More cleavage.

Fedderman gulped. *Heaven help me,*

"I don't know," Rose said. "Girl stuff, is all. And how this place might become a fruit and veggie juice health bar."

"Fruit and veggie juice? You kidding me?"

"Nope. Some idea of the mayor's. He wants a fruit and veggie drink establishment every ten blocks, so one will always be within easy walking distance. S'posed to make New Yorkers healthier. Right now, it's a pilot project. This place has already gone to the dogs. I didn't think we could sink any lower."

"So who was this guy Bonnie thought might be a winner?"

"I don't know if Bonnie thought that. I did. Something about him. He just seemed like a nice guy. Genuine, if you know what I mean."

Fedderman didn't, exactly. "What'd he look like?"

"Average looking, but there was, like, *nothing* wrong with him. Features like they came out of a mold. Everything fit, nothing unusual. I guess that's what makes him hard to describe."

"Go ahead and try, so I won't have to cuff you."

"Hmmm."

"Behave, Rose. This is a murder investigation."

That reminder seemed to sober her. "Average, is what he was. That's how I'd describe him. Not too tall or short, not too fat or thin." She smiled. "Mr. Just Right."

"Hair?"

"He had enough of it and it was brown, I think."

"Eyes?"

"Two. Blue, I think."

Fedderman wrote *Brown over blue* in his notebook, and then a question mark.

"How'd he dress?"

"Put his underwear on first, I would imagine."

"Rose . . ."

"Average. I remember him in a suit, and once in khakis and a blue shirt. Always looked nice the half dozen or so times I saw him."

"Was he always with Bonnie Anderson?"

"I think so. Though they didn't always come in together. They used the Lap Dog as a meeting place, then they'd have a few drinks and head on out to who knows where."

"Not you, I guess."

Rose smiled. "Sorry. I make it a point not to pry into my customers' private lives."

"Now here's a big one," Fedderman said. "Do you know the guy's name?"

"Rob," Rose said, grinning, coming through again.

"Just Rob? No last name?"

"Hey, whaddya want? This is a first-name-only kind of place."

"Ever hear 'Robert' or 'Robin'?"

"Nope. Not 'Roberto,' either. Just 'Rob.' "

"When you saw them leave here together," Fedderman said, "did they usually turn left or right?"

"Right," Rose answered without hesitation.

Toward Bonnie's apartment, which was within easy walking distance. If that meant anything.

Fedderman closed his notebook.

Rose grinned. "Did I do good?"

"A-plus," Fedderman said. "No need for handcuffs."

"Hey, that's not fair."

"What's fair," said a voice from down the bar, "is if you'd sell me a drink."

Fedderman turned to see an elderly man with a neatly trimmed gray beard. He was scrawny but wearing a blue T-shirt that said PAIN AND GAIN GYM in faded black letters across the narrow chest. He didn't look as if he'd ever worked out in his life.

"Gin straight up," he said. "First of the day."

"I believe it if you tell me," Rose said, and moved down the bar to pour from a gin bottle.

Fedderman swiveled down off his bar stool and walked past her, gave her a smile and a wave. Let the old guy with the beard deal with this hungry cougar.

"C'mon back sometime and I'll break the law," she said.

"Just try it," Fedderman said.

Rose laughed. "I'll sew a bigger button on that cuff for you."

When he was outside on the baking, sunny sidewalk, where Rose couldn't see him, Fedderman buttoned his shirt cuff and went on his way.

He put on his sunglasses and walked toward where he'd parked the unmarked car, his ego boosted by Rose the bartender, a definite slouchy spring in his step.

Lookin' cool. Then he noticed that his shoelace was untied.

He stopped, kneeled down, and tied it and the other shoelace in double bow knots. Then he was up and striding toward his car again.

Lookin' cool.

The man watching the woman across the street stayed back in the doorway, where she wouldn't notice him. This was the third time that he knew of that she'd come here. The first time she'd stood motionless and watched the Q&A office door, but left without entering, as if she'd lost her nerve. That interested him enough that the second time, which had been a repeat of the first, he followed her. Found out her where she worked, her name and address. Began his research.

A delivery van the size of a small house drove past, momentarily blocking his view. When it was gone, so was she.

The man watching from the shadows knew she must have gotten up her nerve and entered the building.

He smiled approvingly. That was what life was about, forcing yourself to open doors leading to where you were afraid to enter.

12

The street door made its familiar swishing sound.

Into the office walked a petite, dishwater-blond woman with pigtails.

Quinn was the only one at Q&A not out in the field. He watched her stand just inside the door and look around.

My God, May!

Only it wasn't his former wife, May. But the resemblance was strong enough to be . . . startling.

A younger May.

Q&A was set up somewhat like a precinct house squad room. There were neat rows of desks rather than cubicles, so there could be a free flow of information. Only Quinn's desk was next to a partial cubicle that could be easily rearranged for semi-privacy.

The blond woman, who looked to be in her early twenties, quickly realized that Quinn was the only one in the spacious office and fixed her gaze on him. She was wearing jeans, brown open-toed sandals, and a sleeveless blue blouse with large white buttons. Sunglasses dangled on a cord just above her breasts. She started toward Quinn. The window light playing over her face changed, and suddenly he knew her.

She said, "Hi, Uncle Frank."

Quinn stood up. "You're Carlie! Carlie Clark!" She was the daughter of May's sister. "You've grown up. Last time I saw you was when you were on your way to middle school."

"In California," Carlie said.

"Which is why it took me a few seconds to recognize you. You're not a kid anymore, and you're supposed to be on the other side of the continent."

She gave a tiny mock shiver. "Ooh! You make it seem so far away."

They'd never had a chance to be close, and he actually didn't know Carlie very well. As a kid she'd taken to him for some reason, and used to call him Uncle Frank. Nobody had called him that for years, until a few minutes ago.

She rolled a chair over from Pearl's nearby desk and sat down in it. Quinn got a slight whiff of perfume, which he liked.

He sat back down behind his desk.

"I've only been in New York a few weeks," she said. "Got an apartment in SoHo provided by the company."

"Company?"

"Bold Designs. I'm working for them as a retail designs consultant."

"Wait a minute. . . . You're . . ."

She smiled. "Twenty-six," she said.

He studied her. Bold features. Dishwater-blond hair. Blue eyes. She didn't actually much resemble either

May, or May's sister. He'd filled in the details with memory. And yet . . . maybe without the bangs or pigtails. "You can't be twenty-six," he said.

"I wish."

"And a . . ."

"Retail designer."

"Which is?"

"I lay out floor plans for retail establishments, maximizing shelf space with traffic flow, providing for display and checkout experiences. I'm in New York doing a women's boutique that will specialize in a few name brands that complement each other."

"Sounds interesting," Quinn lied.

She gave him a broad smile.

"Really," he said, doubling down.

"Confession time," she said.

Quinn wasn't sure exactly what she meant.

"I didn't just look you up because we're family," Carlie said. "I'm here because the police in this city seem to think I'm invisible."

"You should go into crime," Quinn said.

"You were always funny, Uncle Frank."

"Your aunt May didn't think so."

"Guess not." Carlie shot him a penetrating stare and suddenly looked very much like May. "Are you still with Pearl?"

"Yes."

"She's a detective, too, right?"

"Right."

"You could always make me laugh, but at the same time, you intimidated me. Still do."

"Intimidated you?"

"In a good way, if such a thing is possible. Maybe

part of it was your size. I was just a kid, so you seemed even larger."

"Well, there'll be no more of that intimidation business, and that's an order."

She grinned, but what he'd said actually did seem to put her at ease in his presence.

"You must scare the hell out of suspects," she said.

" 'Course I do."

The street door opened and Jody walked in. She saw that Quinn was with someone and started back toward the door.

"Wait a minute," Quinn said.

Jody turned, cocked her head at him quizzically, and moved toward him and Carlie.

"This is my ex-wife's sister's daughter, Carlie," he said. He turned toward Carlie. "This is Jody."

Carlie stood up and the two women shook hands.

"I'm here to see my Uncle Frank," Carlie said.

"So you're Quinn's niece?" Jody asked.

"We think so," Quinn said. "She might be once removed or something. I get confused on that kind of thing. Anyway, she's family."

Carlie gave Jody an inquiring look. "And you'd be . . . ?"

"Quinn's daughter," Jody said.

Uh-oh. Quinn caught a whiff of venom in the air. Still, he couldn't help being amused and proud. He had come to regard Jody as a daughter, almost as much as his real daughter, Lauri, who was closer with May out in California.

He decided to let the possessive daughter remark pass. Someone—probably Carlie—would straighten Jody out.

"Carlie's in town as a consultant," Quinn said. "She's in retail design."

"There's a demand for that," Jody said. Quinn would have bet she had no idea what retail design was. She looked at Carlie. "So you're just visiting?"

"Yes. Only for as long as it takes me to lay out and oversee the job. In the few weeks I've been here, I've somehow managed to get in trouble. I went to the police, but they don't seem able or willing to help before something happens. That's why I came to see Uncle Frank."

Quinn saw Jody wince.

"What's the something you're afraid might happen?" Quinn asked.

Carlie sat back down and looked uncomfortable. "It sounds crazy, I know, but I'm afraid I might wind up like that other woman."

It took Quinn a few seconds to realize whom she meant. "Bonnie Anderson?" And as he asked for confirmation, he suddenly saw himself why Carlie had looked so familiar. It wasn't only family resemblance. She actually did resemble the dead woman.

"When I see her photos in the papers or on TV," Carlie said, "sometimes I think I'm looking at myself."

"A lot of women in New York are thinking that," Quinn said. "This killer's got them spooked. Odds are you have nothing to worry about."

"That's more or less what the police told me. They didn't take the fact that I'm being stalked at all serious. To them I'm just another dumb blonde with an overactive imagination."

"They've gotten past the 'dumb blonde' thing," Quinn said. "Really."

"I thought I had, too."

"Fact is, in times like this, there are a lot of women contacting the police, asking for help because they're afraid. And their fear's not unreasonable. But there are millions of women in this city, Carlie. Hundreds of thousand of them at least somewhat resemble Bonnie Anderson, who's been hyped by media as the killer's so-called type."

"But I *do* resemble her."

"Somewhat," Quinn admitted.

"And I *am* being stalked."

Quinn waited, thinking he'd better listen closely.

Carlie said, "I came here a few times but didn't actually enter. I just stood out on the street, trying to make up my mind. I was nervous."

"Why?"

She gave a helpless shrug. "I'd heard so much about you, most of it intimidating. Then something else happened. I noticed a man watching me, outside this place, from across the street. Later I saw him near my apartment. Since then, at least four times, the same man's followed me home from work, on the subway, walking to my apartment. Sometimes I peek outside my apartment window and see him in the street. When I was eating lunch at a diner near where I work, I looked up and there he was staring through the window at me. It's as if he *wants* me to know he's stalking me."

Quinn and Jody exchanged a look. They knew that if this killer was stalking Carlie he would indeed want her to know about it. That was part of his power trip. Act One of the drama he was forcing on an unwilling victim so that eventually she'd be debilitated by fear.

"If you were afraid, why didn't you come in here and confide in us?" Jody asked.

"That's what I'm doing now. Since I've become convinced my imagination's not working overtime."

"So he latched on to you here, where you had an obvious interest, then began stalking you?" Quinn asked.

"I . . . well, I think so. Yes."

Then probably spent the last few weeks learning all he could about you. Making a predator's study of you. "Describe him," Quinn said, picking up a pen and moving a notepad over to where he could reach it.

"That isn't easy. He's average looking. I think he has brown hair. Average height and weight."

"You *think*?"

"Yes. He was dressed in dark slacks and a blue short-sleeved shirt once, on the subway. One morning he had on jogging sweats and running shoes. He wears a beret or a beret-like hat, sometimes a ball cap, sometimes a slouch hat. As if I won't recognize him in a different hat."

"But you do recognize him?"

"Yes. No. Only in a chameleon-like way. If he gets close enough. And he usually does. Once, on a crowded sidewalk where I didn't feel so scared, I turned around to face him. Then a pair of women passed between us. I took my eyes off him for just a few seconds and he disappeared. I tried but couldn't find him. Finally I continued walking home, glanced back, and there he was again. It's . . ." She bowed her head.

"Take it easy, dear," Quinn said in a soothing voice.

"Chameleon like?" Jody asked.

"Yes," Carlie said. "It's an odd thing. I think if he combed his hair differently, wore different clothes, I might not be able to positively identify him. He seems able to change his . . . persona. Honestly, it's scaring the shit out of me."

"That's what the bastard wants," Jody said. She was riled up now. For some reason glaring at Quinn as if *he'd* done something terrible. "Can't this guy be picked up for harassment? I'd argue the case."

Carlie looked at Jody.

"She's an attorney," Quinn explained. He turned his attention to Jody. "You've already got the animal-rights case to keep you busy."

"I shouldn't need a lawyer," Carlie said. "You'd think the cops—" She looked at Quinn. "I know, you don't agree with me about the NYPD."

"I take your complaint seriously," he said. *Even though you'd never be able to pick your stalker out of a lineup.* He lifted up the phone and called Fedderman. "We'll get you some protection, then I'm going to call somebody I know."

"The commissioner," Jody said. Quinn wished she hadn't.

"*Police* commissioner?" Carlie said, surprised.

"They're friends," Jody said.

"Don't lie to her," Quinn said. He swiveled in his chair, concentrating on his phone conversation.

It wasn't with Renz. Not yet, anyway.

"Feds. Got an assignment for you."

While they waited for Fedderman to arrive, Quinn listened to Jody explain her law firm's case for an animal rights organization. The courts had already found that there was a right to sue on the behalf of animals. It was done all the time to stop developments that threatened endangered species. Jody wanted to be able to sue across species, on behalf of *all* animals. A sort of class-action approach.

"I dunno," Carlie said. "Could a person murder a rat? I mean, if an exterminator killed a rat, could you sue on behalf of all rats?"

"Of all animals!"

"Are you actually talking about a murder conviction?"

"Definitely. If there are mitigating circumstances, the penalty needn't be as severe as life in prison."

Carlie wasn't buying into it. "Would it be illegal to step on a roach?"

Jody had heard that one. She smiled. "Would *you* represent a roach?"

"Well, no."

"So it's hypothetical and a frivolous use of the courts."

"I wouldn't represent a rat, either," Carlie said. "And what about the fact that a roach or a rat can't declare that you're his or her attorney?"

Quinn thought about mentioning how difficult it would be to obtain a retainer from a roach or a rat, but decided to keep out of the discussion.

He was relieved when Fedderman walked in.

Quinn introduced Fedderman to Carlie and explained the situation. Not about roaches and rats, but about Carlie being stalked. Fedderman listened carefully, nodded, and assured Carlie she had no worries as long as he was around—and he'd be around.

"First thing we'll do," he said, "is make sure your apartment is tight."

"Tight?"

"Doors, windows, ingress, outgress."

"Outgress?"

They left together, Carlie trailing her effusive thanks to Uncle Frank.

"Pretty girl," Quinn said.

"She is," Jody agreed. "Or she would be without those pigtails. She really needs to do something about that hair."

Said the redheaded woman with hair like berserk bedsprings, Quinn thought.

But didn't say.

He picked up the phone and called Harley Renz, so he could hear the same thing the NYPD had told Carlie.

13

Bland County, Missouri, 1990

The woman from the white van, which had last year been traded for a blue van, gripped six-year-old Dred "Squeaky" Gant by the upper arm and led him toward the house. She had put on considerable weight, but evenly. A big woman, no longer young but still vital. Fleshy but firm. She was what used to be called zaftig. Compared to a six-year-old boy, zaftig translated into superior strength.

They didn't go into the ramshackle house, but instead walked around to metal storm cellar doors set almost horizontally, but at a slight angle tilting away from where they joined the house's foundation. They led to a concrete six-by-eight-foot room that served as a tornado shelter. Tornadoes often roared across the flatlands, chewing up crops, houses, anything in their way. The only real shelter was underground, where the powerful, searching winds couldn't reach you—as long as they weren't strong enough to pluck you out of wherever you were hiding.

The double doors to the storm cellar were clad with sheet steel that was screwed into hard cedar. The doors were heavy, and once barred from inside couldn't be lifted by the wind. Or by desperate neighbors seeking refuge from a nuclear attack, which was something the woman, Mildred Gant, sometimes dreamed about.

Mildred, strong though she was, had to expend some effort to shove the boy to the ground, where he lay in the tall grass with his knees drawn up.

Not much fight in you, Mildred thought. *I raised you right.*

She keyed open a padlock on a heavy chain that ran between the doors' handles, played out the chain through one handle, then hooked beefy fingers around the handle of the right-side door. She grunted loudly as she heaved it open. The doors were wide enough that there was no need to open the left-side door.

Steep wooden steps without a hand rail led to the underground room. There was no other way in or out.

Mildred yanked Squeaky to his feet and led him to the dark rectangle in the bright sunlight. She pushed him ahead of her down the steps.

Some of the breeze found its way into the shelter, but it was still plenty hot and uncomfortable. The small room was dank and smelled like urine, from when Squeaky could no longer hold his water and had to relieve himself in the bucket that was hosed out every two or three days.

There was a pull cord and a screw-in porcelain light fixture mounted on the wall between the storm cellar and the basement proper. The woman pulled on the cord and a sixty-watt light bulb winked on. It was on the basement circuit, and the only source of electricity in the shelter. It provided barely enough illumination when both shelter doors were shut.

Every morning, before the flatlands really heated up, Mildred would take the boy to the storm cellar. There was a small wicker stool there, and an old cane rocker with sturdy legs. She had taught Squeaky how to repair cane chairs, and he was almost ready, almost skillful enough to repair broken chairs that she'd buy at auction, repair, and resell at auction. She used to repair the chairs herself, but her fingers had fallen victim to arthritis to the point where she couldn't work long with the long strands of cane. It was a job that required younger hands. Very young hands could do it well, up to a point. Squeaky would be even better at caning when he was older and stronger.

Not that he'd ever be strong inside.

Mildred didn't completely ignore Squeaky's education. She'd picked up some used textbooks at a flea market. They were marked on with pen and pencil, and a few of the pages were missing, but they were good enough. The infrequent lessons would start with basic grammar and reading comprehension. Squeaky would recite the alphabet, then read aloud a chapter of the book.

"Ain't no one gonna call you unschooled," Mildred said. "Take you away from me."

After the sacrosanct alphabet had been successfully recited, she would barely listen as he read from the book. It was his grammar she was concerned with, not her own.

When the grammar lesson was over, it was time for him to go to work.

Mildred would sit on the wicker stool and watch,

occasionally guiding his fingers to demonstrate. He toiled and learned to work with his hands in the stifling shelter, breathing in the stench of the bucket's contents, and the odor of the woman's rank body along with his own. He worked the cane strands between each other, over and under, over and under, lacing them skillfully as she'd demonstrated, finding the grain and splitting strands precisely down the middle, for finer work. Sometimes, for bends and corners, the cane had to be worked while it was wet and more pliable.

Listening to each other's breathing, Squeaky and the woman he knew as his mother would become lost in their task. Every fifteen minutes or so, one or the other of them would take a swig of water from the glass jug kept on a shelf. Other than that, they worked in silence, she watching the boy and correcting him when he did anything wrong, he learning patience and servitude, as well as a useful skill.

When the heat became almost intolerable, Mildred would strip until she wore only her baggy shorts and a red sweatband. Her shirt she would use as a rag to sop sweat from her broad face. The boy worked only in his white Jockey shorts, which had long ago turned gray. He worked . . . worked . . . worked until his fingers bled.

When the rocker seat was finished, Mildred stood with her hands on her hips and surveyed it. The boy watched her intently, trying to read something in her features.

As usual, her expression gave him no clue.

"Here, here, and here," she said, pointing three times with a blunt finger. "It ain't for shit!" She gripped Squeaky's shoulders and shook him. "Can you do better?"

His head felt as if it might snap off his neck.

"I can do better!" he squeaked.

She dabbed at her forehead with her wadded shirt, then got pruning shears from where they lay next to the jug on the wooden shelf.

In a fury she snipped and struck and bent and snapped the recently woven cane until the chair was in worse condition than when they'd started working on it.

"There's plenty more cane in there," she said, pointing to a long cardboard box set against a wall. "See what you can do with it. I'm gonna check at lunch time, you hear?" She slapped him on the cheek to emphasize her words.

"I hear," he said softly, then again, louder, to be sure that she'd heard.

"You don't do it good enough, you're gonna sit in the shit house till dark, you understand?"

"Understand."

He hated it when she locked him in the wooden outhouse, especially if it was still daylight. He could see out through the spaces between the vertical slats, but the cracks also let the wasps in. There were also plenty of flies, the big ones people called horseflies. They could bite you, and it hurt. But he feared the wasps more than anything, and it seemed he was always recovering from a bad sting somewhere on his body.

He would sit on the wooden bench with its circular hole and try not to breathe the foul odor from below, or to hear the ceaseless buzzing of the flies, and the more militant drone of the wasps. It was the stench, along with the heat, that attracted the wasps, he was sure.

They weren't so bad once it got dark, around the time he'd see the woman coming to release him, wearing her flowing nightgown so white in the night, lifting her Coleman gas lamp high in one hand so she wouldn't trip over the paving stones that were laid unevenly on her way to unlock the outhouse door.

Usually a beating with her leather belt followed his release from the outhouse, but it was so much better than the wasps that Squeaky almost welcomed it.

But right now it was a long time till evening.

"Take a swig of water," she told him.

He did.

"Chore time." Mildred hefted herself up the wooden stairs, into the light of high morning. Against the clear blue sky she looked as huge as a storybook goddess, towering above him.

Then the storm cellar doors clanged closed and he was in dimness.

Mildred hoisted one of the steel-clad doors back up part way and stuck a block of wood under it so it would stay open about six inches, letting in light and air. The heavy chain clattered as she fed it through the handles, then fastened it with the padlock.

There was no way out for the boy, and he knew that.

There was no way out.

Patiently, he used the back of his thumb to rub sweat from his eyes, then he began working again with the cane.

He did know he was becoming more skillful, and he took a certain pride in that.

One of his mother's favorite homilies stuck at the fore of his mind. *A job worth doing . . .*

14

New York City, the present

It was odd the way she met the guy.

Connie Mason was drinking alone in Jill's Joint, a Village club with a sixties theme. Jefferson Airplane was doing background music from the big Bose speakers angled downward around the walls where they met the ceiling. Grace Slick, singing her heart out. Not loudly, though, which was a shame. Grace was made for loud.

The fact was that many of Jill's Joint patrons had actually lived the sixties and now were in the country of the old, where softer music often prevailed.

As for Connie, she was twenty-six and barely noticed the music, and thought Grace Slick was some kind of television sitcom or reality star who was branching out.

A man at the bar, younger than many of the drinkers, caught Connie's attention. She was mildly interested. Not that he looked like a winner. It was more that he didn't look like an obvious loser. At best he was average looking.

She reassessed with a mind dulled by vodka.

Well, no, he was better than average looking. Why was that?

She openly scrutinized the man, which didn't seem to affect him. He returned her stare with a sort of neutral one of his own.

There was nothing you could say was wrong with him. He had regular features, was average height and weight. He had brown hair with a part on the left, and was dressed well enough in gray slacks and a black blazer. Not a memorable-looking guy, but one you didn't immediately look away from. If he were a tune he'd be Muzak.

But there was something else about him that had snagged Connie's attention. The woman he was with at the bar was blond, like Connie, and not overweight but kind of on the plump side. Plump in the right places, that is. Connie automatically compared: she, Connie, had a better turn of ankle than the woman at the bar, a slimmer waist, lusher hair—and she wouldn't have been caught dead in the green dress the woman was wearing. Green did nothing for her color other than make her look like a zombie.

All of this in a glance.

Connie decided she and the woman might be the same type, but it was Connie who won every comparison. The other woman looked like her frumpy country cousin.

Not that Connie actually *had* a frumpy country—or city—cousin.

As she watched, the man smiled at the woman he was with, touched the back of her hand, then seemed to excuse himself.

Uh-oh.

He was walking directly toward Connie.

Connie wished she were somewhere else.

I was too obvious. Made an ass of myself.

She was glad she'd had enough vodka to dull her embarrassment somewhat.

While she stared, he sat down easily across from her at her table, as if she'd invited him. She resisted smiling back at him. It wasn't easy. This was such an obvious trade-up from the woman at the bar, who now was pointedly facing away and paying no attention to either of them.

"You invited me over," he said.

Connie kept a straight face. "I don't remember that."

He gave her the same smile he'd given the woman at the bar just before leaving her. It was a smile that said he could do pretty much what he pleased, and she wouldn't mind. He leaned slightly toward Connie. "When two people like us meet, we should discuss it."

"Discuss what?"

"Why we're meeting."

She grinned. "That would be because you've got the chutzpah to walk over here and pretend fate has drawn us to each other."

"If fate hasn't provided us with each other, what am I doing here?"

"I would say it's because I appeal to you more than the woman you were chatting up at the bar."

He laughed. "Talk about chutzpah! She happens to be my sister."

"Is that the truth?"

"Of course not. What are you drinking?"

"Vodka and water on the rocks."

"Enjoy it while you can. I hear this place is soon going to become a health drink oasis."

"You gotta be kidding."

"Nope. A lot of bars are going to convert. They'll get a big tax rebate. It's part of some pet project of the mayor's. He wants New Yorkers to be healthier."

"Than who?"

"I don't know. The Russians? The Chinese? Texans? It's not a bad idea. For the public good. Your glass is almost empty. May I buy you another?"

"My glass is one quarter full."

"Such incredible optimism." He signaled to the bartender for another round. Connie saw that he was drinking what looked like scotch or bourbon on the rocks.

"I didn't say you may," Connie told him.

"I read your mind."

"You can do that?"

"Yes, but I don't want to embarrass you."

The bartender came out from behind the bar and delivered their fresh drinks. She left his half-full glass and removed Connie's nearly empty one.

He raised his drink as if in toast and said, "My name is Brad."

"Your name is bullshit," Connie said. But she touched her glass to his. "I'm Connie."

He smiled at her. "Nice name. And mine really *is* Brad. I won't tell you my last name, though. It's too early in our relationship for that."

"True," Connie said. "We wouldn't want to be able to look each other up in the phone book."

"Or on Facebook."

They both sipped. He looked at her with eyes she'd thought were blue but in the reflected light of an illuminated beer sign might be brown.

Connie didn't look away.

"Chutzpah and fate," she said. "They're pretty much the same thing."

"Very often," Brad said.

They stared at each other for a few minutes more in frank appraisal.

"Yours," he said, finally. "Mine's a mess."

"We talking places?"

"Places."

"Mine's a mess, too."

"I knew that. I was too polite to mention it. We thinking of the same solution to our problem?"

"Yes."

"That would involve leaving here together," he said.

"We just got fresh drinks."

"Two sips, then we'll go."

So obvious. "Will the lady at the bar who isn't your sister be miffed?" she asked.

"I see no lady. I see no bar. I see only you."

"Do I look . . . healthy?"

"Oh, yeah."

She let him register them at the Barrington Hotel. It was a decent enough place, not far off Times Square. There were lots of potted palms in the lobby, and a huge chandelier that looked like the one in *Phantom of the Opera*.

Connie, who had finished her third only slightly watered down vodka at Jill's Joint, stood silently nearby and let him register at the desk. She watched and listened. *One night. Brad Wilson and wife.* Connie had to smile. *Brad Wilson.* She hoped he'd have a better imagination than that when they got upstairs. She watched as he filled in his "wife's" name on the registration card. *Mildred.* That made her think of the famous bitch in that old movie, *Mildred Pierce.*

As they ascended in the elevator, she thought he could have at least made it "Millie."

15

Fedderman had a boring assignment, but he knew from experience that he'd better not be bored.

He had no trouble staying close to Carlie Clark when she left her apartment and subwayed and walked to work. But he was careful. He didn't want Quinn's niece—or whatever she was—to glance back, not recognize him, and suspect that he, Fedderman, might be stalking her. Also, if she didn't know he was watching over her, she'd be less likely to give him away and prevent him from latching on to the real stalker. If there was a real stalker.

Fedderman watched Carlie enter an office building near the Flatiron Building. It was an old building with a red granite face. Two white marble steps led to a tinted glass entry beneath an art deco fresco. The building had a clean, ordered look, as if it had just been rehabbed but had chosen to return to the thirties rather than be up to date. Inside the building was Carlie's employer, Bold Designs Ltd.

In the increasing heat, Fedderman stood on the sunlit sidewalk across the street for a while and watched to see if anyone else was hanging around who might have tailed Carlie to work. He tried to pinpoint someone average looking. It seemed that all the years he'd been a cop he'd been searching for suspects who were "average" in every respect, because that's the way witnesses often described them. Fedderman had long ago come to the conclusion that your average person didn't appear at all average.

The thought made him smile. He would have to mention it to his wife, Penny, this evening, see if he could get a yuk out of her. Yuks didn't come so easy these days.

When he decided he'd seen enough of the average comings and goings in front of the building entrance, Fedderman walked across the street and pushed through the revolving door into the refreshingly cool lobby. As he did so, he noted a brass plaque informing him that he was entering the Mangor Building.

The lobby was spacious and high ceilinged, with lots of veined gray marble that probably dated back to the thirties, or maybe the twenties, when the building had been constructed. There were slowly revolving paddle fans here and there, dangling from the ceiling like lazy spiders, not moving much air but adding a lot to the ambience. Off to the left was an office directory beneath glass, in a narrow silver frame. To the right of the directory were three polished steel elevator doors. Above each door was an art deco arrow that indicated what floor the elevator was on. Nothing digitalized here. Fedderman wouldn't have been surprised if Sam Spade and Kasper Gutman appeared. The elevators were busy, under the heavy usage of men and women in office attire. There was no sign of a doorman or security guard.

Or Carlie.

Fedderman checked the directory and saw that Bold Designs Ltd., was on the twelfth floor. He walked over, pressed an already glowing UP button, and waited.

When the elevator arrived it was empty. Fedderman stepped aside for a woman who'd been waiting close behind him. He seemed to have lost his place in some kind of pecking order. Immediately half a dozen other people, most of them no doubt employed in offices above, stepped around him and filed into the elevator. Fedderman edged back into the herd, sneaked an arm between two fellow elevator passengers, and pressed the twelve button.

He was the only one who got out on twelve. Another, smaller directory on the wall indicated the offices on that floor. Bold Designs was the third one on his right.

Here Fedderman got lucky. Visible through a large lettered glass door was Carlie, standing and talking to a man and a woman who were behind the long, curved surface of a reception desk. He was looking at her from behind but was reasonably sure she was Carlie. When she turned slightly, laughing at something the man said, Fedderman got a clear look at her profile and was positive.

Safe in your nest.

He returned to the lobby and went back outside.

The sidewalks were still crowded, and the morning was heating up robustly, as if trying for some kind of record. Fedderman crossed at the corner and entered a pastry shop he'd noticed. It was reasonably cool in there.

Though he'd already had breakfast, he went to the counter and ordered a cheese Danish and a cup of coffee. He found a booth by the window from which he could keep an eye on the Mangor Building entrance. The lobby didn't go through to the next block, so if Carlie left the building he'd see her. Quinn had told him that, once inside, she probably wouldn't emerge until lunchtime.

Still, there was always a chance things would change. That the unexpected would happen. He wanted to be ready. So he sat patiently, a cup of coffee before him that he barely sipped, along with an uneaten Danish. Like a hunter intent on his snare.

At ten-thirty, Fedderman gave up. It had been unlikely anyway that Carlie would leave and be followed by her stalker.

Yet not all *that* unlikely, he told himself. If she actually was being stalked, the sicko would most likely latch on to her either leaving her apartment or her place of employment.

Or he might be waiting and watching somewhere, just like Fedderman.

Fedderman slid out of the booth and stood up. His body was stiff, his back slightly sore. He reflected that stakeouts were a younger man's game.

The suspicion was beginning to sneak in that the same might be said of life in general.

He left a generous tip, then paid at the register and

went back outside to cross the street and enter the Mangor Building.

It was time to make his presence known to Carlie.

It would be good to instill some confidence in her, surprising her with the fact that he'd provided security for her from her apartment and had staked out her office building. She hadn't noticed him, even though they'd briefly met. She would be impressed, and would comply all the easier with any request.

As before, the Mangor Building lobby was refreshingly cool by contrast. The rush to occupy offices and cubicles was over. There was an elevator waiting at lobby level with open door. Fedderman stepped inside and pressed the button for twelve.

As he was doing this, the elevator alongside his reached the lobby and three passengers emerged. One of them was a man in a neat gray suit, white shirt, pink and gray tie. His black shoes were buffed to a high gloss. He looked like a mid-level management guy. A typical executive.

Very average.

The door to Fedderman's elevator slid closed before the man became visible to him.

Oddly, Carlie was back at the reception desk, where she could be seen from the twelfth-floor hall. The same man and woman were behind the desk. The man was African American, beefy, in a sharply tailored chalk-stripe blue suit. The woman was petite, with spectacularly piled brown hair that, with her high-heeled shoes, added about a foot to her height. They were all staring at something on the reception desk. As Fedderman watched, Carlie pointed at the object of their concentration. The woman behind the desk shook her head no. The man placed his fists on his hips.

Fedderman opened the heavy glass door and entered the anteroom. Behind the curved desk was a doorway open to a hall leading to more offices. On the wall, too high to have been visible from the hall, were neat block letters reading *Bold Designs Limited*.

All three people at the desk stopped what they were doing and stared at Fedderman. He was glad to see the glimmer of recognition in Carlie's eyes. And puzzled to see that all three Bold Designs employees seemed upset.

Fedderman tried a reassuring smile. It seemed to reassure no one. He flashed the shield that the NYPD gave Q&A detectives when they were working for hire.

"You must be here about this," the man behind the desk said.

"This?" Fedderman asked.

"You *are* the police?" He had a slight accent, maybe Jamaican.

"He's the police," Carlie said. "We've met." She gave Fedderman a smile.

"Good as," Fedderman said. "Detective Larry Fedderman."

"You can talk in front of them," Carlie said to Fedderman. "They know my problem."

"I've been tailing you since you left your apartment this morning," Fedderman said. "Looking out for you."

"I know," Carlie said. "If anyone was stalking me, you probably scared him away."

"Not a bad thing," Fedderman said, a little hurt by the fact that she'd noticed him.

"But *this* is a bad thing," the woman behind the desk

said, pointing again with a tapered, painted fingernail at whatever was on the desk. All of her nails were painted the same bright red color and had a tiny silver star pattern on them. Like many petite women, it was her diminutive size that triggered an assumption of youth. She looked older close up. Maybe even in her fifties.

"What the hell is *this*?" Fedderman asked, getting a little irritated.

Carlie picked up three eight-by-ten color photographs and handed them to him. One photo was of Carlie leaving her apartment building. Another of her walking along the street near her subway stop. The third photo showed her entering the Mangor Building.

Fedderman looked at Carlie. She was wearing the same clothes she had on in the photographs.

"They had to have been taken this morning," she said.

"Did they arrive in that?" Fedderman asked, nodding toward a ten-by-twelve yellow envelope.

Carlie nodded.

Fedderman used a fingertip and lifted the envelope partway off the desk. It was blank on the other side, too, except for *Carlie* in neat blue printed letters.

"A guy came in about ten minutes ago and laid this in front of me on the desk," the woman with the nails and high hair said. "Then he turned around and walked out."

Fedderman felt a stirring of hope. "You see his face?"

"For about a half a second, just before he turned around."

"Would you recognize him?"

"I doubt it. There was a bandage on his face, near

his nose. That's about all I can recall about how he looked."

"The way he planned it," Fedderman said. "How was he built? Tall, short?"

"Neither. He was average height and weight."

"What was he wearing?"

"A gray suit. White shirt. And a pink tie, I think."

"Did he say anything?"

"Nothing. He seemed to be in a hurry."

"I'll bet. Was there anything else in the envelope?"

"Nothing." The woman automatically reached for the envelope to demonstrate to Fedderman.

"Don't touch it," Fedderman said. "Or the photos."

She drew back a talon-like hand. Fedderman wondered what she did when she had to use a keyboard with those nails.

"He must have taken the photos this morning," Carlie said, "then printed them and brought them here. There might be copies."

She was too diplomatic to suggest that Fedderman should have noticed someone taking pictures of her. Fedderman realized that and blushed.

That bastard with his camera! How good he must be at his craft. My craft.

"Copies would be his problem," Fedderman said.

"Evidence," Carlie said.

Fedderman winked at her, this young woman with pigtails already looking ahead to her day in court.

He picked up the phone and asked the petite woman with the designer nails for an outside line. She used a knuckle to press the button for him.

He talked briefly with Quinn, describing the events of the morning.

"Make sure nobody touches those photos or envelope again," Quinn said. "I'll have Renz send a radio car over and pick them up so they can be handed over to the lab. Not that we'll find any useful prints. The envelope flap wasn't licked, right?"

"Right," Fedderman said. "It's one of those where you peel a little strip back and the flap has its own adhesive. It won't yield any DNA."

"Well," Quinn said, sighing in a way Fedderman didn't like, "we'll do the dance, just like this bastard intended."

"Nothing else to do," Fedderman said. He knew Quinn was right: this scene they were playing out had been intended by the killer.

"Stay with the envelope and photos," Quinn said again, and broke the connection.

"Was that Uncle Frank?" Carlie asked.

"You know it," Fedderman said.

"How'd he sound?"

"Unhappy. He'll be even more unhappy if anyone handles the envelope and those photos again."

As he spoke, Fedderman glanced at the photos, lying fanned out near the bottom of the envelope, where they had slid when he'd peeked at the opposite side and seen Carlie's penned name. The top photo was the one of Carlie entering the building this morning. It had been taken at a diagonal angle from across the street. In the foreground was a tall man facing away from the camera, his long arms at his sides. He was slightly out of focus but obviously observing Carlie. There was a blur of white near his right hand, barely distinguishable.

Fedderman looked down and buttoned his shirt cuff.

16

The hotel had been proof enough that Brad Wilson (so called) might be average looking, an imperfect and precise five, but he was anything but average when it came to sex. Connie hadn't realized she had so many erogenous zones, and the variety of things that could be done to them to evoke pleasure.

This was their first date, really. The first time they would have dinner together.

Connie was determined there would be no sex tonight. She wanted to begin this relationship emphasizing just that—a relationship. She doubted that Brad shared her determination. He seemed centered on the purely physical. And there was something oddly fascinating about him. Not on his very normal surface. Know him only a short time, and you realized he was something like a plain family sedan with a powerful engine beneath the hood. While he wasn't overtly intimidating, he gave the impression that there weren't many contests he would lose.

Maybe he'd have his way with her, she admitted.

Connie was learning the true meaning of the word *smitten*.

She studied him across her plate of penne pasta in Hall's, the restaurant he'd taken her to on First Avenue. It was also a corner bar, but the table area in back was remote enough not to pick up any loud conversation from the drinkers or noise from the large TV mounted above the mirrored shelves of bottles.

Connie had arrived first. When he'd entered the restaurant she was surprised to see him carrying a large, scuffed leather briefcase, as if he might have come here straight from work.

He smiled in a way certainly genuine; he was definitely glad to see her again. He didn't mention the briefcase as he slid it beneath the table and sat down in the chair across from hers. The white-clothed table was round and small. They were very near each other. She could feel the briefcase with the side of her foot.

"I'm glad you're here," she said. "I need to visit the powder room and not have them clear the table and give it away."

"Do they still call them that?"

"I do. Watch my purse."

He was glad to do that. She was gone only a few minutes when he worked the purse's clasp. Research, research, research.

"You never did tell me what you do for a living," Connie said, when she'd returned and was sipping her glass of Chablis.

Surprisingly, he didn't hesitate. "I buy and sell antiques."

"What kind of antiques?"

"Old."

Connie grinned at his evasiveness. "So you don't want to tell me."

"I just did."

"I mean, do you work for a large company, or an association of antique dealers, or are you one of those mystery buyers at auctions with secret clients on the phone, bidding up prices?"

"Sometimes I'm one of those phone people. I freelance, and my specialty is finding things. If a dealer, to satisfy a customer, is looking for a seventeenth century French wardrobe, I deliver."

"Would you go to France to get it?"

"I might."

"But how do you know where to find it?"

He smiled slyly. "I have my sources."

"That's interesting," Connie said, meaning it.

Brad smiled. When he did that, he lost his average looks and became, in Connie's mind, quite dashing. "And you?" he asked.

"Nothing so romantic as traveling all over the world searching for French wardrobes. I'm a bookkeeper."

"Whose books?"

"Various businesses around New York. Small ones, usually. Shops, restaurants, diners . . ."

"Restaurants?"

She nodded.

He seemed concerned. "Not this one?"

Connie laughed. "You seem worried that I might embarrass you and say this dinner's on me."

"Oh, nothing like that."

"I don't keep books for this restaurant, or for any antique stores, either," she said. "In case you were wondering."

"I wasn't. But I'll ask around antique outlets. Maybe drum up some business for you, if you're not too busy already."

"Are you kidding? An independent accountant in this economy?"

He smiled. "Maybe you can keep my books."

"Who's keeping them now?"

"I am."

"You know accounting?"

"I have a thing with math," he said. "But I'm more confident assessing the patina on an old firearm."

"Do you shoot, too?"

He raised both hands, palms out. "Not me. If a gun has to be fired, I find someone else to do it. I'm not interested in any gun newer than the nineteenth century."

Connie laughed. "I'm relieved."

When they were finished with dinner, they walked along First Avenue, past shops and diners and blacked-out office buildings. The evening was warm, but there was a slight breeze off the river. Thunder rumbled off in the distance, like the artillery of an army slowly advancing on the city, and occasionally lightning played among the clouds. New Yorkers didn't ask one another if they thought it was going to rain. They had become used to the distant sound and light shows, knowing that Mother Nature was tantalizing but promising nothing. They'd know when she was serious.

Brad and Connie looked over as they passed the UN Building, on the other side of the street.

"Why can't we all just get along?" Connie asked jokingly.

"We could go back to the Barrington Hotel and get along nicely," Brad said, slipping his arm around her.

"Only if the general assembly approves," Connie said.

A taxi traveling uptown crossed three lanes and pulled to the curb alongside them. Its passenger-side window glided down.

"Need a cab?" the driver asked, leaning sideways across the seat.

Connie looked up at Brad. "Did you arrange this somehow?"

"I'd like to take credit, but that would be my first lie to you."

He gripped Connie's elbow gently and guided her into the back of the cab, then climbed in after her and pulled the door shut. Connie could hardly resist. She was still considering it when she found herself already in the taxi.

She was surprised, but didn't object, when Brad gave the cab driver the cross streets closest to her apartment as their destination. So their relationship had moved beyond secret hotel trysts, into a phase more personal and serious. She was pleased.

Beside her, Dred Gant sat thinking about this morning, the photographs, and about the woman beside him. He knew he had a choice to make.

And that for somebody it would be final.

17

Fedderman met Carlie as she was coming out of Bold Designs after work.

"I thought you might want company on the way home," he said.

Carlie smiled gratefully. "Wouldn't at all mind. But mightn't it be better if you stayed out of sight behind me and caught the killer when he made a try for me?"

"You're kidding, right?"

"Damned right," Carlie said. She stopped walking and looked around. "Shall we take a cab?"

"Is that usually how you go home from work?" Fedderman knew that it wasn't.

"Nope. I'm a subway girl."

She must be rattled, if she was considering a cab.

"We can cab it," Fedderman said.

"No, I've reconsidered. If the sick creep is watching us, he'll think he's scared me into a taxi. Then his stunt with the photographs will have been a success."

Fedderman couldn't argue with that. "Then the subway it is," he said.

He didn't try to disguise that fact that he was with

Carlie as they walked to the subway stop, down concrete steps to the platform. He waited while she bought a Metro pass from a machine. He already had a paid-up one that would be good for another week.

The subway train was crowded and warm, and smelled like too many people in too small a space. Carlie was lucky enough to plop down in a seat after a woman with shopping bags rose at the last moment to push her way to the door before it closed. Fedderman wedged between two passengers and stood near Carlie, gripping the stainless steel overhead bar and letting his gaze slide.

He decided that everyone looked suspicious. There were three average-man types. One of them was sitting across from Carlie and reading a foreign-language newspaper. Fedderman kept an eye on all three, but they seemed completely unaware of Carlie. Like most people on the subway, they appeared almost trancelike and didn't make direct eye contact for very long with anyone else. Now and then someone would do a mild double take when they saw Fedderman. He could almost hear them thinking, *Cop*.

He flexed his legs slightly to maintain balance, and spent his time jouncing and swaying along in the subway car by mentally cataloging passengers—especially the three Joe Averages. If anyone in the car showed up again in Carlie's life, it wouldn't be considered a coincidence.

No more than those photographs left with the receptionist at Bold Designs.

Carlie's stop was next. She struggled to her feet as the train began to slow.

Steel squealed on steel, and the train came to a halt,

then did its backward lurch as if rebounding gently off a rubber wall.

Over a dozen passengers filed out, and over a dozen pressed into the car. On the platform, Carlie and Fedderman stayed well away from the drop to the tracks and made their way to the concrete exit steps.

When they surfaced, Fedderman scanned the street and sidewalks and was reasonably sure no one was dogging them. It was one of those times when he was sure he'd *feel* someone's presence if they posed a danger.

When they'd walked the few blocks to Carlie's apartment building, Fedderman accompanied her inside.

They rode the elevator up and he went with her to her apartment, going inside first after she'd unlocked the door. He was glad to see she had a knob lock and two dead bolts, all operated by the same key. Fedderman was glad to see her return the key to her purse. It was surprising how many people, for the sake of convenience, left their door keys under a welcome mat or on top of the door frame. Those obvious hiding places had been a convenience for burglars for as long as Fedderman could remember.

Though Carlie didn't seem to require it, he went through the apartment room by room, even checking closets and beneath the bed. He also made sure all the windows were locked.

When he returned to the living room he noticed how much cooler it was and saw that she'd switched on the air conditioner.

"I should have turned on the unit in the bedroom," he said.

Carlie shrugged. "No matter."

"You're locked in tight," he said. "I'll hang around outside for a while, just to be sure."

"Of what?"

"That nobody else is hanging around outside."

"You don't have to do that," Carlie said.

Huh? "Aren't you the woman who asked for protection?"

"Yes, from a killer. But the way I figure it, whoever took those photographs is a coward."

"So you don't think they were taken by the killer?"

"Probably they weren't. But if they were, he was hiding behind a camera."

"I know that bullies and people who operate in the shadows are supposed to be cowards," Fedderman said, "but to tell you the truth, I haven't found that to be the case."

"No phony reassurances out of you," Carlie said.

"It would be just like a serial killer, driven by compulsion and sadism, to try to spook you by letting you know he's been observing you. This is serious, Carlie. I could show you some other photographs that would assure you of that."

"I understand that he's not playing games," she said.

"No, he *is* playing games! And now and then it's time to sacrifice a pawn."

Carlie cupped her elbows in her hands and gave herself a hug.

Fedderman smiled. "Sorry. I don't want you badly frightened, but at the same time I want you scared enough to take precautions."

Carlie seemed to give this some consideration. "I think we've achieved just the right balance."

Fedderman wasn't so sure.

He went back outside and stood in a doorway across the street, where he could keep an eye on Carlie's apartment building. He could, in fact, see one of her lighted windows, and her silhouette pass from time to time across the drawn drapes.

A nice kid, Fedderman thought. He imagined her as his daughter. He considered what young women in the city had to cope with these days.

He was glad he didn't have a daughter.

Fedderman had been there about an hour, his knees locked the way he'd seen cattle do it in the field, when Carlie came out of the building. She glanced around, and walked toward him. She had on blue shorts and jogging shoes, and a T-shirt with a big yellow arrow on it pointing to her chin above the message *Not Stupid*.

She thought Fedderman was staring at her breasts until she remembered what shirt she was wearing.

"This is kind of silly," she said. "I'm hungry. Let's go down the street to a good Chinese restaurant and I'll buy you dinner."

Fedderman wondered what Quinn would think about that. He'd probably approve. Carlie couldn't be much safer than sitting across from her protector in a restaurant.

"Let's do that," Fedderman said. "But dinner's on me. I've got an expense account."

"All the better," Carlie said, and led the way.

She walked fast. Fedderman had a long, loping stride but had to hurry to keep up.

As he walked, he used his cell phone to let Quinn know where they were going.

* * *

They stayed at the restaurant, drinking green tea and talking. It struck Fedderman that while he contemplated how it would be having Carlie as a daughter, her contemplations might be altogether different.

Come back to earth, he told himself. Besides, he was married and she knew that. Probably.

While she sat across from him, perhaps trying to imagine what he was thinking, he found himself comparing her to Penny.

Penny, he decided.

For me, Penny.

With a certain smugness, he silently congratulated himself on his fidelity. Carlie continued wondering what it was the restaurant put in the sauce that made it taste so good.

A few minutes after ten o'clock, Fedderman saw Sal and Harold enter the restaurant. They remained just inside the door and studied the menu on an easel for a minute, then turned and walked out. Not once had they looked at Fedderman and Carlie.

Fedderman knew that if he left her now, she'd be safe.

And he'd be safe, too.

At that same moment, both of them laughing and still with the taste of wine in their mouths, Brad carried Connie Mason across the threshold of her apartment, and another kind of threshold altogether.

* * *

Quinn was lying in bed wearing nothing but his boxer shorts, feeling the cool air from the window unit play across his body. Pearl had wanted to go to bed early. That was fine with Quinn. They were both exhausted from a hard and hot day. He was surprised when she came into the bedroom in a diaphanous gown he hadn't seen in months.

She slid into bed alongside him. The gown, short to begin with, seemed to follow reluctantly. Somehow one of the straps had come loose, and Pearl's right breast was lodged firmly against his ribs. She scooted this way and that, changing position enough so she could kiss him on the cheek.

"An occasion?" he asked.

"Does it have to be?"

"Never."

"I just feel like it," Pearl said.

"Usually . . ."

"What?"

"I get signals."

"You mean like dots and dashes?"

"You know what I mean"

Her nude breast burrowed more firmly against his side. "You think I'm getting old?" she asked.

"If you are, I am. And I don't feel so old right now." He strained a neck muscle tilting his head forward and to the side so he could kiss her surprisingly cool forehead.

"It's Jody," she said.

"Huh?"

"I wouldn't give up having her around. But there's no denying she ages me."

"Bullshit," Quinn said.

"Older every day," Pearl said. "That's not bullshit. It's simple fact."

"Better every day," Quinn said. "Like fine wine, babe." He kissed her again. "Anyway, Carlie's a year or two older than Jody."

"But she's your niece, not your daughter."

"So?"

"You know what I mean."

And he did. He scooted himself lower on the mattress, turning toward her. A single bead of perspiration was tracking slowly down the breast that had worked out of her night gown, moving toward the nipple. Before it got there, he licked it off with the very tip of his tongue, then kissed her nipple. Her arms snaked around him and he moved a hand between her thighs, feeling her dampness. They kissed with a violence and passion he'd thought they'd lost.

She helped him work the nightgown all the way off. Then she was gripping him with her hands, helping him mount her, guiding him in.

Within a few minutes they rolled on the bed, changing position. Pearl wasn't acting like a woman dreading her advancing age. Or one who placed much value on foreplay.

Another few minutes and she was on top, rocking back and forth in a frenzy. Riding him.

Her muscles clenched and she threw back her head so she was staring at the ceiling. He raised his hips so all of him was in her, and she took full advantage.

She began a lilting moaning that was almost musical, the tendons in her neck standing out in stark relief. Tension tugged at the corners of her mouth.

The old Pearl, he felt like saying, but knew better, certain he'd be misunderstood.

Jody, Carlie, both young and with long lives stretching before them. He'd known what Pearl meant, and it had more to do with time than with anything else.

Women—men, too—had to establish their own personal relationships with time.

Pearl moaned again, lost in her consuming passion, safe from all her fears if not her desperation. For now, anyway.

Another trailing moan.

Pearl.

Afterward, he held her to him as she slept.

18

Connie was awakened by the light from the bedside reading lamp.

She screwed up her eyes and turned her face into her pillow. The pleasures of last night—Brad with his hands on her, all over her, Brad entering her body, pushing into her, ramming her, flooded into her memory. The evening hadn't gone at all as she'd planned. Then, within minutes after entering her apartment, it had gone exactly as she'd planned.

Plan B, she thought. She realized there had always been a plan B.

Thank God he wore a condom.

It seemed to her that the kind of deep and penetrating sex they had might lead to pregnancy almost every time. She knew it was foolish to think that way, but thinking had nothing to do with it. *Feeling*. That's what it was about. It had not been like sex with other men. Not in its intensity. For a while he had turned her into a creature that lived only in a world of sensation. Consideration and caution, morality and logic, none of it meant a thing because none of it existed when he so thoroughly possessed her.

Pregnancy.

She derived some solace from the knowledge of the condom. Still, she couldn't be sure. Condoms breaking or failing in other ways had led to entire industries of alternative means of protection.

She told herself not to be an idiot. She wasn't in such a terrible situation. They'd had sex. He'd used protection. *So be a big girl and don't start to worry 'til you miss a period.* Right now, all over the city, there were plenty of women in more danger of an unwanted pregnancy than she was.

But what if she *did* become pregnant? What would be her reaction? His reaction?

All the while she pondered, a part of her knew that it was something else about last night that was bothering her. What he'd done to her, what he now *could do* to her because of the power he held over her, seemed very much like prologue.

Or foreplay?

The possibility frightened and thrilled her.

She burrowed her forehead and eyes deeper into the pillow to escape the light.

"When you gonna turn the lamp off?" she asked, and for the first time wondered why he'd turned it on. There had been enough ambient light in the bedroom for him to make his way to the bathroom. She shifted slightly so one eye was exposed and could see the clock radio by the bed. Its green numerals indicated that it was 2:17 AM.

"Sweetheart? The lamp?"

No answer.

She felt with an exploratory foot and decided that she was alone in the bed. Maybe Brad was in the bathroom. She scanned the dark rectangle of the doorway and saw that the light in the bathroom was still off.

Connie sighed. Now she was completely awake. With her mind even more awhirl.

"Brad? Honey?"

No answer. But she could hear him—someone—moving around.

She sat up in bed and the room spun.

Really spun. There was a metallic taste in her mouth. She placed both hands on the mattress and clutched at the sheet so she wouldn't fall off the bed.

What the hell?

"Brad?"

"Here, Connie."

She couldn't see him; the room was revolving around her so crazily it was as if a powerful strobe light were making everything lurch with irregular but increasing speed.

"What's going on?" she asked breathlessly. "I'm so . . . It's like a carnival ride."

"Must have been something in that last drink you had," Brad said. She had a fix on him now, saw him in the strobe light as he went spinning past again and again. Nude, the way he slept. But his hands were different. A different color. Pale. White. Gloves. He was wearing white rubber gloves.

And he was closer.

"Drink?" she asked, knowing she'd been drugged.

He laughed. "You want another?"

"No. I . . ."

Closer.

"It will wear off soon," he assured her. "Then you'll know everything that's happening. You'll understand."

He rolled her onto her stomach and she felt his hand encircle her right wrist. Her arm was forced upward. She tried to resist but possessed no strength at all. There was a ripping sound. Something—tape?—was wrapped around her wrist, fastening it to a spindle of the heavy brass headboard. She started to object, but heard an identical ripping sound, what she knew now was a length of tape being torn from the roll. The tape was pressed painfully over her mouth. Her lower lip was bleeding. She was sure of that.

She closed her eyes. She had to. She didn't want to become nauseated and choke on her vomit behind the tape. She tried to reach for the tape with her free left hand, peel it off her mouth. Only she couldn't find her mouth. Her arm and hand felt as if they were detached from her body. Her legs felt the same way, waving about with the elasticity of noodles. Her left wrist was quickly taped to another brass spindle. Then her ankles were taped to the footboard.

Material ripped, sounding almost like the tape. Connie felt her torn nightgown sliding from beneath her body. She knew she was lying nude now, face down and spread-eagle on the bed.

Connie closed her eyes. This—everything—was out of her control now. She could only wait to see what was going to happen, and endure it. Whatever, it would end. . . .

She snapped alert and her body jerked as something acidic and powerful was waved beneath her nose. Her eyes bulged as she attempted to scream and heard nothing but the rush of blood in her ears.

She was completely aware now, no longer dizzy. The room was now stationary. It was so sudden it amazed her.

And her mind. Her thinking. Her thinking was now clear.

Brad—or whatever his name was—appeared as he had earlier when the room had been spinning. Naked except for almost transparent white rubber gloves. He was staring at her with unblinking interest, his intention clear.

Connie watched the news, read the papers. She understood what was going on. Her eyes bulged even wider as she tried a louder scream. All she managed to do was strain something in her neck.

Brad pulled the dresser out from the wall and angled it toward the bed. Then he carefully tilted the mirror so Connie could see herself in it. She tried not to look but stared fascinated at the nude, spread-eagle woman on the bed. The woman who looked like nothing so much as a sacrifice to ancient gods.

Brad had his scuffed leather briefcase. He held it up so she could see it. Then he laid it on the floor and bent over it. When he straightened she was surprised to see that he had a small replica of the Statue of Liberty. He placed it on the dresser so it faced the bed.

He knelt to reach into the briefcase again. This time when he stood up he was holding a coiled whip. It was braided leather and glittered with inserted splinters of steel. He loosened his grip on it and it uncoiled snake-like to the floor.

Connie almost levitated off the bed in terror. She saw the woman in the mirror do the same. They exchanged a glance of horrible knowledge.

Seconds became minutes.

Her tormentor controlled even time.

Later, he turned her onto her flayed and burning back and buttocks, and went to his briefcase for his knife. She caught a glimpse in the mirror of its sharp point and long, serrated blade.

And a glimpse of *him* staring at her.

He would leave her eyelids intact. Bonnie Anderson's eyes had bled and interfered with her vision, he was sure.

Live and learn.

He bent over her.

She didn't believe her pain could be greater without loss of consciousness.

She was wrong.

Her screams were constant and silent.

In the morning Fedderman returned to the street outside Carlie's apartment. Sal and Harold were in their unmarked Ford, parked at the opposite corner.

Harold, on the passenger side, spotted Fedderman and pointed up toward Carlie's apartment. Then he gave a thumbs-up sign.

Fedderman nodded, then took up position in the doorway across from Carlie's building.

Fifteen minutes later, Carlie emerged from the building, took the few steps down to the sidewalk, and strode toward her subway stop.

Fedderman considered catching up with her, then

changed his mind. He was sure she knew he was behind her anyway.

He should do his job. Do it right.

That was okay with Fedderman. Carlie was safe, at
least for the time being. She'd made it through the
night.

She hadn't been chosen.

19

"In the bedroom," the uniformed cop said to Quinn, when he stepped through the open door into Constance Mason's apartment.

There had been no need to tell Quinn. CSU personnel were swarming the living room and what he could see of the kitchen, plucking and tweezering and spraying and collecting. What Quinn often thought of as the dance of the white gloves.

Renz had phoned half an hour ago to tell Quinn that a woman named Constance Mason had been found dead in her apartment this morning. Judging by what was left of her, she'd been the same type as the killer's previous victim, Bonnie Anderson. Blond, firm chin and broad forehead, and curvaceous.

Quinn made his way past the kitchen and bath, to a bedroom at the end of the hall. When he stepped inside he saw a white-gloved tech who'd somehow separated himself from the swarm and was dusting for prints. He nodded to Quinn, and dusted his way out.

It took Quinn a few seconds to take in Renz, and Nift the medical examiner, standing over the bed. On the bed was something Quinn had to force himself to look at.

"Meet Connie Mason," Renz said. He'd mentioned the victim's name to Quinn on the phone.

"She'd get up, smile, and shake hands with you," Nift said, "but I don't think you'd like that."

"Not 'Constance'?" Quinn asked Renz.

"Nobody named Constance isn't called Connie," Renz said. "Even dead."

Nift said, "By the way, Quinn, where's Pearl?"

"She sends her regrets."

"Tell her I said hey."

Quinn ignored him and moved closer to the bed.

A rectangle of silver duct tape had been removed from Connie's mouth but still clung by a corner. Her pale lips were slightly parted. Her eyes were wide and staring, making Quinn momentarily wish there was something to that old notion that killers' images were emblazoned on the eyes of their victims at the time of death.

"At least she still has her eyelids," Quinn said.

"A quality of mercy?" Renz wondered aloud.

"More like throwing shit into the game to confuse us," Quinn said.

Renz shrugged. "You're the one who knows these sleazebags."

Her stomach had been sliced open in a wide U shape just over her pubis, the flap of raggedly cut skin carefully laid back to reveal whatever of her internal organs hadn't been removed and slung all over the bed.

"I took a peek," Nift said, "and her back and ass look pretty much like hamburger. Scourged. I think they did that during the Spanish Inquisition."

"But back then it was the cops," Quinn said.

Quinn noticed something familiar jutting from the carnage of the victim's stomach cavity. Covered with blood was a familiar statuette of the Statue of Liberty.

"Not much doubt who did this," Renz said.

Quinn nodded. "No doubts now, if there ever were any. You've got your serial killer, Harley."

"Not that I wanted one," Renz said.

Quinn believed him. There was no political gain to be had from what was happening, only pitfalls.

Quinn looked up at Renz. "What do we know so far?"

"The victim was some kind of accountant," Renz said. "She had an eight o'clock meeting with a client and didn't show. They were supposed to have coffee at a place not far from here. At quarter to nine the guy she was supposed to meet came here. He found the door unlocked. Opened it part way and called in, but got no reply. He started inside; then he smelled something. He wasn't sure what, but it scared him. That's when he went downstairs and got the super. They came in together, got sick together. The super, guy name of Ike, called nine-eleven. Like that thing on the bed needed medical attention."

"Anybody talk to Ike and the guy she was supposed to meet?"

"Uniforms got statements from both of them. The guy Connie was scheduled to meet owns a jewelry store on West Forty-fifth Street. She kept books for him. Ike's story is essentially what I just told you."

"Where'd you get her ID?"

"The purse over there on her dresser. And there are several identifying papers in and on her desk, in the living room. Also these." He drew a plastic evidence bag from his coat's side pocket and handed it to Quinn, who carefully examined its contents.

"Photographs of Bonnie Anderson," Renz said. "His previous victim. They were on the floor near the bed, where they wouldn't get blood on them."

"He wants unimpeachable credit for the murder," Nift said. "Can't blame him for that."

Quinn was glad Pearl wasn't there to hear Nift. They would definitely get into it.

"Connie have a computer?" Quinn asked.

"Had one. Looks like the killer took it. There was a wireless mouse and a modem on the desk, but that's all."

"Smartphone?"

"Yeah. He took that, too. Call it and you get nothing useful."

"Smart killer."

"He sure as hell works clean," Renz said. "Literally. He wore rubber or latex gloves, and it appears that after he was finished with Connie, he took a shower in the bathroom. There's still blood there, and no doubt some in the drain. But probably it's all the victim's blood. Of course, he wasn't careless enough to leave bloody fingerprints." Renz gave a grim smile that seemed to include his double chin. "Maybe someday he will."

Quinn doubted that. "What about the victim's nails?" he asked Nift.

"Nothing much under them," Nift said. "Nothing suggests a struggle before she was tied up and sliced open. My guess is we'll find drugs in her."

Quinn glanced again at the corpse. "God, I hope so."

And they did find drugs. Traces of Ambien. There was white wine in her stomach, too. To help Constance Mason nap before her ordeal.

They were sitting around Q&A that evening—Quinn, Fedderman, Sal, and Harold—along with Helen Iman, the NYPD profiler. Quinn was the only one in his chair. The others were all simply standing, or perched on the edges of their desks. Helen the profiler, lanky and over six feet tall, with a choppy carrot-colored summer hairdo, was half sitting on Pearl's unoccupied desk. She looked like a girls' athletic director, in baggy shorts and a Knicks T-shirt, leaning back with her arms crossed. She wasn't trying to figure a strategy for the second half, though; she was trying to get a handle on this killer, and share it.

On Quinn's desk were copies of the Bonnie Anderson photographs that had been left next to Connie Mason's corpse, along with current shots of Connie's mutilated body, taken in her bedroom by the police photographer and printed out and disseminated immediately.

"I suppose we're going to find photos of Connie Mason's body next to the killer's next victim," Quinn said. He remembered what Nift had said about unimpeachable evidence. "He doesn't want credit for the murders to go to anyone else."

"Seems obvious he hates women," Fedderman said, "the way he guts them like that."

"But why the Statue of Liberty in the open wound," Quinn asked, "if he's going to the trouble of taking photographs?"

"The photos are his mementos," Helen said. "The Lady Liberty statuettes are ours."

"Being a serial killer doesn't necessarily mean you're un-American," Harold said.

The others stared silently at him.

"So why does he open his victims up like that?" Sal asked.

"Maybe he wants to learn more about them," Helen said. "Maybe what he's doing is a metaphor for spilling all the secrets."

"Looking inside them," Harold said.

"Nobody—I mean, no man—really understands women," Sal rasped. "But we don't go around gutting them with a sharp knife. Most of us don't."

"We're dealing with somebody who does," Helen said. "And that's about all we know about him."

"If we know even that," Fedderman said. "He might have an accomplice."

"Not unless it's his brother," Harold said. "They might have the same background, hang ups, and compulsions. And they wouldn't necessarily kill together. They might take turns."

Quinn thought that Harold now and then showed rare insight. Usually nothing came of it, but occasionally Harold's wild conjectures were accurate. Or at least provided new perspectives. He should leave his brain to science, Harold.

"It would be a first," Fedderman said. "Alternating brother serial killers." He hitched up his belt, but his pants dropped back down to where they'd been. "It'd take a lot of mutual trust."

"Something we can't rule out, though," Sal said.

Helen shook her head and smiled at him. "Men and

their mothers," she said. "Talk about love-hate relationships."

"Their fathers too," Harold said.

"But they usually don't go around killing men who
remind them of their fathers," Quinn pointed out. *Or in
pairs.*

The street door opened and Pearl came in. She'd left
her observation post across the street from Carlie
Clark's apartment after an NYPD radio car arrived.
The police car was still parked outside the apartment,
and would remain there until Sal arrived to take up the
watch.

"Have I got time to stop someplace and get a carry-
out coffee?" Sal asked Pearl.

"We've got foam cups with lids here," Pearl said.
"You can take one with you."

Sal looked as if he wanted to say something, but he
saw no percentage in criticizing coffee brewed by
Pearl. He simply smiled at her and left to drive the unmarked over to Carlie's apartment and set the radio car
guys free to roam.

Pearl made her way down the row of desks toward
her own, where Helen the profiler still lounged with
her lanky six-foot-plus body. Lazily, Helen straightened up and moved aside, ceding Pearl her territory.

As Pearl passed Quinn's desk, she glanced down at
the photos from the Bonnie Anderson murder, lying
next to current police shots from Connie Mason's bedroom.

"So where are the babies?" she asked.

They all stared at her.

"What babies?" Quinn said.

"Both those women have been cut open as if for C-section births," Pearl said.

"But neither one was pregnant," Quinn said. "We know *that*. Don't we?"

"We know it," Fedderman said.

"I don't care," Pearl said. She pointed to the photographs. "C-sections. Performed by a madman, but C-sections nonetheless."

She was tired and moved around her desk corner to sit in her padded chair.

Helen got out of her way.

20

Everyone from New York wanted to kill him.

The killer lay alone in his bed, his head propped on his wadded pillow so he could see the TV on the mass-produced antique dresser facing the foot of the bed. He watched the umpire simply stand with his fists on his hips, staring off toward left field. Threats seemed to fall flat even before they reached him.

The big-screen TV was tuned to a Mets game with the Houston Astros. A pop-fly ball that should have been caught had dropped between two Mets outfielders near the foul line, allowing an Astros player on third base to score a go-ahead run. Replays showed that the ball was clearly foul. The umpires, besieged by Mets players and the Mets manager, stood their ground and seemed to have minds focused elsewhere. The two players who had muffed the play stood off to the side as if they were lepers.

Nothing was going to change the umpires' decision. They turned in unison and walked away from the apoplectic Mets. Every Mets fan in the ballpark moaned as if they'd been stabbed in the heart.

Smiling, the killer sipped his beer, feeling some of it dribble from the corners of his lips because of the awkward position of his head.

Baseball really is like life. Once the play is called, it stands.

Tell it to Connie Mason.

But he had more important things than a ball game to moan about, if he were predisposed to moan.

There was, as always, the gnawing suspicion that he might have overlooked something, left something of himself behind. A bloody footprint, perhaps.

Afterward, it was always blood that bothered him most. Blood science. The police were doing more things with blood all the time. Learning things. The slightest nick on his body could leave a usable sample of DNA.

Another sip of beer. His third bottle. He knew logically that he'd been careful enough. But still, it was so easy to ignore something important and incriminating, like DNA.

DNA evidence was like a two-edged sword in the hands of a fool. So unpredictable. In a world of risk and secrets, it made it difficult to move without getting something lopped off. Something you didn't know was missing until it was too late.

The killer nursed his beer until a Mets player hit an easy pop fly that was caught behind second base, and the game was over. Another Mets loss. There would be post-game analysis, but the bartender knew his customers wouldn't be interested in that. To them, a loss was a loss was a loss.

Three sips of beer and a string of commercials later, it was time for the local news. He separated his feet some more on the bed so he could see all of the screen between them. A world gone mad, bracketed by his bare feet.

Vibrant colors danced over the screen, music blared, and a banner proclaimed BREAKING NEWS. A beautiful African American newscaster appeared on the screen. The killer knew she was Minnie Miner, who had her own quasi-news show, *ASAP*. The show was more journalistic hijinks than factual, though it usually got things reasonably right. The killer was a fan.

Minnie Miner looked solemn as she spoke:

"Another Manhattan woman was murdered last night. Twenty-six-year-old Constance Mason, a consulting accountant, was slain in her apartment in the same manner as last week's victim, Bonnie Anderson. Police aren't saying much, but *ASAP* has learned from unidentified sources that both women's abdomens were sliced open to reveal their entrails, some of which were removed. And in the body cavities of each was placed a cheap plastic statuette of the Statue of Liberty." Minnie looked angry. "That isn't what Lady Liberty was made for, folks. To be a cheap prop in a killer's tawdry tandem homicides." Morgue photos of the victims appeared behind Minnie. "As you folks can see, the victims certainly might, in the killer's diseased mind, be the same *type*. There is at least a superficial resemblance."

Minnie tilted her head to the side, touched her chin, obviously acting curious.

"What makes these serial killers of women tick? Why do certain women, looking a certain way or doing certain things, trigger their insane impulses? Dr. Joseph Westcomber, clinical psychiatrist and former New Jersey assistant prosecutor, has some ideas on the subject, and will appear on *Truth Report* tonight to reveal some startling facts about such predators—and their prey."

Minnie folded her hands. Sighed.

"There you have it—two beautiful New York women, both with so much to live for, both apparently victims of the same vicious killer. The Lady Liberty Killer, who leaves, propped in the gruesome wounds of his victims, plastic statuettes of the iconic female symbol of freedom, and of truth—two things we here at *ASAP* take very seriously. Unfortunately, we might not have seen or heard the last about this insane slayer of women. Yes, the Lady Liberty Killer is still at large, and still *extremely* dangerous.

"Sadly, history tells us this killer will strike again soon. If there are any new developments on this story, you can be assured that *ASAP* will be all over it. Sharing the news with you, *ASAP*!

"Now! Ever wonder what's *really* in those off-brand frozen dinners . . . ?"

The killer pressed his head back farther into his pillow, looking up at the ceiling and away from the TV. *The Lady Liberty Killer*. He thought about that, and decided he liked it. The words had a . . . well, a *legendary* feel to them.

Quinn had assigned himself the top apartments in Constance Mason's building, Fedderman the bottom units. They had canvassed the building for hours, expecting little, obtaining nothing. The building was a prewar structure with thick floors and ceilings, and even some interior brick walls. Almost soundproof. It was only through the ductwork, added decades after original construction to provide central air-conditioning, that sometimes secrets were unknowingly shared with neighbors.

Fedderman was still mildly confused after interviewing an aged tenant with hearing issues. He and the good-humored but less than communicative man had shouted back and forth and read lips, all to the conclusion that the hard-of-hearing tenant had seen or heard nothing the night of Constance Mason's murder. The tenant had watched TV with closed captions until around nine thirty and then fallen asleep.

Fedderman clasped one of his earlobes between thumb and forefinger and shook it in a circular motion, trying to clear his mind. He checked his notepad for the name and unit number of his next interviewee.

He had drawn the apartment of Adelaide Appleton, which was directly beneath Connie Mason's unit.

Fedderman scanned the copy of the cursory statement Appleton had given an NYPD detective the night of the murder.

Something interesting here.

Adelaide had heard something the night of Connie's death, though not necessarily anything of importance. Still, it couldn't be ignored, because she had heard it during the time the police estimated Connie was being tortured and murdered.

When Appleton came to the door after the third knock, she let Fedderman into the modest but comfortable-looking apartment. He showed her the account of her conversation with the detective concerning the night of the murder.

"That looks more or less right," she said, handing the wrinkled paper back to Fedderman.

"This wasn't an actual conversation that you heard?" Fedderman asked.

He watched Appleton's round, lined face as she struggled to make herself understood. She was a roundish woman, as her name suggested, thick-waisted and with a large bust. In her mid-forties, she was attractive in a sweet and gentle manner. She wore dark bangs and seemed to peek out from beneath them like an animal peering out from where it had found refuge.

She seemed nonplussed as to why Fedderman had to hear her statement after he'd read the account of the original statement she'd given to that other detective.

"It's as the other policeman wrote," she said patiently, smiling at Fedderman as if he were a slow student. "I heard only one voice. That would, I believe, make a conversation impossible."

"A man's voice?"

"I think so."

"And you heard it through that vent?" Fedderman motioned with his head toward a vent set low in the wall near a red leather recliner. Anyone reclined far back in the chair would have an ear very near to the vent.

"Did the speaker sound old or young?"

Adelaide sighed. That was okay, Fedderman thought. Let them get bored and itchy, and sometimes all of a sudden they remember something.

"In the middle," she said. "Maybe forty—though to tell you the truth I think it's a silly question. It's often impossible to guess someone's age by listening to their voice."

"It is a stupid question," Fedderman agreed. He kept a poker face. Conversational jujitsu.

"Yet you asked it."

"Your answer might not have been at all stupid and imprecise. You might have said he sounded sixty-seven years of age."

"That would be worse."

Fedderman smiled. "Yeah. Then I'd figure you were fibbing."

Adelaide thought about that. "Okay, I suppose you're right. And a woman who is my New York neighbor—which is to say, we hardly knew each other—has been horribly tortured and murdered. I suppose any question is allowed."

"And any answer is allowed to be questioned," Fedderman said.

"Isn't *that* reassuring?"

A rhetorical question, Fedderman decided. "You say you happened to hear voices through the vent—while sitting in that chair?" He pointed toward the red recliner.

Adelaide nodded. "I sit in that chair when I watch television. Sometimes I fall asleep there and wake up in the wee hours. Life isn't a cabaret for me."

"Is that what happened the night of Constance Mason's death?"

"No, I *had* dozed off watching this reality show about a group of people trapped on an island."

"Like Manhattan?"

"Very much so, except for the bridges and tunnels." She smiled sweetly. "Are you pulling my chain, Detective Fedderman? Hoping maybe gears will mesh and some pearl of knowledge will come rolling out and drop into your hand like a gum ball?"

"More like I'm trying to push your buttons, hoping I'll find the right one."

"Does that sort of thing work often?"

"Not really. But it's part of the job, to be a smart-ass with some people so they'll get emotional and reply in a way they wouldn't if they were calm."

Adelaide gave him her sweetest smile. "Are you married, Detective Fedderman?"

"Yes. And now you're trying to press *my* buttons." He touched the tip of his pencil to his tongue, then pretended to jot something in his notebook. "What you heard through the vent," he said, "were probably the last words spoken by a woman nearing her death."

Adelaide tilted back her head and surveyed the ceiling, rolling her eyes slightly as if seeing images up there, showing Fedderman that she was thinking. Then she abruptly shifted her bountiful body forward. Fedderman thought she might shout *Eureka!*

"I think you might have pressed one of those buttons," she said.

He leaned toward her. "How so?"

"It wasn't a woman's voice I heard—I'm positive now. It was a man's. And I realize now what he was saying."

Fedderman waited, encouraged. "So what *did* he say?"

"That's the thing about it. He said nothing."

"I thought you heard his voice."

"I did. And I'm sure now what he was doing. He was reciting the alphabet. Even if I didn't hear some of the letters, I could tell by the lilt of the voice, the old rhyme that we all learn at an early age. I almost thought he was going to finish and break into 'Now I Know My ABC's.' He was reciting the alphabet. Not fast, but slowly, as if he were testing his memory."

Tell me what you think of me. Fedderman couldn't resist reciting the last line of the childhood jingle in his mind.

"Maybe he was teaching someone. A kid. Or someone foreign trying to learn the language."

No." Adelaide shook her head. "It was more as if he was performing, trying to impress someone."

"But there was no applause? No complimentary remarks?"

"Nothing. Only silence."

"Are you sure the voice wasn't Constance Mason's?"

"Positive. It was a man speaking." Adelaide gazed at him in a way that made him uncomfortable. "You absolutely positively sure you're married?"

Fedderman said, "It isn't the kind of thing you forget."

He thanked Adelaide Appleton for her time and extended his hand to shake.

"If you don't mind," she said. Smiling her apple-sweet smile, she deftly tried to button his shirt cuff. Fedderman managed to avoid that, and she brushed some imaginary crumbs off the front of his suit coat.

Fedderman thanked her and got out of there.

21

When Harold showed up outside Carlie's apartment, to take his shift sitting in the unmarked Ford and watching her building, Sal moved over to make room behind the steering wheel. The car was parked half a block down from the apartment, in a dark space between the ranges of two streetlights.

Harold handed a carry-out coffee in through the window to Sal, and then got in on the driver's side. No interior light showed in the car, as the bulb had been removed. The seat was still warm from Sal.

"Anything going on?" Harold asked.

"The usual." Sal pried the plastic lid off his coffee, appreciated the rising steam for a moment, then took a sip that made a slurping sound.

Harold looked at the illuminated hands of his wristwatch. Ten minutes past midnight. Sal would start home in a few minutes, where he'd settle in for something like a night's sleep. Then Harold would be alone, tired, and bored out of his skull.

"I wouldn't mind switching shifts," Harold said.

Sal grunted. "Too late for that."

"How so?"

"One of us would have to work two shifts in a row."

"You," Harold said.

"Why?"

"To be fair."

"I don't deal in fair," Sal said, irritated. Why couldn't Harold simply do his job?

"We need a third guy," Harold said. "That way nobody would do a double shift."

"Then you'd bitch about doing your third of a shift."

Sal opened the car door and prepared to leave. He was exhausted, his back ached, and he'd had enough of Harold, though he was grateful for the coffee.

"Who's that?" Harold asked.

Sal looked and saw a man going up the steps to the entrance to Carlie's building. Average-sized guy. Wearing dark clothes. Glancing around.

"He looks furtive," Harold said.

"Could be a tenant who keeps late hours," Sal said, thinking he couldn't remember hearing any other cop use the word *furtive*. He placed his coffee in the car's plastic cup holder. "Or something else."

He and Harold waited until the man was inside the foyer, then got out of the car simultaneously, closing the doors but not slamming them and making noise that might attract attention. They walked fast toward the apartment building.

They'd taken only half a dozen steps when the building's door opened and the average-sized man in dark clothing came back outside.

"Surprise," Harold said softly.

The man immediately noticed Sal and Harold ap-

proaching and bounded down the steps, touching only
the middle one, and was running hard away from them.

"Jesus!" Sal said. "Why can't the bastard have average speed?"

"We can get him," Harold said, and turned to run in
the opposite direction.

Sal knew what he was doing, running the short distance to the corner behind them, then cutting left on
the cross street. If the guy they were chasing made a
right turn, he and Harold might run into each other.

But just as Harold's strategy seemed like a good
idea to Sal, the man ahead glanced back. He knew
there was only one pursuer now, and if he was smart
he'd figure out why and go straight or run left at the
corner.

He chose left, crossing the intersection, picking up
speed.

Damn it!

Harold was out of it now.

Sal continued to give chase. He tried using his two-
way to summon backup, young cops with young legs.
But he was bouncing up and down too hard to control
his grip and figured the hell with it. If he stopped and
called, the man would surely outdistance him far enough
to disappear. Maybe he'd even snag a late-running cab.

When he approached the corner, Sal made his left
on the diagonal to pick up a step or two. At this hour,
he didn't bother looking for cars.

A shadow flitted among darker shadows on the sidewalk ahead. The average guy, not as far ahead of him
as Sal had assumed.

But this was getting to be agony.

Sal lowered his head and tried breathing through his nose so he wouldn't get winded.

His lungs were working like noisy bellows, and his heart was pounding. Not only that, he was developing a stitch in his right side. He knew what might be up ahead of him, and hoped if he did catch up, he'd have something left with which to fight.

He was considering firing a warning shot, right here in the middle of Manhattan. The streets were almost empty.

But there were windows. And people turned up when and where you least expected them.

And who knew where a ricochet might go?

Sal began to wobble, then faltered.

A horn blared, jolting his senses, and a patrol car roared past him, the light strip on its roof sending out dancing bolts of color. The man ahead looked back and began to slow down, realizing he couldn't outrun a car.

The car's siren yelped once, like a dog's warning bark. Sal watched the man stop altogether and stand, leaning forward with his hands on his thighs.

You're out of breath, too, you bastard!

Sal slowed to a steady walking speed, hoping he'd reach the NYPD car and the possible killer before his heart gave out.

Ahead of him, the police car veered toward the man and angled in to the curb. Car doors opened and two uniforms got out. The runner raised his hands as if he were in a cowboy movie. One of the uniforms yelled something, signaling with his drawn gun, and the darkly dressed man stooped low and then lay facedown on the sidewalk.

Within seconds, both uniformed cops were over him. One of them was cuffing his wrists behind him.

Footsteps behind Sal made him turn.

Harold was chugging along behind him, breathing hard, looking as pale as his gray mustache.

"We're getting too old for this stuff," he said.

Sal made a growling noise to disguise the fact that he was panting. "We got him, didn't we?"

"We got somebody," Harold wheezed.

Both men continued trudging toward where the Lady Liberty Killer might be, lying on the sidewalk with two cops standing over him. Both cops had their arms crossed. One of them was staring down at the suspect, and the other was watching the approach of Sal and Harold.

Sal and Harold broke into a steady jog, side by side, putting up a pretty good front but actually moving more slowly than when they were walking.

"One of us should have gotten into a foot race with him," Sal said. "The other should have gone back to the car and driven after him."

"Easy to say now," Harold said.

"No," Sal said, "I can barely breathe, much less talk."

Sal flashed his shield and explained to the two uniforms who he and Harold were, and why they were there.

"So this asshole might be the Lady Liberty Killer?" the younger of the two uniforms said. He sounded awed. He wore his cap tilted forward and looked like a young Clint Eastwood. His partner looked like no one in particular but was larger than Clint. Not good casting.

"No, no, no . . ." the man lying awkwardly on the sidewalk said. He began to move.

"Maybe, maybe, maybe," Harold said.

The older, larger uniform helped the handcuffed suspect stand up, while his partner opened their patrol car's rear door. They loaded him into the backseat, which was separated from the front of the car by a steel mesh divider.

Sal gave Carlie's address to Eastwood and his partner, and they drove to the apartment building and waited while Sal and Harold walked the three blocks to join them.

When the two walking detectives reached the parked police car, they were still breathing hard.

"Tough night for you guys," the younger cop who looked like Eastwood said, half sitting and propped against a front fender.

"See what you got to look forward to?" Sal rasped, and spat off to the side.

The young cop grinned.

"It's not so bad," Harold assured him.

Sal could have kicked Harold.

"Don't I know you from someplace?" Harold asked the young cop.

Eastwood shook his head. "I don't think so. Why? You feel lucky?"

"What's that supposed to mean?"

Sal thought about straightening Harold out, but what was the use?

Instead, he went into the apartment building and woke up Carlie Clark.

* * *

Carlie was wearing jeans, a blousy red tunic, and slippers, when she emerged from the building with Sal. Her eyes looked swollen from sleep, and her blond hair was tousled. The young cop stared at her appreciatively.

She flinched as Sal gripped her elbow gently and guided her toward the back of the police cruiser.

There were reflections on the slightly tinted car windows, and she leaned forward so she could see into the dim, meshed-in confines where the suspect sat. Sal could feel the vibrations of fear running up her arm.

"He's cuffed," he assured Carlie, "even if he could get out."

That seemed to relax her, but not a lot.

"This the guy who's been stalking you?" Sal asked.

She leaned slightly farther forward.

"Jesse Trummel!" she said, and straightened up, wearing a surprised expression.

Sal was surprised, too. "You know him?"

"Yes. He works at Bold Designs."

"I guess he had designs on you," Harold said.

He was ignored.

The large cop inside the car had been listening. The back window glided down.

Carlie moved back a step. There was nothing but air between her and Jesse Trummel now.

"You don't have to be afraid of me, Carlie," Trummel said. He had a high, phlegmy voice.

"What were you doing in her apartment building?" Sal asked.

Trummel made a point of looking him directly in

the eye, not realizing that was what most liars did. "Leaving her a note, is all. Honest!"

"You just happened to be in the neighborhood?"

"Not far from here, actually. I was drinking at a friend's house. You can check that and see—there was a bunch of us. When the party broke up and everyone started to leave, I remembered that Carlie lived nearby."

"So what?" Sal asked.

"I . . . I admired—I mean, I admire Carlie. I don't know if she knows that. But . . . well, I was drinking and not thinking straight, and I decided to let her know how I felt."

"Past midnight, and you were going to surprise her and declare your love?" Sal asked.

"No, no. I wouldn't do that. I left a note in her mailbox, is all."

"Weren't you going to see her at work tomorrow?" Harold asked.

"Sure, I was. But like I told you, I'd had enough to drink that I wasn't thinking straight."

"Thinking with the wrong head," Eastwood said.

Sal looked over at him. "You want me to include that in my notes?"

Eastwood shrugged and leaned farther back against the car. He tilted his cap down low on his forehead and looked even more like the movie star.

Sal led Carlie away from the car, out of earshot. Harold knew the routine and stayed near the car, like the uniformed cop. Leaving Sal and Carlie alone so they could become buddies and confidants.

Sal moved closer to Carlie and glanced over as if to

make sure they were far enough away that they wouldn't be overheard.

"Were you aware of the way this guy thought of you?" he asked.

Carlie seemed slightly embarrassed. "To tell you the truth, it's been hard not to be aware of it. I mean, the way he stares at me . . ."

"He looks average enough. Is he the man who's been following you?"

"No. Definitely not."

"How can you be so definite, if your stalker is so average looking?"

"I see Jesse every day at work. He's a draftsman. He works at a desk and computer setup not far from mine. Makes renderings."

"Which are?"

"He works from plans or blueprints and shows what projects will look like after they're completed."

Sal leaned toward her so their foreheads were almost touching. "Understand, I have to ask you this. Have you and this Jesse guy ever—"

"Never! Our relationship—or at least what he'd like to be a relationship— is platonic and only one way."

Sal knew that people often fibbed about this. "So you and he aren't in a romantic situation."

"Not in the slightest. I don't dislike Jesse. But . . ."

"So you don't think of him *that* way?"

"Of course not."

"Okay. I had to ask. I mean, Trummel's not a bad-looking fella."

"I suppose not," Carlie said. "He's just . . ."

They looked at each other and spoke simultaneously: "Average."

While the others stood and watched, Sal went back into the building with Carlie. To be on the safe side, he went up to her apartment with her so she could get her mailbox key and come back down to the foyer

Her brass box contained only a single folded sheet of white paper. It was nothing the Postal Service had delivered. Sal slipped on a pair of white gloves and removed it from the box before she could.

"There might be fingerprints," he said. "Or something else. You'd be surprised what a police lab can come up with."

"But we know Jesse wrote it. He said he did."

"We don't know exactly what we know," Sal said. He was glad Harold wasn't here to make this conversation more confusing.

He carefully unfolded the note. It contained a single sentence written in blue ink.

Sal held it out so Carlie could read it:

I think about you all the time.

It was unsigned.

"Short and sweet," Sal said. *And anonymous.*

Carlie felt her face flush. She reached out for the note, but Sal refolded it on the seams and held it at the edges with his fingertips.

"Sorry," he said. "I've gotta keep this. I'll take it outside and put it in an evidence bag. It's part of the investigation, even if it doesn't lead anywhere."

She jammed her hands in her baggy tunic's pockets. "I understand."

Sal thought she didn't. Not really.

They returned to where the patrol car was parked. Sal showed the note to Harold, who looked at it without touching it, looked inside the car at Trummel, and grinned.

Sal refolded the note with care.

I think about you all the time.

"You're a genuine heartthrob," Sal said to Carlie, smiling.

"I don't see myself that way," she said.

Sal said, "There are at least two men who do."

Harold said, "Rawhide!"

22

Outside Kansas City, Missouri, 1996

Mildred Gant drove her black Dodge van into the rest stop off the interstate, listening to the loud squeal of front brakes that needed new pads. She backed off slightly on the pedal, muting the squeal so as not to attract attention. Next to her, Dred "Squeaky" Gant sat staring straight ahead out a windshield that was scarred by the arc of a worn-out wiper blade.

He had recited the alphabet at least a dozen times since they had set out this morning. His mother didn't believe in time wasted, and as she had often told him, the alphabet was a good thing to occupy his mind. She wondered sometimes herself if she could recite the damned thing after listening so often to Squeaky. Some things could become *too* familiar,

There were half a dozen parked cars nosed into the curb near the restrooms and vending machines. Beyond the restrooms was a larger blacktop lot area where trucks were parked. Not just big eighteen-wheelers, but smaller straight vans as well. Recently mowed grass surrounded the stop, and its scent still hung in the air. A woman walking a brace of white poodles was the only thing moving out there in the heat.

"Out," Mildred said. She watched while Dred unbuckled his seat belt; then she unbuckled hers and climbed down out of the van. She waited for Dred to walk around the front of the van to join her.

She looked at Dred in his Missouri Tigers T-shirt, worn-out jeans, and moccasins. He was average height and weight for his age, but looked strong enough. He was staring at her expectantly.

Off to the left of the restrooms and vending machines were a wood picnic table and some trash barrels—one of them for recyclables. Beyond that table was a small stretch of woods.

"Sit yourself over there and wait," Mildred said.

She stood and watched while Dred silently obeyed. Then she went to the vending machines, used her forearm to wipe sweat from her forehead, and dug in a pocket of the smock-like dress she wore for some loose change. She fed some quarters into a machine and bought a couple of orange sodas in cans. The machine messed up giving her change and didn't respond when she kicked it and rattled the coin return. Mildred's world.

She walked out of the shade of the vending machine kiosk and crossed the grass to where Dred was sitting patiently at one of the wooden tables. There was a small charcoal grill there on an iron post. Mildred wondered who the hell would grill anything on it. Who wanted to eat at a rest stop?

She gave the soda can she'd been sipping from to

Dred, then sat down next to him on the bench seat, hoping she wouldn't get a splinter in her ass. It had happened to her once before at this stop.

From where Mildred and Dred sat they could see the truckers' side of the rest stop. Three eighteen-wheelers were parked over there. The round metal lids capping their vertical exhaust pipes were dancing, and diesel fumes from their idling engines wavered in the humid air.

One of the trucks growled and moved forward, rolling slowly away from where it had been parked. The engine changed tones as the driver worked through the gears. When the truck reached the long ramp back up to the highway, it picked up speed. Mildred watched it merge with traffic, off in the distance.

"You know what you're gonna do?" Mildred asked.

"Sure."

Neither of them spoke as a tractor-trailer with a dusty blue cab rolled into the truck stop. It slowed, and with much hissing of air brakes it parked in the space vacated by the truck that had just left. This rig (as Mildred had come to think of them) looked as big as the law allowed, with a sleeper behind the cab. It was pulling a long trailer with a blue stripe painted on it front to rear. The trailer was lettered HOGAN GASS CARTAGE. Mildred had researched it and learned it was a small outfit based in Memphis.

The driver-side door opened, and a husky man in coveralls and no shirt swung himself down from the cab. He was bald and wearing sunglasses. Even from this distance he looked big. He stood for a moment looking around, then swaggered toward Mildred and Dred.

When the man got closer, Dred saw that both of his huge arms were covered with tattoos. So many tattoos that it was impossible to single out any one of them and know what it represented without staring hard. And Dred didn't want to stare at the man at all.

"I'm Rudy," he said in a smoker's harsh voice. "If you're Mildred, we talked on the phone."

"I'm Mildred," Mildred said. "And this is Dred."

Rudy looked at Dred appraisingly. "Named after your mother?"

"I s'pose." Dred had never considered that. Now that he had, he didn't like it.

"To some folks he goes by the name Squeaky. 'Cause he bitches and whines too much."

The driver looked him up and down. "I'll call him something other'n that."

"Suit yourself."

"I expected somebody older and bigger," the driver said.

"He's big enough. Don't matter how old he is."

"Guess not," Rudy said. He trained narrow dark eyes again on Dred. "You strong, kid?"

"Strong enough."

Rudy grinned. "He a smart-ass?" he asked Mildred.

"If he is," Mildred said, "let me know."

"I'll behave," Dred said.

"You bet your ass you will," the driver said. He glanced around, then took a roll of bills out of a coverall pocket. He peeled five of the bills off the roll and handed them to Mildred.

She counted them deftly and slipped them into a fold of her dress.

"You got a money belt in there?" the driver asked.

"Or a knife or a gun," Mildred said, grinning to show she was kidding, they were just joking around. Maybe. "Either way, you'll get your money's worth." She nodded toward Dred. "He'll go with you and unload your truck while you sit on your ass. Then he'll load your trailer for your return run. Just drop him off here and we're done. If you like the service, you can use it again."

"Sounds fair."

"Is fair."

"To everybody but the kid."

"Like you give a shit."

Rudy nodded. "Let's go, kid."

Dred wriggled his way along the bench to where he could swivel and stand up without getting his legs tangled up under the table.

"How much of that hundred is he gonna get?" the driver asked Mildred.

She smiled. "He likes to work."

"Lives for it, I'll bet," the driver said, signaling with a sideways motion of his head that it was time to walk.

Mildred watched the two of them cross the grassy rise toward where the truck with the blue cab was parked. The driver absently rested a hand on Dred's shoulder.

They could have passed for father and son.

Five miles west of the rest stop was a restaurant and gas station popular with travelers as well as truckers. The lot was crowded with cars and eighteen-wheelers. Mildred steered the van over to the pumps and filled the tank with some of the money she'd been paid for hiring out Dred.

When the tank was full, she went inside and paid cash, then returned to the van and moved it onto the restaurant side of the parking lot. She felt pretty good, with a full tank of gas and a pocketful of money.

She got out of the van and locked it carefully out of habit, from hauling antiques she bought and sold at auctions. There was an old tiger oak dresser back there now. She should have used Dred's help unloading it before driving to the rest stop. They could have moved it into the storage shed, where it wouldn't be rained on, so the van would be available for whatever they might buy at an auction scheduled in two days where a farm was being foreclosed on.

They could move the dresser as soon as Dred returned, she decided. He shouldn't be too tired. Better to wrench his young back than her older one.

She went into the restaurant and had a large piece of coconut pie and a glass of milk. After wiping a milk mustache from above her upper lip, she scooped up the check and made her way to the cashier to pay. She didn't leave a tip.

On the way out, she bought a lottery ticket.

23

"What if something had gotten in the paper or on TV news?" Carlie asked Jesse Trummel the next morning at work.

They were alone in the Bold Designs employees' lounge, a pale green room lined with vending machines that dispensed soup, sandwiches, tasteless cinnamon rolls, and coffee. There was a table with half a dozen gray metal folding chairs around it. Hardly anyone actually ate any of the food here. They drank the coffee only because they had no choice.

"I'm sorry," Jesse said for the tenth time. "I screwed up," He was dressed in a brown suit, blue shirt, and plain red tie. Decades ago he might have been a faceless advertising executive over on Madison Avenue. Now he was a faceless draftsman with delusions of gossip and grandeur, and the executive's unisex restroom that required a key.

The key, Carlie mused, was what Jesse would always be searching for.

"We can be colleagues and friends," Carlie said. "That's all."

"I think that was pretty much drilled home to me last night."

As he spoke she noticed a curious thing. One of his ears was noticeably larger than the other. Oddly, that took away some of his boring sameness, his *averageness*, even made him remotely attractive.

Carlie cautioned herself not to dwell on the mismatched ears.

"Can I at least buy you a coffee?" Jesse was asking.

Not giving up. Something else she had to admire, despite herself.

"No," she snapped. "Nothing. It isn't real coffee, anyway. It's piss."

She turned and went out the door.

"I know it is," she heard him saying, as the door swung closed behind her. "But it's all we've got."

His words echoed in her mind. *All we've got . . .*

No, no, no!

"A paycheck for your thoughts," a male voice said.

She stopped, startled.

Floyd Higgins, one of her many bosses at Bold Designs, was smiling at her. "You looked so preoccupied," he said, "it made me wonder."

"I was thinking we need to move the changing rooms closer to the middle of the store in that Cuddled Cougar account."

"The closer the customers are to the changing rooms, the closer they are to trying it on," Higgins said.

"And to parading around and showing it off to whoever else is in the store, gauging other people's reactions before they commit to buying it."

"Strangers' reactions?"

"Especially strangers' reactions."

"Ah, the female insight."

"Like you guys with hats."

Higgins grinned. "Okay, you get your paycheck."

Carlie couldn't help noticing that both of his ears were exactly the same size. Boring.

Dora Lane had watched another condo deal come unraveled. The prospective new owners had ordered a home inspection—not a bad idea, or unexpected—and found plenty to bitch about. The seller offered to adjust the price downward, but not enough. Another commission lost.

Dora was a sales agent for The Walker Group. Old Herman Walker, the owner and manager of the firm, had already laid off half the sales force, and those left were now working on a commission-only basis.

No sales, no commissions, no paycheck. Dora's savings were shrinking fast, and her credit cards were almost maxed out.

She stood now on the subway platform, waiting for the uptown train—any train. It would be painful but simple and fast to die beneath the wheels of a roaring, shrieking subway train that would still be traveling near top speed when it got to where Dora was standing.

She had moved as far down as she could get on the platform. So far, in fact, that there were no other passengers around. That was fine with Dora. She didn't want to upset anyone. She simply wanted out.

Out of sight now on the platform was a crusty-looking guy playing the sax, with the case laid out open before him. As she'd walked past him, Dora had noticed that there were two lonely dollar bills in the worn velvet lined case, probably put there by the sax player himself as an ice breaker.

He was playing something sad that Dora had heard before, but whose title she couldn't recall. Something about Sunday-morning love. His worn clothes, battered instrument, and mournful tune reminded Dora that there were people worse off than herself. But so what? Wasn't there always someone in a worse situation? Maybe this guy with the sax should follow Dora's lead and end his ceaseless desperation.

An incomprehensible voice blared from the public address system, speaking with an accent Dora couldn't place.

The air began to stir as a train approached, pushing a breeze ahead of it through the narrow tunnel. Dora moved to the edge of the platform, where it was painted yellow, leaned forward, and peered into the black tunnel.

Still she couldn't hear the train, but she could see its distant twin lights piercing the darkness.

She gathered her final thoughts as she began to hear the muted roar, watching the twin lights become brighter and farther apart.

And there the train was, bursting out of the darkness, drowning out the sad song of the saxophone.

Or had the plaintive tune ceased earlier?

Just her luck, not even being able to die with musical accompaniment.

The great steel front car was gigantic now, closing fast.

Dora shifted her weight forward. She had the balls to do this. She did!

As she leaned forward, a grip like steel closed on her arm just above the elbow and pulled her back.

The train screamed and squealed to a stop, to disgorge and take in passengers. Dora heard a voice in her ear.

"A pretty girl like you doesn't have to do that."

She moved half a step away and turned. And was looking at the sax player. Same tattered jeans, duct-taped sneakers, stained black *Phantom of the Opera* T-shirt.

Otherwise she wouldn't have recognized him. He was such an average-looking guy.

She glared hard at him, told him to mind his own business, then walked to the stairwell and stomped toward the world above.

Half an hour of hard walking later, Dora said, "What the goddamn hell are you doing?"

She'd found herself at the farmer's market and had reached for the last apple pie, and another, larger hand closed on the pie just as she touched it. Neither she nor the man who had reached for the pie withdrew. It had been something of a tie.

Their fingers remained in contact. He had strong-looking hands with prominent veins. They were warm, and the hair on the backs of his knuckles was dark and slightly curly. Dora looked up from the pie display, into his face, and there was the interfering bastard from the subway. Mr. Sax Man.

He was smiling. It didn't light up his face. "Apple pie happens to be my favorite," he said, "and considering what you have in mind, why not let me have it? Don't try to tell me you weren't going to do a swan dive in front of that train."

"I don't have to tell you or not tell you anything. You were probably gonna steal the pie anyway." She moved her hand slightly so it wasn't touching his, but she could still feel a slight tingling on the backs of her fingers. As if electricity played there.

He was still smiling. He was getting some kind of charge out of this. As if he sensed a mutual attraction. Dora kept a poker face. *Dream on, asshole.*

His smile stayed. "I'm not as down and out as you might think," he said.

"Or as I might care." Dora wrenched her arm away from him.

"Let me buy the pie and we'll go someplace and share it. We can talk this thing over."

"The pie thing?"

"The other thing. You know what I mean. What were you going to do, gorge on the pie because calories no longer mattered?"

That was precisely what she'd had in mind. The lesser sins hardly concerned her at this point.

"There is no *other* thing," she said. "And I don't want to share *your* apple pie with you."

He shrugged. "So you pay for the pie. What's it matter to you, if it's gonna be your last meal?"

He showed infallible logic there. And another train wasn't due for more than twenty minutes.

And there would be one after that.

"All right," she said. "I've got enough left on one of my credit cards for a hamburger."

"You should use a debit card. You can run through your money much faster that way." He did a graceful little dip and picked up his saxophone case, which

Dora had forgotten even though it was close enough to trip over.

"You aren't going to change my mind," Dora said.

"About the debit card?"

"You know what I mean."

"I don't want to change your mind," he said. "I only want to enjoy your company, what's left of it. And my pie."

He stayed beside her as they walked toward the register, paying for the pie with a twenty-dollar bill and waving away the change as if he were Rockefeller. Out on the sidewalk beyond the stalls, he stayed close to her, as if he didn't want her to get away from him.

They settled into a diner on Sixth Avenue. It had blue vinyl booths, gray Formica tables, and oak-paneled walls displaying autographed photographs of famous but older Olympic athletes. Dora had heard of Wilma Rudolph and Mark Spitz, but that was about it. Who the hell was Cassius Clay?

She'd placed the pie, shrink wrapped and in a paper bag, on the seat beside her.

"We can't very well eat this in here," she said.

"We'll have it for dessert somewhere later."

There aren't going to be very many laters, she almost told him.

When a waiter came over from behind the counter, Mr. Saxophone ordered for both of them a cheeseburger, fries, and coffee. Dora wasn't crazy about the cheese but let it go. Mr. Sax removed his Mets cap when the waiter walked away, and placed it next to him on the booth's blue vinyl seat cushion, where his saxophone case was leaning.

Dora continued to assess the man. Couldn't help it. Brown hair, parted on the left, no gray in it yet, not a bad haircut. Even features. Some might say a reasonably handsome man. Others not. It would average out to about fifty-fifty. She wasn't sure which side she came down on. If he acted in the movies, it would be in forgettable everyman roles. The star's best friend who gets the homely girl as a consolation prize.

"You should take advantage of this opportunity," Dora said. "Get some good, nourishing food in you."

"You're concerned about my health?"

"Not really."

He placed his elbows on the table and laced his fingers. Dora noticed that his nails were clean and trimmed. "Meat and potatoes," he said. "Not to mention a bun. That should help me somewhat."

It took Dora a few seconds to realize he was talking about the meals he'd ordered for them. He made them sound like part of a health regimen.

Dora played with her napkin-wrapped knife and fork until the waiter returned with their coffees, each with a spoon balanced on the saucer.

She added cream. "Is playing sax in the subway more lucrative than I think?"

He gave her his average smile. "Probably."

"Are you one of those talented musicians licensed to play there?"

"No, no, I'm strictly illegal."

"What would the cops do if they caught you?"

"The first time, they'd just give me a warning and chase me away."

"Then what?"

"I don't know. There's never been a first time."

"You're actually pretty good on that saxophone. You teach yourself?"

"Nope. A truck driver taught me, long time ago."

She laughed, surprising herself. "You are *so* full of bullshit."

"That would be true."

The waiter came with their food.

Dora realized she was hungry and wolfed down her hamburger. She noticed her companion took his time eating and had reasonably good table manners. Better than hers, in fact.

After eating, they had coffee, neither mentioning the apple pie.

She studied him. "You're not one of the homeless."

"Didn't say I was. But matter of fact, right now, I am."

"Oh?"

"I was subletting. Well, borrowing, actually. An old friend let me stay in his apartment while he was in London on business. He unexpectedly returned yesterday, with a British lady love."

"And you were a third wheel."

" 'Fraid so. It was sickening to be around them, anyway."

Dora drummed with her fingernails on the side of her coffee cup, thinking. The prospect of dying wasn't so appealing now. Sometimes things were meant not to happen.

Not to say there was a God, necessarily.

But *something*.

24

Things could happen, if you were patient and waited for the opportunity. Dreams as well as nightmares could be real.

Sixteen-year-old Dred "Squeaky" Gant sat alone in a ten-by-ten-foot visiting room and waited. He was in a plain oak chair, facing the table, also oak, and an identical chair, now empty. Both chairs and the table were bolted to the concrete beneath the gray tile floor. Overhead was a fluorescent light fixture encased in heavy wire. There was a single window in the room, but it faced out on another room that appeared slightly distorted because of the thick, shatter-proof glass. The walls were painted institutional pale green. The institution was the Chillicothe Correctional Center, a state prison for women in Chillicothe, Missouri. The room was uncomfortably warm. Dred was especially warm because he was wearing a long-sleeved shirt even though it was well into May.

Dred's mother, Mildred Gant, had stolen nine hundred dollars cash from an auctioneer. It was money he'd received for an antique knock-down wardrobe. He'd made the mistake of leaving his office with the roll of bills exposed on his desk. He'd called the police immediately, and the money had been found beneath the seat of Mildred's parked van. It had still been tucked into an envelope with the auctioneer's name and address on it.

That would have been serious enough, but Mildred had jumped into the van and tried to drive it away, seriously injuring a highway patrolman in the process. It appeared that she'd swerved deliberately and tried to run him down.

A pubic defender in Jefferson City had helped Mildred plea bargain her sentence down to twenty years.

Though Mildred retained custody of Dred, he was now living in a foster home, along with four other foster children. The farm couple who ran things there worked the five foster children, but not unduly hard. Dred was becoming used to the place at last, and had even begun to speak, though in abbreviated sentences that were mostly mumbled.

The problem was that he'd become restless there. Nothing ever really happened, unless you counted the corn growing. He'd been considering running away, but that wasn't a practical solution. While in the foster home before this one, he'd been accidentally shot in the thigh while he was stealing eggs to sell to a pig farmer's wife down the road. He thought the egg farmer, a man he'd lived with and worked for, had shot him on purpose. It was only a .22 long rifle bullet, but it had lodged in his thigh, been removed by a doctor who was usually drunk, and left him with a slight limp.

When Mildred had been told about the "accident,"

she'd said not to bother her with such news unless the wound was fatal.

Today was the third time Dred had come to the prison for a visit with his mother. The pig farmer's wife, a wiry, hard-eyed little woman named Irma, had driven him in the family pickup truck and now waited in the prison's main building for the visit to be ended.

A slight sound made Dred look up.

The door opened and Mildred entered. She had on a drab prison outfit that looked like it should be on a man. Her straight dark hair was stiff and slicked back, but dangled down over one ear. She wore no makeup. None had ever worked an improvement, anyway.

A large uniformed guard with massive hands accompanied her. He watched in that detached way of guards everywhere while she slid into the chair opposite Dred's. The guard fastened and locked the handcuffs on her wrists to an iron ring bolted into the table, so she could barely move her hands and could stand up only halfway. She posed no danger now.

The guard left the room, closing the door behind him. He almost immediately reappeared outside the window and stood watching the room's two occupants.

Mildred sat staring at Dred, noticing the way he was looking at her.

"Ain't I pretty?" she said, with a gap-toothed grin. She'd lost a front tooth two weeks ago in a scuffle with another prisoner.

Dred said nothing.

Mildred sneered at him. "Heard you was shot. You okay?"

"Healed up, mostly."

"You been behavin', after that, I trust," said Mildred.

"Been trying," Dred said.

"I suspect it learned you a lesson."

Beneath the table, he began fidgeting with his left shirt cuff, using the fingers of his right hand.

"How those folks you're livin' with been treatin' you?" Mildred asked. "Other than shootin' at your sorry ass?"

"Okay, I guess."

"Social workers or the like ever come around?"

"They do. I don't talk to them unless they ask a question, then I don't say much. Like you told me."

He could smell his mother's stale perspiration, feel the heat emanating from her bulky, sweaty body.

She tucked in her chin and hunched a shoulder to absorb perspiration from around her eye.

She gave him another grin. "You miss your old mom?"

"Time to time, I do."

Dred continued kneading his shirt cuff with his right hand. Visitors had to endure a body search when they arrived at the prison. It was feared that they might slip something dangerous or illegal to the prisoners.

That wasn't exactly what Dred had had in mind. No one had noticed the flexible, string-thin jigsaw blade inserted out of sight in the rough material of his shirt sleeve and cuff.

"I get outta here," Mildred said, "and we can pick up where we left off."

"Yes, ma'am."

"First thing'll be to make sure that auctioneer, Larry, is sorry enough he crossed me that he won't do it again." She turned her head for a second and spat on the floor. "You be thinkin' about that."

"Sure will."

Something narrow and silver appeared below a tiny hole in Dred's left shirt cuff. The fingers of his right hand continued to manipulate against his thumb, gradually working the jigsaw blade out from between layers of material.

"You don't slip back into your lazy habits while I'm gone, you hear?" his mother said.

"I never been lazy."

Mildred blinked, slightly surprised by his positive statement. It wasn't like Dred to disagree with her even slightly. He should know better. Definitely he would need retraining.

Beneath the shirt cuff the slender silver jigsaw blade protruded, under the table where the guard couldn't see it. It was about a foot long, supple, and finely sawtoothed. When drawn taut in the frame of a saw, it could swivel and cut fine patterns in wood. Gripped at the final inch, where Dred held it tightly between thumb and forefinger, it dangled down like a whip, with more spring and flexibility than a hickory switch.

"I get outta here, you better believe you're gonna get a talkin' to," Mildred said.

"I don't believe so, ma'am."

"There are such things as parole," Mildred said.

"Not for you, ma'am."

She looked at him curiously. He stared back at her in a new way, without fear. More like with a deadpan decisiveness, as if he'd flat made up his mind about something. There was a tiny bright glint in his right eye, like a bit of broken glass catching the light.

"I hope you're not thinkin' about—"

Dred drew the supple jigsaw blade up and back as he leaned across the table. He slashed with the blade.

Blood flew from Mildred's face and splattered against the window. On the other side of the thick glass, the guard was standing with his jaw dropped, momentarily frozen by surprise.

Mildred struggled to get up and defend herself, trying desperately to avoid the whipping, slashing blade. But her wrists were cuffed firmly to the table. She couldn't even stand all the way up. Couldn't get her head, her face, out of harm's way.

The supple blade continued to slash, back and forth, whipping across mouth, nose, and eyes, leaving horrible, gaping wounds. Dred could see the white glisten of teeth and bone.

He hardly noticed the door flying open and the guard rushing in. Heard the guard say, "Ow! Goddamn it!" as the blade caught his arm.

He managed to grab Dred's wrist, slender but strong, and twist his arm back.

Dred dropped the whipping, bloody blade.

Across from him, Mildred was still seated, screaming over and over, her hands cuffed close to the table and stiffened in grotesque claws.

"Holy Christ!" the guard said.

A loud alarm bell began to ring.

"Get a doctor in here!" the guard was yelling.

Mildred continued to scream, staring with one bulging eye at Dred through a curtain of blood.

"A doctor!"

Dred thought that, what with the screams and the clanging bell, it would be a while before anybody heard the guard.

He wished he hadn't dropped the flexible steel whip.

He'd rather be making good use of his time.

25

"And he became Muhammad Ali," the forgettable-looking guy with the sax said.

They were still in the diner on Sixth Avenue, the one with the autographed Olympic athlete photographs on the wall. Somebody must have ordered something with fried bacon. The scent of it filled the air.

Dora made a little *Oh* with her lips. "*Him,* I've heard of." She sipped at her third cup of coffee and looked out the window at the increasing pedestrian traffic streaming past. So many people. So many strangers. That's what made the city so lonely. Right now, her loneliness was like a knife. She knew that was why she was pursuing an acquaintanceship with this man, but she continued anyway. "We never did introduce ourselves. I'm Dora."

"We using just first names?"

"For now, yes."

"Okay. I'm Brad."

She considered. "Nice name."

"So's yours. It must mean something."

"It's an old Romanian name meaning *gift.*"

"I was thinking more like 'open the Dora.' "

Dora was in sales, so she understood people and had met all kinds. This one was trying to keep her off balance with what, in his mind, passed for wit and charm. The problem was, knowing that about him didn't keep him from succeeding with his dumb-ass humor.

He did have a certain heavy-handed wit and charm. Dora couldn't deny that.

"You told me you were a saxophone player," she said. "I never mentioned what I did."

"You're an aviatrix, I'll bet."

"No, I'm a real estate agent here in Manhattan. Do you know what that means?"

"You're broke?"

"I meant what else it means?"

He sipped and swallowed the last of his coffee. Smiled. "I give up."

Like hell you do. "It means you're not actually homeless. Or dependent on your friend with the new British lover. But all that doesn't matter."

He seemed interested. "How so?"

"It also means I have a master key to the lockboxes of condo and co-op units all over the city. That's so I can show the units if the owners are at work, or playing, or out of town." She smiled. "Some of the units are furnished and unoccupied, and have been for a long time."

Brad touched his fingertips together lightly, as if to check and see if they all matched with their counterparts on the other hand. "Is what I'm thinking you're thinking legal?"

"Sure. Long as you're a prospective buyer and I'm showing you the apartment."

"But what if we're caught . . . making ourselves at home there?"

"Whoever walked in on us would think I'm trying really hard to sell you the unit."

Brad looked thoughtful and absently used one hand to play with his spoon that had been resting on the table, unused near what was left of his black coffee.

"The honest truth is," he said, "I've been thinking about buying an apartment in Manhattan."

She gave him a knowing grin. *The honest truth.*

"Have been thinking about it for the last ten minutes," he said. "I'd like for my real estate agent to show me something."

"What are your preferences?"

"We talking real estate?"

"For now."

"Something vacant and furnished, where we wouldn't be disturbed."

"I think I've got exactly what you need."

"We still on real estate?"

"I'll take you by and show you the apartment," she said. "Then you can make up your mind."

"I think," he said, "it's already made up."

She paid at the counter while he left a tip, placed his Mets cap back on his head, and slid out of the booth with his saxophone case in one hand, the sack with the apple pie from the farmer's market in the other.

She held the pie while he went into a liquor store and bought a bottle of wine.

The condo was on West Fifty-seventh Street, in a pre-war building that had been completely rebuilt except for an ornate stone entrance. There was a key pad off to the side, near one of the glass double doors that were topped with brass arches.

Dora had memorized the simple five-number key code. She pressed buttons on the pad, and the door on the right clicked open a few inches. Brad started to open the door all the way for them, but he was holding his sax case and the bag containing the wine. Dora closed her hand around the brushed metal grip and held the door open. She was used to doing that for clients, and on a certain level was pretending that she was showing this apartment to a potential buyer. It helped her to believe there should be no trouble in doing something impulsive and, some would say, outrageous.

The lobby was done in pink marble and more brass. The elevators were centered in what looked like flat brass ovals overlaid in an open fan design.

"Swank," Brad commented. Actually thinking the lobby was overdone.

Dora was obviously glad he was impressed. "Swank as I could make it when it came to a building without a doorman."

He didn't question her about why they didn't want a doorman on the premises. It was best if they got upstairs and into the apartment without being seen, if they intended to be secret tenants for a night.

Possibly more than one night, Dora thought. She was a romantic and a dreamer.

A man in his sixties, wearing a gray suit and black beret, entered the lobby not far behind them. He nodded to them but other than that didn't acknowledge them, as the three of them got in an elevator. Dora pressed the six button. The man in the gray suit reached in front of her and pressed the button for the tenth floor. Brad stood at parade rest and fixed his gaze on the floor indicator above the doors sliding.

The man in the gray suit did likewise, and paid little attention to them as they left the elevator on the sixth floor.

"It's a big building," Dora said, leading Brad along the carpeted hall. "Nobody pays much attention to anyone else. It's not like it was on *Seinfeld*."

"The real New York," Brad said.

"There is no one real New York. It's all in the eye of the beholder."

"Deep," Brad said.

Dora laughed. "Sorry, I didn't mean to be."

"When we get inside, I'll open the wine and we can take care of that."

"Maybe I get deeper the more I drink," she said.

"That would be interesting," Brad said.

Dora glanced at him to reassure herself. She saw an ordinary-looking guy, harmless. Even if he did get a little kinky, she was sure she could handle him. Besides, what was wrong with a little kinky?

She used her master key on the agency lockbox that held a door key and prevented the knob from turning. When she'd removed the metal lockbox, she put it in her purse and opened the door.

The apartment greeted them with the silence and stillness of a place that had been sealed up for a while.

"How long's this unit been on the market?" Brad asked.

"Too long. The owner won't come down on price."

"I won't even ask how much it is," Brad said. He

stood a few feet inside the closed door and glanced around. The walls were white, with framed prints of impressionist paintings. Monet's water lilies calmed the spirit. Van Gogh and Brad exchanged a glance. Both mad.

"Hardly anyone inquires about this unit anymore," Dora said, "but the best thing—for us—is that the owner is in London and probably isn't going to return to New York, ever. Imagine—he doesn't like this place." She made a sweeping motion with her arm.

The furniture was traditional, a low cream-colored sofa, matching chairs with reading lamps on stalks peeking over them, a long walnut coffee table, blue and red cushions stacked before a fireplace containing fake logs.

"Other than that there are no clothes in the closet, it's like somebody still lives here," Dora said. "Dishes, flatware, and glasses are still in the kitchen. Somebody with a lot of money could move right in."

"Somebody has," Brad said, grinning. "At least for a while."

"I'll go wash my face," Dora said, "while you open the wine."

Moving closer, he kissed the tip of her nose. "Good plan."

He put down his saxophone case on the floor, and the apple pie on a nearby end table, and watched her walk into a hall that presumably led to a bathroom and at least one bedroom. Carrying the brown bag that contained the wine bottle, he went into the kitchen.

It was what's sometimes called a European kitchen, all white sink and appliances, with a pale granite countertop. The refrigerator and dishwasher had dark front surfaces, which didn't match the rest of the décor. Poor taste, Brad noted. He knew about taste. He'd learned about it as he'd moved higher and higher in the world of rare antiques, learned to act and talk like the people who knew good taste, because they had grown up with it. He had come to recognize it himself, and had put that knowledge to good use.

Sure that he hadn't absently touched something in the kitchen, he removed a pair of skintight Latex gloves from a pocket and slipped them on his hands, snapping them like a surgeon who'd prepared for countless operations. He removed the bottle of wine from the bag, a Chardonnay that Dora had mentioned she liked. He'd brought a cork remover, but he wasn't surprised to find a superior one in a kitchen drawer that also held silver-plated flatware. The silver design was supposed to make it look turn-of-the-century, but it didn't fool Brad. The stuff was available at Bloomingdale's.

There were no wineglasses, so he got down two water tumblers of the sort used in lots of diners and mid-priced restaurants. From his shirt pocket, he withdrew a small plastic bag containing white powder made from crushed pills. He poured half an inch of wine into one of the glasses, sprinkled the powder into it, then added more wine. In the other glass, he poured only wine. He got a spoon from the drawer where he'd found the cork remover and gently stirred the powder into the wine.

He removed his gloves and put them back in a pocket. Before he put the gloves back on, the bottle and two glasses would be the only objects he'd touch, and not take with him, that would bear fingerprints if not wiped.

* * *

Something ripped. Dora heard it quite distinctly.

My dress?

No. Impossible.

Was she having a dream?

Another, identical ripping sound brought her all the way out of sleep. Though she didn't open her eyes, she realized where she was. And how she'd gotten there.

Dora remembered she'd been drinking right after they'd come to the apartment, but still it was strange. That first glass of wine she'd had just minutes after they'd arrived had struck her like a hammer.

She became aware of a sound now, like someone working a bellows over and over, the way her father used to do when trying to get a flame to grow in the fireplace.

He never could get a fire started without using more and more crumpled newspaper. Dora had often wondered why he didn't simply begin the process that way.

She realized something odd. It was herself that she heard, breathing heavily through her nose.

Dora attempted to move, and immediately got a painful cramp in her right thigh.

Oh, God that hurt!

What the hell?

Where's Brad?

She tried to verbalize the question and discovered that her mouth was taped, which was why she was breathing through her nose. She worked her lips, pushed with her tongue. The tape stayed firm.

Finished with the tape, she realized that she was nude. And what an awkward position she was in. Something—she assumed some of the tape that she guessed now had made the ripping sound being torn from its spool—was holding her wrists fastened tightly to her ankles, her arms within the confines of her thighs. It left her in a three-point position, knees and head against the living room carpet. Face, rather her right cheek, was pressed flat into the carpet fiber. She must present an undignified and vulnerable position this way, her back exposed, her thighs spread wide, and her rump raised.

She felt herself becoming angry. *Very angry.* And it didn't take her long to find a focus for her rage. Brad had done this to her. He must have.

Where the hell was he? What kind of kinky non-sense was this?

She tried again to scream, but what small amount of noise she made was muffled by the tape and carpet.

There was Brad!

He was naked. Surprisingly muscular. He had an erection. When she looked away from that, she saw he was wearing tight latex gloves—the kind surgeons wore. He was smiling down at her.

For a few seconds, he disappeared from sight. When he returned he was carrying his fake leather saxophone case.

He placed the case on the floor, where she could see it. And where he could see her as he removed whatever he had inside the case in addition to his saxophone.

The smile never left his face as he opened the case and placed back into it the roll of duct tape he'd used to secure her. Then he took things out of the case. A knife with a long, serrated blade. Like a bread knife but with a sharp point. While Dora was still staring wide-eyed at the knife, he laid it on the floor and removed from the case a coiled leather whip. Dora saw flecks of silver glinting among the braids of the whip. Bits of sharp metal. Brad stood up and let the whip uncoil to the floor.

Dora could feel her heart hammering. She tried to scream again into the carpet. She kept up on the news. She understood now what was happening. What she had picked up in the subway and brought here, where no one would disturb them.

My own, stupid fault!

I deserve this!

I caused it!

If only there were someone she could apologize to. Say how sorry she was. How she despised herself for what she'd done.

For everything I've done. Ever!

The killer was staring down at her. The look on his face terrified her. She knew he was getting what he wanted, feeding off her fear. There was nothing she could do about it. Nothing.

He said, "You belong to me now."

For everything I've ever done . . .

She felt her bladder release as, dragging the whip like Satan's tail, he casually walked behind her and out of sight.

A minute passed. It must have been a full minute. Would he ever—

She heard the whip sing through the air.

It began.

Much later, on the way out, he picked up the apple pie.

26

"He's making them live longer," Nift the ME said, with something like admiration. He saw Quinn and Fedderman looking at him. "They suffer more for a longer period of time. He displays a very refined technique."

"Hooray for him," Fedderman said.

Standing over Dora's bloody remains, Nift smiled. "He's a craftsman. Gotta admire that. Even if we don't like what he's doing, we have to acknowledge he's good at it. That's his goal, to make them suffer while they're barely holding on."

"We know that," Fedderman said. "We still think he's a sick fu—"

"Something on the bathroom mirror," one of the techs interrupted.

Quinn and Fedderman followed him into the tiled bath, where the killer apparently had cleaned up after the murder.

Scrawled in blood on the bathroom mirror over the basin was a simple but infuriating phrase: FREEDOM TO KILL.

"Not enough there that we have a handwriting example," Fedderman said.

Quinn led the way out of the bathroom. The crime scene unit wasn't finished in there.

They took a quick look into the bedroom before leaving. There were a few techs in there. Nift was still probing at the ruined body with one of his gleaming stainless steel instruments. It was almost as if she were being tortured twice.

Quinn and Fedderman started moving carefully toward the apartment's hall door, leaving the place to the techs until they were finished searching it for clues that probably weren't there. They would come back later and root through drawers and closets.

Fedderman glanced back in the direction of the dead woman.

"I wish I was wearing a hat," he said, "so I could remove it."

Quinn thought at first he was joking, then saw that he wasn't.

Carlie slid into the booth in the Red Line Diner so she was facing Jody across the table. She had to admit that Jody was attractive in her unique way, with the springy red hair that she probably couldn't tame even if she tried. She also had a face that featured good bones, so that a more serious bearing neutralized the red tangle that resisted ribbon or barrette. There was also a sharp intelligence in her blue eyes, coupled with a good-natured challenge. This was a woman who would do something just for the hell of it.

Which might be why she'd invited Carlie to meet for breakfast.

"I took the liberty of ordering you a coffee," Jody said.

As if on command, one of the countermen came over with a hot mug. Jody already had coffee. Cream and sweetener were on the table, along with a fresh napkin and spoon. The attorney taking care of details.

"I'm not sure this meeting is such a good idea," Carlie said, adding cream to her coffee and stirring.

Jody glanced around the diner. It contained the usual New York mix—an elderly couple who looked like tourists; a guy with an orange Mohawk; four teenage girls in a booth, fortunately out of earshot; a blind woman with a service dog; two somber guys in business suits; a bearded man who might be homeless; a frenetic woman surrounded by shopping bags; a man playing chess by himself.

"Seems normal enough," Jody said. She looked out the grease-stained window, where morning traffic was a slowly moving parking lot. "Maybe it seems wrong to you because it's possible that you're being stalked?"

"I was thinking about you. Why endanger yourself?"

"I'm not the killer's type," Jody said.

"Maybe he likes variety."

"Killers don't."

Carlie smiled. "Quinn tell you that?"

"More or less."

"Did you get his permission for this breakfast meeting?"

Jody looked at her as if she must be insane. "I don't need permission, Carlie. I passed the bar."

Carlie knew some lawyer jokes that could flow from that statement, but held her silence. It was a subject that should be changed. "We gonna order food?"

"I'm on a diet."

"Me, too."

They regarded each other over the steaming coffee mugs.

"I wanted to clear the air," Jody said. "First of all, I admire what you're doing. You aren't satisfied to sit on your ass and wait for somebody to save you. You're taking an active part in a counter strategy."

"I don't know if it's a strategy," Carlie said.

"Then you don't know Quinn."

Careful not to burn her tongue, Carlie sipped her coffee. "You mean I'm being used as bait?"

"It comes to that. It isn't Quinn's idea, though. It's something that's been forced on him by circumstances. He wants to protect you more than he wants to use you."

"You like him, don't you?"

"Yeah. More importantly, I respect him."

"You're jealous of me," Carlie said.

"I'm not."

"Is he like a father to you?"

"Something like that."

"You don't have to be jealous."

"I'm not."

"You are."

"I am."

They grinned at each other.

"We're not blood sisters, but we're sisters nonetheless," Jody said. "I wanted to meet with you and let you know I'm with you in this, or anything else. I've done some work for Q&A, and you need to understand how dangerous and ugly things can get."

"I think I understand."

Jody knew she didn't, but why push it?

"Whatever questions you might have," she said, "you can come to me."

"Are you my lawyer?"

"If you pay for breakfast, that will be my retainer, and everything we say will be privileged information."

"Are you sure you passed the bar?"

"Passed it going away."

Carlie decided she'd play. "All right. We've got a deal."

Jody raised her almost nonexistent eyebrows. "Questions?"

"Quinn and your mother—"

"Except questions about Quinn and my mom."

Carlie smiled. "Fair enough. I'll ask my questions as they come up. What do I need to know?"

"When Quinn gets into a case, he becomes obsessed. These aren't just words. He *really* won't give up until the killer is stopped."

"Arrested, you mean?"

"Stopped."

Carlie understood.

"You can trust everyone at Q&A," Jody said, "and you can trust Quinn all the way to the bank."

"And inside the bank?"

"He *is* the bank. Trust him. Trust my mom. Trust the rest of them. Feds and Harold might make you wonder at times, but don't underestimate them. They'll die for you if it comes to that."

"They don't even know me."

"They know Quinn."

Carlie knew what Jody meant. She smiled broadly as she reached across the table and squeezed Jody's bony hand. "From now on, we behave like the sisters we are."

"Twice removed or something," Jody said. "Maybe three times. Not that it matters."

"Sure you don't want breakfast?"

Jody said, "Let's order French toast."

"I want in on the Lady Liberty case," Jody told Quinn and Pearl.

She had gone to Q&A immediately after leaving Carlie at the diner.

Quinn looked at her from where he sat behind his desk. "What about your cross-genre animal suit?"

"I'm not really worried about that anymore. The Supreme Court is on our side. They decided years ago that animals have constitutional rights. They've been litigating since then over what creatures are animals."

"I don't guess insects would qualify," Quinn said.

Jody looked, for a moment, angry. "Some people think that if it experiences pain, it fits the legal definition of animal."

Quinn knew better than to get into this discussion with Jody. Insects aside, he did wonder how livestock could hire an attorney. Probably, though, they would if they had the means. The pigs for sure.

"Why the Lady Liberty Killer case in particular?" Quinn asked.

"I talked with Carlie, and I don't like what some asshole is putting her through."

"You two . . . I mean, you aren't actually sisters."

"Sisters enough," Jody said.

"So what would you suggest?" Quinn asked.

"I could keep an eye on her, make sure she doesn't get surprised by the sicko who's killing, whipping, and eviscerating women in this wacko city."

"Not in that order," Quinn said.

Jody made a face as if she'd bitten into something unexpectedly bitter.

"And who'd be keeping an eye on you?" Quinn asked.

"One: I'm not the killer's type. Two: I can take care of myself."

"Sal and Harold are her angels," Quinn said.

"Twenty-four hours a day?"

"Almost. They take shifts."

"Then let's make it twenty-four hours a day."

"What about your job at Prather and Pierce?"

"I talked to them. They'll give me a leave of absence. They think that eventually they'll get some billable hours out of this. There's already enough interest in those murders to get a book contract."

"And the proceeds would go . . . ?"

"To various animal causes."

"Causes generally result in legal action."

"That's what the courts are there for." Jody smiled at Quinn, for a second looking like Pearl. "They need me even more than they think, but not every hour of every day."

"And your mother?"

"She's on board."

"What about your sort-of sister?"

"I talked to her."

"Seems you saved me for last,"

Jody grinned. "I knew you'd be hardest to convince."

"There's one condition," Quinn said. "Your mother has to approve of you getting involved in this case. And I want to hear her say so."

"She will," Jody said confidently. "I told you, I already talked to her about this."

Quinn was defeated. "I'll work out a schedule where sometimes Carlie will have three guardian angels."

"Good enough for me," Jody said. "For now."

Quinn pulled a murder file from a top drawer and laid it on the desk for Jody.

"Homework," he said.

She opened the folder and glanced at its contents. Autopsy photos were on top. One photo Quinn had removed from the folder was the one he wanted to keep as tight a secret as possible, with Renz and a few others. It was a shot of the medicine cabinet mirror, taken at an angle, so the message FREEDOM TO KILL was visible, scrawled in blood. After a sample of the blood had been removed and photographs had been taken, the message had been rubbed out. Some of the pursuing detectives would know it, and of course the killer. But not the public. FREEDOM TO KILL would be the test to weed out the many people who for whatever strange reason confessed falsely to such crimes. If a confessor knew about the bloody message, he'd be taken much, much more seriously.

"Those photographs supposed to make me puke?" Jody asked.

"Works sometimes," Quinn said.

"Well, not this time. Remember, I've seen blood and death before."

She thumbed through the photos and laid the case file down, then walked toward the half bath at the rear of the office. Faster and faster. Quinn heard the door slam. Then he heard her choking and gagging. The exhaust fan started running.

Jody was paler than usual when she returned to Quinn's desk.

"Not next time," she amended.

He smiled and handed the case file up to her.

He believed her.

"What do you think of your daughter giving up the legal world to play Spenser?" Quinn asked Pearl.

They were in the brownstone's living room, for once not using the air-conditioning, because the place had great cross ventilation and a cooling breeze was wafting through front to back.

Pearl, lounging on the sofa, paused in leafing through the contents of the Lady Liberty Killer murder book and said, "What the hell are you talking about?"

"Spenser. The famous tough guy P.I."

"I know who he is—the guy you are on your best days."

"Maybe your daughter's like Spenser."

They were in the office. Jody had been gone about ten minutes. Her energy field still seemed to electrify the place.

Quinn filled Pearl in on what Jody had told him.

Pearl looked nonplussed. That was the only word Quinn could think of that fit.

"She has this thing about running the bad guys to ground," Pearl said.

"Like her mother."

"More likely it's because of your dubious influence. Do you think we should stop her?"

"Kind of like trying to stop the tide," Quinn said. "Was her father like that?"

"About his music, yeah." Pearl's eyes took on a distant expression, as if she were looking inward, and back. She seemed ambivalent about what she was remembering.

"Obsession can be a good thing," Quinn said.

"If it isn't fatal."

"I didn't tell her about the Lady Liberty Killer's 'Freedom to Kill' message on the last victim's mirror."

"Good," Pearl said.

"Our psycho is in the game-playing phase," Quinn said.

"Because?"

"He's feeling the pressure and thinks he can handle it if he reduces it to a game."

"Maybe the most dangerous phase," Pearl said.

Quinn said, "Maybe you oughta tell your daughter that."

"What I think," Pearl said, "is that my daughter and your niece need to know the facts of death."

She returned to her foraging and reading, then looked over at him. "Doesn't Spenser have a dog?"

"I wouldn't know," Quinn said.

27

"We making progress?" Renz asked Quinn.

Quinn decided not to tell Renz that Jody was now also on the case.

"By inches," he said.

"Anything more on Dora?"

"Not unless you count that everyone who knew her even slightly thought she was angelic, even though she was a cutthroat real estate agent."

"There's nothing like dying young and violently to attain instant sainthood," Renz said.

"What about Carlie?"

"You mean Carlie as bait?"

"If you want to be so crass as to be truthful," Quinn said.

"I have nothing against the truth if it's useful."

"I think someone really is stalking her. It might be our killer, playing games. Or it might be Jesse Trummel."

"The guy she works with? How do you figure that?"

"He's kind of acting like her wingman," Quinn said, "ready to swoop in and save her if anyone actually does go for her. Which will probably result in two dead instead of one."

"Try telling the Jesse Trummels of the world that."

"Useless," Quinn said. "We're looking out for him. He really does seem ready to lay down his life for his fair maiden. You ever been in love like that?"

"I was always more interested in sex."

"I don't think Trummel has made it to that particular base." Quinn knew that Renz would have a hard time understanding that. But he was wrong.

"The Madonna-whore view of women," Renz said. "He respects her too much to screw her. My feeling is, find a whore who's a true believer."

"You would know where to look."

"If you're going to be pejorative I'm going to hang up."

"I was just starting to be pejora—"

Renz broke the connection. He loved to do that, demonstrate that he and technology were the alpha couple.

As Quinn was replacing the receiver on his desk phone, Jody walked in. It was hot outside. Her hair was a springy jungle and her nose glistened with perspiration. Her blue eyes were red rimmed and swollen, as if she'd been rubbing them, and her freckles were vivid. She was wearing jeans cut off just below the knees, and a faded red T-shirt that proclaimed she was a virgin and wearing a very old shirt.

She plopped down the murder book on Quinn's desk.

"You could have kept that," Quinn said.

Jody slumped into one of the chairs angled toward the desk. "I read it thoroughly, then copied everything in it."

"That should have made it evident that you've become involved in something dangerous."

"Uh-huh."

"You saw the photographs," Quinn said.

"And I read everything in the file you gave me."

"And?"

"It's always possible what Helen the profiler says about gamesmanship is true. The killer, like so many of them, likes to play games with whoever he sees as leading the pack that's trying to hunt him down."

"And I'm the leader of the pack," Quinn said.

Jody smiled with what looked like tolerance. "If you say so. But it sounds like a teenage song."

"It should."

He waited for her to speak, but she didn't. "And I'm smart enough to listen to your mother," he added.

"What about my mother's daughter?"

"She has my respect."

"And you have hers," Jody said.

"Have you come to some conclusion after sifting through all the material on the Lady Liberty Killer?"

"It isn't patriotism that motivates him," Jody said.

"We'd already decided that," Quinn said.

"And I don't believe Carlie—or I—are in as much danger as you seem to think. Unless, of course, Helen the profiler is right and he's playing mind games with *you*, personally."

Quinn hadn't been kidding about respecting Jody's intelligence. Not to mention her intuitive powers. "Helen might be right," he said. "But I suspect it's still too early for him to force some kind of end game."

"Is that how he'd see it?" Jody asked. "An end game?"

"He knows he's going to be caught. In some ways, he wants it to happen."

"But on his terms," Jody said, "so he can claim a kind of victory."

"Yes." Quinn had to smile. "Very astute of you."

"Then you assign some credence to my suggestion that Carlie and I might not be in such grave danger."

"Some," Quinn said. "Not enough to be unafraid for you. This kind of killer isn't predictable. He knows all the rules, too. And he enjoys breaking them. Sometimes making new ones."

"Still," Jody said, "compulsion trumps game playing."

"Usually."

"What's even better," Jody said, "is if the killer can combine the two."

"True. But compulsion still trumps. That, in the end, is how he gets caught."

"Then Carlie's safe because Dora Lane has been murdered. And I'm not slated to be murdered until sometime in the intermediate future."

Before she'd finished her sentence, Quinn understood what she meant.

"The victims were taken in alphabetical order," he said.

"Starting with *B*, for Bonnie." Her eyes bore into Quinn's. "There must be an *A* out there we don't yet know about."

Quinn felt like saying, *That's my girl!* But he didn't. After all, he had another daughter, out in California. And a niece, or whatever the hell she was, here in New York with Jody.

Jody was beaming at him. She said, "I understand."

Jesus! She does understand!

"It's time to talk to Jerry Lido," Quinn said, sounding a little throaty.

"The alcoholic computer genius?"

"He's all of that," Quinn said. "And he has an intimate relationship with Google, not to mention Lexis-Nexis and every search engine on the Net."

"He's one up on me, then," Jody said. "I don't seek around."

28

They sat in comfortable padded chairs with red cushions so brilliant they hurt the eye. They were in the all-purpose room at Golden Sunset Assisted Living. It was a large room, with a chocolate-brown carpet and strategically placed groupings of chairs and tables where various factions and family of the tenants could meet and visit.

Where Jody and her grandmother sat, no one could overhear their conversation. The nearest human ear was forty feet away, where half a dozen gray-haired men sat at a table before a large window. They seemed to be playing an odd kind of game with dollar bills while they enjoyed various non-alcoholic beverages.

Jody's grandmother, Pearl's mother, had known Jody was coming and was wearing a satiny blue dress that, with all the jewelry, might have looked more suitable on a younger woman. Her hair was recently done, and had been dyed an entirely different hue of blue, with undertones of the entire color spectrum. She was wearing moderately high-heeled shoes that had brass buckles and looked as if they must be causing distorting injuries to her feet.

She smiled at Jody, seated attentively across from her, and said, "Pearl." Pronouncing her daughter's name as if it were an answer on a quiz show.

"You mean Mom?" Jody asked. As if they had other Pearls in common.

"Yes, our own and dearest Pearl who—and I do keep fastidious and accurate count—hasn't been here in almost a month. I can't tell you how, being my flesh and blood and not with a tendency to avoid one's elders, you bring such comfort with your visits."

Jody, genuinely pleased, smiled wider and said, "Good!"

"Family is God's way of binding human beings so they are not alone, placed like game pieces put away too early in the closet, in places like, I am sorry to say, this."

"It seems okay here," Jody said, glancing around.

"It is my own opinion—and I must say, in most respects, also that of the other inmates—that we here find ourselves with no escape in a way station on the road to hell."

"Mom says she checked the place out and it was the best available."

"If the choice is between arsenic and strychnine, *the best* is hardly a matter of consequence."

"Well, if you put it that way . . ."

"Your mother has lost her perspective, in part due to holding so closely and dearly a job rather than a husband and children. *Her* choices, I am afraid, were not of the wisest and—if I may venture to express my opinion—she had her chances. A blessing such as yourself, for instance—"

"There's no need to go into that," Jody interrupted.

"Of course not, dear." Jody's grandmother leaned far forward to grip and squeeze her hand. "Often fate steps in and forces people to make the only choice they seem able to make. But I wonder sometimes that, if Pearl had listened to me about a certain *Doctor* Milton Kahn, things might even now be different for her, and perhaps different for you."

"I think she's with the right person in Quinn," Jody said.

Her grandmother threw up her hands. At first Jody thought it was a gesture of protest.

But she was wrong. Her grandmother was rolling her eyes heavenward. "Thank all the powers that be for *that* man, a mensch to the rescue when your poor mother most needed one. I won't say she was drowning in her troubles and going down for the third time, but sharks were circling. You tell Pearl her mother said, whatever else happens, not to get into one of her uppity moods and walk out on that good man."

Jody said. "Don't worry about that, Grandma. But you said—"

"It's vocation and—let's be realistic—salary that is the problem. The income of an established and respected dermatologist like *Doctor* Milton Kahn, compared to the meager earnings of a retired policeman and private detective, no matter how much of a mensch he is, determine quite different lifestyles, dear. No one shoots at a dermatologist."

"You have a point, Grandma."

Jody's grandmother smiled. "It's so nice to hear that word."

"Point?"

"No, the other. 'Grandma.' And it's so good to have you here with us, where, after tossing on the stormy oceans of life, we have found each other."

"See?" Jody said, feeling somewhat like driftwood. "None of this would have happened if Mom had married Dr. Whoever. If she'd never met Quinn. Life just works that way sometimes, Grandma. So many things we have no control over simply happen to us."

"So wise you are beyond your years, dear. Please remind your mother that fate plays its mysterious—not to say it doesn't now and then need a nudge—role in bringing us together. We are like moths seeking heat and light and then one day finding flame, or one of those loud zapping devices suburbanites place on their patios."

"I promise to remind Mom," Jody said. She squirmed in her chair, getting antsy.

"You might want to stay for lunch, dear. It's Italian wedding soup, and we don't know what that's going to be."

"I wish I could, but I can't," Jody said. "I'm working on an important case."

"Like Perry Mason."

"I remember him," Jody said.

"Of course you do, dear."

The group of gray men playing the game with paper money let out hoots and hollers at the table over near the large window.

Sunset Assisted Living wasn't so bad, Jody decided. Boredom punctuated by periods of elation. And occasionally by tragedy.

Like life in the outside world.

29

The beautiful TV newscaster, Minnie Miner, was on the TV above the shelves of assorted gourmet coffees in the Underwater Brew, an establishment that had nothing to do with water, or with beer. The killer had heard people talking about the owner calling his coffeehouse "Underwater" in reference to his real estate mortgage. The killer doubted the story. People didn't have a sense of humor about losing money.

"This killer," Minnie Miner said on the flat-screen TV, "is becoming increasingly vicious." Her big dark eyes widened beneath her bangs. Her astonished look. "Police say the details of this latest murder are too awful to describe." Astonishment became anger. "I say we deserve all the facts. We the people are strong enough to endure anything—even a monster in our midst."

The killer, seated at the coffee bar, thought about being referred to as a monster and decided he didn't mind. He'd heard great athletes referred to as monsters. Sometimes the word was used to describe people of great talent, with daring and abilities so far beyond those of most mortal beings they were . . . monstrous.

"You've got a nice smile," a woman's voice said.

He turned and saw an attractive—attractive enough, anyway—woman who'd been sitting at a nearby table. She'd moved to sit next to him while he was absorbed in *Minnie Miner ASAP*. She had a slightly overweight but sexy figure, the top button of her blouse undone to reveal the cleavage of generous breasts. Her eyes were the proper blue, her hair adequately blond, her jaw firm. She was still in her twenties, maybe.

The killer sipped his latte and decided this meeting was fated to occur.

"I wondered what you were smiling about," she said, her voice revealing a little uncertainty as to how he was going to react to her.

He smiled back. "I was thinking about baseball," he said, "so I wouldn't have to listen to any more on the news about that serial killer. I've seen and heard so much about him that I'm sick of it. He's awfully famous."

"Which team?"

"Huh? Oh. The Yankees."

Both of them looked again at the TV above the coffee display. Minnie Miner was still discussing the Lady Liberty Killer's latest victim, the horrible things that had been done to her. Minnie looked slightly ill, but that was probably an act.

"What do you suppose *ASAP* stands for?" the woman asked, as an SUV commercial came on the screen.

The killer thought. "A sudden appearance of a phenomenal person," he said. "In the Underwater coffeehouse."

She laughed. "Did somebody come in I don't know about?"

"I think we both know I'm talking about you."

She frowned, surprising him, and moved closer. "But see, I know I'm okay, but not phenomenal. So you're . . . exaggerating. And that means you might exaggerate about other things."

"I will out and out lie if it means making any progress in getting you to like me," he said.

"See, there it is again."

"No. You're an exceptional beauty. I'm right about that because I'm the beholder. That's all there is to it. If you and millions of other women wouldn't finish first in the Miss USA pageant, so what? To the guy here sipping coffee—that's me—with the speeded-up metabolism and discerning eye—me again—you're phenomenally beautiful and should have been first in any beauty pageant you ever entered."

Not quite sure whether she'd been insulted or complimented, she chose, "Phenomenally beautiful?"

"Yes!" he proclaimed, as if he were Professor Higgins and at last she'd gotten it right.

The pimply kid behind the coffee bar might have overheard them. He moved father away, shaking his head. A coffee bean grinder began to growl, but not loud enough to impede their conversation.

"Quite a charmer, you are," she said. "Like magic coming into my life. You can see why I don't think any of it is true."

He made a face, as if she'd injured his feelings. "I wouldn't say such a thing unless I thought it was all true."

"But if you would," she said, "that would be quite dangerous."

"To you or to me?"

"Me."

"Then raise your right hand."

She did. So did he.

"What's your name?" he asked.

"Let's call me Scarlet."

He looked at her as if trying to read something on her forehead.

"Doesn't fit," he said.

She laughed. "Okay, you choose a name."

"I'll tell you your real name."

"You mean the one on my birth certificate?"

"No. Your *real* name." He placed his forefingers against his temples as if waiting for inspiration. "You're Eva," he said.

She couldn't see why not, if he wanted her to be an Eva. "Amazing that you knew that," she said.

"Eva and Brad pledge never to lie or even exaggerate to each other, ever again, under penalty of life without each other."

The new Eva thought about that. "Sounds reasonable."

"Brad is my actual given, birth certificate name," he lied.

"And mine is Evelyn." *True. Just in case.*

Wonderful! he thought. *Fate again.*

He touched his fingertips to the bare back of her hand, and she felt something pass between them that surprised her.

"Now we've been properly introduced to each other by each other," he said. "You know what that means?"

"Yeah." She sounded slightly breathless. "That we

want our experimental relationship to work." As she spoke, she felt a pang of doubt. "We need to go slowly," she said.

"Agreed. You know where Mon Gourmet Ami is?"

"Yes. On Second Avenue. One of the best French restaurants in New York."

"Not too good for us," he said. "Let's meet there tomorrow at eight o'clock. I'll make the reservation under Brad. We're not yet ready for last names, and there's no need to rush."

Eva had been stood up before and knew how it felt. "You're sure about this?"

"No. We could eat Italian."

"You know what I mean."

"I'll be there, Eva. Please don't doubt me. Not already."

She reached over and squeezed his wrist. "I don't," she said.

But she did.

After Eva (as they both thought of her now) left the coffeehouse, the killer waited a minute or two and then followed. He'd watched which way she turned, and it didn't take long to spot her up ahead, making her way along the crowded sidewalk.

He hung back, easily tailing her to her apartment. It was on the West Side, not far from Columbus Circle.

Traffic was heavy as they negotiated crossing the roundabout, and he imagined that he smelled her perfume as he stayed well out of sight behind her. He was being extra careful, but he needn't have been. She didn't once glance back. A sign of a trusting soul, he thought.

She entered a redbrick and stone six-story apartment building, perhaps a converted great mansion of one of the long-ago very rich. He waited, counting slowly to fifty, and then cautiously entered the lobby. Eva either lived on a lower floor, or had safely gone up in the elevator. The floor indicator above the elevator door suggested she'd gotten in and was rising. He watched the tremulous brass arrow to see where the elevator might stop.

On the number three.

And it stayed there.

The killer didn't follow her up. It was too soon for that. You didn't long for something so strongly that you ache, and then appease your hunger with huge immediate bites. The experience was to be savored. He walked to the bank of painted-over mailboxes just inside the street door.

Above the mail slot for 3-B was a metal framed window holding a card identifying the box as belonging to one *E. Donavon*. Nothing else was close. The killer did make a mental note that three of the six apartments on the third floor held names revealing only first initials before surnames. Probably they belonged to single women, not revealing their gender. It was a simple, much used precaution. Only one first initial was *E*.

Everything was falling neatly into place. That was because it was meant to happen.

The killer imagined: Upstairs, Eva would be standing in front of her refrigerator, drinking a canned soda or bottled water. Or maybe she was undressing for a cooling shower. Or was slumped on her sofa watching television. Mind turned off. Guard down. Vulnerable.

The way the killer figured it, this kind of building,

these units, were potential hunting grounds. The lairs of his prey.

The killer knew that he and Eva were really not that much alike. In fact, in one important way, they were complete opposites.

He was on this earth to take. She was here to be taken.

They did have at least one thing in common: they enjoyed drawing out the pleasures of a burgeoning relationship. Beyond the bright smiles and forced clever patter, deep in the recesses of their brains, where instinct ruled, they both knew their respective roles.

They weren't thinking about their relationship in the same way, though their hearts knew its true purpose.

The details were immaterial. Eva would become fuel for the fire growing in the killer's soul. The obsession to possess and then kill, which he'd controlled and ridden as if it were a wild but manageable steed, was becoming stronger within him, almost as if there were no reins.

When he felt that way, the killer began to watch, to search, to assess. He couldn't get to the woman he yearned so much to destroy. She was in an invulnerable fortress, guarded by a small army behind stone and iron.

Proxies would have to serve his purpose.

Evelyn "Eva" Donavon fit the mold well enough. He would play her, use her, and then take her soul.

But only to sate himself before taking his most desired objective that *was* vulnerable. A woman who *didn't* fit the mold. Whose obvious death at the hands of the Lady Liberty Killer would throw Quinn's investigation into a whirlwind of pure speculation and scant actual knowledge.

They would know then that he wasn't the usual serial killer, that like them he had read the literature, familiarized himself with the canon. He'd know what they were thinking almost before they did. Some of it would be right, and some wrong. They would try to outguess him, comprehending only gradually that he was better equipped to outmaneuver an opponent.

Quinn and his detectives sometimes made the killer smile. When it came to the game they were playing, he knew the same rules they did, the same supposed tendencies. When his mind began to bleed, and to need, he would kill for a purpose as well as to assuage his need.

His was an appetite with claws and fangs. He knew that if he ignored it, it would begin to feed on itself and everything around it.

And *everything* included its host.

But there was no reason to ignore it.

Just as there was no reason for him not to take and use, and make his own, one of Quinn's women.

The killer was having fun.

The game had barely begun.

PART TWO

To wit, that tumblebugs and angleworms
Have souls: there's soul in everything
    that squirms.

—WILLIAM VAUGHN MOODY, *The Menagerie*

30

"What I'd like to do," Jody said, "is help."

They were at the table in the brownstone's spacious dining room, with its wainscoting, high ceiling, and original gas and electric brass chandelier. It was the sort of dining room where servants might be dispensing exotic dishes on bone china. They were eating takeout pizza off paper plates.

"You mean help people, as opposed to animals and insects?" Quinn asked.

"The law doesn't make the distinction," Jody said, and took a huge bite of cheese-dripping pizza.

"Between people, animals, and insects?" Quinn asked.

"Yep. The cute little kit fox and the snail darter can both halt huge construction and destruction projects."

"I was thinking more of how people figured into the equation," Quinn said.

Pearl, seated directly across from Jody, had heard about enough of their verbal give and take. She swallowed her last bite of pizza and washed it down with Diet Pepsi. "What are you trying to say, Jody?"

"I'm thinking of putting aside the rats' rights-as-legal-squatters case, for the time being."

"Why?"

"So I can be of more help with the Lady Liberty Killer case."

Quinn said nothing.

Pearl said, "Is this because of Carlie?"

"Well, she *is* my sister."

"In a limited kind of way," Quinn said.

"She's part of the family."

Quinn smiled, shrugged. "Yeah. She is."

There was a lot Pearl wanted to say, but she limited herself to, "You are a trained attorney, Jody. Not a trained detective."

"I did all right on the last case, which was my first."

"Can't argue against that," Quinn said, "though I'd like to."

"Are you *sure* your law firm approves of this?" Pearl asked Jody.

"I've already cleared it with Prather and Pierce. They want to expand their criminal defense department, and they have me in mind as the principal attorney. Eventually." She gave them her naïve but indomitable crooked grin. "So can I help more?"

Quinn studied pizza crust crumbs.

"Yeah, you can," Pearl said.

Quinn repeated her words. Pearl glared at him, knowing he'd let her answer Jody first. Knowing, if anything happened to, or because of, Jody, how the blame would be shared. Pearl knew how he hated bureaucracies, and sometimes she thought he'd survived in one too long.

Quinn dabbed at his mouth with a paper napkin, then glanced at his watch.

"Yankees game on TV?" Jody asked.

"Even better," Quinn said. "Helen the profiler's going to be on local television. The *Minnie Miner ASAP* show. Starts in five minutes."

"We should hear what she says," Jody said.

"And what she doesn't say."

They cooperated with each other without being told. Quinn put the grated cheese and other condiments in the refrigerator. Pearl gathered paper plates, wadded napkins, and plastic utensils and dumped them in the trash. Jody ran what was left of the pizza through the garbage disposal, then used a damp dishcloth to wipe down the table. Quinn enjoyed watching Jody's face while they all worked. Obviously she enjoyed this ballet of family cooperation.

Together they went into the living room, where Quinn opened wooden panels to reveal the flat-screen TV. He sat on the sofa next to Pearl. Jody curled up in the chair that had customarily been his before she'd arrived.

On the TV, Helen appeared seated calmly, her long legs crossed in a chair angled to face three quarters of an identical chair. In that chair, beaming into the camera, sat Minnie Miner. Helen was casually dressed in Levi's and a gray pullover. Minnie Miner was festooned with bracelets and necklaces and rings, and was about half the size of Helen. She looked, in fact, like a pretty, grinning doll that Helen had brought onto the set.

Until she began to talk. Then there was little doubt as to who was the ventriloquist.

"So no progress has been made in the Lady Liberty Killer murders," Minnie said.

Helen said, "I wouldn't—"

"And another victim was found only days ago, horribly mutilated. Tortured by this elusive madman that the police can't figure out. Would it be safe to say that he has this city totally horrified?"

"Well, he is killing—"

"And it could be any one of us. You're a profiler, Helen. What is there in this killer's profile that makes him so badly want to destroy women?"

"My belief is that it's his mother. She—"

"Why the woman? Isn't it the father who usually molests a child?"

"Well, we're not talking about—"

"But it goes back to his childhood."

"We can't know that for certain, but almost always—"

"As the twig is bent," Minnie said.

"More like as the seed is—"

"Who *is* the mother? For that matter, who's the father?"

"We don't know. We can only—"

"And what is it that makes this killer especially terrifying, that reaches into the dark corners of every woman's soul and creates fear and sleepless nights?"

"I wouldn't say no one is sleeping," Helen said. "But there's no denying—"

"That he's a monster," Minnie finished.

"We agree," Helen said quickly, finally catching on that she was going to have to jump right in, elbows flailing, if she wanted to be heard.

"Our thanks to Helen," Minnie said, swiveling in her

chair to face away from Helen. "A real profiler with some real information about the Lady Liberty Killer."

Her expression went from tragic and puzzled to deeply concerned and knowing, somehow without any of her features seeming to move. "Speaking of killers, a killer tornado slashed through the small town of—"

Quinn pressed buttons on the remote and the Yankees game appeared. There was no score.

"That was informative," Pearl said.

"Had to watch it," Quinn said.

"Why?" Jody asked.

"Because, almost surely, somebody else was watching."

When Carlie left Bold Designs to buy lunch from a street vendor, she couldn't help but notice Jody lurking nearby. Carlie bought a knish and bottled water and walked directly toward where Jody was standing in the doorway of a luggage shop across the street.

She and Jody exchanged smiles.

"If you're trying to be unnoticeable," Carlie said, "you could be doing a better job. Unless you're really interested in buying luggage."

"Don't need luggage," Jody said. "Also don't care if the killer spots me, if he happens to be stalking you. The object is to keep you alive."

"But we might be doubling the desirability of the target."

"How so?"

"If it's the killer's intention to send a message to Quinn, isn't he just as likely to try for you?"

"I'm as different as possible from his type," Jody

said. "A scrawny redhead with freckles and corkscrew hair. Also, I'm an attorney. Everybody says they'd like to kill all the lawyers, but nobody ever actually does it, even to one. They might need to sue someone someday."

"Well, that sounds logical."

"It does when you consider that I'm not new to the detective business. I've been taught by experts. And I carry this." She raised her tunic a few inches to reveal a belt holster holding a compact handgun.

"Is that legal?" Carlie asked, slightly unsettled by the sight of the gun.

"It's legal and I'm licensed," Jody said. "And I've spent time learning how to use it. And when not to use it."

"Okay," Carlie said, unscrewing the cap of her water bottle. "I feel safer with you here. Really." She peeled the paper covering the cardboard container holding the knish. "I'd have gotten you something, but I wasn't sure what you'd want," she told Jody.

"I've already eaten," Jody said.

"Then let's sit down."

Carlie moved toward a small concrete ledge where several other people were perched eating food from the kiosk. The ledge was hard and not the cleanest. There was plenty of room for two more. Carlie and Jody sat at the far end, where they wouldn't be overheard.

Carlie offered her water bottle to Jody, but Jody shook her head no. Carlie took a swig, then started on her knish. Jody wondered how she could eat anything that was flavored by the low-lying exhaust fumes from the nearby traffic.

After chewing silently, Carlie swallowed some water and put bottle and knish on a white paper napkin that had come with her lunch order. She drew a sheet of paper from her purse.

"I thought you'd be interested in this new 'professional woman' line that the company I'm designing for is bringing out next month," she said. She deftly unfolded the glossy paper with one hand and gave it to Jody. "High style and very severe. For every woman from attorney to dominatrix."

"Pretty much the same thing," Jody said. She made sure the paper was right side up and stared at it. "Keep an eye out for the killer while I study these," she said almost absently.

In fact, that was exactly what Carlie was doing.

31

The killer bought a cheap throwaway cell phone from a chain drug store in Williamsburg. He thought it would be safe enough, especially if he thoroughly destroyed it immediately after his call.

He would call from a relatively quiet place in Times Square (or at least a place where the din was manageable), and keep his conversation brief.

Not too brief, though. He'd call just past the top of the hour, when *Minnie Miner ASAP* usually took listener calls. Minnie enjoyed arguing with or commenting on her show's callers. The Lady Liberty Killer smiled, thinking Minnie didn't know it, but she was in for a treat. ASAP.

"For God's sake, put him on!" Minnie said.

Her producer, Hal Divet, wasn't so sure. He was an overweight, florid man, given to wearing sweaters in the cool studio even during the summer. "We don't want to set off a bunch of numb nuts calling in for nothing other than to get a few minutes in the spotlight."

Minnie, seated like an angry patriot in the middle of her red, white, and blue set, was fuming. "Maybe you didn't notice, Hal, but we already have that!"

"Not like this guy," Hal said. He seemed actually frightened. "I mean, there's something about this caller. You don't want him to get to know you, or even think he does."

"If our viewers feel the same way, fine. If he's genuine, what can the competition in our time slot do? I want *them* to be the ones caught sitting with their thumbs up their asses! Not us!"

Hal sighed. "Yeah, I guess you're right, Min."

"All the goddamn lines are lit up. So where is he?"

"Line four," Hal said.

The director gave his cue. ". . . two, one", and the commercial was over and they were live on TV again. Well, that was if you didn't count a seven-second delay. In case somebody said something truly politically incorrect.

Minnie presented her good side to the camera, leaned in close to the mike, and pressed the glowing white four button.

Being Minnie, she got right to the point:

"Is this really the Lady Liberty Killer I'm talking to, or just another imposter looking for temporary fame?" She glanced at the camera, smiling slightly, showing her audience that at this point they should be skeptical.

"I'm real," said the voice on the line. The camera moved in on Minnie, a tight shot of her somber face. With a high-definition TV, you could see her pores. "And you know I'm real." There was nothing distinctive about the voice. No way to fix the caller geographically.

"How do I know that?" Minnie asked. But the chill that ran up her spine for no apparent reason was how she knew.

"Freedom to kill."

The camera stayed tight. "I don't understand."

"The police do."

"You seem to be availing yourself of such a presumed freedom, but I don't see how you've offered any sort of proof that you really are the—"

"It's something I wrote in blood on a mirror. The police didn't inform media parasites like you because they wanted the knowledge used to determine the genuineness of confessions to the Lady Liberty murders. A test."

"I didn't know that," Minnie said.

"Of course not. Only the police and the killer know it. Well, now we'll have to include you and all your loyal viewers. Gosh, that sure might make the police's job more difficult."

Minnie was signaling frantically to her director. Hal nodded and pointed. He was already on the phone to the police.

"So what prompted you to call the show?" Minnie asked. "Was it only to make the police's secret information public?"

"Not at all. I called because I want to get *my* story out. The part of it I want people to know, anyway."

"What about the other part?"

"Well, everyone has a private life they want to stay that way."

"So why choose me as your means of communication?"

"You have a lot of viewers. And you're tough. The

police can't muffle you and put out some kind of story that saves their reputation. Quinn and his detectives. Really, they haven't kept up."

Minnie figured time was running out. This character was too smart to stay on the line long enough for his call to be traced. Better get to the point. "Okay. Now another question: why did you kill those women?"

"They had the devil in them."

"Many of us do."

"Actually, I wanted your viewers to know their city isn't safe. I do as I please. Go where I please. Kill as I please."

"Is it true that killers like you are really slaying their mothers over and over?" *Keep this sicko on the line, even if it means insulting his mother.*

"My mother was one of the kindest, gentlest women I have ever known."

"Well, you'd say that."

"And I'd tell you why, but it's time for me to leave."

"You say *was*. Is your mother dead?"

"How could she be, if I'm killing her over and over."

"Who says you are?"

"Much of the media. Like you. Didn't you just say that?"

"I don't think so. I simply asked a question."

"I think," the killer said, with a soft laugh deep in his throat, "that you are trying to keep me on the line, talking as long as possible."

"Not true! Believe me!"

"Check and see if your pants are on fire."

Minnie actually found herself glancing down.

"Freedom to kill," the caller said. And was gone with the connection.

Freedom to kill?

Minnie had to make sure he was no longer there. "You never gave me your name," she said inanely.

Her reply was silence.

"Your first victims were in alphabetical order," Minnie said. "Is there a reason for that? Is there an *A* the police don't know about? Should women whose names start with E be worried?"

Again, silence.

The director signaled for a commercial, then did a countdown from five. A spot for an underarm deodorant came on, a woman standing on a mountain peak with her arms spread wide. Eagles circled her.

"The police said it was true about the 'Freedom to Kill' line," Hal said. "Our caller *was* the real killer." He hugged himself as if he were cold. And he might have been, despite his unseasonable powder-blue sweater.

The director signaled that there was a phone call for Minnie.

She picked up, shooting a glance at the monitor. The deodorized woman was hang-gliding now, soaring with the eagles.

"This is Police Commissioner Harley Renz. You off the air?"

"We're in a commercial break, Commissioner. Will be for another minute and twenty seconds."

"Was that guy for real?"

"You tell me," Minnie said.

"He knew about the 'Freedom to Kill' message, so we gotta assume he's the killer."

"You gonna be able to trace the call?" Minnie, still trolling for news.

"We already did. It came from somewhere in Times

Square, and the phone's one of those cheap toss-aways. It's no doubt broken apart and dropped down a storm sewer, or some other place where we can never find it. Not that it would do much good if we did."

"There might be fingerprints."

"Not with this guy. He's too careful to leave prints."

"Can I quote you?"

"Can I prevent it?"

Minnie had to smile. "Well, no. It's news. But I assure you the story is about the killer, not you."

Renz wasn't sure he liked that, but he hadn't figured out yet how to use this latest development to promote himself.

"I'd love to talk to him some more," Minnie said. "I'm sure I could get him to open up."

"If he does call," Renz said, "we want to be in on it from the get-go. And I want any contact of any kind between you and the killer to be taped. Or digitalized. Or whatever the hell it is you do. Then I want it to find its way to my desk, and fast."

"Of course. We want the same thing. For the killer to be stopped. And for credit to go to the proper people. My show seems to be the way the killer has chosen to talk to his fans."

"His *what?*"

"His public, I meant to say. *The* public. I'm sure you know what I mean, Commissioner. We have to face the fact that this case has captured public imagination. We here at *Minnie Miner ASAP* are a news organization. What we want out of this is a wider viewership so we can better inform people. Ratings. And of course for the killer to be caught."

"By the by," Renz said. "You did mention credit going to the proper people?"

"Of course. Such as yourself. And that entails exchanges of information. Facts."

Renz was silent.

"Do we have a quid pro quo?" Minnie asked.

"We do. Only because I don't have much choice." They both knew that wasn't true, but people on both ends of an agreement should be allowed their delusions.

"Fine," Minnie said. "I look forward to talking and sharing with my new friends."

"With friends like her—" Minnie heard Renz say, as he was lowering the phone and breaking their connection.

Probably by now, Minnie thought, the killer had shattered his disposable cell phone into as many fragments as possible.

The commercial break was over. Minnie thought she'd mull over her recent conversation with Renz and decide when, how and *if* she'd use it. There was no reason quid pro qu*o* couldn't simply be quid.

Minnie was back live.

"Wow! Wasn't *that* something? Inside the mind of a serial killer. And we have good reason to believe that won't be the last time the killer calls.

"Something special for you now, folks. We have a guest who believes serial killers can and *do* affect the stock market. He's going to tell us how to take advantage of that phenomenon and, just as importantly, how and when to get off the gravy train."

The gravy train, the killer thought. *Where do you board that one?*

32

"So who's this Jesse Trummel?" Jody asked Carlie, as they had breakfasts of bacon, eggs, toast, and coffee in a diner on Amsterdam. Someone in the kitchen had screwed up and burned some bacon, or maybe they'd done it as a ploy to increase customer appetites. If so, some genius had then put onions on the grill.

Carlie swallowed a bite of toast. "I assume you got his name from the Q&A case file."

"Yeah. Quinn asked me about him. I know he's a draftsman at Bold Designs. But I mean *who* is he?"

"A bit of a nerd, but not a bad guy."

"Does he have the hots for you?"

"I'd have to say yes," Carlie said. "For a while, he had it in his mind he was going to be my silent and secret protector."

"Maybe jump out of the shadows and beat up your attacker, then you two could go from there directly to bed."

Carlie smiled. "Something like that."

Jody nibbled on a charred twist of bacon and studied her. "You like this guy?"

"I don't hate him. But like I said, he's sort of nerdy."

"Nerdy can be sexy."

"So the nerds would have us believe." Carlie sipped coffee and checked the time on her smartphone. She'd have to get out of here in about ten minutes if she was going to be at work on time.

"Did you ever do anything to encourage him?" Jody asked.

Carlie sputtered and coughed, dribbling coffee but catching most of it with her wadded paper napkin. "Not a chance!"

"I think his photos make him look like a reasonably handsome guy."

"Jesse? I don't think so."

Jody was grinning.

Carlie shrugged. "It's an office crush, that's all. You must've had that kind of experience. You see a guy as a friend, but he sees everything you do together as the beginning of a love affair right out of *Casablanca*."

"My guys are more like out of *Night of the Living Dead*," Jody said.

Carlie checked the time again on her phone, which she'd left lying on the table next to her water glass. "Whatever Jesse Trummel does, or however he feels, I'm gonna do this assignment for Bold Designs, then probably head back to California. The nutcases there are more at street level and not stacked up in tall buildings. I like it better that way."

And Jody's place in the family will be secured.

They had that same thought simultaneously, but neither woman voiced it.

"Does Trummel pretty much keep the same hours you do?" Jody asked.

"Yeah. It's a nine-to-five job, occasionally with over-time."

Jody thumbed through the notes she'd brought with her. She squinted rather than put on her reading glasses.

"I've already got his home address," she said.

"Jesse's?"

"Jesse's. While the rest of Q&A is keeping tabs on you, I'm going to make myself useful by watching him."

"Why?"

"To make sure he's not still watching you."

"I don't think it's a problem. He's been warned."

"So has the Lady Liberty Killer," Jody said. "He gets warned every day."

Four hours later, Fedderman approached Quinn, who was seated at his desk battling paperwork.

Quinn sensed Feds's looming, unkempt presence and looked up. "Something?"

"I was keeping a loose tail on Carlie," Fedderman said, "and found myself also tailing Jody."

Quinn sighed, laid flat the paper he'd been about to read, and sat back in his chair. "Why does it have to get so complicated?"

"People," Fedderman said. "They're the problem."

"Jody knows the plan, and knows we've got Carlie covered. So why is she following her?"

"She isn't following Carlie. She's following Jesse Trummel."

"That kid who works at Bold Designs?"

"Yep. She followed him from Bold Designs to a Peruvian restaurant, where he ate alone. From there he walked south, into the Village. Went to a sex shop."

Quinn was interested. "What kind of sex?"

"All kinds, really. He seemed particularly interested in leather bondage equipment."

"For males or females?"

Fedderman rubbed his chin. "That's kinda hard to say."

"So what'd he buy?"

"Nothing. Just browsed for about fifteen minutes, then left. Went straight back to work."

"Jody take all this in?"

"Yeah. She didn't spot me. I kept an eye on her, though. Soon as Jesse left, Jody went into the shop and asked the clerk if he'd bought anything. A few minutes later she scrammed out of there and caught up with Trummel walking up Broadway. Timed it just right, and didn't do anything that'd draw attention to herself. She's pretty good, for somebody who's never been trained to tail."

"A born huntress," Quinn said.

Fedderman said, "Well, yeah." Maybe thinking of Pearl and the genetic pool. "Sal and Harold took over the watch on Carlie when I took off after Jody and Trummel. They're still on it."

"Good. This sicko has to be feeling the pressure."

"According to Helen, anyway."

"Helen knows pressure."

But Fedderman wondered if she did. There weren't too many cases of profilers being shot or stabbed in the course of an investigation.

"I been thinking," Fedderman said. "Well, Penny's been thinking, actually. She came up with an idea."

Fedderman's wife, Penny. Quinn thought that was just what this case needed, another wily female.

"So what's Penny's idea?" he asked.

Fedderman smiled, knowing what Quinn must be thinking. Leave the detection to the pros. If the normal tension between a cop and his or her spouse became too much of a burden, then the people involved had to learn to deal with their problems, or walk away from the relationship.

But Fedderman didn't spout nonsense, and he didn't launch into a long explanation of why his wife wanted him to go into some other business. One that didn't involve guns and knives and the people who used them.

"We know why Carlie is the particular victim the killer wants," Fedderman said. "She belongs to you, and in the killer's mind, he and you are engaged in a deadly chess game for the championship of the universe."

"More or less," Quinn said.

"Penny thinks that maybe Helen should ask to be a guest on *ASAP again*. Minnie Miner would probably salivate at the chance to do another lopsided interview with her. Helen could twist the knife in the wound. That's if we really want to yank this guy's chain."

"Which we do," Quinn said, not at all minding the dueling metaphors.

Quinn thought it was a pretty good idea. He was wondering about the way to get the most out of it. Timing would be important.

"Tell Penny thanks," Quinn said.

"Something else," Fedderman said.

"Always, Feds."

"I went back to that sex shop and talked to the clerk.

When Jody was in there earlier, she bought a dog collar that was displayed with the S and M merchandise. Big black leather one, with spikes. She got a dog?"

"Cat," Quinn said.

"Oh."

Quinn thought, *Good Lord!*

33

Helen said, "Quinn sent me."

She was in the *Minnie Miner ASAP* studio reception room with a wooden table and chairs on one side, and matching green armchairs and a walnut coffee table on the other. The air was cool but didn't smell good, as if there were crossed electric wires sizzling somewhere. There were *People* magazines on the coffee table. On the walls were framed photographs of Minnie Miner smiling and interviewing famous guests on her show, or smiling and bracing herself against a stiff wind that had blown years ago, when she did the weather for one of the major networks. Or smiling and standing in front of fires or crime scenes or damage from earthquakes or tornadoes, when she was doing local news in the Midwest. Or simply smiling.

Minnie seemed pleased, but slightly suspicious.

"Why Quinn sent me," Helen said, "is he wants to make sure you understand a few things before I go on with you again, or before the killer calls you again. He thought I might be the best person to talk to you."

"Why?"

"To the degree that it's possible, I understand serial killers."

"You're awfully tall. You sure you never played basketball?"

"I'd remember," Helen said. She was sprawled lanky and lean in one of the armchairs, smiling.

"I often ask people off-the-cuff questions like that," Minnie said. "It surprises them. You never know what's going to pop out."

"Well, you've found out I can't make free throws."

"So what don't I understand about serial killers?" Minnie asked.

"What the rest of us don't understand. Why they kill."

"I thought we'd settled that last time you were here. Their mothers mistreated them, right? So they're killing substitute mothers over and over."

"Often that's the reason, and it seems to be with this killer. But at this point we can't be sure. I've done this kind of thing before," Helen said. "When he calls again, sort of let the killer determine where the conversation goes. He'll forget that he needs to be cautious. He'll make a slip. That one slip could mean the end of him."

"Why don't they simply kill their actual mothers?"

"Sometimes they do. Sometimes the actual mother reaches such iconic proportions that they're afraid to try to kill her. She's achieved, in their minds, immortality."

"Or she's already dead."

"That, too," Helen said. "You've done your research like a good journalist, but the knowledge we have isn't always precise. The Lady Liberty statuettes, the manner in which those women were killed, do point to a maternal fixation. Why that is, we won't know until we catch the killer. Or maybe we'll never know. At a certain point, they often choose the violent way out. Suicide seems to them a logical conclusion, the completion of a dramatic arc."

"As if they're in a play."

"They are in a play," Helen said, "and now you're in it, too."

"You're saying I'm in danger?"

"Oh, yes. The thing about this play is, he's the director."

"Listen, Helen, I've been in danger plenty of times. You don't reach the level I have in the news business without risking your hide. I have my own security, and even if they're not around, I know how to handle myself."

"We know that," Helen said. "What we want to know is whether you'll cooperate if we ask for your help. You're in a unique position to influence the killer."

"Of course I'll help to catch a serial killer."

"Incidentally," Helen said, "was the killer's mention of his 'Freedom to Kill' message something you'd heard anywhere before?"

"No, that was the first I heard of it, during our on-air interview. He sprang it on me just like he sprang it on you guys."

"He'll probably call again. When he does, put him on. He'll try to forge a bond with you. And because of your efforts to gain his trust, you might feel that helping us to apprehend him is a form of betrayal. It would be only human."

"Human? What the hell is that? I've seen the world without its makeup, Helen."

"Then you know the face of betrayal can be pretty ugly. You might not want it to be yours."

Minnie smiled like an ingénue and said, "Helen, I'm not gonna form any bond of friendship with a serial killer. I'll throw him under the bus and personally back over him. We don't have enough toes and fingers between us to count all the people I've betrayed in order to get a story."

"That's reassuring," Helen said dryly.

"It should be. I'm glad you came by the studio, because we need to understand each other. The killer's trying to use me, and I'm using him. That's what's happening here, and nothing more. I'm on the side of God and sunshine and the law."

Helen nodded and stood up. "That's what we had to make sure of, Minnie."

"Be sure."

"These guys get by in the world by becoming charmers. He'll try to make you fall for him."

"He can believe I've been charmed, if he likes. If he keeps talking. That's my method, Helen. Keep them talking until the mouth runs faster than the brain. That's when the truth spills out. *Oops!* You can see it in their eyes. 'I've said too much.' That's a sweet moment."

"You and I," Helen said, "we're pretty much in the same business." She stood up.

"No need to run," Minnie said, looking up at her. "Hang around. Do some more Q and A."

"No," Helen said. "I'm afraid I might say too much."

* * *

The wasps were stinging him, again and again. They were getting larger, too. Now they were as large as flying roaches.

He peeked out between the boards of the outhouse, rattled the door, screamed for help. The heat and the stench were overwhelming. The stench. The pain. He banged on the rough wooden door. Saw nothing outside but darkness. The wasps were even larger, brushing against his legs, crawling along the back of his neck. Flying hard into him.

God! If only he could fly out of here!

He crushed his face against the splintered door, peering through the crack, watching for her, watching for her . . .

She must come soon, with her lamp.

The Lady Liberty Killer woke listening to the trailing noise of his own frightened gasp.

Awareness and relief rushed in.

He was safe in his sweat-soaked bed.

Not there! Not then!

Somewhere else!

Thank God!

He opened his eyes and stared around at a darkness that wasn't complete. He could see hulking, shadowed forms of furniture, make out a rectangle of moonlight marking the edges of a window shade. A larger, darker rectangle that was the door to the hall, bathroom, and living room.

Familiar objects.

He was in his apartment. Not in Missouri. In New York. In the now and not the then. He mentally reached out and felt cool iron bars, rough concrete and brick, a lock, a knob.

Another door. A small window in it, with iron bars.

This one he wanted to open, not to get out, *but to get in*. He gripped the bars and tried without success to rattle them. He screamed and begged to be let in.

He wanted in!

He wanted in!

He woke up all the way and lay breathing hard, staring at a pale ceiling that was a tilting plane miles above him.

A dream within a dream.

Then how can I know I'm awake?

The thought filled him with dread and he hurriedly reached into the darkness and found the bedside lamp, its switch.

With a familiar click, the light came on, a hundred watts to chase away the shadows and demons of his dreams.

Outside, the city stirred restlessly in the night. Distant car horns blared. A siren like the wail of something woeful sounded far away in the dark. There was a muffled shout, a muted clang of metal. A bus or truck roared and rumbled down in the street.

Still, with every breath, with every heartbeat—fully awake and in the actual and coherent world—he wanted in.

34

There was a trusty who trimmed prisoners' fingernails and toenails, while the prisoners' hands were cuffed behind them, but Mildred Gant never availed herself of those services. She used her teeth to keep her nails chewed down to the quick, and she secretly saved the trimmings.

Late at night, when her cellmate Isabella was asleep in the top bunk, Mildred would lie awake in the bottom and let one hand dangle down to the concrete floor. Doing the fine work by feel, she would gather the nail trimmings and sharpen them on the rough concrete surface. She saved the sharp trimmings in a folded sheet of paper, which she kept rolled up and tucked in a crack where the plumbing ran into the wall behind the toilet bowl.

Mildred's cellmate Izzy, as the other women in detention called Isabella, was not a cooperative person. She didn't share. In fact, she made everything, including the top bunk, her own. She chose to dominate.

She was ten years younger than Mildred and trimmer and more solid, with muscle developed in the prison gymnasium and on the exercise yard. In fact, she did push-ups in the cell, while Mildred dutifully watched and counted. Forty, fifty push-ups. Sometimes one-handed push-ups. Impressive. Though her forearms and shoulders were bulky, she still appeared feminine, mainly because of her long auburn hair. Her hair cascaded in waves and ringlets around her ears, then fell almost straight to the small of her back. Izzy's hair was obviously her pride.

Mildred fantasized about getting on top of Izzy and stuffing handfuls of her hair into her mouth with one hand while she held Izzy's nose with the other, so the dumb-ass woman would inhale and choke to death on her own hair. She would no doubt give Mildred quite a ride before she succumbed.

Sometimes Mildred would fall asleep thinking about that, and not the dangerous side of Izzy.

Izzy was inside the walls for giving her third husband a severe beating that began after he'd lost consciousness. He was completely paralyzed now, as well as divorced. Izzy's lawyer had enough pull to have her charge reduced from attempted murder to intent to do great bodily harm. She still had five more years to serve of a twelve-year sentence.

Nobody messed with Izzy. Least of all Izzy's cellmates, who tended to come and go.

Some evenings, for amusement, Izzy would tell Mildred how her husband used to beat her. Then she would show Mildred how she'd turned the tables on her assailant. And she would beat Mildred. The trick was to inflict pain without leaving incriminating bruises. That called for a lot of internal injury. If the assailant knew how, such a beating could be administered without leaving much of a trace.

While she was inflicting pain on Mildred, Izzy would always ask the same question: "Where's the money?"

Mildred's answer was more or less always the same. "Ain't no money."

The conversation that developed would also be much the same:

Izzy: "Said on the news it was paid out."

Mildred: "Said wrong."

Izzy: "News don't lie."

Mildred: "Neither do I."

Izzy: "That hurt?"

Mildred: "Some."

Izzy: "I can make it hurt more."

Mildred: "Go ahead and have your fun."

And Izzy would.

When she was finished with Mildred, for the time being, she would stand in front of a small all-steel mirror and use a brush with rubber bristles to brush her long hair. The hair made a soft crackling sound with every stroke.

Mildred knew it was only a matter of time before she'd be forced to brush Izzy's hair. She wouldn't endure that.

Like Izzy's former cellmates, Mildred had taken to walking bent forward at the waist, so as not to awaken the pain.

Prison staff and administration knew of the situation but did nothing to stop it. Compared to some of the other problems they had to cope with—drugs, gang affiliations and wars, suicides, shower homicides—Mildred getting her ass whipped from time to time was nothing to them.

So Mildred suffered, and Mildred planned.

Thursday, supper was often a pathetic mix of cut vegetables, meat chunks of dubious origin, and pieces of potato. All half submerged in greasy brown gravy. The prison called it stew.

Mildred thought of it as opportunity.

She chose Thursday at dinner to slip a handful of razor-sharp finger and toenail clippings into Izzy's food, which Mildred was as usual made to carry to their customary places at one of the long tables. The cell block guards not only didn't mind Izzy bullying Mildred, they approved of it. They figured that without Izzy, Mildred would be hell and a handful. Though nothing was ever expressed in words, Izzy received extra candy bars and privileges in exchange for making sure Mildred stayed manageable.

Mildred had soon learned there was a hierarchy in prison. The guards pretty much left it alone to work. Thanks in part to Izzy, Mildred was at the bottom of the pecking order. Too bad for Mildred.

And Izzy.

A few hours before dawn, Izzy awoke with a horrendous stomach ache. Mildred could hear her groaning in the bunk above. Then Izzy began to cough and gag.

Mildred got up to take a look at her cellmate in the dim light. She could see that Izzy had spit up some blood and was curled in on herself with pain. The fetal position. That pleased Mildred.

The sharpened nail trimmings had done their work before becoming softened by swallowed food and stomach acid. If left alone, Izzy might bleed to death internally. But only *might*. Mildred had seen a dog poisoned this way when two fellas made a bet, and it had survived. Never barked much thereafter, though.

Izzy's groaning and gagging wasn't a problem. If any of the guards heard it, they would assume they were listening to Mildred suffering at the hands of Izzy, and stay away.

When Izzy had been administering her beatings to Mildred, Mildred had been learning. She knotted blankets around Izzy's legs and arms, leaving her midsection bare. Then, using the tips of her stiffened fingers, she drove the wedge of flesh, bone, and fingertips deep into Izzy's innards, shoving with a scooping motion, just beneath the rib cage and up. Over and over again.

Izzy couldn't catch her breath at first, and was angry as hell. She began to scream, and she knew she had to be plenty loud and identify herself to get any results. Mildred was ready for that. She forced one of her socks, full of swept-up dirt, into Izzy's gaping mouth. No sound emerged other than a muffled squawk.

That was it for Izzy's screaming.

"You comfortable, bitch?" Mildred asked.

Izzy shook her head violently, making her long hair fly in all directions.

Mildred laughed, but softly, so no one in the dim cell block would hear. It remained quiet out there beyond the barred door. A lot of the women were snoring, which also helped to cover up any noise Izzy might make.

There was a lot of time left before daylight. Mildred set about going to work in earnest, enjoying herself.

Letting Izzy almost die.

Prison doctors couldn't make a precise diagnosis of Izzy's problem. There was considerable internal bleeding. It was as if she'd suffered serious damage, but X-rays showed no significant injuries except for possibly severe bruising.

How this had occurred was impossible to know. No one, including Izzy's cellmate, Mildred, had any idea as to how this had happened. Mildred said Izzy had been experiencing dizzy spells lately, and suggested that she might have had a bad fall.

Izzy was hospitalized for over a week. She wasn't the same after she returned, whiling away her time in the cell with Mildred.

Who slept in the top bunk.

35

Eva lay spread-eagle on her back on her bed, gazing up at the ceiling light fixture. It was an old one, with a bowl-shaped frosted glass cover. It was also switched off. The light in the room was from the bedside lamp and the smaller lamps on Eva's dresser.

She knew who Brad was, *what* he was, and through her terror she wished she could ask him a thousand questions.

She could ask none. She could barely make a sound through the thick tape plastered over her mouth.

She listened to herself breathing hard and rhythmically, fearfully, through her nose. Oddly enough, her terror was at a distance. That was because she simply couldn't believe this was happening to her. She had picked up a serial killer in a bar, liked him, had been looking forward to good sex with him. Then, no doubt because he'd put something in her drink, she'd passed out.

And here she was.

Good God! Here she was!

Her body became rigid and momentarily levitated slightly off the mattress as she was assailed by a wave of panic. Her heart battled to escape her chest.

Then a curious calm came over her. Like something small caught in the jaws of a tiger, she accepted her fate and wanted her ordeal to be over.

That didn't seem to be Brad's idea. She craned her neck and watched as he placed a Statue of Liberty, obviously plastic and no more than six or seven inches tall, on the dresser, facing Eva. As if he wanted the thing to have a clear view of what he was going to do.

What is he going to do?

Her mind spun away from what she'd heard and seen on TV and radio news, read about in the papers.

Brad came into clearer view, naked except for white rubber gloves and baggy shoe covers of the sort nurses and surgeons wore in operating rooms. Indeed, he went to the switch and turned on the overhead fixture, as if to illuminate a surgical procedure.

Eva knew which procedure.

He set his briefcase on the floor and she watched him bend over it, then straighten up. He was smiling, holding something.

Knife!

Serrated. Sharply pointed.

She wet the bed. This was when they always lost control of themselves, when they first saw the knife.

He leaned over her and traced a wide C on her stomach with his gloved fingertip.

"Just about there," he said, meeting her horrified gaze as if trying to find something in her bulging eyes.

Her body was vibrating now with raw fear that took over every part of her body and mind.

The knife was all she could see. She couldn't look away from it.

The knife!

And he held it up where she had a good view of it. He wanted her to see. To know. She wanted to deny him that, but she couldn't look away.

She heard herself making a muffled, whimpering sound behind the tape. He touched the tape lightly, then pressed it to make sure it was adequately tight. They both knew she was about to scream.

He steadied himself, bending over her, and she watched his shoulders move and felt the cold blade and heard a ripping sound and knew what it was.

And she did scream. She heard only a pathetic humming, like that of a bee sealed in a jar.

Pain washed over her. She raised her head and looked.

She shouldn't have.

She hadn't realized she'd passed out, but he was holding something beneath her nose, waving it back and forth in protracted arcs, making her smell it. She coughed, almost strangling on her phlegm.

Unable not to, she looked down again.

This isn't happening to me!

Her stomach was laid open, and he was slowly and systematically removing things. The pain bored in like a separate rapacious creature with teeth and claws. She tasted blood, and was afraid she might drown in it behind the impenetrable wall of tape. She thrashed her head back and forth, managed to breathe, and willed herself to lose consciousness again. When finally she did drift away from the horror of reality, he brought her back again.

And again.

And again.

Until she no longer came back.

Another crime scene. Another FREEDOM TO KILL message in blood. Another tortured and destroyed woman. If anything, the killer was becoming more vicious and expert in his torture technique. Nift didn't hesitate to point that out.

Quinn wondered for the first time if he'd be able to go on seeing and thinking about the carnage. Dreaming about it.

There really wasn't any choice.

Not if he wanted to continue living with himself.

36

All Quinn knew about Harlan Wilcoxen at first was that he'd phoned and said he'd only be in New York for a few days, staying at the Hayden Hotel.

Quinn was familiar with the Hayden. It wasn't classy enough to be called a boutique hotel, but it was okay, and well located on Seventh Avenue near Times Square. Wilcoxen said he'd like to talk to Quinn about the Lady Liberty murders. He'd also said he was formerly a U.S. marshal in Bland County, Missouri.

When Quinn saw Wilcoxen walk through the door of the Q&A office, he was impressed. Not that Wilcoxen was physically intimidating. He was easily in his seventies, a little under six feet tall, whipcord lean, and moved slowly, as if he had a sore back he'd long ago learned to accommodate. It was his cool blue eyes under gray brows, the rock-hard set of his jaw, and something about the steadiness of his gaze, that lent him a definite authority. He was wearing gray slacks, and a white dress shirt with a plain blue tie held by a silver clasp. After shaking Quinn's hand, he sat down in the chair in front of Quinn's desk. Quinn sat down across from him and waited.

"Hot enough for you?" Wilcoxen said.

"Hot enough for me to do what?"

Both men smiled, recognizing that neither believed in embellishing what they had to say with small talk.

"I read the *Times* here a while back, 'bout those Lady Liberty murders?" Apparently Wilcoxen was one of those people who ended some of their declarative sentences with question marks. "I didn't think much of it at first?"

"And then?"

"Then I knew that if I didn't do somethin' about what was ticklin' the back of my mind, I might never forgive myself?" He smiled thinly, as if holding high cards. "You ever had that problem?"

"Often enough," Quinn said.

Wilcoxen drew a small cigar from his shirt's breast pocket and held it up. "You mind?"

"I don't," Quinn said, "but that detective over there might shoot it out of your mouth."

Wilcoxen shifted in his chair and stared across the office at Pearl. Shifted back. "Yep. She looks like she might." Back in the pocket went the cigar. "She a good cop?"

"Yes."

"I thought as much."

Pearl seemed to sense she was being talked about, fixed her gaze on Wilcoxen, and stared him down.

"God almighty," Wilcoxen said.

"No," Quinn said, "just Pearl Kasner."

Wilcoxen and Quinn both chuckled. Pearl gave them both a look.

"Anyways," Wilcoxen said, "I been followin' those Lady Liberty killings an' my memory got itself jogged? They're sorta similar to something that happened in Missouri some years back."

"Similar how?"

"Young lady was found with her belly cut open, just like your victims here? Didn't take us long to find out she'd been more'n eight months pregnant. Didn't make any headway with the case for some time? Then it turned out—or at least it seems—a woman name of Mildred Gant had cut her open and stole her child right outta the womb. Musta done it almost on a whim. But suspicion ain't evidence, 'specially in some parts of the country, so Gant was let alone. Didn't hurt her either that she was scary as hell."

"We're not getting actual extreme C-section births here. So far, none of the victims was pregnant."

"Oh, yeah. I know. Anyways, we never found out what happened for a long while? I was in on the investigation because it was a possible kidnappin', makin' it a federal offense? Never did find out for sure what occurred, though. Nothin' much in the way of a clue. Just like it happened all of a sudden between strangers—an' maybe it did. Anyways, this Mildred Gant was arrested a few years ago for swindling an antique dealer out of some money, got herself a spell in prison? I still got connections with the feds. Seems Mildred had a son, name of Dred—D-R-E-D—and there's no birth record. Plenty of people seen 'em together, though, over the years? We learned he was a super smart kid, educated mostly at home. Then a truck driver that dealt in antiques took a shine to him, taught him all about the business? So much so, Dred impressed some big-time dealers, who hired him. Rumor is he quit them after a while an' made himself rich."

Quinn had been taking notes. "We need to talk to this Dred Gant."

"I looked up the truck driver that knew him? He was killed in 2005 when his truck ran off the road in an ice storm? Woman he lived with said that from time to time he mentioned Dred. He did say the boy was smart as they come, and real gentle."

"I think we've both seen gentle people do some very ungentle things," Quinn said.

"Yep. Some smart ones, too. Especially if they been beat down over time when they were a kid?"

Wilcoxen was actually defending the killer, or at least making excuses for him. He must feel strongly about this case. Strongly enough to be in New York sitting and talking with Quinn.

"Is it your feeling the truck driver's partner told the truth?" Quinn asked.

"It is. Dred disappeared some years back? He'd be pushing thirty now."

"You mean he just disappeared?"

"Completely. Like a man runnin' away from his life an' lookin' for another. An' maybe he found one? Last anyone seen of him, he broke probation an' left everything behind in some shit-hole apartment in Kansas City."

"Probation for what?" Quinn asked.

"He visited his mother in a Missouri state prison in Chillicothe, an' in a conversation room commenced trying to kill her with a jigsaw blade. A guard pulled him off just in time? Disfigured the woman somethin' terrible, though. Hell of a way to treat dear ol' Mom."

"I'll say. And for this he was only put on probation?"

"Judge heard what his mother done to him over the years, felt like saw whippin' the woman himself, and showed a little mercy?"

"Was Mildred that much of a monster?"

"Yep. Near as I can tell."

"Where exactly is the monster incarcerated? We need to talk with her."

"Too late for that," Wilcoxen said. "That's what prompted me to come talk to you. Six days ago she knocked her cellmate unconscious? She didn't have any kinda blade, so she yanked most of the woman's long hair clear outta her head, then braided it to make a short rope and hanged herself dead."

"Good Christ!" Quinn said.

"They tried to get hold of the son but couldn't find him?" Wilcoxen pulled his cigar halfway out of his pocket without thinking about it, then slid it back in. "I doubt he'd have laid claim to the body anyways, an' he sure wouldn't have been interested in a funeral."

"So nobody knows where Dred is?"

"Not to my knowledge," Wilcoxen said. He shook his head. "An' we sure as hell can't ask his mother. Usin' your cellmate's hair like that . . . Mildred Gant was a resourceful sort. We gotta give her that."

"I give her nothing," Quinn said.

"Yeah," Wilcoxen said. "I can see why you might have such feelin's." He placed gnarled hands on both knees and stood up. "I guess that's all I can tell you for now? Mildred Gant is dead, an' her son is in the wind, so I don't know if I been any help to you at all."

"You know how it works. We might not know for a while."

"Yep. I do know. But I'm curious about this one? Have been for a long time."

"I'll let you know where things stand," Quinn said.

Wilcoxen nodded and turned to leave. "An' I'll let you know, 'specially if I hear anything new on Dred Gant." He shrugged. "Might be somethin'; might be nothin'."

"Wait up," Quinn said. He reached in a desk drawer and drew out a wrapped cigar. He stood and handed it across the desk to Wilcoxen. "They're Cubans, and damned good. Just make sure you're in a safe place before you light up."

"Much thanks to you," Wilcoxen said. As he slid the cigar into his pocket next to the other, he and Quinn both glanced over at Pearl, then at each other, and smiled.

Pearl shook her head as if having witnessed clueless boys at play, then went on with whatever it was she was doing.

At his desk, Quinn decided that treating Wilcoxen's information as something had little downside. Gant was a violent and dangerous criminal who had broken probation and disappeared. If he objected to being the prime suspect and presumed Lady Liberty Killer, let him come forward. A lesser crime would be solved, a lesser criminal brought to justice.

Meanwhile, Dred Gant was in the wind.

And Quinn would test the wind.

* * *

"Hanged herself with her cellmate's braided hair," Pearl said, later that night in bed. "My God, what a world!"

They had both brought books to read in bed, mystery novels of the sort so divorced from reality that they provided a welcome change. Pearl's novel wasn't exactly a book. It was on an electronic reader she'd recently purchased. The print was enlarged so it was easier for her to read. She'd gotten used to the enlarged print, then dependent on it.

"Imagine the cellmate," Quinn said.

Pearl shivered. "I'd rather not imagine." She lay back and let her gaze roam around the brownstone's spacious bedroom, with its high ceiling and ornate crown molding, the tall windows, the furniture they'd bought to match the period. She felt safe here, and safe next to a man who loved her.

How lucky she was, and how tenuous it all could be for her and for Quinn. Considering the people they dealt with, almost anything could happen. How terrible it was, the swamps good people could wander into, and the things that occupied those swamps.

She set her electronic reader aside, leaned over, and kissed Quinn.

He kissed her back, harder, using his tongue.

She waited until he'd placed his book on the nightstand and turned off his lamp, and then she came at him like a fury.

37

Helen had taken to her occasional appearances on *Minnie Miner ASAP*. She had her hair done, wore girly clothes, and on television looked feminine and smaller than she was. Always she kept in mind that perhaps the most ardent of the show's followers was the Lady Liberty Killer. That was the reason she had to be extremely careful. Serial killers often sought their own end in spectacular fashion. Even though they prized and needed anonymity, it was fame and recognition they craved. All the more so toward the end, when they knew the only escape from themselves was death.

And for this killer, a singular event might well mark in his mind the total futility of his quest.

"You're saying," Minnie Miner was telling Helen, "that the killer, murdering—in his mind—his mother over and over, was being driven mad because he couldn't get at his own mother, because she was in prison?"

"Correct," Helen said. "Alleged killer. He—"

"So for the Lady Liberty Killer, prison was a fortified castle keeping him out, wherein his mother lived sheltered and protected from him."

"Exactly. He was frustrated because he had no way to get at the much despised woman who raised him," Helen said, "so he killed substitutes instead. At least that's one theory."

"It certainly seems the most accurate one. It's like a dark fairy tale that gets more and more menacing."

"I'm not sure—" Helen began.

"I *am* sure this animal needs to be stopped."

"Of course he does. But I—"

"It's fascinating that an amazing event occurred that made things not better but worse for the murderer. His mother committed a crime and went to a place even more remote from him, where he could never reach her. That must have driven him mad."

"He was already mad," Helen reminded Minnie and the audience. "And we can't be sure—"

"So now, his compulsion and sense of defeat and frustration all the stronger and more overwhelming, this killer still walks our streets. If he was irrational and random in his choice of victims before, he might be even more so now."

"Count on it," Helen said. "Though I wouldn't say he chooses his victims entirely at random."

"The killer has become more deranged, and much more dangerous." Minnie said. "No woman in this city is safe."

"You could say that," Helen said.

Say anything you want—you will anyway.

"It certainly must send chills down every woman's spine . . ." Minnie was saying. She gave a slight shiver.

Helen was listening to her just attentively enough to be able to answer without making a fool of herself.

Minnie was locked in now, holding her audience's

attention in one sweaty little palm. "The real target of his hate and fear—yes, fear—has escaped this grisly killer's grasp by going where he can't reach her even if he follows. Yes, I said *her*. His mother, if you can believe it! How desperate and cheated he must feel! How betrayed and useless, now that his reason to exist no longer *herself* exists. The proxies he chooses as his victims now will be mere shadows of a shade, not representatives of a live and malevolent being taunting and living safely behind stone walls and iron bars, where he couldn't get at her no matter how hard he tried."

Helen thought that maybe her theory was correct and Quinn had been right in asking her to go on TV and stir the pot. To increase the pressure on the killer to act to reduce the angst he must be suffering. Minnie Miner was certainly stirring.

"The thing he wanted to kill has herself denied him that satisfaction," Minnie said. "Incredible!"

Helen nodded sagely. "All the cruelty and pain the monster visited upon him can no longer be avenged. It's as if she removed herself from the board while the game was still in progress. It isn't fair—at least in the alleged killer's mind. It isn't fair to cheat him out of despising her, blaming her, and eventually killing her."

"Yes!" Minnie said. "I can imagine him feeling *exactly* that way!"

"What he might be thinking now," Helen said, "is that somebody has to pay. His other victims, all of them, were only prelude."

Minnie gave one of her mock shivers. "It's creepy that you're so *into* this killer's mind."

"My job," Helen said.

She heard Minnie mention a commercial break and

thank her for coming. Helen made nice. She was glad
this television appearance was almost over. For a
while, anyway, she'd be back in the real world. She
wanted to get out of the studio and go home, where she
could change into her sweats and joggers and kick off
these high heels.

Only prelude . . .

The killer was mesmerized by Helen's concise and,
for the most part, accurate analysis of his mental
processes. At least in so much as he could determine
them. She was by far the most interesting and intelligent guest he'd seen interviewed on *Minnie Miner
ASAP*.

And she was close to his adversary, Quinn. Maybe
even his lover. (*Alleged* lover. Why couldn't the killer
also let his imagination serve him?) The thoughts she
voiced had to be much like the thoughts harbored by
Quinn. Listening to Helen gave the killer rare insight
into the mind of his pursuer. It confirmed what the
killer had known all along: Quinn would never give up.

After the commercial break (in which a lot of beautiful people laughed heartily and allegedly drank the
same brand of beer) Minnie Miner talked in glowing
terms about Helen and alerted viewers that her very
special guest was scheduled to be on again tomorrow.

The killer made a note of that.

38

Rapunzel, let down your hair. . . .
The killer had his dream again.

The one he'd had every night since learning his mother died.

But the fairy tale had it backward. It was Rapunzel who was kept prisoner in the tower prison. And she let down her incredibly long hair so her lover could use it to scale the tower wall and propose marriage.

It hadn't worked out well in the fairy tale, either. The lover climbed into the tower and encountered the witch.

There were several interpretations of the fairy tale, but in none of them did Rapunzel dangle by a hair noose from the tower with her eyes bulging, an evil smile on her face even with her distended tongue.

Rapunzel!

He awoke with a start.

Another dream within a dream . . .

But why stop with two dreams?

* * *

The killer poured his third cup of morning coffee and sat down on the sofa, watching the flat-screen TV mounted on the wall.

Minnie Miner ASAP came on as scheduled. Minnie wore a lightweight gray suit with a fluffy white blouse and very high heels. She would be standing up when she introduced Helen and didn't want to be dwarfed. A few fans had e-mailed that they hadn't known Minnie was so small, not knowing that Helen was a god-damned jolly *un*green giant.

An enthusiastic Minnie announced that after the commercial, police profiler Helen Iman would be on to talk more about the Lady Liberty Killer.

The studio audience matched her enthusiasm with its applause.

But Minnie didn't say *immediately* after the commercial.

The killer had to sit and sip his rapidly cooling coffee while a young actress talked about how her fourth trip to rehab had saved her life. (*For now*, the killer thought.) After the actress came a recently fired newscaster who was angry as a hornet about the direction of news in America and was going to write a book. Both the actress and the former anchorman vowed never to quit their personal crusades.

The killer thought these people were obsessive, and not very plausible.

Finally, after the angry anchorman and a blast of short commercials, Helen Iman was introduced. The killer paused in his sipping as he regarded her towering height and beanpole figure. Wrong color hair. Definitely not his type. *Lucky for her.*

Helen had talked with Quinn about today's interview, and they'd decided they didn't want the killer to enjoy his publicity too much. He mustn't mistake public fascination for public support.

"Do you or the police think it's possible this killer has what we would consider a normal personal life?" Minnie asked, once she and Helen were settled into their chairs, Helen trying to figure out what was different, then realized her chair's legs had been shortened.

"Is 'normal' code for sexual?" Helen asked.

Minnie grinned. Maybe Helen knew what ratings were made of. "More or less."

"What we would consider a normal sex life isn't likely," Helen said, "unless he's playing at a normal relationship with a woman. That would be in order to enhance the camouflage that these sick people need in order not to be noticeable for their madness."

"Maybe the killer himself will call and set us straight," Minnie said. "He's called *ASAP* before. And I might add he's not so crazy that he stayed on the line long enough for his call to be traced." She winked. "For those of you who were wondering."

The killer didn't like the way this was going. Not that he was blaming Helen, whom he'd come to admire. Quinn the puppet master was the one to blame. He was the one making things happen. Telling his people what to do. The killer thought about Pearl. He'd enjoy telling *her* what to do. Then there were the other two—Jody and Carlie. They might serve a purpose.

Quinn wasn't the only puppet master in this game.

The killer drummed his fingers on the sofa arm. Maybe he *would* call in to the show. He knew Minnie would let him talk, though he wasn't sure she'd allow a three-way conversation. For that matter, something about Helen frightened him. He wasn't sure he wanted to speak to the towering profiler directly. The words *sick* and *madness* bothered him. Did Helen think she was a medical doctor or a psychologist? She was a goddamned profiler, that's all. Sure, she knew her job, but it was one step up from handwriting analysis.

Then why do I fear her?

"What I'd like to talk about today," Helen said, "is the nature of the victims' injuries."

"Sounds lurid," Minnie said, with obvious anticipation.

"It is, I'm afraid, but I think it might help your viewers to better understand the sort of individual we're dealing with, and who's still walking the streets of New York."

Minnie smiled and leaned back in her chair. "We're listening."

In a calm and unemotional tone, Helen described the nature of the damage inflicted on the victims before and after their deaths. She spared no horrendous detail, and the matter-of-factness of her voice made the injuries seem all the more horrible. For the most part, Helen looked into the camera as she spoke. Now and then, she'd glance over at Minnie Miner.

Minnie was turning green.

"I know this is strong stuff," Helen said to Minnie and to the audience, "but I'm not here to entertain. I'm here to inform, and to alarm. Because we should be alarmed. Not panicked, but alarmed. A monster who looks and acts as we do, who blends into his environment like a chameleon, is stalking some of the women of this city. And what I've just described is the result of only some of the earlier encounters. I've left out the most vivid and gruesome."

"We can imagine," Minnie said, swallowing. Her lipsticked mouth arced downward. She appeared ill.

The unexpected had happened. Her show had become real, and reality lived in her stomach.

Helen was glad to see Minnie make it through her polite thank-you to her guest, and then introduce the next commercial break. As the picture faded, viewers who looked quickly could see Minnie stand up, then double over with her arms crossed tightly against her abdomen. Some of her cast and crew hurried over and supported her so she wouldn't fall.

Nobody was paying much attention to Helen.

The killer, ensconced before his flat-screen TV, noticed what was happening and wondered what all the fuss was about.

Quinn remembered there was a voice mail message on his cell phone, but he didn't have time to listen to it before his desk phone jangled.

"You see Helen on TV this morning?" Renz asked, when Quinn had picked up.

"Sure," Quinn said. It was only eleven o'clock, but already the offices of Q&A were heating up toward what weather forecasters promised would be record high temperature.

The air-conditioning units, set in the windows, were humming and banging away, fighting the good fight against the heat. Not losing quite yet, though Quinn was sure at least one of the units would ice up and stop operating before the sun went down and all that baking concrete outside would begin to cool.

"Helen about made me barf," Renz said.

"That's the plan. We don't want the killer to get the idea the public sees him as some kind of underdog hero."

"That seems unlikely."

"In this city?"

"Well, yeah, I see what you mean. Also," Renz said, "I didn't hear the word *allegedly* on Minnie's show."

"You think a serial killer is going to sue for libel?" Quinn asked. He didn't say there might be a remote possibility the killer was insane enough to attempt just that.

"Not if we got the right guy," Renz said.

"We do," Quinn assured him. "Otherwise he would have come forward all lawyered up to dispute the allegations. Anyway, we can't lose either way."

"My kind of odds," Renz said. Then the tone of his voice changed to one of officiousness. "Reason I phoned is I called in some chits with the FBI and got the file on that old Missouri case where the infant was ripped out of its mother's womb."

"The FBI?"

"Yeah. As long as the kid was thought to be alive, the Bureau viewed the crime as a possible kidnapping. According to the file, they showed up right away to assist the locals while they told them what to do."

Quinn understood. He remembered that Harlan Wilcoxen had mentioned the Bureau's involvement.

"They did do a good job of finding more information on the dead woman and her baby," Renz said.

"What kind of information?"

"The victim's full name was Abigail Taylor. Her folks were farmers," Renz continued. "Country girl through and through. Never got in any trouble to speak of. Made decent grades but dropped out of high school her senior year to take a job as a waitress in a spaghetti joint. Told her folks she was bored with school."

"Sounds familiar," Quinn said. "I wish you could tell me now that a movie producer stopped in at the restaurant where she worked, saw her, talked to her, and offered her a screen test. Stardom followed."

"I can't tell you that, but you're sorta right. That's how she met the father of the child that was taken from her. He came in and ate lunch, then came back for supper. The next day, he returned for breakfast and the waitress. They got involved, moved in together. She got pregnant."

"Not a movie producer?"

"That's where it went wrong. The father was an auto mechanic, worked at a repair shop and drove a tow truck."

"Ambitious, anyway."

"Not so's you'd notice. Word was the pregnancy showed so soon after the wedding it was unlikely the mechanic could have been the father. He and Abigail fought some, maybe about that, according to the file. The FBI saw him as a suspect for a while."

"What made them eliminate him?"

"He and another fella were talking on hubby's landline phone at the time of the murder-kidnapping, about Hubby being too hungover to come into work to do a brake repair job." Quinn listened to Renz breathe for a few seconds. A fat man, and getting fatter, his weight was starting to drag him down. Finally Renz said, "The daddy didn't have anything to do with what happened, Quinn. Day after Abigail was found, he drove his car straight into a bridge abutment. There were no skid marks. The speedometer was broken in the impact, stuck at ninety-seven miles an hour. Witnesses said it sounded like a thunderclap."

"Christ!"

"Kid finds out he's lost his woman, his baby, all in the same day, and in the worst way. Next day he took his own life."

Quinn thought for a while. "I suppose the FBI made sure later on about the father. I mean, with DNA testing and all."

"They did. Got blood from the placenta at the time of the crime to test for type. Tested some of it later for a DNA match. The kid was the daddy, all right. It'll all be in the file I'm sending over. Name's right there, supported by modern science. 'Father: William James Wilcoxen.' "

Quinn pressed the phone tighter to his ear. "Say again."

"Supported by modern science."

Quinn said, "Not that part."

39

Quinn saw that the message on his cell phone was from Harlan Wilcoxen. He sat back and listened:

"That conversation we had the other day?" Wilcoxen's laconic voice said on the phone. "I gotta admit I didn't play quite square with you. I kept some things from you, like why I was so interested in the Lady Liberty Killer case? Truth was, I wasn't so interested in givin' information *to* you as in gettin' information *from* you. There was one piece of information I knew you'd come across once you got far enough into the FBI file. The dead woman's husband? Billy Wilcoxen? He was my son, and it was my grandson who was ripped from his mother's womb. It was my grandson that became Dred Gant, an' who killed all them women. I'm hopin' what additional information I've given you will be of some help. An' that when you find Dred, you'll remember Mildred Gant."

That was the end of the message. There was no good-bye, but still it gave Quinn the creeps.

He motioned for Pearl to come over from where she was working at her desk.

"Let's take a ride," he said, when she got close.

"One I'm gonna like?"

"Probably not."

"Let's go then, before things get even worse."

On the drive to the Hayden Hotel in Quinn's old Lincoln, he filled her in, and then let her listen to Wilcoxen's message on his cell phone.

"I don't like any of it," Pearl said, handing the phone back to Quinn. "From the content to the tone of his voice."

"He always uses uptalk," Quinn said.

"Uptalk?"

"Says things that end in question marks when they aren't questions. Kind of an upward glide. Must be a Missouri thing."

They stopped for a red light on Broadway. A guy in a ripped T-shirt and khaki shorts rapped his knuckles on the Lincoln's hood and pointed to let Quinn know the front of the car was inside the crosswalk. Quinn unconsciously edged the big car forward even farther while waiting for the light to change. The look on his face scared Pearl. Scared the guy who'd tapped on the hood, too, judging by the way he picked up his pace. Quinn had a way of figuring out things before he realized he'd done so, before he put on his dead-eyed cop's face.

"You think we oughta call Renz?" Pearl asked. "Get a radio car over there before Wilcoxen checks out?" But she knew he wouldn't check out; he'd simply leave. Probably he already had left. Wilcoxen was an old hand and knew the moves.

"Let's see what we got first, when we get to the hotel."

"Optimist."

"I don't feel like one," Quinn said.

The light turned green and the Lincoln swooped across the intersection, causing a man wheeling his bike along the crosswalk to stop cold and make an obscene gesture. Pearl smiled. The pedestrians were frisky today.

Quinn leaned on the horn, getting impatient. They were about fifteen minutes away from the hotel. Traffic was getting heavier as they moved downtown. Pearl phoned the Hayden. Wilcoxen was still registered, but he wasn't in his room.

"Maybe he's in the bar, waiting for us to show up," Quinn said, jockeying for position in the traffic.

"Or maybe he doesn't want to lend any more help to someone trying to get his grandson caught and shot to death or executed."

"Or maybe he does want to lend a hand in finding his grandson before more women are tortured to death."

"I'd guess both," Pearl said.

Quinn said, "There's the problem."

The Hayden was a small hotel on Seventh Avenue, near enough to Times Square to have enjoyed some of the area's resurgence. The lobby was more cozy than imposing, with walnut paneling, potted palms, and black leather armchairs that were unoccupied. A mildewed scent tainted the air, as if someone had just come up from a damp cellar and left the door open.

There was a bar off the lobby, and Quinn detoured

and glanced into it on his way to the front desk. Six people occupied bar stools or chairs. Two of them were women. None of them was Harlan Wilcoxen.

Over near the desk, Pearl was using a house phone to call Wilcoxen's room again.

She put the receiver back on its hook and shook her head. Still no answer.

Quinn saw no point in wasting time. He talked to a bellhop, who directed him to an attractive Hispanic woman behind the desk.

The woman listened to Quinn, then called the manager on the phone. After a brief conversation, she made a subtle come-hither motion that produced a large, shambling man in a brown suit who looked exactly like what he was—the house detective. He said his name was Bert Salter.

The manager appeared from a doorway behind the desk, then disappeared and emerged from another door on the lobby side of the desk. He was a lean, nervous man and introduced himself as Larry Castleman.

Quinn, Pearl, the manager, and the house detective walked in a tight group to the elevators and rode one to the tenth floor, where Harlan Wilcoxen was registered in room 1057.

Castleman knocked gently on the door, waited, then knocked harder. The house detective, Bert Salter, inhaled so his barrel chest swelled, then sighed loudly. Quinn thought Bert would have enjoyed kicking in the door, but the manager, a man of milder temperament, produced a card key and swished it.

The card worked the first time.

Bert moved to enter first, but Quinn eased in front of him, and the big house detective shuffled to the side.

They moved cautiously at first. Then, satisfied that there was no immediate problem, they walked in and found the room unoccupied.

A black leather suitcase rested on a foldable luggage stand. A wrinkled blue shirt was draped over the desk chair. Either the maid hadn't been there yet or Wilcoxen had gone back to bed for a while. The spread and covers were mussed and turned back, and the rough outline of a human head was indented in the pillow.

"Nothing," the manager said, sounding relieved.

"Both card keys are on the dresser," Bert the house detective said.

Quinn stood still. He'd smelled something. So did the others. All except the manager.

It was subtle, but easy to identify. Blood. And a lot of it.

Harlan Wilcoxen was in the bathtub, which was three-quarters full of an approximate mixture of half blood and half water. His eyes were closed, but he didn't look peaceful. He looked pale and in troubled deep sleep. One of his hands was turned palm up, floating on the surface of the devil's mix in the tub, and the broad cut in his wrist was visible.

"Opened up his wrists," Bert said. "Whatever kinda blade he used is underwater, where it isn't visible." He talked like a man who'd seen this kind of death before.

On the closed toilet lid was a Bible that looked as if it had never been read. It was probably from the hotel nightstand drawer. It was weighting down a fat file folder that looked as if it contained copies or originals of everything that was in the file Wilcoxen had given to Quinn earlier.

"Don't anybody touch anything," Bert said. He was an ex-cop, and this was his beat, after all.

The manager looked at him as if he must have lost a gear somewhere, giving orders. "We've got a suicide here," he said.

Bert looked at Quinn, waiting.

"We can't be sure yet what we've got," Quinn said.

They all moved toward the door to the hall, while Quinn used his cell phone to get in touch with Renz.

The killer, scanning the *Times* and *Post* at breakfast the next morning, saw an item about a former law enforcement officer from Missouri committing suicide in a Manhattan hotel yesterday.

There were few details. Suicide wasn't all that uncommon. The item would be of only passing interest to anyone other than the man's family members, who, if they existed, weren't mentioned.

40

Quinn sat at the dining room table in the brownstone with the two files on Dred Gant's kidnapping from his mother's womb.

It seemed to him that three important things were made clear in the file that Wilcoxen had left in his hotel room.

The first was that Dred Gant had somehow learned that Mildred Gant wasn't his biological mother; but he still had no idea as to the identity of his real mother, or his father or grandfather.

The second was that a week before she'd stolen the auctioneer's money and injured the highway patrolman thirteen years ago, Mildred had bought a state lottery ticket. It had turned out to be a winner.

She hadn't been the big winner, but big enough, especially considering her finances. Her winnings were a quarter of a million dollars. It was estimated that after taxes, this would amount to approximately one hundred and seventy-five thousand dollars. Some of it she used to make bail. Most of it she hid somewhere.

Dred had been a teenager at the time. He might have

learned about the lottery winnings, or he might not have. It would have been like Mildred to make sure he didn't learn of it, so he couldn't somehow get his hands on it.

In the file was a yellowed newspaper clipping announcing Mildred's good luck, along with that of some other winners. She'd bought her ticket at a combination gas station and convenience store off of Interstate 70 just outside of St. Louis, where she'd gone for an estate auction. The jackpot winner, an attractive unemployed schoolteacher who had lost her job after posing seductively with a nozzle for a firefighters' calendar, had received three million dollars, and almost all of the newspaper ink. There was no photograph of Mildred, or any of the other lesser winners.

The third important thing?

Wilcoxen had been of the opinion that Mildred Gant not only had acted as a pimp for Dred, but had also molested him herself.

Quinn sat back in his chair, mulling all of this over.

Good God! How might that have affected a young boy, being sexually abused by his mother? Or the woman he assumed was his mother?

A mother like Mildred Gant?

And how must he have felt when, protected from him by prison walls, she took her own life?

He had mauled her with a whip-like saw blade, but she had denied him his final ecstasy and release. His closure.

Two questions: What had happened to Mildred's money? And should any or all of this information be released to the media?

Quinn thought the FBI might be sitting on much of

the information, though he couldn't be sure. The Bureau played whatever cards it held close to the vest. It was unlikely that they'd seen Wilcoxen's expanded file, but they might have pieced together the information from other sources. Despite the jokes and feigned disdain about the "Feebs" that was present in a lot of metropolitan police departments, the Bureau was good at its job.

Quinn considered lighting one of his Cubans, to help him think this over. If he opened one of the tall dining room windows looking out on West Seventy-fifth Street, and sat near it so the smoke would escape outside, would Pearl still know?

Probably.

Quinn sat cigarless, staring at the clutter of the files' contents, wondering what Renz knew. Renz was tight with the feds, in his Machiavellian way.

His cell phone chirped and he dug it out of a pocket. He saw that it was Sal calling. The Sal and Harold team was keeping a loose watch on Carlie.

Quinn switched on the phone. "Whaddya got, Sal?"

"Carlie and Jody are in a place called Twiggy's on Varick, kind of a pick-up health-drink bar." Sal's voice was made even raspier by the tiny cell phone.

"A pick-me-up health—like a juice bar?" Quinn was trying to understand that.

"Literally, I guess yes. It's part of a pilot project. The mayor wants there eventually to be at least one every ten blocks or so. Keep New Yorkers healthy. They seem to be popping up all over the place. You haven't noticed?"

"No."

"Anyway, the two girls have been here a while, sipping drinks that look like they're mostly fruit juice."

"A health-drink bar? Really?" This city, this mayor, had the capacity to keep surprising Quinn.

"Health-drink *pick-up*. That's the word on it with folks who wanna—you know, hook up romantically and physically."

"Jesus! Sex and asparagus."

"Well, I thought you oughta know. Carlie and Jody don't seem to be here looking for romantic possibilities. They're minding their own business. They chased away a couple of nerdy-looking guys, ten, fifteen minutes ago, who had drinks with what looked like sprigs of vine dangling from them. Seems to me the girls are just relaxing with a couple of sprout drinks. On their second round, is all."

"I don't like it," Quinn said.

"It's just another one of the mayor's pilot programs. Like the fire hydrant taxi stop thing. Probably nothing'll come of it. You know what I mean."

"I was thinking about Jody and Carlie."

"Yeah. Thing is, the place isn't an opium den. And the girls act like old friends gabbing at each other. That's all that's going on here, Quinn." Sal waited a beat. " 'Course, I can do something about it, if that's what you want."

"I don't know that you could do much, Sal. They're both adults. They'd probably both be pissed off if you interfered with them."

"That's what I figured you'd say. How about I don't do anything overt, but I keep an eye on the situation? I'll turn it over to Harold when he shows?"

"Do that, Sal. And let me know if either one of them . . . hooks up."

"Sure. I'll call you right off."

Quinn broke the connection. *Girls! Women!* He had to remind himself that Jody and Carlie weren't a couple of kids. He saw them that way sometimes, but he knew he was wrong. One was a retail designer, the other an attorney. He was lucky they listened to him at all. Or to Pearl.

Sometimes all of life seemed to be a goddamned conundrum.

He told himself that Jody and Carlie would be okay with Sal and Harold looking after them. Then he sat at the table, staring at the Dred Gant files' contents, trying to determine what information he might put to use. It could help if he located an auctioneer who'd dealt with either Mildred or Dred, or both. He remembered a name in the file, and started shuffling papers looking for it. An auctioneer in Missouri. Vernon something . . .

Vernon Casey.

That was it. He soon found the folded flyer, printed in the nineties, advertising the auctioning off of a farm house and barn's contents in Missouri. Vernon Casey had been the auctioneer. There was a black and white photograph of him, a man with cherubic features, grinning with his mouth open wide as if emitting a loud volume. He was wielding a gavel like a judge about to adjourn court. He didn't look like a young man. Quinn hoped he was still alive, and that he knew something about Mildred or Dred.

He checked on Facebook and Twitter and found nothing on Casey. That would have been too easy.

When he phoned the Missouri State Police he had

better luck. Casey was still alive, and still auctioneer-ing. He lived and worked in and around Columbia, Missouri, a city of about a hundred thousand in central Missouri. Quinn thought that was where the state uni-versity was located.

He got Casey's home and work phone numbers. Then he glanced at the kitchen wall clock. Missouri was an hour behind New York. It was still early enough to try to get in touch with Vernon Casey.

He used his cell to call Casey's home number.

Harold had relieved a weary Sal. Now he sat almost out of sight at the far end of the bar in Twiggy's Health Drinks and watched Jody and Carlie. They amazed Harold. These two barely knew each other, yet they found endless things to talk about. Even from where he sat he could see that they were interrupting each other, so eager were they to trade information and view-points.

They seemed to be having a good time, and Harold could be sure they weren't the slightest bit tipsy. Judg-ing by their drinks, they were mostly in danger of im-bibing too much vitamin D.

At least Harold wouldn't have to call Quinn and re-port that his sort-of daughter and his niece were inebri-ated. They wouldn't be driving anyway. They'd met here after taking the subway to the stop three blocks away, and then walked. Harold presumed they'd go home the same way in reverse.

It occurred to Harold that the subway must have saved a lot of lives. Imagine thousands of DUIs behind private car steering wheels, jousting with all those taxis. Pure chaos. Maybe the mayor had something, with his fruit-and-veggie juice bar project. Harold sipped the strawberry-avocado-almond drink he'd been nursing, thinking about the ratio of people who'd avoided fatal car crashes to the people who'd fallen or were pushed beneath the wheels of subway trains.

While he was considering this and trying with his tongue to force a morsel of almond from between his teeth, he noticed in the corner of his vision a figure approaching Jody and Carlie's table. An average kind of guy, not bad looking but not a matinee idol. Conservative haircut. Dressed well enough—gray slacks, white shirt with no tie, and the top button unfastened, blue blazer. Average size. Nice smile. He was casually holding a half-full glass of something green in his right hand. The thing about him was, there was nothing off-putting about him. He was too average to be threatening.

Harold stopped thinking about subways and car crashes.

41

Quinn sat at his desk, his chair eased over so there was a direct breeze on him from the air conditioner, and worked the landline phone. The struggling window unit was picking up a scent from out on the street, sweet, occasionally cloying. Probably some overripe trash that hadn't yet been collected by the city. Garbage and commerce. New York.

He couldn't reach Vernon Casey at either his home or work number. He assumed the work number was a cell phone.

He tried the home number again, and this time a woman answered.

"I'm trying to get in touch with Vernon Casey, the auctioneer," Quinn said, after the woman had said hello.

"You've gotten in touch with his wife," the woman said. "I can give you his work number."

"I tried there and got voice mail."

"What's this about? If it's business, I should be able to help you whether you're wanting to buy or to sell. Been working in those capacities for Vernon for years."

"Neither," Quinn said. "I'm a detective in New York,

and some information was given to me by Harlan Wilcoxen."

There was a long silence.

"New York?"

"The one on the Hudson."

"Where everything's expensive."

Quinn smiled. "Do you or your husband, Vernon, know Harlan?" He thought it best to proceed on a first-name basis.

" 'Course we do. Have for years. I'm Wanda, incidentally. I ain't seen Harlan Wilcoxen in a coon's age. How is he?"

"How well did you know him, Wanda?"

"I don't much like that question, nor the tense nor tone you asked it in. Has something happened to Harlan?"

"I'm afraid so. He—"

"Hold up," Wanda Casey said. She sounded apprehensive. "Jus' hold up, please. I'm gonna let you converse with my husband."

Quinn listened to them talking in the background but couldn't make out what they were saying. There was the sound of movement, of paper rattling.

A deep male voice said, "I'm Vernon Casey, Detective . . . Quinn, is it?"

"It is," Quinn said.

"You with the NYPD?"

"Yes." The short answer.

"Now what's this about Harlan?"

Quinn told him.

Vernon Casey didn't say anything for a while, then said, "Lord almighty!"

"How well did you know Harlan?" Quinn asked.

"Well enough. He was a U.S. marshal where we lived in Bland County some years back. Pretty much the law there. If you knew Harlan, then you know what I mean. Haven't seen him in years."

"What about Mildred Gant or her son, Dred?"

"Now them I recall real well. Dred never said much. Acted kinda withdrawn. Smart as a whip, though, you could tell."

"So how did you know Mildred?"

"She bought and sold antiques. Got real good at it, too. Made some money 'cause she was no dummy. She knew real antiques from the merely collectible or plain junk. Real aggressive bidder. I liked that about her, but that was the only thing I liked."

"Why do you say that?"

"She didn't treat her boy real well. He had bruises sometimes that came from more than falling off his bicycle. I wasn't the only one that thought that. Marshal Wilcoxen did, too. But he couldn't do a thing about it without proof. And most everybody knew Mildred wasn't the sort who'd leave proof lying around. Harlan didn't like doing nothing about it, but that was all he could do—nothing. Nobody else would help. Wasn't nobody in the county wanted to lock horns with Mildred Gant. She's a real spitfire. Last I heard, she was in prison. That in New York?"

"Chillicothe," Quinn said. "She cheated some people having to do with antiques, then ran over a state trooper and damn near killed him."

"Yeah, we heard about that. Antiquers talk amongst themselves. She was bold as brass when it came to going after a piece she really wanted. Say . . . you said *was*. She ain't—"

"She is," Quinn said. "She hanged herself in her cell." He didn't explain how.

"Now ain't that something!" Casey seemed astounded. 'Maybe the estate'll finally auction off that old house and all the junk inside it."

"Old house?"

"Mildred's house. Over in Bland County. Nothing in it's worth much, and the house itself is rundown, partly because of weather and lack of care, and because people been sneaking in and out of it for well over a decade now."

"Trespassing?"

"You betcha! They figure it's worth the risk. Place has been trampled inside and out, some of the walls knocked clear in to studwork, holes dug all over the yard. Time passes, and just when you think folks have forgotten, somebody shows up with a shovel or a pick-axe and starts searching again."

"Searching for the lottery money?"

"So you know about that."

"Sure," Quinn said. *But I can always learn more.*

"You betcha, that's what they're searching for. I think they're wasting their time. If they knew Mildred they'd believe she could spend and gamble away all that money in the short time before she went to trial. Any gambling addict would tell you that. She wasn't used to having so much money, and she didn't know how to handle it. She could squeeze dimes till they bled, but paper money was for burning."

"So she was a compulsive gambler."

"Yep. That's the reason she bought all those lottery tickets. Won all that money weeks afore she went to prison. Just in time to spend big on legal expenses.

Hell, being Mildred, she'd hurry to spend it all afore she had to start doing time."

"Was she always a risk taker?"

"Long as I knew her. Horses, fights, cards, slots, wherever she could place any kinda bet, she laid it down. Spent a fair amount of time in Vegas, I know."

"I thought you said she was smart."

"Smart's got nothing to do with gambling. For somebody like Mildred, it was a sickness. She had to keep at it even though the odds were against her. She thought she was special and that somehow she'd win. She always thought she could quit at the right time, only there was never a right time, and there was never gonna be."

Quinn decided it might be best not to identify Dred to Vernon Casey as a suspected serial killer, but he wanted to probe to see what Vernon knew.

"What about her son, Dred? Did he ever look for the money?"

"I doubt that. Hell, he was just a teenage kid at the time. Said about three words a year. Real withdrawn. Wrapped up in his own little world. And I can't see Mildred telling him about the money. She wasn't one to share. Also, 'bout the time of the trial, he was hustled outta the area and put in a foster home. Heard he ran away after a week."

"You don't think he came back here to look for the money."

"Oh, I'm sure he would've if he'd known about it. My guess is he headed east, your territory, maybe. Dred was a bright enough kid to get the hell away from here or anyplace else that reminded him of Mildred. Rumor was he got sort of adopted by this truck driver, put some money Dred's way, got him an education. A kid like Dred, he could do the rest. Scholarships and such. I heard he's in the antique business somewhere in the Northeast, but it's real money antiques, not weather vanes, depression glass, and pie safes. Fancy European stuff, art. Well, I say more power to the kid. He rose up outta the ashes and more power to him."

"Would you know anyone who might be able to locate him?"

"No, no. Like I said, we don't travel in the same circles. I never even dreamed I was in Sotheby's."

Maybe Dred hadn't either. Maybe he dealt with a different set of buyers who didn't mind if all of their collection was illegally obtained.

"Anything else you might tell me about Mildred Gant?" Quinn asked Vernon Casey.

"We talking fact or rumor?"

"Either one. We're not in court."

"Rumor, is all. For what it's worth."

"Pretend we're chatting over the back fence," Quinn said.

"Well, years back, something mighty bad happened to Marshall Wilcoxen's daughter-in-law that was married to his son, Billy."

"What might that have to do with Mildred Gant?"

"Maybe nothing. The daughter in law was pregnant with her and Billy Wilcoxen's baby. Then she got murdered and the baby took from her womb before its time, but when it was alive. Somebody killed that poor woman and sliced her right open, probably afore she was all the way dead. The law never did find the killer, nor the baby. A while later, still in his grieving, Billy Wilcoxen ran his car at high speed into a concrete bridge abutment, died instantly. It wasn't no accident, though it was recorded as such in state records."

"So what might Mildred have to do with all that?" Quinn asked, knowing the answer but wanting to hear it.

"Rumor was that about the same time all this was going on with Billy Wilcoxen and his wife and baby, Mildred went and gave birth. She was a heavyset woman to begin with, and people didn't see her all that often, so it was plenty possible. I mean, the times work out with what happened to the Wilcoxen baby, and all. But that could be coincidental."

"What do you think?"

"I'm like everybody else. I don't know what to think. People talked and talked about it for a while, then the talk died down."

"So who was the father?"

"Of Dred? Mildred's baby? There was speculation, is all. Birth certificate said father unknown. And for sure, nobody with a pecker walked up and claimed the kid."

"Dred would be about the missing Wilcoxen baby's age," Quinn said.

Vernon Casey said, "Exactly his age."

42

Jody and Carlie talked for a while with the average-looking guy in Twiggy's Health Drinks. Harold watched the three of them gab and grin. Then the two women stood up. The average guy seemed to be saying good-bye to both of them, even touched Jody's upper arm for a moment. She obviously didn't take to that but didn't do anything to remove his hand.

When Jody and Carlie left, the average guy took their table. He looked around, as if maybe they'd forgotten something, then ordered another juice drink.

Harold knew Sal would fall in behind Jody and Carlie, who would almost surely walk back to their subway stop.

But maybe not.

Harold had his choice. He could stay in the fruit drink bar and confront the average-looking guy who was probably just that—an average, innocent guy searching for life-enhancing vitamins. Or he could do what he was supposed to be doing, following and protecting Jody and Carlie.

Harold belched and went out into the warm night.

He jaywalked, quickened his pace for a while, and eventually saw Sal up ahead of him. And ahead of Sal, Jody and Carlie.

They seemed to be headed back to the subway stop, all right. Harold turned a corner and jogged a short block, then continued half jogging, half walking. He figured he'd make the next cross street before Sal and the girls. Then he could keep up his steady pace, faster than theirs, and reach the subway stop before them.

There'd be nothing to connect him and Sal when they boarded the same train.

In Harold's coat pocket was a packet of religious pamphlets proclaiming the Rapture would be next November the third, when the world would come to an end. Harold thought that if he was following someone who seemed to suspect he was a cop, he could pull out the pamphlets and start handing them out to his fellow passengers. That would allay suspicion.

It might work, if he was sure he'd been spotted and pegged for the law.

Harold had never mentioned this fallback plan to anyone.

Sal would shoot him if he knew about the pamphlets.

The killer sat in the sunlight on a bench at the edge of one of the area's urban "pocket" parks. He didn't mind Carlie and Jody leaving a similar bench facing another direction. He knew where to find them.

He had for the last ten minutes flirted with an attractive blond woman struggling to straighten her slightly bent front bicycle wheel. She had her legs spread for leverage, and with her short skirt was creating quite a show. She didn't suspect that he'd stuck out his foot and given her bike a shove to cause her wobble and crash.

The killer's gaze didn't linger on her legs for long. It was her face that most interested him. Her blue eyes held a kind of cruel light, and her square chin lent her a vaguely defiant expression even at rest.

My type.

The killer watched Jody and Carlie stand up and leave, undoubtedly still being trailed by the overconfident but not very bright cops who were assigned to watch and protect them.

They were so predictable that the killer almost yawned. Now the women would go to the same subway stop, take the same train. They would get off at separate stops, close to their respective homes. That's when their guardian angels would also split up, to make sure each woman would make it home alive, Carlie to her apartment, Jody to the brownstone on West Seventy-fifth Street. The killer had to smile.

Blondie with the bike thought he was smiling at her. She tried again, feebly, to straighten the bike's handlebars, then gave an elaborate shrug.

The killer got up, walked lazily to her, and easily aligned the handlebars. "Good as new—almost," he said.

She said, "Fiona."

The killer gave her the kind of amiable grin that was every salesman's ambition.

"Is that the password?" he asked.

"That's my name."

"Is that the password?" he asked again.

She laughed.

"First or last name?" he asked.

"I thought, after the kind of looks you were giving me, that by now we could be on a first-name basis."

"First names are good enough. I've met a Betty and a Zelda while I've been sitting here. You're the first Fiona."

"It's not a common name."

"You're not a common girl. That's Fiona with an *F*?"

"Uh-huh." *As if he has to make sure. What did he expect, a PH?* "You friends with the women who just left?"

So she'd noticed he'd been watching Jody and Carlie. He didn't like that.

"No. I thought I knew one of them from work."

She leaned on her bike, flexing her legs to put on a show. "Let me guess—you're an advertising executive. Or a trader who works on Wall Street."

The killer smiled. "I was thinking *you* might be one of those things. Or an important CEO of an international company."

"That doesn't surprise me. Most men assume I'm some kind of executive. Even dressed casually, riding my bike, I just look . . . businesslike."

"I'll say."

"It's a curse."

"Not necessarily."

"I guess not if you mean business," she said, grinning. She got a plastic water bottle from a bracket on the bike and unscrewed the cap. She held the bottle out to the killer, who shook his head no, he wasn't thirsty. She was. She tilted back her head and guzzled water. He watched her throat work, fascinated.

She noticed his interest and gave him what she no doubt thought was a dazzling smile as she capped the water bottle and replaced it on the bike.

"We on a first-name basis?" she asked.

"Why do you ask?"

"Because it doesn't often happen that I fall off my bike, much less in front of a perfect stranger who I have to admit I'm drawn to." She shrugged, making it cute. "It could be fate."

"Or you ran over a rock."

"I'd rather go with fate."

"It certainly makes life more interesting," he said. "It's Brad."

She tilted her head as if rolling the name around in her mind. "I'm not surprised. That's a nice name, Brad. And you look nice. Like you'd be nice, anyway."

"Oh, I'm known for nice."

"You in the area?"

He grinned. "Sure. I'm right here."

She laughed. "You know what I mean. Do you live in or around here?"

"Nope. Upper East Side."

"That's what men say when they want me to think they're rich."

"I'm rich."

"That doesn't matter to me. I only care about your mind."

"I'm nice as well as rich."

"That's why I'm drawn to you, Brad. That and your modesty."

"Are *you* rich?"

"Yes, I am," she said. "And I also live on the Upper East Side, near Second Avenue."

"That's why we're here tonight in SoHo, isn't it?"

" 'Splain, please."

"Hooking up with someone who isn't from our *very* expensive neighborhood," the killer said. "Though God knows it's gotten expensive enough around here. Taxes are going up like an elevator."

Fiona got her water bottle and helped herself to another drink, doing things with her tongue the killer couldn't help but notice.

"I wouldn't care to agree with that," she said, then smiled. "Even though it's true."

"About the property taxes?"

"No. The hooking up. That's why most of the people here come to this little park, though they'd never come right out and admit it. This park has sort of a reputation."

That was news to the killer. He made a mental note of it.

"You can admit it to me," he said. "We're on a first-name basis." He touched the back of her hand lightly with the tip of his forefinger and traced a gentle pattern. "We're both here looking for someone interested in a first-name-only relationship. We both found someone."

"You speak the simple truth, Brad."

"Oh, always. Another truth I sense is that we should get to know each other even better. Who knows where it might lead?"

"Maybe nowhere beyond tonight," she said. "I like to keep that option open."

"It's open, for both of us."

She leaned toward him, and her loosely buttoned

white blouse parted, showing considerable cleavage. "I believe in fate," she said.

"So do I."

"I'm glad I'm not a Betty or a Zelda."

"Who are they?"

"The women you decided not to pursue. The ones you were watching earlier."

"Oh, them. Do you know them?"

"Enough to know they aren't for you."

"I did talk to them earlier. They gave me different names."

"Ah! Already they fibbed to you."

He liked the way this woman lied. So smoothly and confidently. Kindred spirits.

"Fate led you to a Fiona," she continued. "There aren't many of us, and I'm the one you approached. Not a Mary or a Sandra or a *Sondra*, but me, a Fiona."

"You approached me. Fell down in front of me on your bicycle, anyway."

She shrugged. "Well, you weren't approached by a Frances. That might have made a difference."

"Maybe. I can honestly say that I wouldn't care if Frances happened to be your name." He touched her hand again. "Not that I don't believe in fate. Fate and I are old friends. He's done me another favor tonight."

"You are *so* nice. But sometimes fate needs a little help. Now it's up to us to acquaint ourselves with each other."

"What we should do along that line is visit each other's apartments, see how the other half lives."

"Yes, that would facilitate our relationship," Fiona said.

The killer considered kissing the hand he was touching, but decided that would be oddly inappropriate with this frank and unapologetic liar. "Your place first," he said. "If things work out okay, my place next time."

"Why start with my place?"

"I'd like you to be comfortable, surrounded by familiar things. You could know you were safe."

Her lips arced in a wide smile. "You are so *very* nice."

He moved closer and gently took the handlebars from her so he could walk the bike.

"You know what my ambition for tonight is?" he asked as they walked.

"Hmm. I think so."

"It's to make sure you don't change your mind about that 'nice' remark."

"See," she said, smiling wider. "What a nice thing to say."

But he seemed to be thinking of something else.

A Zelda. Doesn't that boggle the mind?

43

Quinn and Pearl visited their fourth antique shop of the day. This one was actually a mall, with various dealers renting stalls stuffed with merchandise. It was on Second Avenue, near a diner where they'd stopped for lunch.

Prices here were high, as they'd been at the other three antique shops. In front of Pearl was a set of Fostoria crystal champagne flutes for three hundred dollars per stem. A Stickley chair that looked god-awful uncomfortable had an asking price of a thousand dollars. Pearl thought it would be a good place to sit a suspect down for interrogation. Anyone would confess to anything just to get out of the chair.

"Beautiful stuff," Quinn said.

"You're talking about me?"

Quinn smiled. Having Jody and Carlie around had certainly lit some kind of fire under Pearl. As if youth were contagious.

"It should be beautiful," Pearl said, "at three hundred dollars per stem."

"I wasn't talking about your legs. I was talking about the chair."

"Really something," said a man's voice. It belonged to a chubby, balding man in a suit patterned in olive-green plaid. What hair the man had was gray and combed in wings above his ears. The grayness picked up the green in the suit.

The suit itself was outrageous, yet somehow the chubby guy pulled it off. Pearl figured that was because the material was so obviously expensive that the outfit had to be taken seriously despite the ludicrous pattern.

"It looks uncomfortable," Pearl said.

"I was talking about the Mayan bust," the chubby guy said. "It's pre-Columbian."

Quinn had had enough of this. He showed the man in the absurd suit his ID. "What we're really in the market for are answers."

The man handed Quinn a richly embossed white business card with gold printing. "I'm Jacob Thomas," he said, and the card confirmed that. Thomas smiled. "I sort of thought you were police."

"So you have an eye for more than antiques," Pearl said.

As if she'd just requested it, Thomas gave her another of his cards. "I have an eye for what I know about," he said. "No one has all-encompassing knowledge of antiques and their value." He pointed. "The Mayan bust, for example, is a museum-quality piece. It's been verified by an expert in pre-Columbian statuary."

"Museum quality means expensive," Quinn said.

"Means desirable, which is pretty much the same

thing." Thomas motioned toward the bust with a well-manicured hand. "Myself, I think it's rather ugly. But there's no denying that it's old and rare." He looked around the wide area and smiled. "We don't sell junk."

"Maybe expensive junk?" Pearl asked.

"Not knowingly." Thomas frowned. "I have a feeling you might think we have some stolen merchandise here. If we do, it's quite by accident, I assure you."

"No," Quinn said, "we want to ask you questions about somebody you might know." He grinned in a way that was oddly menacing. "Unless you'd like to unburden a guilty conscience."

"No, no!" Thomas waved his hand as if swishing away a pesky insect. "It's just that in this business, there *are* imitations. And sometimes excellent ones. Now and then we get fooled." He shuffled his feet and looked nervous. "*Have* we been fooled?"

Quinn laughed and rested a huge, rough hand on Thomas's shoulder. "Not that we know of, Mr. Thomas. By the way, how do you obtain your merchandise?"

"We have various sources. We purchase estates, deal with heirs, buy from other dealers, or at auction. There's a surprisingly fast turnover with items in this price range. They tend to increase in value over time, whatever the economic news. Investors as well as collectors are among our customers. And we do sell to some museums."

"Your obviously upper-crust inventory," Pearl said, "suggests you deal with upper-crust sellers and buyers."

"We run some items through Sotheby's or Christie's, if they show well in their catalogs, and if the market is right."

"Have you heard the name Dred Gant?" Quinn asked.

"Why would you ask that?"

Quinn and Pearl were surprised.

"You're not supposed to answer a question with a question," Pearl said. "You've seen the TV cop shows and know the rules."

Thomas smiled, but he looked worried. He made a sweeping motion with his arm, inviting them over to a small, carpeted area where there were two armchairs and a mauve upholstered love seat, a conversation area for hushed negotiations.

Quinn and Pearl sat in the chairs, Jacob Thomas in the love seat. He rested one arm of the extreme suit over the scrolled wooden back, obviously hoping to appear at ease.

"We find it best not to reveal ourselves when we purchase merchandise at auction," Thomas said. "So we use telephone buyers, sometimes nameless, faceless proxies, to relay their bids to representatives at the auctions. You've no doubt seen anonymous bids phoned in at auctions."

"Only in the movies," Quinn said. "I don't hang out at Sotheby's or Christie's."

"Until a year ago Dred Gant was a buyer for us," Thomas said. "He'd travel to various places and relay our bids."

"Secret bids?"

"As to the identity of us as the perspective buyer, certainly. The people who ran the auctions knew of course who we were, but none of their clientele knew. When the item would go up for sale in our shops, no one would associate it with the auction—or the auction price."

"I can see the reasoning," Quinn said. "When did you hire Gant to do this?"

"We never actually *hire* such a person," Thomas said. "Not only would Dred bid via phone for us, he would appear now and then with a valuable piece that we bought from him to add to our inventory. He was self-employed in that capacity. Then, when we came to know and trust him, we used him as a telephone negotiator assessing merchandise and relaying bids."

"You said *until a year ago*," Quinn said.

"Yes. Last summer it seemed he simply disappeared. As if he left the area."

"Without contacting you?"

"Exactly."

"Isn't that a bit unusual?"

"Well, it wasn't as if he was a nine-to-five employee in an ordinary office job. But still, yes, it was unusual."

"Did you ever hear from him? In any way? From anywhere?"

"No. We called his cell phone number, but everything went to voice mail and he never replied. And then the number went out of service."

"How long ago was that?"

"Almost a year."

"You never reported his disappearance to the police?"

Thomas shrugged. "It wasn't that kind of business arrangement. He was a freelancer. He came and went. Like some of the others. Usually they pop up again somewhere in the world of antiques, maybe in foreign lands. The antique scene, in this price range, is world-wide."

"How lucrative is it?" Pearl asked.

"For someone as shrewd and experienced as Dred Gant, it could be very lucrative."

"Six figures?"

"Maybe seven."

"What *do* you have concerning him?" Quinn asked. "Surely you had him bonded."

"No. We looked into him, but couldn't get back very far. We did a credit check on him, made sure he lived where he said."

"Which was?"

"In the Village, on Bank Street. He's moved from there. We checked. No forwarding address." Thomas looked at both of them. "This isn't so strange. We didn't want him bonded because we wanted our private negotiations to stay that way. You'd be surprised how people snoop."

"Us?" Pearl said, acting surprised.

"But surely you had a file on him," Quinn said.

"Certainly. We still have it."

"Does it contain a photograph?"

"Sure," Thomas said. "Wait right here and I'll get it for you."

Jacob Thomas went to a small cubicle of an office that contained a desk and chair, and a laptop computer lying open on a table. On another, smaller table, sat a combination printer, tax machine, etc. Quinn contemplated the technological smorgasbord and wondered if it also brewed coffee.

Thomas walked over to a bank of square black file cabinets with hidden drawer handles. The entire open and visible modern office, surrounded by all the antiques, looked as if it had dropped there from the future.

Quinn didn't see what Thomas did, but he'd obviously pressed a button or in some way triggered a signal, because the second drawer on the nearest cabinet slid smoothly open.

It didn't take Thomas long to find the file on Dred Gant. It was fat and legal sized, contained in a green folder. Thomas laid it on the otherwise bare desk and flipped it open. He withdrew a five-by-eight photograph from the file's front pocket.

Quinn picked up the photo, and he and Pearl stared at it.

Dred Gant had a neatly trimmed mustache and beard, large black-framed glasses, and longish hair with a part in the middle. It was difficult to know the color of his eyes behind the reflections in the lenses of the oversized glasses. His hair was blond with dark roots.

"He might as well be Elton John," Pearl said.

"Or Justin Timberlake," Jacob Thomas said.

Quinn said, "Who the hell is Justin Timberlake?"

44

Fiona was startled to wake up next to a warm male body. Then remembrance of last night came to her in a rush that made her dizzy. The time in her apartment, here in her bed, the depleting of her supply of vodka.

My God! She shouldn't have had so much to drink. She would have kicked herself, actually, only she feared waking the nude man next to her in her bed. At least she assumed he was nude. The wrinkled, turned-back sheet came up to his waist.

No, she thought back. She knew he was nude.

Her mind grasped for facts. She had left him alone in the kitchen to put ice in the glasses and pour their drinks. Straight vodka because that was all Fiona had where she kept the liquor in a cabinet above the refrigerator.

Beyond that, Fiona couldn't recall much.

Demon rum, she thought. Though she couldn't remember even tasting rum.

Moving slowly and carefully, listening to the man's easy breathing, she rubbed an eye that was sore from being mashed into the pillow. What the hell was his name? Brandon? No, Brady! No, Brad. First-name basis. And he knew her only as Fiona. Or as some of the things he'd whispered to her last night, when he wasn't being rough. Brad liked it rough, but not too rough. She probably didn't have a bruise on her body. But he'd known how to play her, have her eating out of his hand.

She regarded him through only one eye. His brown hair was barely mussed, and he seemed to be sleeping peacefully. Almost smiling.

He was no great prize, but a girl could do worse.

Fiona decided not to get up yet and shower. She'd wait for him. She was comfortable enough, with only a light sheet over her and the ceiling fan ticking away and providing a soft breeze.

In fact, she was *very* comfortable.

The killer knew Fiona was awake, and he was sure she thought he still slept. He maintained a neutral expression, with his eyes lightly closed, carefully regulating his breathing. His sensory perception was on high. He was aware that she was staring at him, but he didn't mind. He'd practiced feigning sleep. It was a skill that had often proved useful.

He put the woman out of his mind for now and recollected last night. He hadn't touched much in the apartment, and he remembered precisely where and what he had touched.

Sometime after midnight, when he was awake and Fiona still slept, he'd gone into the bathroom down the hall. He'd wiped all the fixtures and smooth surfaces down with a damp towel. Being extra careful to make sure there would be no fingerprints for the police to find.

Before returning to bed, he'd gone into the living room and found his briefcase where he remembered placing it at the end of the sofa. He'd withdrawn a pair of tight, flesh-colored rubber gloves, and slipped and snapped them deftly onto both hands as if they were second skins.

He'd be using them shortly. Though he didn't want to rush. He enjoyed the anticipation almost as much as the act.

He lay there in the dark, in the soft breeze, giving his imagination full play. Waiting for the dawn. This time his victim wasn't going to be drugged. He wanted her to anticipate and feel every nuance of her torture.

When he heard her soft voice, he knew he'd dozed off.

That was okay. He was instantly all the way awake and alert, although he hadn't opened his eyes or moved a muscle. Even with his eyes closed, he could tell it was morning and the room was full of light.

He realized his left hand rested on top of the sheet.

"What's that on your hand?" she asked again, in a fond and amused whisper. He felt her lips brush his cheek.

"Rubber gloves," he said.

"What on earth for?"

"I'll show you," he said.

*   *   *

Fiona lay face up on the bed. Her arms and legs were lashed to headboard and footboard with ties from a robe and dress the killer had gotten from her closet. A rectangle of gray duct tape was plastered over her mouth. In the center of the tape was an indentation in the shape of a small *O* from her last, futile breath. She had died on the up beat, the killer mused.

He was still nude except for green disposable paper booties of the sort surgeons and OR nurses wore. They fit well enough over his bare feet. He was cleaning up after himself carefully. He dipped the forefinger of his gloved right hand into blood that had pooled in a low spot on the mattress, then he padded into the bathroom. He scrawled his FREEDOM TO KILL message on the medicine cabinet mirror and smiled.

Mustn't forget Quinn and his minions.

For a moment he thought of adding that this time his victim had been fully awake and aware of everything he did to her. Then he thought better of it. Economy was safety. Deviation was danger.

He rinsed the blood from his gloves, then went to his briefcase, which he'd brought into the bedroom so he could have his implements within reach. Fiona's bulging blue eyes seemed to follow him. He enjoyed that.

Bending over the briefcase, he withdrew a seven-inch-high plastic statuette of the Statue of Liberty. It was like the others that he'd bought at different places, over time.

He propped Lady Liberty in Fiona's abdominal cavity at an angle so she seemed to be peeking out over the wide flap of stomach skin, her torch held high as if in a signal.

Freedom to Kill.

The killer used the bathroom to shower, scrubbing himself carefully. He wore a plastic shower cap from his briefcase and made doubly sure that no hair went down the drain that might be retrieved for DNA purposes. He knew that there might be a hair or two somewhere in the apartment; healthy people lost quite a few individual hairs per day. But his DNA wasn't in any of the data banks. A match could be made only *after* he was apprehended, and he didn't plan on that happening.

When he was sure he was leaving behind nothing that would provide an unintended clue, he stood at the foot of the bed, holding his briefcase. He drew a deep breath and took one last long look at Fiona, fixing her in his mind.

She stared back at him, looking appalled.

Well, that was too bad for her.

Murder was actually so easy. Simple as ABC. If everyone knew that, there'd be lots more of it.

He thought about leaving some other taunt for Quinn, maybe something relating to Jody, sweet Carlie. Or Pearl. Quinn's vulnerabilities.

Then he reconsidered. It didn't take much to push Quinn's buttons. Mustn't overdo it, though.

Wouldn't want to press the wrong button.

As he left the apartment, the last thing he did was peel off his gloves and wipe down the doorknob. He took the elevator down, knowing he would soon simply be another of New York's faceless millions. There was such contentment and security in anonymity.

No one took any particular notice of him as he left the building, and within seconds the teeming city enveloped and protected him.

He was one of its own.

Quinn thought the Fiona crime scene was like another installment in a running nightmare. The killer exercised the usual care not to leave any real clues, and he employed the usual techniques that Nift so admired. The only difference was it looked as if this one might have fought back a little. Not that it mattered.

Quinn went into the bathroom and wasn't surprised to find the usual message scrawled in blood on the mirror.

He went back and looked down at the usual victim. Yet she wasn't like any of the other victims. They would all have been different from each other once you got to know them—if they were still alive. Catching sight of his reflection in the dresser mirror, he was startled by the expression on his drawn features and found himself wishing he were anyplace but here.

Nobody ever really gets used to this.

The killer knows that.

Quinn strode toward the hall door. He had to get out of there. In a corner of his vision he saw a surprised Fedderman, the pale forms of the techs haunting the scene like curious ghosts,

Nift's voice: "Leaving so soon? I'm just getting to the good part."

The killer Quinn couldn't stop had done this. A killer who had to be aware that the torture went on long after he'd left his victims. He knew the heartbreak and broken lives he was leaving in his wake. The years of furious impotence.

Rage rose in Quinn like an angry sea. He knew it would never completely recede.

45

Helen sat in the chair across from Minnie Miner on the *ASAP* set. The leather arms of the chair were stained and stiff from hundreds of perspiring guests. It surprised Helen how clean and new the chair appeared on the TV studio monitors and on her television in her apartment.

"Fiona!" Minnie said, squirming around to get comfy in her own chair, not nearly as scuffed and stained as Helen's. "The killer continues his gruesome march through the alphabet."

"I think since we've made it to F that we can assume that," Helen said. "It is beyond coincidence."

"Of course, many of us in the media were saying that weeks ago."

Minnie was getting on Helen's nerves. "The media can speculate and be wrong. The police have to be sure. One wrong assumption and they can soon be miles off course. Like the explorer who was off by one degree at the beginning of his voyage but sailed hundreds of miles beyond his destination."

"What explorer was that?"

"Santo Vincenti Diego."

"I've never heard of him."

"There you are."

Minnie gave Helen a look, not quite knowing if she'd just been had. She was gaining respect for Helen, who had a knack for taking control of an interview without seeming to do so.

"The killer is doing what you predicted," Minnie said, as a kind of peace offering. "He's becoming more sadistic. More vicious and grisly. I mean, the things he did to poor Fiona, the F girl."

"What he did that was worst of all," Helen said, "was to keep the woman alive as long as possible once he began to work on her."

"And there was no sign of—"

"No sign of rape or forcible entry, but there had been sex, with a condom."

"Is it possible that they knew each other?" Minnie asked. "That they'd been lovers?"

Helen shrugged her broad shoulders. "Anything's possible. This killer thinks he's intelligent, so he leaves few, if any, clues for us to work with."

"*Thinks* he's intelligent?" *Easy*, Minnie told herself. *Don't do anything that makes it seem you're defending a killer. Ratings, ratings . . .*

"I know he's baffled the police so far," Helen said. "But what he's doing isn't an intelligent risk. He doesn't seem smart enough to understand that time isn't on his side. If he makes only one mistake, overlooks only one thing, we might have him. And when we do, if he's convicted, that will be the end for him. Game over."

"Whereas if you don't get him today, you simply start over again tomorrow."

"Until eventually he's ours," Helen said.

Minnie raised a forefinger, gazed off in the distance, and then touched the finger to the hearing device in her ear.

"Excuse me, please," she said to the camera displaying the red light.

She unclipped her miniature mike from her lapel and spoke softly into it so no one could hear other than whomever she was talking to.

Then she said, "Yes, yes," quite clearly and looked at Helen and then out at the studio audience. Back to Helen.

"The killer wants to talk to you," she said. She could hardly contain her emotions as she pronounced the words.

A prop man walked hurriedly out and handed a cell phone to Helen, who sat shocked.

But not for long. Who did this asshole think he was, trying to rattle her?

"Helen Iman?" asked the ordinary male voice on the phone.

"Yes," she said, and waited. She'd noticed that her voice resonated with a slight and immediate echo. Sound was being fed through to the studio audience.

Minnie whispered loudly in *sotto voce* that the killer was on the line with her guest—really!

"I can't talk long without my call being traced," the killer said.

"Your paranoia is showing," Helen said.

"I called to remind you that after F comes G, and after G comes H."

Helen felt her blood rush to a small cold place in her

core. She almost dropped the phone. Suddenly the studio became even more uncomfortably cool.

"Listen—" she began. But she noticed immediately that she was talking to herself.

There had been no click, but the background hush of the call had changed and she knew she and the caller were no longer connected.

Minnie was staring at her, almost vibrating with excitement. This was quite a *coup*. The killer and perhaps one of his future victims, right here on her show.

Ratings were going to—

She saw Helen stand up and detach her lapel mike, then gently lay it and its transformer on the chair. Obviously she was leaving the set.

Minnie hadn't nearly milked this situation dry.

"Helen! Helen! I know you're shaken. Who wouldn't be, after that last, *incredible* remark? But you mustn't—"

But Helen continued to walk away.

No one tried to stop her. No one so much as touched her or even looked directly at her. It was as if she had something that might be contagious.

The killer had marked her.

Out on the sidewalk, her cell phone chirped. She hesitated even removing it from her purse.

The electronic chirping continued. Whoever was calling was determined. Reluctantly, she put her hand into her purse and withdrew the phone.

The chirping went on unabated.

She didn't answer until she saw that the caller was Quinn, and the fluttering bird that was her heart became calm.

"You might want to watch Minnie Miner tomorrow,"

he told Helen. "I've just given her some instructions concerning an interesting news item about a woman who won the lottery just before going to prison, and her house in the country."

And he explained to Helen the trap they were going to set.

"It could work," Helen said thoughtfully.

"*Could* is enough to make it worth a try," Quinn said.

PART THREE

Oh, write of me, not "Died in bitter pains,"
But "Emigrated to another star!"

—HELEN HUNT JACKSON, *Emigravit*

46

Fate remained on the side of the Killer. Dred Gant was in a rental car, driving toward Jefferson City, Missouri, where there was going to be an auction in pre-1899 firearms.

He was using his 3G phone to listen to *Minnie Miner ASAP* on the Internet. Because he was out of town didn't mean he had to miss what had become, if not his favorite, the most interesting of the TV shows he watched. He wasn't actually *watching* the show, though it was visible on the phone on the seat beside him. He had to be careful driving, the way the traffic weaved at speeds over eighty miles per hour on Interstate 70.

As soon as he heard Minnie Miner relate the story of a woman from a small town in Missouri, who in 2000 had won a lottery jackpot and then gone to prison, he knew it was a trick. His pursuers would know that *he'd* know the story was related to that of the Lady Liberty Killer.

This was not coincidence. Minnie would use her

show to broadcast any sort of bait that would result in a catch. Her adoring audience would patiently assume the relevance and be delighted with the outcome.

Minnie described how people had searched the woman's ramshackle house and yard for traces of the money, but had found none. Now, however, there were rumors that some money had been removed, stolen, but much of it hadn't.

That "rumor" had also not been a coincidence.

The coincidence could be that he had heard this news when less than two hours from his boyhood home.

And, according to Minnie Miner, there might be money he hadn't found in the dilapidated house.

His money. Not his mother's now. Or anyone else's. *His*.

The killer decided that *might* was reason enough to run the risk. There came a time in any game when one of the players must seize opportunity. Safety here would be in acting first and directly.

He stayed on Interstate 70 and drove toward the orange setting sun.

Night had fallen, and it was almost ten o'clock.

Dred Gant sat out of sight in the dim moonlight, gazing down the hill at the house where he'd grown up.

He was comfortable in a shelter among the ancient pines that were scattered on the sloping hill beyond the house. There were fewer of the trees than he remembered, but they were much larger.

From where he'd positioned himself, he could see the house's front porch, and off to the right, not as far

from the porch as he recalled, was the old wooden outhouse. He felt the bile of anger rise bitter in his throat
and swallowed it noisily. As he had so many times here
at . . . home.

It bothered Dred at times, knowing strangers, and
some people he knew and despised, had rooted through
his old home. One he would no doubt inherit, if the au-
thorities could find him. Well, they could keep the
house and the rocky, hilly land around it. He'd keep his
freedom, and his mission.

The money was another story. Whether it was dimes
or dollars, it belonged to him. He would use it to maintain his lifestyle.

He remembered watching old movies and television
shows, fascinated by the way how, while the projectors
or DVDs were running, their stars seemed to lead lives
pertaining only to the roles they played. Those people
on screen led precisely the lives they wanted. Or that
the script demanded. Of course, being fictional, they
could do that.

But at a certain point Dred had come to see himself
in a similar situation. It was simple, really, if he used
his initiative. His role would be himself. The drama
would be of his making. The ending . . . well, he would
choose the when and where of that. And the means.

He wouldn't, like the ordinary fools in this world,
have to think first and foremost of earning money.

He knew where to find money, cash that, legally,
should be his, anyway. The only problem was that he
wasn't . . . legal. He certainly wouldn't want his name
and photograph in the news as inheritor of a lottery
win.

But he *would* like the money, his spendable trophy.

And he *had* found it, once, where he knew it would be and where others wouldn't think to look. And it had been enough money to fund what would eventually become a profitable business in antiques.

So here he was, poised in the darkness so near the darkness of his past. For the oldest reason in the world—personal gain.

The rest of what was his.

When the moonlight was unbroken with clouds, he shifted his gaze through his high-powered binoculars from the pockmarked dirt yard to the slanted steel doors of the storm cellar. They were slightly askew, allowing a narrow shadow of an opening, as if beckoning anything that yearned for the dark. All anyone would find down there were spiders and junk, but it was no surprise to Dred that even from this distance he could see that the padlock on the heavy, rusty hasp was broken. Someone had forced his or her way into the claustrophobic storm cellar, seen nothing of value, and no doubt gotten out of there in a hurry. It was the kind of place you visited only in nightmares, when you had no choice.

But there was something in the cellar that attracted Dred now. It was time to satisfy his curiosity.

Had he left behind some of the lottery money?

He was sure none of the money was in a bank. No surprise. Mildred had had a virulent distrust of banks. And just to be positive, he'd surreptitiously checked the house long ago,

But he'd been in a rush that night. And he'd been eager to flee the storm cellar. It was certainly possible he'd overlooked some of the stacked bills.

He'd been gone long enough for the embers of fear and gossip to have cooled. The old house, and the violent woman who'd lived in it, had slipped into local lore, and existed only on the edges of people's minds. By now, they needed something else to talk about. To think about.

Minnie Miner's "report" would soon spread throughout the area, and the pickers would be back, some of the same ones who'd dug up the yard and broken through the wallboard years ago.

Another reason to move fast. Immediately.

There were a lot of places to hide money in any house. Dred knew all of them in this house, from the times he'd had to look for Mildred's hidden booze or weed.

But he was thinking about the storm cellar in particular. The hell hole had served only two purposes that he knew of—a tornado shelter, and a dungeon. But Mildred Gant had found yet another purpose.

He stood up slowly and brushed pine needles from his pants legs. An owl hooted nearby, and he froze and glanced around. Nothing was moving in the night but dark smudges of clouds in a gray half-moon sky.

The law—maybe the state police; maybe Quinn himself—would soon be closing in, if they weren't already here.

But the killer knew the hills and the woods around the house. He sensed that he was the only human being in the vicinity. Nothing out of the ordinary was moving, breathing, stalking nearby.

Time to take a chance.

He slung the binoculars crossways on their leather

strap, so they rested just above his hip. Then he left the thicket of pines and began making his way down the hill toward the house.

As he got closer, the crickets' ratcheting cry seemed louder. He listened carefully to the sound, feeling through it with his mind for a warning, but he found none. When he reached level ground, he circled away from the outhouse and approached the west side of the house. The storm cellar doors.

Dred saw that the steel double doors were rusted, in some spots all the way through.

He bent forward so he could see the heavy padlock more closely. It had been sprung, all right. He closed his fist around it to twist it out of the bent hasp, and the hasp broke in his hand. Rust again. Some water, at least, must be getting into the cellar.

He grabbed the hasp again and levered one of the wide doors open. It yowled on its hinges, hesitated at the vertical, and then fell to the side with a clang.

He opened the other door.

47

The cellar yawned before him, a black pit that for all he knew sank to the center of the earth. A damp, sickening odor rose out of the cellar, as if something had died there and was in the final stage of decomposing.

Dred put on rubber gloves, then his plasticized paper booties of the sort surgeons fit over their street shoes to keep the floor sterile. He dug from a pocket the small Maglite he'd brought and switched it on, aiming its beam into the cellar. There were the old wooden stairs, one of them missing. He played the beam of light around slowly. Saw the metal pail that had been his sometimes toilet. He smiled. Too much time had passed for the odor to be coming from there.

He blinked, and from where he stood played the narrow beam of light around the cellar. Near a stone wall was a broken and useless wooden bookcase, and next to it a decrepit cane rocking chair with a twisted back and one runner broken in half.

Junk.

A, B, C, D . . .

Dred became aware of the alphabet thrumming through mind and memory. Quickly he switched off that part of his brain.

He caught a shape off to his left and aimed the beam that way. The corpse of a small animal lay on its side in a corner. It might have been a fox, or a dog, that had gotten trapped in the cellar, or locked in by someone with a cruel sense of humor. If it was a fox, Dred didn't care. But a dog? No one should treat a dog that way.

He made himself chance the broken step and go down into the cellar.

L, M, N, O, P . . .

At first he couldn't breathe, and he was surprised to find that he was trembling.

Then a great anger came over him and he clung to it, converting it to righteousness, and he was in control.

Moving carefully, he found himself standing in a shallow puddle. That was okay; the treated paper boot was waterproof. The odor down here wasn't any worse than up top. The dog, or whatever the remains were, had been dead too long to be overpowering.

Dred followed his flashlight beam across the cellar, and to the old cane rocking chair. Even in its disabled and broken condition, he recognized it. Oh, he knew it well!

The trembling began again, but he got it in hand. He was almost finished here. Soon he'd know if he was right.

He saw that the rocker's seat was somewhat worn, but the cane still looked tight. The younger Dred who had woven the cane, sometimes with bleeding fingers, had done a solid job.

It was easy to turn the chair upside down.

What Dred knew, that no one else would suspect, was that there was a space between the top and bottom of the seat, created by a wooden framework that separated the two cane surfaces and allowed the one on top to give and stretch.

He saw immediately that the bottom of the rocker seat was as he had left it years ago, cut and pried open so he could remove the money, a dozen packets sealed in plastic with rubber bands around them. Each packet had been made up of hundred-dollar bills.

There was no sign that he'd forgotten any of the packets, or money that had been hidden by itself.

Dred could hear the hissing of his breathing now. It made him smile.

Rumor. The speculation of more hidden and unfound money was only that. Rumor, or a plant.

And here he was, almost buried in what had almost been his grave. At least he had thought so, from time to time.

Getting out of the storm cellar was no problem. He felt as if he might fly out.

He didn't even remember surfacing, but here he was standing in the wide night alongside the home of his childhood. He couldn't resist going inside and glancing around. It did seem that every possible place anything could have been hidden had already been investigated.

He spent about twenty minutes in the house anyway, making sure, eliminating one potential hiding place after another. The space behind the panel in the bed-

room closet; the loose floorboard in the living room;
the space above one of the kitchen cabinets, large
enough to contain a bottle on its side. He had to break
some molding to reach that one and find it empty.

Finally satisfied, he performed one small task, then
went out into the night and began jogging away from
the house. It would have been nice to have actually
found more money, but he had satisfied himself that
there was none. Quinn had devised a trap, and with the
help of fate and coincidence the killer had entered it
and left it before it could be sprung.

His rental car was parked out of sight among some
sycamore trees, off the dirt road a quarter of a mile
away, a black Chevy Impala that would not show in the
night.

He unlocked it with the key fob, then slid in behind
the steering wheel. Within seconds he had the engine
running and pounding like his pulse. He sat motionless
for over a minute, forcing himself to surface from his
dream and use good sense.

By morning, possibly before, they would be here.
The police and perhaps some treasure hunters who
would be sadly disappointed. Not many treasure
hunters yet. News didn't spread that fast from New York
to an isolated place in rural Missouri.

It was 10:45 PM. Clouds slid across the moon, casting among the trees the moving shadows of things gigantic.

Dred drove carefully, well within the speed limit,
acutely aware of leaving the house and the storm cellar
behind him.

He began to laugh.

He turned on the radio at high volume to music he had never heard. Laughed louder.

A move had been made.

Then an immediate counter move.

Like lightning chess.

He was winning.

48

New York City, the present

Hoo-boy!

Carlie, alone in her office and deeply involved with how to fit the maximum number of display gondolas among half a dozen supporting posts in a proposed electronics display retail area, let down her guard and told the assistant to put the phone call through.

A moment later, she pressed the receiver to her ear, identified herself, and her heart plunged.

The caller was Jody's grandmother.

"How nice to hear from you," Carlie said. Not exactly lying. She liked the woman, but a little of her went a long, long way.

"Are you a busy beaver, dear?" Jody's grandmother asked.

"Not desperately so, but—"

"We are family, dear, or I wouldn't take up your time, knowing, as I do, that you are a modern woman with a modern skill set and must, as we all must, appease certain inexorable needs."

Like talking for hours on the phone, Carlie thought.

She laid aside her plastic ruler, calipers, and calculations on customer patterns. Figures rushed out of her head.

This was, to be fair, only the third time today that Jody's grandmother had called her from Sunset Assisted Living. The woman and Carlie weren't even actually related, yet Carlie had been drawn into this blatantly manufactured, suffocating family intrigue.

How must it be for Jody?

But Jody didn't seem to mind. Perhaps because she was dealing with an actual blood relative.

Jody's grandmother continued firing salvos from New Jersey:

"I don't like it that Jody is unsafe, being as she is, in many respects, Captain Quinn's own daughter as well as my dear daughter Pearl's. Of course *I* have a horse in this race, as some might say, though God knows I don't regard Jody as any sort of animal. But I *am* her grandmother and want, as you might imagine, to see her safe so she can live through her golden years but not, God forbid, in a place like this. I know the joy of having a grandchild—two, I would like to say, dear, including you—and wish for both of you the same satisfaction and success in life."

"Your being where you are doesn't seem to interfere with your enjoyment of having a granddaughter," Carlie pointed out, using the singular to try to pull back a little.

"I've been made a gift of two such wonderful creatures and every hour of every day count my blessings, such as they are. In this dreadful place, if you count your blessings and get to two, you're doing better than most doomed souls."

"It really doesn't seem that terrible," Carlie said, trying to cheer her up. "I mean, with assisted living, think of all the things you *don't* have to worry about."

"You mean like death?"

"Well, no, but—"

"Mr. Cammeralter, three doors down, is an example."

"Of what?

"He seemed, poor man that he was, happily unconcerned, but his heart was unaware of his state of bliss and exploded in his chest. He passed three nights ago."

"That's truly a shame. Still—"

"It's a simple favor I'm imploring of you, dear."

"Favor?"

"Yes. Help me please to convince my headstrong granddaughter Jody to move out of the city. Her place should be here in New Jersey, where she is nearby and safer. Being Captain Quinn's surrogate daughter makes her a natural target for this horrible killer who has, for twisted reasons of his own, limited his victims to Manhattan. At any time his grim and grisly plan—and they do plan, such people—might include Jody. Jody would, like so many young women of independent and dangerous means in Manhattan, be safer in New Jersey."

"I don't believe," Carlie said, "that I ever heard of someone moving to New Jersey to be safer."

"Think about it statistically, dear."

Carlie had to admit that Jody's grandmother might have something there. With this killer. Statistically. But Carlie knew how Jody would feel about her grandmother's suggestion. Thought she knew, anyway.

"Jody's a working attorney in the state of New York," Carlie said. "I'm sure she'd be grateful that you have her welfare at heart, but it seems to me it would be impossible for her to live in a different state from the one where she's licensed to practice law."

"Oh, look at the expensive areas of Connecticut and New Jersey and even Philadelphia. All within easy commuting distance. In any of those places you couldn't close your eyes and shoot off a gun without hitting a New York lawyer. Or for that matter, physician. Did I ever tell you about *Doctor* Milton Kahn?"

"Yes, yes," Carlie said.

"Jody's mother's repetitive avoidance, and in fact rejection, of that fine man is another example of her headstrongness that works against her so that she's her own worst enemy and doesn't realize it. Jody seems to have inherited that persistent oppositional outlook. Such opportunities as *Doctor* Milton Kahn come along rarely. Missed opportunities are the plums of life."

Carlie wondered what that meant.

"They eventually become tiny, shriveled prunes."

Ah!

"Jody is exactly like her mother in her obstinacy. We might blame heredity, dear. Itself a close sibling of fate."

Carlie hadn't though of it that way, but it made a certain kind of sense.

"Well," Carlie said, "I'd better get busy here or they'll fire me." She laughed to make it clear she was joking.

"They would be utter fools to fire a woman of your caliber."

What am I, a gun?

"Though the place is probably run by men who hire

and fire women for reasons all the time unconnected to work, though they themselves are too obtuse to recognize the turn of mind it takes to sacrifice willingly quality home life for the cause of quality work—"

"I wouldn't want to put my boss to the test," Carlie said, not mentioning that her boss was a black woman who knew full well how men thought. Or didn't.

"You *will* speak to Captain Quinn about Jody's increasing vulnerability?"

"I promise I will."

"That horrible woman with the TV news show doesn't help any. Molly—"

"Minnie."

"Miller."

"Miner."

"Whatever she calls herself, she should be taken off the air."

"Many people agree with you." *But a couple of million don't.*

"Do talk to—"

"I will. I promise. Please don't worry. Oh-oh . . . darn! You're beginning to break up. The old phone lines in this building . . ."

"Captain Quinn will see the train at the end of the—"

Carlie hung up her phone, feeling guilty, guilty. . . .

49

Quinn and Pearl, and a dozen Missouri State Police officers, held their positions around the ravaged shack that had been the home of Mildred Gant and her son, Dred. They had been on station since a few minutes past midnight, waiting for the killer to come for the rest of his money.

A Captain Milligan was crouched next to Quinn in a small clearing halfway up the hill from the front of the rundown house. It was a moonlit night, but with fast moving clouds. Quinn knew night vision goggles and scopes were being used; it was doubtful the killer could make his way into the house without being seen.

And as soon as he was inside, the signal would be given to advance on the house.

It was a solid plan, if the killer didn't suspect it was a trap.

And it wasn't a hopeless plan if he did suspect. The temptation to remove money—if he had some idea of where it was hidden—and outwit Quinn and the rest of his pursuers would be strong in the killer. He was like the rest of them, playing a game. Life was a game. Death was a game.

Luck was the wild card.

Dawn arrived, but not the killer. Not unless he'd somehow managed to sneak in and out without being seen.

It had been only around six hours since the possibility of hidden money had been revealed by Minnie Miner. Quinn and Pearl were on a red-eye flight that laid over in Pittsburgh and then continued to Kansas City. They'd rented a car in Kansas City. Pearl drove, while Quinn talked to the state police about how and when to set the trap. Wasting no time getting here.

SWAT members in body armor advanced on the house first. They cleared it and then one of them came out front and waved a safe signal to the others.

The yard was full of holes.

"Looks like a mortar attack went on here," Milligan said.

"Treasure hunters with shovels," Pearl said.

Milligan wiped his arm across his perspiring forehead. "Looks to me that if there was anything valuable buried out here, somebody must have found it."

Quinn looked over at the wooden outhouse, now with its door open after being cleared by the SWAT unit.

"In case you're wondering," Milligan said, "SWAT guy told me that the ground's been dug out under the outhouse some time ago."

"I was wondering," Quinn said.

With increasing belief that the killer had failed to show, Quinn walked over to the front porch.

"Wait up a minute," a SWAT guy said. He was a beefy man with a drinker's nose, but Quinn doubted if the man was much of a drinker, judging by the shape he was in, and his career. Quinn heard him called Schweitzer.

Quinn, Pearl, and Milligan froze.

"Been somebody here," Schweitzer said. He pointed. "See that footprint." He pointed at a number of footprints on the dusty porch floor. They all looked pretty much the same, except for one. No, two! Schweitzer pointed again. The two footprints had been made by someone headed away from the front door. Someone leaving. "Our team's all wearing the same kind of regulation shoe," Schweitzer said. "None of us made those two prints."

"But they're recent," Pearl said.

"Damn right they are, ma'am."

"He beat us here," Pearl said.

"That's doubtful," Quinn said. "More likely some local's been here."

"Why?" Pearl asked.

No one had an answer.

"Pretty remote spot," Milligan said.

"Shoes are about the same size and shape as that bloody footprint we got. The one looked like it was made by a surgeon's OR paper bootie."

"Nobody else would wear paper booties around this place," Pearl said. "It's almost sure to have been the same guy."

"No," Quinn said. "He wouldn't have left a footprint."

"Unless he did it on purpose," Pearl said.

"Coulda been somebody around here with a helluva TV dish," Milligan said. "One that'd pick up a local New York City news channel."

"Pearl's suggestion is more likely. About him leaving the footprints on purpose."

"Maybe he picked up the news somewhere on the Internet," Milligan suggested.

"Could be," Pearl said. "Anything's possible on the Internet."

Quinn let out a loud, trailing breath of frustration. "If he somehow learned about this and got here before we could set the trap, he might not have given a damn about footprints."

"This guy sounds like a real shit kicker," Milligan said. "Shit-kicker ego, anyways."

"Let's see what we got inside the house," Quinn said.

They carefully stepped around the footprints on the way in.

"Somebody's been here fairly recently," Milligan said, pointing at a piece of wooden molding that had been broken from the back of a cabinet door. "Looks like a fresh break."

Quinn saw that the splintered molding was a lighter color than similar breaks in the wainscoting.

"Can you tell how fresh?" Pearl asked Milligan.

"Could if I was a termite."

Quinn gave Pearl his straighten-up look. This wasn't the time or place for desperate questions.

"No dust on it, neither," said Milligan, sliding the tip

of his finger with the grain of the broken wood and avoiding a splinter. He held up his forefinger to show that it was clean.

"Looks like something was hidden in the space behind the cabinet," Pearl said. "Maybe when we had Minnie lie, we were unknowingly telling the truth."

"If money was hidden there," Quinn said, "it wouldn't be much, even in large denomination bills."

"How much you New York people get paid?" Milligan asked.

The SWAT guy, Schweitzer, stuck his head into the room. "You better come see this."

Quinn, Pearl, and Milligan filed into the hall, then moved toward the bedroom door.

But Schweitzer stopped them and pointed into the tiny bathroom.

Half the medicine cabinet's mirrored door was broken. The half that remained was coated with dust. The scrawl made with a fingertip in the dust was familiar: FREEDOM TO KILL.

"We must have just missed the bastard!" Quinn said.

"Maybe he didn't keep that finger moving and left a print," Schweitzer said.

"If you want to bet money on that," Quinn said, "it's the only way I can think of how this place will show a profit."

50

Harold was surprised when Carlie left work almost an hour early. He hung well back so she wouldn't spot him, but tailed her with care and caution. Any break in her routine or the rhythm of her surroundings might mean something pertinent.

Now and then he got this creepy feeling, the notion that as he was following Carlie, he was being watched. Or used sometimes as an indicator of her whereabouts.

It could have been his imagination, but experience had taught him that it probably wasn't. And it meant that Carlie might be in real danger, and he'd better keep a close watch on her.

Be her guardian angel, as the cops sometimes said. But Harold didn't feel like an angel. He felt more like a hunter who had, to some degree, become prey.

He stopped without warning, turned, crossed streets he didn't have to cross, checked reflections in car and show case windows. He saw nothing irregular. If he was being tailed, it was by an expert.

And he *was* being tailed.

His best course, he decided, was to tend to the business in front of him.

Carlie strode to her usual subway stop, not far from Bold Designs, but this time crossed the street and descended the narrow concrete steps to the uptown side of the platform.

A train had just pulled in and was screeching to a halt alongside the platform. Harold managed to board the same crowded car, but was standing toward the back, while Carlie had one of the few remaining seats up in front. As the train roared and swayed through darkness, he watched Carlie's reflection in a window opposite where she sat. She was slouched and seemed tired. Her eyes were half closed. Occasionally she closed them all the way. Like many seated passengers, she might be feigning half sleep to withdraw from the cramped and speeding world of the subway, to discourage drunks or solicitors or the mentally precarious from approaching her. No right-thinking person wanted to deal with some of the people on the subway. So the walls stayed up; the gates stayed closed. Harold, watching carefully, knew Carlie wasn't anywhere near falling asleep.

The train slowed slightly, approaching the Seventy-ninth Street station. She jerked to full attention but stayed seated. The train continued to slow, then finally stopped and took a lurch backward as momentum shifted. The doors slid open. Carlie stood quickly and got off quickly onto the platform. Harold got out behind her. He kept his distance as they climbed the steps toward the light and noise of traffic above.

Carlie stumbled at the top of the steps and almost

fell. It was dangerous, the way the concrete slanted up there. She might have fallen right into the traffic on Broadway.

It was a dangerous city, Harold thought. One full of ways to get hurt.

Carlie didn't have far to walk to the offices of Q&A. Harold waited until she'd entered, then followed.

She must have called first, because it appeared that Quinn had been waiting for her. As Harold entered half a minute behind Carlie, he looked over and saw her seated in front of Quinn's desk. Quinn didn't so much as glance in his direction. Carlie saw him and nodded. Harold didn't know what to make of that.

Something passed between Harold and Quinn without either man even looking at the other.

Harold went over and poured himself a cup of coffee and pretended Carlie wasn't there.

When Carlie was finished describing her phone conversation with Jody's grandmother, Quinn sat back and absently twirled a pencil through and around his fingers. He'd learned to do that with poker chips as a young man, and it had stayed with him.

He noticed Carlie watching the pencil and stopped. He rolled his desk chair a few inches toward her.

"Jody's a freckle-faced redhead," he said. "Not at all the killer's type."

"But she is your daughter," Carlie said, "which makes her a likely target of this killer. I do think Pearl's mother is right about that."

"Right as far as it goes."

"What does that mean?" But part of Carlie's mind

suspected what it meant. The icy suspicion trickled down her back.

"If you were to dye your hair a much blonder color, and wear it differently, you'd be even more the killer's type. And there's your middle name."

"I never told you my middle name."

"For God's sake, Carlie, you have a Facebook page." She fidgeted. "I forgot about that."

"People tend to, Grace."

"All right, so my middle name is Grace. So what are you getting at?"

"If this were a chess game, you'd be almost as tempting a piece as Jody, even without the fact that in the killer's mind, you are the way to Helen."

Carlie hadn't thought of that. *G before H.* "My God! The killer's twisted alphabetical mind . . ."

"The alphabet might be the only thing about him that isn't twisted. His adherence to it is an exercise in orderliness, part of what Helen calls the backbone of his obsession."

"So it's not Jody. It's *me* you want to use as a lure." Carlie wasn't really that surprised. It only made sense.

Quinn nodded.

"Because Helen would be alphabetically premature, and I'm only slightly less valuable a chess piece than Jody."

"I wouldn't put it that way. Jody simply doesn't figure into his plans, either by type or alphabet. With you, the alphabet works. And to the killer, you could hardly be a more desirable type." Quinn smiled, but with only the slightest edge of humor. "He does have good taste."

Carlie didn't smile. "Thanks for *that*, anyway."

"We're going to continue our protection for Jody,

just in case. The thing that would take her, and you, completely out of danger is if the killer were apprehended."

"No denying that," Carlie said. Still, she wondered how Jody would feel about this conversation. About this strategy.

"Jody could leave the city," she said.

"We suggested that. Jody *won't* leave. Says her life and her work are here, and she won't be scared away."

"Runs in the family," Carlie said.

Quinn knew where Carlie's musings would eventually take her. He thought he might as well get there first. "Pearl doesn't like this, either, but she figures it's the best way to go."

"And so do I," Carlie said.

"Minnie Miner has said she'll help to set up the situation," Quinn said.

"I'll bet she will," Carlie said. "Do you think she can be subtle enough to fool the killer?"

"No," Quinn said. "He'll know what's going on. He'll try for you anyway."

"The ego thing?"

"More the id."

Carlie felt ice travel down her spine again. It was the id that made her flesh crawl. There was something primal about this killer, in the torture of his victims and in his birth and twisted maternal fixation. How callous and violent the human race must have been in order to persist. How near the surface lurked those primitive but powerful instincts and impulses so necessary for survival. Perhaps that was why serial killers so fascinated the public. We weren't so far removed from the ancient past as we'd like to think. Or maybe not removed at all. Some of it we dragged along with us.

The killer knows and is showing us how base and vicious we can be. The reptilian killer in the primal forest is immortal.

"We can protect you," Quinn said. "But I wouldn't lie to you and pretend there isn't any danger. There's plenty of that. But . . ."

"What?"

"We might have help from an unexpected source. The killer himself. He might have reached the point where he wants to be stopped."

"That actually happens outside of books and movies?"

"Oh, yes. Killing weighs heavier and heavier after a while. It's a burden that can be gotten out from under only one way."

"Don't killers like this usually choose to go out in a blaze of gunfire, gore, and glory?"

"They like to see it that way. But sometimes they don't have the balls. Other times a sniper's bullet to the head puts an end to them."

"But they don't give up."

"No," Quinn said, "they seldom stop on their own. They have to be stopped."

"You and they have that in common."

"Yes," Quinn said.

"Which is why you're so good at what you do."

"Part of it."

"When do I start?"

"You've already started. He's been watching you."

* * *

Helen worked to make Carlie as likely a lure as possible to the killer. Carlie's hair was dyed an even blonder shade, and worn in a style more suited to the eighties. Her clothes, too, were backdated stylistically without it seeming too obvious.

"I'm not sure what more I can do," Carlie said, "other than go around whistling outdated Beatle songs."

"Weren't they more the sixties?" Harold said.

"The Beatles were never outdated," Sal rasped, obviously annoyed with Harold. "Never will be."

"I've got some old Beatle T-shirts," Pearl said.

Helen looked inquisitively at Quinn.

"Yeah, yeah, yeah," Quinn said.

Fedderman said, "Just don't say 'Boop, boop, e-doop.' "

This is fun, Carlie thought, *dressing up to be murdered*.

51

The killer made sure the blinds were closed in his second-floor apartment in the East Village.

The building was a six-story walkup that he'd rehabbed and rented out. There were stairs down to a small courtyard out back, made private by foliage and sections of stockade fencing, and backing to a paving stone walkway to the next block, where one of several abandoned warehouses squatted, deteriorating unused near the river.

He spent much of his time elsewhere, and barely knew the neighbors, even those who were his tenants. This part of the Village was friendly enough, but privacy was respected, and Dred had long ago politely but firmly made it clear that he valued his privacy.

He dumped the money he'd taken from his safety deposit box out on his bed and stared at it.

Fifty thousand dollars.

He'd kept it as a safety net while he used the rest of what was left of the one-hundred-and-seventy-five-thousand-dollar lottery winnings to establish his antique business. The money was in hundred-dollar bills, small enough and negotiable. They were easily safe to spend, especially here in New York, where prices were geared to customers with expense accounts. Hundred-dollar bills were common. A cab ride with a generous tip could cost you more than half that, and the cabbie always had the change in small bills.

Mildred had accepted the lump sum from the state rather than monthly payments, and had probably simply cashed her check at one of the large banks. There would be no reason to mark the bills, or make any sort of record of their serial numbers. Still, Dred was glad to see that none of the packets of cash he'd held in reserve were made up of bills with sequential serial numbers.

He would be safe spending this money, as long as he didn't draw undue attention to himself. For now, though, he would keep it hidden beneath the sink, where he could get it quickly and easily if he had to run on short notice. The adventure at the old house might have turned out much differently were it not for his good luck. It had made him more cautious. No, not more cautious—more meticulous. Certainly not more afraid.

Meanwhile, it was time that he spent this money.

Antique trading upper-end merchandise was a loosely taxed business that depended a lot on the honesty of the taxpayer. Payoffs like the one Mildred had enjoyed were taxed even before the money was made available. Dred could leverage it tax free as long as he didn't buy or sell big-ticket items at exclusive houses like Sotheby's or Christie's. Beyond that, he knew plenty of private collectors who would pay cash, ask no questions, and give no answers. Money in whatever form moved easily in a vacuum.

The private art and collectible market was a healthy, long-running shadow economy, impossible to stamp out. Simple, and sometimes secret, possession was everything to the kinds of buyers Dred knew. More than mere connoisseurs, they were what they owned.

The wonderful thing was that he wouldn't have to actively pursue his business for a while, and he could instead pursue prizes much more interesting.

Like Carlie Clark. Close enough to Quinn to hurt him, but with several prime targets left—like Jody and Pearl.

Something to think about.

Always let them believe nothing worse can happen to them—until very near the end.

The killer had been stalking Carlie with extreme care. One of Quinn's detectives was always near her. The killer had to be especially alert to the fact that if he made the slightest mistake, he might be seen, identified somehow, and apprehended.

No. Not apprehended.

A mistake on either side could exact the ultimate cost.

That made the exercise enjoyable.

Here came Carlie now from Bold Designs, not knowing that he had bold designs on her.

What was this? She'd had her hair dyed a much lighter blond, and it was hanging straight and curtain-like, partially concealing one side of her face or the other as she moved. A beautiful woman, presented simply to the world as such. There was almost a spirituality to her earth-mother blond beauty. Peter and Paul had to be around here someplace with a couple of guitars.

She was dressed more boldly, too. A blue summer matching outfit with a short skirt, navy blue, very high heels that added inches to her height and flashed in the sunlight as she strode along the sidewalk toward her subway stop. She appeared tall, statuesque, and was carrying a small black attaché case this evening. Homework?

Or homicide?

At least there was no sign of the idiot Jesse Trummel. He was an amateur who could throw all sorts of unexpected shit into the game. At least the police seemed to have done their job and kept Trummel away from Carlie, and alive for a while longer. Trummel might thank the police in the future, if he ever gained sense enough to understand what had happened.

The one called Sal was Carlie's guardian angel today. He was short, which made him slightly more difficult to keep track of in a crowd. The killer was almost certain of where Carlie was going, anyway. Home to her apartment. Maybe she'd stop at a deli down the street from where she lived and get some takeout. She didn't look dressed for the kitchen.

He decided to cross the street and hurry ahead of Carlie and Sal. The subway trains ran closer together in the early evening, when people were headed home from their jobs. He could train ahead and wait for Carlie, and Sal, near the deli.

Or he could simply go directly to stand across the street from her apartment and observe her. She'd be approximately twenty minutes later if she stopped in at the deli. He'd been tracking her carefully, noting times and places, letting his plan fall into place on its own. It worked best that way, letting fate determine his method, his unconscious seeing possible chinks in whatever protective armor Carlie was supposed to have. An overarching plan, but with adjustments on the run.

Eventually opportunity would present itself in its entirety—the best way for him to spend quality time with Carlie.

That was because fate was on his side.

Not luck, mind you, but fate.

52

Dred Gant knew that lately he was drinking more, but not *too* much more. He had control of booze rather than vice versa, and it helped to relax him.

He sometimes wondered what he'd do if his drinking became a problem. A membership in Alcoholics Anonymous? *My name's Dred Gant and I'm a serial killer. I also have this problem with alcohol.*

He sat in his favorite piece of furniture, a Victorian wing chair that would have been valuable if some clod hadn't "restored" it by replacing its nineteenth-century frame with pine lumber from Home Depot. The one thing about the chair that hadn't been ruined was its comfort.

Jack Daniel's, Queen Victoria, and high-definition television. Not a bad combination.

Usually.

Dred couldn't believe it when Carlie appeared on the evening airing (were news programs still *aired*?) of *Minnie Miner ASAP.* It was only a brief appearance. Carlie, dressed as she had been when she'd left Bold

Designs, was one of half a dozen women briefly interviewed on the street by Minnie Miner.

Minnie asked them the predictable questions: "Are
you aware of the Lady Liberty Killer? Have you taken
extra precautions to be safe with a serial killer on the
loose? Are you more likely to stay in at night? Do you
go places in groups for safety's sake?"

Then the killer's favorite: "Are you afraid?"

All of the women gave the expected answers. They
kept up on the news and were aware of what was happening. They took precautions, sure. But they still went
out at night, and lived their normal lives. None of the
women admitted to being afraid. The city was no more
dangerous a place than usual, as long as you behaved
sensibly.

The killer liked that slant on things. His quarry didn't
realize that *sensibly* was another word for *predictably*.

Prey animals, he thought. Women were prey animals. But dangerous ones if given the upper hand. He
considered phoning in to the show. He was important
to them and they would put him on the air instantly.
Minnie Miner would be happy to have him chat while
seconds ticked away.

Then he decided he was better off as he was, relaxed
in his favorite chair, sipping good bourbon, and view-
ing his TV as if it were a window looking out on a city
he had mastered. He could watch terror growing from
the fearsome seeds he'd sown.

He didn't really feel like talking with Minnie Miner,
anyway.

It was actually the made-over and statuesque blonde,
Carlie, that he longed to communicate with, in his own

special way. More and more often, at unexpected times, he found himself thinking about her. He did wonder, had there actually been a change in Carlie, or was he simply seeing her that way because she was becoming more desirable the more he looked at her? Was her increased desirability only in his mind?

He mentally shook his finger at himself. He knew the answers to those questions.

She was enhanced bait, of course. Nothing more. Made more vulnerable and especially tempting.

A Frank Quinn creation.

For days the killer ignored the bait. Carlie Clark had become something of a regular guest on *Minnie Miner ASAP*. She was getting good at being interviewed, and demonstrating a kind of casual disdain for the killer. Helen the profiler was pleased.

Quinn wasn't as sanguine about the plan as Helen. Last night someone pretending to be the Lady Liberty Killer had phoned in to the show and scared the hell out of him. A man's voice, cold enough to have icicles.

The caller stayed on the phone too long, and was surprised when an army of cops descended on his lower Manhattan apartment and made a wreck of it, and almost of him.

He turned out to be a seventy-year-old former light-heavyweight boxer who had fought too long. He seemed to *think* he was the killer, but he was a serious alcoholic confined to a wheelchair. For him to leave his loft apartment in a four-story walkup was impossible without someone's help.

This turned out to be the most recent of many

crimes he'd confessed to, possibly because he wanted to be in prison where the food was doubtless better and there was no rent.

"Is this really going to work?" Quinn asked Helen, hanging up the phone after Renz had told him about the latest confessor. Time was wasting here.

"It will work," Helen assured him.

"Poor Carlie's nerves are going to snap."

Helen raised an eyebrow. "Not before yours, I'd bet."

"We're asking a hell of a lot of her."

"She wouldn't have it any other way."

"And Jody's starting to bug the hell out of Pearl and me."

"Explain to her that police work requires patience."

"Is there a way we can make this become police *work?*" Quinn asked. "Some way to make something happen sooner?"

"Maybe," Helen said, looking at him in a way he didn't like.

Saturday morning, on her walk to Q&A, Pearl was enjoying the sunlight and the smell of exhaust fumes. Her cell phone began chiming the four opening notes of the old *Dragnet* TV series, over and over.

Without breaking stride, Pearl pulled the phone from her purse and answered the call before thinking about it. Nothing much could interfere with so bright and promising a day.

The caller was Pearl's mother.

"Jody and I have been talking," she said, without a hello.

Pearl continued walking, but slower. "Is this Mom?"

"You know that it is, dear. Your phone has that little thingamajig screen."

"I thought it might be the serial killer we're trying to apprehend."

"Don't joke about such things, dear. You should be so lucky, that you could meet him on the phone rather than in person. However, your choice of subject is eerily accurate as to the reason for my call. We—that is Jody and I—feel that you have a certain imperative to disengage from the menial job you hold and that might kill you."

"Menial?"

"Due to its danger, dear. Like working in a coal mine."

"Mom—"

"What you do for a living is, at this point, particularly dangerous because of the monster who walks our streets, and who might, in his fevered mind, see you as an essential element of his gruesome plans."

"I thought you were going to warn me about black lung disease."

"That would, at least, be gradual."

Pearl was getting irritated. "Someone has to do this job, so why not me?"

"Why not *you?* Because you have family, as do Jody and I. And that is the same family, when last I looked."

"Almost everyone has family."

"That is a big *almost*, dear. And they don't have *your* family."

"I'm on my way to work now, Mom. This isn't a good time to discuss these matters."

"Discussion? I am simply stating a position of eminent sense. We—Jody and I—feel that, all things considered in ways nonjudgmental, you and she, instead of working at times like this fine Saturday morning, could be with family here, in New Jersey. Or—and here I cross fingers and toes until the dreaded cramps develop—I should be back in my own place in New York."

"It's been leased by a taxidermist." Pearl didn't know this; she thought that if the conversation became more unpleasant it might end.

"He might not notice, then, that I moved back in, accustomed as I am to sitting for endless stretches of time, as I do sometimes here in purgatory. Jody and I—"

"I'm tired of hearing that, Mom. 'Jody and I.' "

"We are jealous, are we?"

"We are busy. We don't need to waste time talking about you and Jody planning my life behind my back."

"Not your life, dear. Only some essential parts of it that you seem unable to recognize as instrumental to your happiness as opposed to simple cheap thrills you might receive through the perilous nature of your present employment. Nothing need be permanent. There are choices to be made even as the clock continues its inevitable—"

"I'm quite content as I am, Mom. I like my job. I like my life. It took me a while to get over things, but I'm happy."

"Some of the deadliest poisons are some of the sweetest. You need to learn the truth of that in order to discern the barely discernible—and very often temporary—paths to true happiness. *Doctor* Milton—"

Pearl switched off her phone. She'd had enough.

She had simply had enough.

She stopped at an intersection to wait for a traffic light to change to *walk*. A knot of other pedestrians gathered around her. The *Dragnet* theme wafted again from her purse. She at first was going to ignore it; then she yanked the cell phone out and answered the call: "I'm not interested in *Doctor* Milton Kahn!"

"Neither am I," Quinn said.

The traffic signal changed, and the people surrounding Pearl surged forward, jostling her. Pearl got herself in gear.

"Sorry," she said into the phone.

"Not as sorry as Dr. Milton Kahn, I bet."

"Don't you forget that."

"I called to tell you we've got a plan," Quinn said. "Helen has a plan, really. Helen and Minnie Miner, actually."

"More planning behind my back."

"Happens all the time," Quinn said. "You almost to the office?"

"Another five minutes."

"Then I'll fill you in when you get here, instead of over the phone."

"When is this plan going to be put into effect?"

"Soon as you get here. You bringing doughnuts?"

"No."

"Come anyway."

"Quinn?"

"Yeah?"

"I'm glad I answered the phone."

53

Helen leaned her lanky body against the doorframe leading to the small alcove where Q&A's Mr. Coffee sat. There was a drip or a run from somewhere onto the electric burner, because every half minute or so there was a hiss and a strong smell of burned coffee.

Today Helen was wearing beige knee-length shorts, a matching silky armless pullover that looked as if it should have a number on its back, and worn down jogging shoes. Muscles rippled in her upper arms and shoulders. She looked more than ever as if she should be coaching a girls' basketball team.

Pearl looked at her, wondering.

Helen looked back at her and winked.

She waited until Quinn, Pearl, and Jody were comfortable before she began to talk. Fedderman wandered over to where he could hear. Sal and Harold were in the field and would be filled in later.

"We've got some interesting elements going that might enable us to lure the killer into a trap," Helen began. "One of them is Minnie Miner."

"Not to be trusted," Pearl said.

"True," Helen agreed, "but then neither can the killer trust her. And he does seem to, at least to some extent, put his trust in her. She's his chosen link to the media and the public."

"That's important to him," Quinn said.

"Not only that, we can pretty much predict that while *Minnie Miner ASAP* is on the tube, he's somewhere watching it instead of committing a murder."

"Or maybe he's calling in," Fedderman said.

"Yes," Helen said. "The show is in a sense his public voice."

"So how is that useful to us?" Jody asked. "I thought he was supposed to be stalking Carlie."

"We can be sure that he is stalking her. That is, obviously, another useful element that helps to make this killer more predictable." Helen pushed away from the wall and stood hipshot with her long arms crossed. "Carlie, with her dye job and new hairdo, looks like the archetypal Lady Liberty Killer victim. With her help, with Minnie Miner's, and with what we already know, we should be able to put ourselves in the same place at the same time as the killer. This is especially true if we use someone else's help."

"And who might that someone be?" Pearl asked.

"Lady Liberty. She's been at every crime scene. If she could speak, we'd have our killer's motive, name, and whereabouts."

"Too bad she happens to be a plastic figure," Quinn said.

"I'm talking about the real Lady Liberty. For some twisted reason she holds some significance for the killer. Therefore she holds some significance for us.

We need to find out what. But we do know a very valuable fact about the real Lady Liberty. She lives on an island."

"And a small one at that," Quinn said. "Not a lot of places to hide."

"Not for a three-hundred-and-five-foot tall woman, or a killer she draws like a magnet." Helen smiled. "I know kind of how she might feel."

Pearl wondered if she was referring to her height or her magnetism. It occurred to her that the Statue of Liberty was made of copper and wasn't magnetic, but she decided to keep that one to herself.

"So we need to get the killer onto the island," Quinn said.

"For that we need someone else's help," Helen said. "Minnie Miner's."

"I'm uneasy with her involved," Quinn said.

Pearl glanced over at him. "Give it a chance."

"Anyway," Fedderman said, "she's already involved, whether we like it or not."

Helen nodded gratefully to him. "I propose we let it slip that Minnie will be taping part of one of her shows near the Statue of Liberty, and she might be interviewing some potential victims there, asking about their fears and what they're doing to allay them."

"One of those potential victims will be Carlie," Jody said.

Helen nodded.

Quinn leaned back in his desk chair and laced his fingers behind his head. "He might not be able to resist."

"And as you noted," Helen said, "it's a small island."

No one noticed until she spoke that Carlie had come in and was standing just inside the door.

She said, "I think I can improve on that idea."

"I'm not sure I like it," Quinn said, when Carlie finished talking.

Carlie looked him in the eye. "It has a better chance of working."

"But it doesn't give *you* a better chance of coming out alive."

"If we do it Carlie's way, the killer is much more likely to select her as a victim," Helen said. "It narrows down his choices."

Quinn looked over at Fedderman.

"I think we should go for it," Fedderman said. "But my vote in this doesn't count as much as if I were family."

"That's what I was thinking," Quinn said.

Pearl and Jody looked at him as if he'd just shot Fedderman. But Fedderman understood. He smiled sadly but triumphantly, knowing Quinn was trapped.

"I think it's a brilliant idea," Jody said. And Quinn knew he was lost.

Brilliant idea or not, there *was* something about the strategy the others might not have considered. Something Quinn knew would work to their advantage.

Commissioner Harley Renz, who could translate publicity into political glory as skillfully as anyone Quinn had seen, would be in position to do exactly that, if Carlie's modified version of Helen's idea worked. For that reason alone Renz would get behind this plan. Also, if it failed, Renz would suffer only minimal damage. He'd go for this, all right, but leave no fingerprints on it unless it was successful. The enthusiastically corrupt commissioner was careful about his political prospects.

Quinn decided to wait and tell Renz about the plan only when it was too late for Renz to stop it. Deniability was the object of the game here. Deniability was important in Renz's life. If things didn't work out, Renz could huff and puff and pass the blame.

To Quinn.

"Renz is a force that will wear itself out," Helen said, seeming to know what Quinn was thinking.

"Like a storm," Quinn said. "Complete with wind and lightning bolts."

"Good God!" Jody said. "Brilliant idea or not, does this really have a chance to work, with people like us in charge?"

"I can see why you're an attorney," Helen said. "You know exactly what questions to ask."

"I want you to meet an impressive young woman," Minnie Miner said, after the lead-in to *Minnie Miner ASAP*. "She's been on this show before, but this time it's different. Because of the—I must say attractive—way she looks, there's something special about her you might have already realized. Because of the 'type' of woman she is, she's very much a potential victim of the Lady Liberty Killer."

The killer, who had been dozing with the help of two fingers of Jack Daniel's, opened his eyes and sat forward in his antique wing chair.

Minnie Miner was so right. He was impressed, even

though he'd been stalking Carlie and was already aware of her new look.

This seemed strange, though. Personal. There was Carlie Clark on his TV, seated in the armchair angled to face Minnie's. The camera was crazy about Carlie. The long curtain of hair (the new do), the defiant tilt of her head, her finely chiseled jaw. The slightly irrational glint in her eyes. She showed so well! And she was up to something.

"If you haven't already, meet Carlie Clark," Minnie said. "This young woman has volunteered to do something incredibly brave."

The killer was actually grinning. What kind of move was this? He had to admit he was taken completely by surprise by this television news gambit. That was the kind of thing he enjoyed, in certain measure. His opponents thought they might be outwitting him, when in fact they were keeping him entertained.

Minnie had on her pasted smile that meant a lot was going on behind her eyes.

"Tell us," Minnie Miner said. "What exactly is your mission, Carlie?"

"I want to demonstrate to the women of New York that there's no reason to live looking over their shoulders. In a city the size of New York, the odds of a maniacal, mentally ill killer choosing you as a victim are miniscule."

Dred smiled again. *Miniscule* . . . He was thoroughly enjoying this—except for that *mentally ill* remark.

"And there's another reason," Carlie said. "We're a free people, and we don't bend to anyone trying to scare us into behaving the way he or she chooses rather than the way *we* choose. If we start altering where we go, when we go, who we see, what we do, for this sick creature, we've lost. We've surrendered. . . ." She leaned forward and visibly tightened her grip on her chair arms. "And I don't intend to surrender."

The killer raised his glass in a toast.

"What I plan to do," Carlie said, "is visit various New York landmarks. Minnie, who is herself not the surrendering type, has been so kind as to agree to cover me while I demonstrate that it's relatively safe to go *anywhere* in New York City."

"*Anywhere* is a big word," Minnie said, shaking her head in admiration.

So's relatively, the killer thought.

Minnie still looked awestruck. "So we'll be able to see you in Central Park, at Grand Central Terminal, MoMA, a Broadway play . . . places like that?"

"Exactly," Carlie said.

"But you *will* have police protection."

"Some," Carlie said. "Some of the time. But we—and the killer—know the police can't protect anyone every minute. It's too big a job. It's impossible."

"I'm afraid you're right," Minnie said. "There's still plenty of danger. Have you paused to consider that you might actually be taunting the killer?"

"If that's what it takes to move about freely in my city, in my country, then so be it."

The studio audience applauded mightily. Minnie Miner joined them, applauding with her arms raised, egging them on.

The killer himself felt like standing and applauding, but he was about one drink beyond actually doing so.

"For starters," Carlie said, "I'm going to go to the

main library, outside, and visit the two lions at Fifth Avenue and Forty-second Street. Their names happen to be *Patience* and *Fortitude*, two qualities we should keep in mind these days."

"*Patience* and *Fortitude*," Minnie said. "I think I knew that. And when will that appearance with the famous lions be?"

"Tomorrow. Then my next stop, the next day, I'll be speaking to your viewers from the Statue of Liberty."

Deep in the killer's mind, something turned.

"After that, the Empire State Building."

The killer doubted that.

"You are an amazingly courageous woman," Minnie Miner said. "I know the gender is wrong, but it's still true. Kid, you got some real brass balls on you!"

Minnie stood up. Signaling that the interview was over and a computerized commercial break was coming at them as certain as death.

Carlie also stood. They embraced.

After about ten seconds, they stepped back from each other and grinned at the camera. A slow panning shot showed the studio audience—about fifty people—giving Carlie a standing ovation. Tears glistened in more than a few eyes.

Patience and Fortitude.

The killer loved it.

A commercial that wasn't at all credible, about a generous, humane bank, came on, and his hand darted to the remote and switched off the TV.

It seemed a sacrilege, to showcase greed and capitalism so soon after a display of genuine heart and courage.

54

The next morning broke bright and cloudless, though already quite warm. Shadows were still long and sharply angled.

Carlie's tousled blond hair and flawless flesh showed brilliant in the sunshine. She was on the steps of the main library at Fifth Avenue. A brace of fierce-looking lion statues, *Patience* and *Fortitude*, guarded the library entrance. At Minnie Miner's suggestion, Carlie had chosen to stand near the concrete lion *Fortitude*.

Five blocks away, the killer sat in a diner over a breakfast of bagel and coffee and observed all of this on a TV mounted high behind the counter. The killer's was one of several booths positioned where the TV was visible. He was familiar with the diner and had made sure such a booth was available before entering. He really didn't want to have to return to his apartment and watch Carlie Clark on television there. That wouldn't tell him what he wanted to know.

One of the things he wanted to observe was how other people reacted to what she was doing. The other booths that gave visual access to the TV were occupied, one by two men in business suits, worrying over cups of coffee. Another booth contained three young women and a young man with his head shaved. They had substantial breakfasts in front of them and talked as if they were employees at the same place and often met here before work. The other booths contained single diners; an elderly overweight woman, a black man in a suit and tie, a middle-aged Jewish man wearing a yarmulke, an attractive young woman in a running outfit, built like a dancer.

A fair cross-section, the killer thought.

As he watched the TV, quite a crowd gathered on the library steps. More than a few people recognized Carlie and waved and cheered her on. Minnie Miner was yammering away in a microphone, but no one seemed to be paying much attention. The sound on the TV was muted to almost complete silence.

When the camera stayed on Carlie and she was obviously getting ready to speak, one of the white-clad countermen, who looked Middle Eastern and had the accent, veered in his hurried chores and turned up the volume on the muted TV. He then moved down the counter and stood where he could watch and hear, while he absently moved a wadded towel in aimless circles on the stainless steel surface.

In her brief talk on courage and the freedom of women to pursue happiness without fear, Carlie pointed out the lion *Fortitude*, using it as a model for all New York women. She mentioned the noble *Patience*, in repose across the wide entrance steps. Fortitude and patience made an unbeatable combination, according to Carlie, and most New York women possessed both. No one seemed to notice that neither of the lions was female.

When Carlie mentioned *Fortitude* again in her speech, the businessmen in the diner were silent, perhaps mulling over a major deal. Most of the others cheered or at least reacted positively. The dancer raised her coffee cup in a toast. They were getting into it, all right, though one of the girls and the man with the shaved head seemed to regard what Carlie was doing as a joke.

The killer felt a ripple of annoyance.

A few of those in every crowd.

A string of commercials came on, a talking turtle, an aging movie star urging people to buy gold, an insurance company showing people with the wrong kind of insurance (not theirs) clanking about in cumbersome medieval suits of armor. The killer remembered the gold. Maybe something he should look into.

The camera panned the crowd on the library steps. No one seemed to have left.

In tight for a two shot:

"Inspiring words," Minnie said, moving close to Carlie so they would both appear in the shot.

Carlie thanked her appropriately. She seemed surprised now that so many people had come to see her, and slightly ill at ease. All very genuine. It went down well with the crowd.

"Remember what this young woman says," Minnie exhorted the crowd. "She's standing up for all New York women. The toughest, most self-sufficient women in the world!"

More cheering.

Carlie mumbled her thanks into the microphone Minnie had thrust at her to make her even more ill at ease. The trick was not to be too slick. This was selling well. Ordinary women could identify with Carlie.

"Remember!" Minnie yelled at the dispersing crowd. "The first part of our show will be broadcast tomorrow from Liberty Island, home of Lady Liberty—the *real* Lady Liberty."

This last remark seemed to have been directed at the killer personally, especially if you considered the sort of obscene jab Minnie made with the microphone.

Since the show was doing a special and shooting live all day, he thought that maybe later this morning he'd phone in to *Minnie Miner ASAP,* let Minnie and the other women of New York know what he thought about this latest Quinn stratagem.

Then he changed his mind.

There was always tomorrow.

Tomorrow would be too special to miss.

After tomorrow, he and Minnie could have quite a different conversation.

55

The next morning was not so clear and sunny.

Perhaps the heat wave and drought would be broken. The sky was low and leaden, and a light mist threatened to morph into a steady drizzle. Of course, New Yorkers, and some of the tourists, had seen this kind of morning before during the past month, and knew how rapidly it could turn into a sauna with no measurable rainfall.

By this time, they'd come to regard Mother Nature as a trickster. Allegorical maternal love wasn't in fashion.

The killer, wearing jeans, joggers, and a light tan water-repellent jacket, boarded the ferry to Liberty Island. He could barely make out some of the larger islands. The Statue of Liberty itself he couldn't see in the mist.

A surprisingly cool breeze danced over the water in gentle gusts, and there was a slight chop as the ferry, about half full of tourists, chugged away from its dock and out to where the sea was greenish gray except for successive lines of low white caps.

Without seeming to notice, Dred Gant scanned and classified the other passengers. A few of them could be undercover cops. In fact, it was almost certain that they were.

He knew he was being led into a trap, and Carlie Clark was the bait. The thing was, he couldn't resist. There were, he had learned, different kinds of addictions.

One of his was a certain kind of woman. Another was besting an arch enemy.

Farther out on the bay, it was cooler and the water was choppier. Feeling slightly nauseated from the boat's motion, Dred stood leaning back on the rail and looking around. There were two uniformed cops on board, standing and talking near the wheelhouse.

As the ferry neared the dock, the killer heard a low tone, like an expensive auto horn, and the rhythmic slapping of water against the hull was broken. While slower, the slapping sound gained in volume. The ferry was tossed about, but gently.

Dred looked over and saw a blue and white NYPD Harbor Unit patrol boat glide past. It wasn't nearly as large as the ferry, but it was much faster and more maneuverable.

God help us if they ever arm them with torpedoes, the killer thought. He was fervently anti-war, and had marched in more than one political protest.

The nimble blue and white patrol boat passed the larger and less bumptious ferry and disappeared in the gray mist. It was already tied at the dock when the ferry arrived.

With the other passengers, the killer gravitated toward where a ramp led to the dock. They hadn't yet gotten the signal to leave the boat. Even tied at the dock, the ferry still rose and fell slowly with the lapping waves. The human stomach wasn't made for this. Dred's nausea had lessened, but it would be a relief to be on stable land.

After a few minutes, a signal he didn't see or hear was given, and eager passengers surged toward the dock, land creatures that had experienced too much of the sea.

"We have a rare treat today," a guide's amplified voice said. Dred couldn't see him, or very many other people, so gray and thick was the mist. About half the passengers had opened umbrellas, though rain wasn't actually falling.

The speaker continued: "A television show some of you locals might have seen, *Minnie Miner ASAP*, is interviewing a young woman who is in open defiance of the serial killer unfortunately named after our great lady—the so-called Lady Liberty Killer." A few people groaned their objections, but others applauded as if they'd already heard of Carlie Clark and what she was doing. New Yorkers needed encouraging news these days, and Carlie was supplying it.

Dred walked farther on shore, until he heard a repetitive clinking and slapping sound. He realized he was standing next to a thick metal pole, near the top of which an American flag whipped in the breeze off the water. The flag was flapping like a loose sail, causing ropes and pulleys to clink against the metal pole.

Then, though the sky remained gray, the mist momentarily cleared, and directly ahead of him *she* loomed.

The sudden sight of her weakened Dred's knees and paralyzed him where he stood. She was facing away from him as if he were unworthy of her attention, rising over three hundred feet, her torch raised high.

She seemed to dwarf *everything*.

He hadn't expected to be so strongly affected. No one could have. He heard people around him express their awe.

The Lady Liberty Killer was helpless. He couldn't move one step closer to her. *He couldn't!*

His plan had been to stab Carlie Clark to death as she stood talking and taunting, live (so to speak) on television. Then, in the resultant tumult, he would slip away. He was wearing dark pants and, beneath his buttoned shirt, an NYPD pullover nylon jacket. His NYPD billed cap was rolled up and tucked in a pocket. He'd obtained the items weeks ago, paying cash, knowing that someday he'd have a use for them. They were knockoffs, sold all over Times Square, and were impossible to trace.

After the attack, he would become one of many cops, running this way and that, futilely trying to find the killer. Despite the daunting nature of his plan, Dred couldn't help but find some humor in it. The old Keystone Cops. He could picture them rushing here, there, and everywhere in panic, and all because of what *he* had done. It would be a challenge not to smile.

Getting through security had been no problem. He'd had no bags or packages to check and leave in a locker. The innocent-looking camera he'd been allowed to carry onto the island was altered so part of its metal framework could be detached and used as a sharply pointed knife.

It had been a daring but thoughtful plan of action

that would work by virtue of its audacity. He had faith in it. Faith in the odds. Faith in fate.

But Dred's awe and paralysis, complete and unexpected, changed all that. He should never have come here. He had underestimated *her*. The effect *she* would have on him, his plan, his fate.

The odds.

What he had to do now was get away—and fast.

If he could make himself move at all, he must speed up his escape. He wouldn't be evading only the police; he'd be escaping *her*.

Forcing himself to walk, he stumbled toward a nearby complex of buildings where a restroom might be found.

One foot in front of the other. That was what it took.

"You okay?" a voice asked.

He stood straighter, made his stride looser. "I'm fine."

He sensed that whoever had asked about him was still watching.

Inside the nearest building, where souvenirs were sold, he found a men's restroom, went into a stall, and sat slumped on the commode with his head in his hands.

This wasn't the way it was supposed to be. He wasn't going to kill Carlie Clark now. Not today. He wouldn't have the opportunity, and wouldn't be able to seize it if he did have it.

Another time, another time . . .

The towering statue, which he'd read was smaller than many people imagined, didn't look at all small to him. It stood facing the sea as if it owned all water everywhere and was raising an arm in triumph. The immensity, the audacity of the thing, forced out all other thoughts.

Escape. That was all that occupied the killer's mind now.

Escape.

Dred removed his outer shirt to reveal his official-looking NYPD pullover wind shirt. It was so dark a blue it was virtually black. The same color as his NYPD billed cap. The pullover was three-quarter length, which changed or disguised his build. The cap? Almost everyone looked like everyone else in a baseball cap.

He used a dime to loosen a screw on the left side of the camera, and levered out a five-inch pointed blade. The camera itself would serve as the makeshift knife's handle.

He now had all he needed—cursory NYPD identification clothing, his courage and guile, and a knife.

He folded the stiletto-like blade back to rest at the bottom edge of the camera and slid the removed screw into his pocket. It would take seconds to turn camera to knife, and the best thing was that if he happened to be asked about the camera, it still functioned as exactly that—a digital camera. He would snap the questioner's picture and show the image to him or her.

He checked himself in the mirror, drew a deep breath, and then left the restroom.

From this point on he would think of himself as a cop, act like a cop, walk like a cop—and if he must, he would talk like a cop.

Dred knew the tiny island would be teeming with undercover cops, as well as cops dressed much like him. Not to mention Quinn and his detectives.

The best thing would be not to go any farther onto the island. He would be at a disadvantage; he understood that. The more people he encountered, the worse for him. He wasn't himself.

Or he *was!*

He couldn't return to the restroom. There was a limit to how much time he could spend there without attracting attention.

He looked back at the ferry boat, tied up now at the dock. It probably wouldn't return to shore without passengers, and not all of those passengers would be the ones who'd just arrived.

He edged sideways where he could see a sign that noted departure times. The next departure was in almost half an hour.

Could he make himself inconspicuous on the tiny, flat island, pretending to be a cop, for half an hour? What were *those* odds?

He didn't like the answer to that question.

Dred figured the farther he stayed away from the statue, the better. He didn't know if he had the nerve to approach *her*, anyway. Certainly he didn't want to test himself.

He knew what his best chance would be, and it would take nerve. He would wait until the boat was about to finish boarding passengers, and then simply walk on board. His expression would have to be neutral, his stride loose. He would *belong* there. Simply one of many New York cops, leaving the island to return to the city.

He'd have a story—something he could make up about a scheduled court appearance—if he needed one. He always had a story.

And if he didn't have a good enough story . . . ? Things could get ugly.

For the next seventeen minutes he stayed in the vicinity of the dock, moving around with feigned casualness, avoiding clusters of people.

Somehow, for seventeen minutes, it worked.

But a pair of uniformed cops had walked past him five minutes ago, nodded, and given him a funny look. He didn't have a badge showing. Other cops might think he was undercover, but not quite. Undercover light. Did such a thing exist?

Semi-undercover?

Not hardly.

A cop on holiday?

If they believed that, it wouldn't be for long.

It was time for a different tactic.

Dred walked directly toward the docked ferry boat, striding more purposefully as he got closer. As if he belonged here.

Damn it, I do belong here!

Believe!

When he reached the docked boat, he walked to the ramp, gave a casual salute to the captain—or whatever he was—in the wheelhouse (or what he thought of as the wheelhouse). Then he deftly ducked under the chain and strode across the ramp onto the boat.

The captain was busy talking on what looked like a cell phone. The call wasn't about Dred, because he'd been talking when Dred came up the ramp. So no worry there.

Dred began to roam around, as if checking the boat

for stowaways or anything else that was suspicious.
The guy in the wheelhouse stared at him for a few seconds, then looked away. Some kind of big deal was
happening on the island; that was all he knew. Dred
was simply a New York cop doing his duty. Always on
the lookout for terrorists. More power to him.

A blue and white NYPD Harbor Unit patrol boat appeared out of the mist with its bow pointed toward the
dock, causing Dred to hold his breath.

But the boat swung north and continued past the
dock, heading toward Ellis Island, leaving a long,
curved wake and gentle waves that rocked the ferry.

Dred began to breathe again.

The watery growl of the patrol boat died in the distance.

The ferry boat captain remained concentrating on
his phone conversation. He was trying to wrangle theater tickets for a play tonight. For a change, *really* good
tickets. Third row center, orchestra. Normally the play
would be sold out, but because of the serial killer wan-
dering around the city, theater business was down.
Tickets for great seats were plentiful.

It's an ill wind . . . , the captain thought.

Though he was a weekend sailor and didn't buy into
that old saying, or very many others.

Still, orchestra-level Broadway play tickets . . .

Dred remained shocked by his strong reaction to the
statue. He had to get farther away from *her!* And as
soon as possible. He stayed near the boat's stern, where
he was least visible to the captain. He could see
through tinted glass that there was someone else on

board, a man with his back to Dred, seated and watching a big-screen TV. The screen showed a long shot of the Statue of Liberty. It zoomed in on the statue's base, then on Carlie, her stance bold, the sea breeze whipping at her hair. She gesticulated as she spoke, and it struck the killer that she was a natural public speaker. There was a shot of a sizable crowd, applauding. Dred had no way of being sure what she was saying, but he had a pretty good idea.

There was a scuffing sound behind him. Soles on the deck.

He looked away from the TV, and there was a genuine NYPD cop, in full uniform, standing and grinning at him.

"You watching the little sweetie shooting off her mouth?" the cop asked.

"Yeah. She's got some guts," Dred said.

"What she's saying though, it's all bullshit."

Dred wasn't sure what to say to that. Here he was finding himself about to defend Carlie Clark, who wanted him dead.

The cop cocked his head at him, wearing a half amused look, and half something else that Dred didn't like.

"You're from the two-oh, ain't you?" the cop asked.

"You think I can get a picture through this glass?" Dred asked, raising the camera and flicking out the blade.

The cop's gaze automatically went to the tinted window.

Dred stabbed him in the heart, three times, hard.

The cop dropped without making a sound. He bled a lot at first, and then the bleeding slowed. Nearby was a container of some sort with canvas lashed over it for a lid. Dred raised an edge of the taut canvas and found the container full of yellow life preservers.

No help there.

But there was a narrow space behind the container, right now in shadow. Something shoved back there might not be noticed.

Dred quickly jammed the cop's body into the shadowed space.

After standing up straight and glancing around, he stooped low again and removed the cop's badge, then picked up the cop's eight-point cap where it had dropped on the deck. For good measure, he removed some of the life preservers from beneath the canvas and laid them over the body to help conceal it. A few more to cover some blood.

Then he pinned the badge on his NYPD wind shirt and replaced his knock-off billed cap with the dead cop's genuine NYPD cap. It had some small bloodstains on it, but they were dark like the cap, so no problem.

He wandered farther astern, glancing at his watch. The ferry would board soon.

In an odd way, things were looking up.

56

Dred Gant was feeling safe again, in a bar near Columbus Circle, on the substantial and densely populated island of Manhattan.

Much of the talk was about the rain, though there hadn't been much. It was mostly a mist, actually. There was talk of a brief but genuine rain in Lower Manhattan, where it was said that a few large drops had fallen but sizzled and disappeared when they struck the street or sidewalk. For all anyone knew, it wouldn't rain again for another month. Or, for some of us, a lifetime.

A group of twentysomethings was about to leave the bar. They were milling around, making noise, and he wished they'd shut up. He was still steadying his nerves after yesterday's close call.

She had almost gotten him killed.

He had to admit he was unnerved by what had happened. He stared at his fingers encircling his glass. They trembled slightly.

He'd thought she was dead in every way. That she couldn't have this kind of effect on him. Yet there was that tremor, signifying vulnerability.

"Coming with us, Gigi?"

The killer looked up from his beer.

"Gigi!" called the voice again.

Gi . . . gi . . .

Phonetically, double what the killer wanted. *Very good*. His world was still spinning as it should.

"I'll stay here a while," a woman's voice said. "Then I got important things to do."

The half dozen or so twentysomethings made their way out the door. A few of them grinned and waved to . . . Gigi. One of the men threw her a kiss.

Dred knew fate when it stood directly in front of him and shook him by the lapels.

He found the woman who had important things to do reflected in the back bar mirror. The *G* woman. She was at one of the round tables, alone now.

His stomach clenched with fear and hate and something like lust. Without openly staring, he sized her up.

She was almost blond—certainly close enough—and her features were perfect. Blue eyes, broad cheekbones, and the sharply defined jaw line of youth. Her hair, which showed some dark roots, was worn in an unflattering cut. If she brushed it back from her forehead it would be okay.

It would do, anyway.

He swiveled slightly on his bar stool to get a better perspective.

You've had too much to drink, a warning voice said. *Be careful*. It was a voice he'd come to regard with respect.

Gigi was dressed like the ones who had just left. Young executive types, probably from one of the office buildings in the area, on their way home after a day on

the job. Close friends, apparently. Probably fellow employees. She was wearing a light gray skirt and a blue
blouse with shoulder pads. The skirt's matching blazer
was draped over the back of her chair.

The soft look of her skin, her face so smooth and
unlined, made her appear younger than the others.

Might she be more naïve?

Dred dismounted his stool and, drink in hand, walked
toward her table. His stride was steady and straight. He
thought so, anyway.

He could see her assessing him as he approached,
and he read in her expression her curiosity as it tugged
against her better judgment.

It's so easy to know what women are thinking.

"Mind if my friends and I join you?" he asked. He
watched as she responded to his smile the way women
usually did. He was doing okay.

"I see only you," she said. Composed. Almost disdainful. Her problem was, he knew she was putting on
an act.

"There is only me. I thought that if you didn't mind
me and my friends, you surely wouldn't mind just me."

She cocked her head and grinned at him, looking at
him as if he might be crazy, but maybe it was *good*
crazy. Just the thing to cheer her up. Maybe even . . .
well, who knew?

He seized the opportunity of her indecision and sat
down next to her. There were two empty glasses near
her. It took her a few seconds to focus on him. She
might even be a little drunk.

I'll play, said her expression.

"You and your friends could buy me a drink," she
said.

"That's what we had in mind."

Dred motioned, and one of several white-aproned women behind the bar worked the pass-through and came over for their order.

"The same for the lady," he said. "I'll nurse this beer."

The server gave him a look, knowing what he was up to. Dred couldn't care less.

Gigi ordered another Grey Goose and water on the rocks.

More letter G's. So many signs. Fate sending messages.

"Nothing for your friends?" Gigi asked, as the server walked away.

"They're teetotalers."

"Not like us." She finished what little was left of her previous drink. Mostly diluted booze and oval remnants of ice.

She placed her new glass on its coaster, which was puddled from overuse. Neither of them said anything, and he let the silence gain substance and weight. He knew if he made her speak first, something good might come out.

"Would you believe," she said, "that I got fired today?"

Ho-ho! "That's terrible."

He felt his facial muscles work into the expression he'd selected. *So concerned!*

Half drunk and recently fired. Something easy has been delivered to me. She's almost literally flopping around with a broken wing.

Gigi gave an elaborate shrug, but looked for a second as if she might cry. *Such conflict.*

"It happens," she said. "Like catching a cold. Sometimes you catch unemployment. I tell myself that, anyway."

"What kind of job was it?"

"Human resources."

"Sounds like something that provides hospitals with body parts."

"They used to call us personnel managers."

"You were a personnel manager?"

"Not exactly that. I didn't have the seniority. But I worked in HR for Homestead Properties."

"I've heard of them," he lied.

"Prob'ly seen their ads." She moved to pick up her glass and lifted what was left of her previous drink instead. When she saw that it contained mostly melting ice, she simply gave it a circular motion so the one-time cubes swirled around. Condensation from the glass dribbled down her arm. "Is it getting hot in here?" she asked.

"It must be you." He winked. "I'm surprised everything around you doesn't melt."

She ignored the compliment. "This is the unluckiest day of my life."

He laughed. "I should be hurt."

"No, no, no . . ." she said. "I didn't mean that. I meant . . . at work."

"Maybe we can change your luck."

The server dropped by and took Gigi's almost empty glass and moved her fresh drink over so it was in front of her.

That brought a smile.

* * *

"He never showed," Pearl said. "The bastard had us all figured out and never set foot on the island."

"We can't say that for sure," Quinn said. He was at his desk at Q&A. Pearl was pacing, not so much pissed off as frustrated. It was still warm in the office, and he watched a bead of perspiration run down her tanned forearm. She idly slapped at it as if it were a tiny insect.

Fedderman, the only other Q&A detective working late into the evening, came over from where he'd tricked Mr. Coffee into making tea. He sipped from his initialized mug. "Maybe the security cameras picked up something."

"They haven't revealed it yet," Quinn said. "Jerry Lido is still going over them with the Harbor Unit and island security." Lido was Q&A's high-tech expert. If there was something suspicious on the tapes, he'd spot it. And he'd know how to get the most out of it.

"I doubt they'll find anything useful," Pearl said. "Let's face it—Helen was wrong about this one. There was no irresistible magnetism rooted in the killer's youth that drew him toward Lady Liberty." She stopped pacing, perched on the edge of her desk, and crossed her arms. "I never had high hopes for this from the beginning."

"There was never a guarantee," Quinn said.

"Not a lot of those in life," Fedderman added. "In fact, none."

For the next twenty minutes thunder rolled like cannon fire across the heated city, but no rain fell.

57

The killer watched Gigi Beardsley (which turned out to be her name) open her big blue eyes, and then open them wider.

He studied her face as it dawned on her: *I've never drunk so much that I passed out.*

But then, I was never fired before.

Still . . .

He put something in my drink!

She struggled to reassert sanity and logic.

This . . . problem is more serious than losing a job. Way more serious.

Slowly, realization began to enter her mind, along with fear. Then it came with a rush. The pieces tumbled into place, and in order. *There's no way out of my predicament.* Her soul was in her eyes. He watched her closely. This was one of his favorite moments.

But she hadn't surrendered to her fate. Not quite yet.

Brad had moved out of sight, but she still sensed his presence.

Gigi experimentally tried to move her right arm,

which was raised over her head, and couldn't. Of course, it wasn't exactly raised, because she was lying flat on her back in her bed. Her left arm was stretched to its limit and bound with gray tape to the brass headboard, like her right. Her legs were spread wide, and she knew her ankles would be similarly bound even before she tried to move her legs and confirmed that she couldn't.

She was as nude as she'd been when he'd carried her into the bedroom.

She did remember that. Also, before that a walk, holding hands. A subway ride?

Maybe.

Maybe to all of it.

She couldn't recall even being placed on the bed.

How the hell did they even get in here? But she knew the answer to that. She'd mentioned to him that, even though she'd been fired, she still had a master key for apartments like this, for the lockbox that real estate companies used so any employee could show any listed, unoccupied property. She'd forgotten to turn the key in, and no one at Homestead had asked her for it.

The killer saw this as another nudge by destiny. Gigi would be his second victim with access to someone else's apartment; obviously this was fated to happen. Not that Manhattan wasn't rich with people occupying other people's apartments, usually subletting or borrowing. New Yorkers tended to travel or move often, and why should the most expensive commodity in the city, space, be allowed to sit vacant?

Gigi recalled an acute sense of trespass and betrayal when letting him, and herself, into this listed unit. Neither of them belonged here, even though she'd figured the company owed her something more than paltry severance pay and a good-bye. The use of this apartment might lessen the debt.

And heighten the sexual experience.

Had they had sex? She couldn't remember. She *felt* as if they had.

She tugged with this limb and that, twisting her head around, exploring again to see how firmly she was bound by the unyielding thick tape.

Very firmly.

Brad—or so he called himself—came into sight again, not so much shocking her as making her mind more muddled. He was naked except for what looked like surgeon's rubber gloves, the kind you could almost see through and were like a second skin. And he was wearing blue plasticized paper booties of the sort that surgeons wore in operating rooms.

"What the hell?" she almost said. It came out as more of a croak. She realized she'd shaken off enough of her sluggishness that she might muster a lusty scream. She strained to do just that. The result was the same croak. Sound that traveled about ten feet, and surely not beyond the walls.

Brad smiled down at her. "You shouldn't drink so much. It's bad for your complexion."

Anger surged up in Gigi. She tried to thrash around in the bed but couldn't manage even that. "Listen, you bastard. If you think—"

She heard a ripping sound, and he slapped her in the face, across the lips.

No! He'd *fastened* something—tape—across her mouth. He used the heel of his hand to press the tape tight to her flesh. She began breathing raggedly, forcing herself to inhale and exhale through her nose. She tried again to scream, but merely made a soft mewling sound.

He grinned, liking that. The way he was gazing down at her, studying her, gave her the chills. Kids looked that way at frogs in biology class.

Gigi tried to suppress her growing terror and make herself think. *Think!*

She knew who Brad was, of course. The Lady Liberty Killer. And she knew what he did—at least what the police had released about his insane behavior. She was sure what was in store for her would be even worse.

Squirming desperately, she managed to see that the gray duct tape, that had also been used to bind her wrists and ankles to the brass headboard and footboard, was so tight that her hands and feet were turning white from loss of circulation. And they were becoming numb.

Gigi watched as he laid the large roll of tape on the bed. He bent over, and from down on the floor—probably from the big leather briefcase he had been carrying and had lugged here from the bar—he withdrew a knife. It had a long, slightly curved blade that was pointed and serrated and scared the hell out of her. She couldn't take her eyes off it.

She craned her neck and stared as he moved down along the side of the mattress, and she was sure he was going to cut her ankle.

Another thought came to her.

My toes! Is he going to cut off one of my toes?

She heard the sound of the blade severing the tape.

Her right leg was free, but only for a second. He gripped it with both arms and leaned hard on it so it was forced up as far as it would go. She tried to bend her leg so she could find leverage and push him away. The strain behind her knee was agonizing.

He let her struggle for a while, enjoying it, then he jammed one of his thumbs deep, deep into her calf muscle, and the leg was paralyzed by pain from the knee down. There was no strength in it. She made the strange mewling sound again as he taped her ankle next to where her wrist was bound.

He stood up straight, breathing hard and grinning. After moving around to the other side of the bed, he repeated the process with her left ankle and wrist. Remembering the pain of his probing thumb, Gigi didn't resist.

Acting quickly and knowledgeably, he spent less than a minute on that leg.

She was left contorted and horribly exposed, and she hated Brad whatever-his-name-was with every cell of her being.

With the hate came curiosity. With the curiosity came stark terror.

What was he going to do? Mount her and rape her? Use the knife on her?

She did know she was having trouble breathing in such a taut and extreme position, and with the tape across her mouth. Each breath was a struggle, both in and out.

He sauntered back around to the other side of the

bed, bent down approximately where she thought the
briefcase must be, and took something else from it.

When he straightened up, she saw that he was holding a coiled black leather whip. Tiny flecks of metal
glinted sharply among its braids.

He let the whip unwind to the floor, loomed over
and checked her wrists and ankles to make sure they
were tightly bound, and then stepped back to where she
was looking up at him framed within her outspread
legs.

He positioned himself carefully, hefted the whip
handle in one hand, and with the other blew her a kiss.
It was much like the kiss blown to her by one of her
friends as he'd exited the bar with the rest of her group,
leaving her alone and vulnerable.

She clenched her eyes shut. The blackness was complete. Not the tiniest amount of light entered.

This isn't real! Isn't happening!

The whip whistled through the air.

She tensed and felt it cut the air inches above her
taut flesh.

Wake up, goddamn you! Wake up!

It whistled again and did not miss.

Quinn's desk phone was jangling. The one on the
landline he refused to replace. Fedderman stopped
drinking tea in mid sip. Pearl quit bitching about Helen
being wrong.

Quinn picked up the phone, said the caller had
reached Q&A Investigations, and then was silent.

Pearl watched his expression change and she became afraid.

A full minute passed, and he placed the black receiver back in its cradle without having said a word.

"Something important?" Fedderman asked.

Quinn let out a long breath. "That was Renz. The ferry that runs to and from Liberty Island, they found a dead cop on it."

58

Misty with pain, her eyes were only half open now. The only sounds that came from her were those muffled mewlings, like the last laments of a dying kitten.

Slowly, skillfully, he used the knife on her. The mewling became a slightly louder sound, a prolonged "*Aaawwww*" that might have been an expression of hopelessness and surrender, of supreme disappointment. As he worked the knife, removing things, her body began to bounce, and then was still.

He bent over her, watching her eyes, *watching, watching.* . . .

The moment came and went.

They had shared the experience.

From his briefcase he withdrew one of the plastic Ladies.

There was enough blood that he wouldn't need any more lubricant.

* * *

It was still hot in the Q&A offices. Humid and op-pressive. Maybe not so much because it was a warm morning, and the city's concrete still radiated heat. Maybe more because of the mood. Or maybe it was be-cause the office smelled like the inside of an old jog-ging shoe.

"You got any spray air freshener in here?" Jody asked. "Even if it's bug spray."

"No," Pearl said simply.

"Phew! How can you—"

"Back it up," Quinn said. Then: "There!"

They were all looking at Liberty Island ferry secu-rity tape, and there, according to Quinn, was Dred Gant.

But was it really Dred Gant?

Quinn stared at the man frozen in mid stride on the flat screen. He'd recognized the way he walked, with an al-most imperceptible hitch. It was from the time years ago when the egg farmer had shot him in the leg. Quinn knew this because he'd been shot in the thigh himself. When the bone healed, it drew in part of the gouge the bullet had made, leaving one leg slightly shorter than the other, or set at a slightly different angle. Quinn had seen tape of himself walking. He had the same slight but distinctive hitch in his stride.

Judging by the people around him, Gant was aver-age size and weight. Nothing at all distinctive about him except, maybe, that walk.

The problem was, Quinn couldn't see Gant's face because of the spread and bill of the NYPD eight-point uniform hat he was wearing. He was also wearing the pullover the Harbor Unit called a wind shirt.

"It's Gant, I'm sure," Quinn said. "I recognize his walk."

Fedderman shook his head, staring at the TV. "No one else would be sure."

Quinn knew that was probably true. There really were no gradations of *sure*.

"You can't see much of his face because of the hat's bill and the downward angle of the security cameras," Pearl said.

"They mount the cameras high that way to get a wide angle," Fedderman said. "Then they can't tell what the hell they've got. Someday they'll learn."

"That's him," Quinn said. "He was on the island."

"We know that," Pearl said. "He killed a cop on the ferry. Name of Bill Straitham. Stabbed him three times in the heart. Stole his badge and eight-point hat."

"No, he was *on* the island, not just on the boat."

"He was trading up when it came to clothes," Fedderman said. "I've done that in Goodwill."

"Meaning?" Jody asked. She was seated in one of the client chairs, knees drawn up, hugging both legs, listening and learning.

"He was looking more like a real cop, every chance he got," Pearl said.

Quinn said, "The same guy, on the earlier Island security tape, had on an NYPD blue baseball cap."

"Meaning?" Jody asked again.

"Earlier cap, earlier tape. We know he was on the island *before* he killed the cop."

"Mean—"

"Meaning he was spooked and ran. Something made him change his plans. Helen was right. We've got a hold on this bastard. We just have to figure out how to use it."

"What hold?" Jody asked.

"We moved him onto that island, almost nailed his ass, and he knows it. His confidence has to be shaken. If we moved him there, we can move him somewhere else, and be there at the same time."

"Guy like that," Pearl said. "I doubt if he sees it that way. He's probably enjoying playing games."

"Enjoying it so much he can't resist it," Helen said.

She'd come in without anyone noticing. Quinn was surprised again how she moved so silently and smoothly for such a big woman.

"We were just talking about how we owed you a tip of the hat," Fedderman said. "We got the killer where we wanted him. Spooked him so he rabbited. Then he got lucky."

"Resourceful and lucky," Helen said. "Renz told me there's security tape, and he sent it over."

"It's on the screen," Quinn said, "stopped where it's important."

Helen squinted at the image on the flat screen. "You sure that's him?"

Quinn told her about the limp.

"Pretty scant," she said.

"He doesn't know that," Jody said.

They all looked at her.

"Any ideas?" Quinn asked the room in general, having one himself but waiting for someone else to come up with it. Wondering who it would be.

Jody?

"What we do now," Helen said, "is call Minnie Miner, and then make sure she gets a copy of that tape."

Quinn smiled inwardly. *Helen. He should have guessed.*

Quinn made the call.

Minnie Miner was so overjoyed she would have crawled through the phone line, if she hadn't been on her cell.

"Who authored this strategy?" she asked.

"Helen Iman. But there's nothing in writing."

"You know what I mean. I'm going to see that Helen gets a raise in pay."

"But she doesn't work for you."

"I'm a taxpayer," Minnie said. "She works for me."

"Minnie . . ."

But Minnie was gone from the ether.

"She was happy?" Helen asked, when Quinn had hung up.

Quinn nodded. "Orgasmic. She thinks you should get a raise. Thinks she can give you one because she's a taxpayer."

"Damn right."

Pearl was about to say something when Quinn's desk phone jangled. He picked up quickly so she'd think twice if twice was needed.

The caller was Renz, and he spoke up before Quinn was finished with his brief "Q&A Investigations" phone greeting that was by now as automatic as if it were electronic.

"Guess what we got," Renz said.

"Yankees tickets?"

"Sort of. Murderers Row."

59

Quinn and Pearl took Quinn's old Lincoln and drove to the address Renz had given them.

By the time they got there, the rest of the troops had been called out. One side of the street had been cordoned off. There were patrol cars parked at careless angles to the curb. An ambulance was backed in, lights out. Quinn and Pearl knew it was waiting for the body to be released. From what Renz had said on the phone, there was nothing here to be revived.

Beyond the ambulance, neatly parked at the curb, was the black Ford that the nasty little ME Nift drove. If Pearl noticed it she gave no sign. They got out of the parked Lincoln and walked toward the building's entrance.

THE PADMONT BLDG, proclaimed an engraved brass plaque mounted near the doors.

"Nice address," Pearl said. "The victim had a lot to lose."

A uniform was on station in the marbled lobby. He pointed toward the elevator, said, "Fifth floor."

Quinn and Pearl rose to Five.

The murder apartment was two doors down from where the elevator door slid open. Another uniform was standing guard in the hall outside the open apartment door. Beyond him, inside, they could see shadow movement, now and then a person, as the crime scene unit did its meticulous work.

Pearl entered first, followed closely by Quinn. A CSU guy handed each of them a pair of thin rubber gloves, which they fitted to their hands as they made their way to where the body was, in the bedroom.

The main bedroom, actually, because the apartment had three of them.

The other two bedroom doors were open about halfway, but straight ahead was the largest bedroom, beyond a fully opened door.

They entered. The CSU was finished in there, and the only other live people in the room were Harley Renz and his sometimes flunky and spy, Nancy Weaver. Quinn hoped Renz wasn't going to sic Weaver on them to gather information he could use to blame anyone but himself if they failed to stop this killer. That would be like Renz. And like Weaver.

Weaver was an attractive woman with a devilish glitter in her brown eyes. Her dark hair was straight and worn in severe bangs that for some reason made her look vaguely Egyptian. She smiled and winked at Quinn and nodded to Pearl. Pearl had never much liked her, but at the same time they understood each other. Women of the world.

Renz was standing back a few feet, his hand cupped to his chin in what was an obvious pose, staring at what was on the bed.

"Good Christ!" Pearl said.

The woman on the bed was on her back with her wrists and ankles bound together to the headboard so that she was rolled back and her buttocks were exposed. What was left of her buttocks.

Nift the ME got busy, probing the corpse's pubic area with a pointed steel instrument. He looked over at Pearl, amused. Nift was one of the few people Quinn knew who could get under Pearl's skin.

Nift grinned at Pearl. "Ass looks like hamburger," he said. "The killer's usual ritual, scourging them. You know the kind of whip I mean, Pearl. Badasses in medieval times tortured their enemies with them."

Pearl knew. She'd seen a whip of the sort used for scourging. It had bits of sharp metal braided into it and caused horrible pain and damage.

"He didn't forget her tummy," Nift said.

The corpse's stomach had been cut C-section style, as with the other victims, and some internal organs and lengths of intestine lay beside her.

And there was something else.

"That's this victim's Lady Liberty statuette," Renz said, seeing where Quinn was looking. "Hard to recognize under all that blood and what have you. This time he inserted it in his victim's anus."

Quinn looked at the mess of blood and feces, and the object protruding from it.

"That's the technical term," Nift said to Pearl. "Must've hurt like blazes."

Pearl gave him a look. "You should know."

Quinn rested a hand on her shoulder, gave her a squeeze. Their signal for her to shut up.

When he was sure Pearl had her temper under control, Quinn glanced around. There was something about this room, about the part of the apartment they'd been in. Nothing was out of place or set at a wrong angle. The walls were too bare. There were no small items lying about.

Weaver had been watching him with half a smile, as if wondering when he was going to catch on. "Nobody lives here," she said. "The dead woman's name was Gigi Beardsley. She was in real estate. She still had her master key that unlocks those clunky metal box things they put on vacant properties so all the agents can show them. Door key is inside the box. A real estate key was needed to get in the box and then to get in here."

"You said '*still*' had her master key," Quinn said.

Renz spoke up. "Seems Gigi was fired yesterday, not long before she was killed."

"But she still had her key."

"Yeah. All longtime employees have master keys. But Gigi hardly ever used hers. She was in human resources and rarely showed property, so giving it back must have just slipped her mind."

"Not her lucky day," Nift said, putting away his instruments in a plastic bag so he could keep them separate and sterilize them back at the morgue. "Except it was her good fortune Lady Liberty didn't go in torch first."

This time Pearl ignored him. "Gigi spelled with a *G*, I take it," she said to Renz.

"Two *G*'s, actually. Our guy is still alphabetically inclined." Renz motioned with his head in the general direction of the bathroom. "There's a 'Freedom to Kill' message scrawled on the mirror in blood, like at the other scenes. CSU took samples, but it's no doubt the victim's blood. The killer probably uses his gloved finger to dip into blood and write."

"You can see where he dipped," Weaver said, pointing. There were half a dozen swipes in the spilled blood on the mattress.

"He used his writing finger to get blood from her ass," Nift said, glancing at Pearl. He smiled. "Fecal matter is present on the mirror."

"Must have gone back and forth, between bedroom and bathroom," Quinn said. "Took his time."

"Or he coulda loaded up with blood once and gone with it into the bathroom," Nift said. " 'Specially the blood from her ass. She was still alive when he put that statuette to her. That had to have been a fountain."

"The letters would get lighter as they were written if he dipped his finger only once," Quinn said. "They don't."

"Very good," Nift said, as if Quinn had done well noting something he, Nift, had known all along. Sort of a test.

"Is there a doorman for this building?"

"No," Renz said, "but I bet there will be."

"So she had the keys to this apartment and knew it was unoccupied," Quinn said.

"It was with more keys on a big ring. Lab's got it. And the lockbox itself."

"So who actually owns this place?"

"Belongs to some guy who's out of the country," Renz said. "He won't be happy to hear about this."

"Odds are she came here with the killer willingly. She was the one with the knowledge that it existed— and she had the key."

"Odds are *she* seduced *him*," Nift said.

"You wanna try her for murder?" Pearl snapped.

Nift shut up and concentrated on bagging his instruments. He closed and latched his black case, then put on the suit coat he'd carefully folded and draped over a chair back.

"Got an approximate time of death?" Quinn asked him.

"Between one and five a.m.," Nift said. "Looks like the torture started before midnight, though." He smiled in a way that made his face particularly ugly. "This killer must have studied the Spanish Inquisition or something. Our Gigi must have suffered horribly before he let her die."

"Nice to know you're concerned," Pearl said.

Nift shrugged. "I'd always heard real estate is a tough business."

"When you have more on this," Quinn said, "give me a call. No matter what time it is."

"Will do." Nift adjusted his cuffs and buttoned his suit coat. "You understand that all of this, at the scene, is preliminary."

"Sure. Everything we goddamn do is preliminary."

"Okay to release the body?" Renz asked.

"If the CSU people are finished, no reason not to," Nift said. "But I should tell you there's something a little different about this murder. I've seen the other victims, the nature of their wounds—especially the torture wounds. There was a special rage behind this. He was mad at her."

"You talking about the statue up her ass?" Renz asked.

"Among other things."

"They'd only just met," Quinn said. But even as he spoke, he realized he was assuming. He'd imagined a brief scenario: woman fired from her job, depressed, goes drinking, meets man who will love and console her, at least for one night.

Gets a surprise.

Nift shrugged. "Okay, don't listen to what I got to say. But just remember, he was extra-special mad at this one."

"That makes sense," Helen said.

She was wearing baggy sweatpants this morning, and a loose-fitting T-shirt. The clothes made her look not just tall, but larger. A scent of slightly perfumed heat and perspiration wafted from her. It wasn't unpleasant. More a healthy scent. She might have jogged here, for all Quinn knew. He thought Helen might have lived earlier as some kind of Viking warrior queen.

"Makes sense how?" he asked.

"The killer would possess a special rage for this victim. So soon after what almost happened on Liberty Island. That had to be a close call for him, a reminder of what *can* happen. Of what almost inevitably *will* happen."

Pearl was seated on the front edge of her desk so she could be part of Quinn and Helen's conversation. "Because he wants it to happen," she said.

Helen nodded. "In his own sick way, yes. He wants it more and more, even though he tries to deny it."

"It's what they all want," Quinn said. "They finally get frustrated with it *not* happening."

"Being so close to her, though," Helen said. "It must have been quite an experience. It must have triggered a lot of horrible reactions in his mind. Maybe she scared the hell out of him."

"No doubt she did," Quinn said, imagining.

"We talking about the Statue of Liberty?" Pearl asked.

"We are," Quinn said.

"His mother," Helen said.

60

Legwork time.

In the heat.

Quinn assigned Sal and Harold to canvass the apartments around the one where Gigi Beardsley had died. They had a police sketch artist's rendering of antique dealer Jacob Thomas's photo of Dred Gant, if Gant were clean shaven and with dark hair. Average looking, to be sure, but quite a different person without the blond beard, mustache, and black-framed glasses. No longer somebody who might score you some drugs in a club restroom.

They had also been given copies of the original photo, featuring the hirsute, scruffy Dred Gant. Disco Dred.

Good luck with that, Quinn thought.

But it had to be done.

A call to Homestead Properties, Gigi's former employer, quickly provided them with Gigi's home address, on the West Side near Columbus Circle. The woman Quinn talked with seemed genuinely distressed over Gigi's death. Quinn was told, predictably enough, that everyone at the agency had liked Gigi. The deceased was an earthbound angel, with a kind word for everyone. It wasn't for lack of friends that Gigi had been fired, but lack of funds.

Quinn tended to believe that last part was true.

Armed with more of the sketch copies, he decided to drive to Gigi's address with Pearl and Fedderman. Jody wanted to accompany them, insisting and insisting, until Quinn finally said it was all right, all right, and assigned her to the backseat of the Lincoln with Fedderman.

The old car's air conditioner was going to have a hard time keeping up with the heat, especially with four people inside.

Feds, even more disheveled than usual, was morose and had been having trouble at home—again. Basically about him being a cop. Busy bickering, leaving no time for much else. Neither he nor his wife, Penny, had been doing the wash or visiting the dry cleaner's for a while, even though they were in the middle of a heat wave. Served Jody right.

Quinn parked the Lincoln in a loading zone across the street from Gigi's apartment building. He saw Sal and Harold's unmarked, also parked illegally, near a fire plug on the opposite side of the street. Who were the bad guys in this city?

The building was an obviously expensive one, four stories of engraved stone and then twenty or so more of brick. The lower windows all had green awnings. There was a fountain outside, a sort of gargoyle perpetually vomiting water. Quinn thought that Gigi's company must have been doing well before the market had gone sour.

"We should be selling real estate, maybe," Fedderman said, gazing out the car window at the imposing tower of stone and brick.

"The crime market doesn't go up and down," Quinn said.

"And down," Pearl added.

"I'd rather go to court than to real estate closings," Jody said. "Borrrring."

"You sell real estate, you don't have to lug around a gun," Fedderman said.

"And nobody tries to kill you," Quinn said.

"So what are we doing here?" Jody asked.

Almost everyone had a good laugh.

Quinn fumed.

Pearl and Jody traded slight smiles.

Just in the brief time since Quinn had switched off the engine and AC, it had gotten uncomfortably hot in the car.

They all climbed out of the Lincoln and gingerly pulled the material of their sweaty clothing away from where it was stuck to bare flesh. Before they crossed the street, Quinn left his NYPD placard where it was visible on the dashboard.

There, he thought. *Legal.*

The lobby of Gigi's building was mostly oak paneling, potted plants, and fox-hunting prints, with tastefully disguised elevators almost impossible to locate.

"What did the victim actually do where she worked?" Jody asked seriously. Trying to match victim with environment.

"Human resources," Quinn said. "It paid well until it didn't pay at all."

A uniformed doorman who looked like a German field marshal directed them to one of the maintenance staff, a short man with a bulbous nose and incredibly baggy green pants. His pin-on name tag identified him simply as Harry. He accompanied them upstairs and worked the locks on Gigi's apartment door.

There was no crime scene tape on the door, though Quinn knew the NYPD had been here. Probably they had found nothing of interest. Or worth preserving.

Of course it was, as British TV cops said, early days. If anything had been obtained here it was doubtless still being analyzed.

"Her computer still here?" Jody asked.

"Police lab's got it," Quinn said. The victim's computer was always one of the first things the lab set to work on. "They already pronounced it useless, unless somebody was planning to buy into New York real estate. Gigi hadn't been online for ten hours before we have her at the bar meeting the man we assume killed her. Her drinking friends and former coworkers could make nothing of that sketch. They did recall a man at a nearby table giving her the eye, but they didn't get much of a look at him. They described him as average this, average that."

"He might not have been the killer," Jody said.

"Did we have to bring her along?" Fedderman asked.

Jody kicked him in the ankle, not hard, but it hurt.

Harry the maintenance guy asked them to lock up when they were finished.

"If you remove anything," he said, moving toward the door, "make sure you let me know. I'm supposed to make a list."

Quinn assured him that they would, then asked if there was anything already on the list.

"Nope. Nobody but you guys has been here since the cops left."

He gave them a half salute and then left.

The apartment seemed to go quiet and still after the door to the hall closed. No traffic noise from outside. Nothing but dust motes swirling in silent riot in the sunlight.

"Damn near soundproof," Fedderman said. "Pre-war building with thick walls."

Quinn wondered when people would stop using the expression "pre-war building." Which war were they talking about?

"Smells like death in here," Jody said. "Even though she died somewhere else."

The others knew what she meant and didn't comment.

"Pearl and I will go through the apartment," Quinn said. He then assigned Fedderman to canvass Gigi's neighbors in the building, even if Sal or Harold had already interviewed them. Jody he gave some copies of the photos from antique dealer Jacob Thomas's files—the ones of Dred Gant with blond hair, mustache, beard, and glasses. Her job was to cover the nearby neighborhood merchants.

Both of them also took copies of the NYPD sketch, and—in case they wanted to jolt someone's memory and disturb their sleep—postmortem photos of the victim that had been faxed over to Q&A from the morgue.

* * *

Jody was having no luck. By the time she entered Sam's Spirits, on Eighth Avenue, she was sweating like crazy and her feet hurt.

Sam's was a liquor store about the size of a closet. Besides booze, there were also racks of impulse items, everything from plastic police whistles to beef jerky.

Jody looked around and didn't see any plastic Statues of Liberty.

A man Jody assumed to be Sam himself stood behind a wooden counter, intent on counting money. He was small, middle-aged, bald, and wearing red suspenders over a blue short-sleeved shirt with perspiration crescents below the armpits. In his left hand he held a large roll of money while his right thumb effortlessly and rapidly folded back the bills one by one. Jody thought he would have looked just right with sleeve garters and a green visor. As he worked his talented thumb, the bills made a swishing, snapping sound.

He glanced up at Jody. She didn't seem threatening, so he continued counting money the final few precious seconds, until he was finished.

Makes the world go round, Jody thought.

He placed the money beneath the counter and smiled at her. "Please feel free to look around," he said, motioning with his arm as if there were vistas of booze instead of his limited stock.

"I want you to be the looker," Jody said with a return smile.

"So I'm looking." He regarded her carefully, and she realized he thought she wanted him to look at her. "I see a cop," he said.

She laughed and flashed her Quinn-supplied temporary NYPD shield. "There is no prize. You the Sam on
the sign?"

"That Sam I am."

She moved up to the counter and laid the NYPD
artist's hypothetical and questionable sketch on the
counter. The guy in the sketch even looked slightly familiar to Jody, but maybe that was because she'd seen
the sketch so many times. "Ever seen this man?"

He stared at the sketch. "Can't say I have. Can't say
I haven't. Average-lookin' fella."

"I know, I know." Jody reached into her purse and
pulled out a copy of the Jacob Thomas photo of Dred
Gant in what might have been a false beard and mustache, blond hair, thick black-framed glasses. She laid
it on the counter next to the NYPD sketch.

Sam studied both likenesses. "Same fella?"

"You tell me."

He pointed to the beard and mustache photo. "I
think I might have bought a joint from that guy back in
nineteen-sixty-nine at college."

Jody waited.

"That's all I can tell you," Sam said.

Jody gave him a spiteful look, but thanked him
nonetheless.

"He do something?" Sam asked.

"We're pretty sure he did." She gathered up photo
and sketch and turned to leave.

"Wait a minute," Sam said. "Bring back that first
one. Something about the second picture kind of triggered something about the first."

That sounded plausible to Jody.

She returned to the counter and laid the two likenesses side by side again, hoping whatever had triggered Sam's memory once would do it again. She said nothing. Didn't even move. Didn't want to create bias.

Sam studied them.

Finally he raised his gaze and looked at Jody with bloodshot eyes. "He might've come in last night, about nine or nine-thirty. Maybe a little later. Had a blond girl with him. She might've been a little tipsy. He bought a bottle of Grey Goose vodka."

Jody felt her pulse quicken. Suddenly she was having fun here. A certain kind of fun.

"They say anything?" she asked.

"Not as I can recall. Just him ordering the vodka from where it's displayed there behind the counter. They was sort of leaning on each other, obviously *with* each other, if you know what I mean."

"Lovers?"

"I wouldn't go so far as to say that. Or to swear it wasn't so."

"How'd he pay?"

"Cash, I think. A fifty-dollar bill."

"Could you recognize that individual bill if you saw it?" She recalled cashiers who always marked big bills when they accepted them, so the customer couldn't claim he or she had given them a bill of even larger denomination and demand more change.

"C'mon!" Sam said, looking incredulous. "Booze ain't cheap. I get fifties all day long." He shrugged his bony shoulders. "You gotta realize that, till you came in here, those two were just some of yesterday's customers, is all. I didn't think there'd be any *reason* to identify them, or their money."

"Which way'd they turn when they went out the door?"

"That I couldn't tell you."

Jody considered the place where Gigi's friends and former coworkers had had drinks, where they'd left her despondent and vulnerable. It was a short walk from there to here, which was about halfway to a subway line Gigi and the killer could have taken to a stop very near the furnished but unoccupied apartment where she'd died.

Though she'd been fired, Gigi had still had her key to the agency's lockboxes. She and the man who'd picked her up—or vice versa—would have gone to an apartment like that to have sex.

She reached in her purse and got out another photograph Quinn had given her. Gigi Beardsley's morgue photo.

She laid the photo on the counter, in front of Sam. "Seen her before?"

Sam stared. "Jesus H. Christ!"

"Not *Him*," Jody said. She pointed to the morgue shot. "Her."

"That's the girl," Sam said. "The one who was in here with the guy that bought the vodka. I could and would swear to it." He shook his head sadly. "She's dead, ain't she?"

"Completely," Jody said.

61

Nobody liked a surprise visit by the cops.

Bobby Aikins, medium height and weight, aveage-looking guy, well on the way to losing all his hair on top, was no exception. Aikins lived six blocks from where Gigi Beardsley had been killed, which was far afield from Sal and Harold's assignment to canvass the neighboring buildings.

What had prompted the visit was the fact that Aikins was managing director of human resources at Homestead Properties, which had sacked Gigi on the day of her death. Probably it had been Aikins himself who'd given her the bad news.

Aikins moved back to let Sal and Harold enter his apartment. It was a nice one on the tenth floor, with a view down Broadway. He motioned for the two detectives to sit on the sofa. Sal sat. Harold remained standing. Aikins settled down in a buttery tan leather armchair that matched the sofa.

There was a lot of tan leather and shiny chrome about. The apartment gave the impression that all the furnishings had been bought recently at the same time and place. They seemed to suggest that the occupant wasn't there very often, but spent most of the time in his office or on business jaunts.

Aikins was having trouble looking either of the detectives in the eye. Hiding something. Sal saw that as a hopeful sign. The more people were hiding, the better.

"I guess this is about Gigi," Aikins said. He shook his head from side to side, staring at the cream-colored carpet. "Damned shame, what happened."

"It's funny," Harold said, "how the apartment she was murdered in is just down the street from yours."

Sal thought Harold was pushing a little too hard here; then he realized what was going on and determined to play good cop.

"Six blocks," he said. "Not so funny, really."

"It isn't funny at all," Aikins said. "Nothing about what happened is in the least bit funny." He looked at Harold now, shot him daggers. "And six blocks isn't all that close. Not in Manhattan."

"Six short blocks," Harold said.

Sal thought of leavening that, but decided not to jump in here. It was kind of fun seeing the mild-mannered Harold playing bad cop.

Harold pretended to consult something in his note pad. "You're the director of human resources at Homestead Properties?"

"Managing director."

"Just what the hell does that mean?" Harold asked.

Sal almost smiled. Harold turning it on.

"Means I'm in charge of personnel."

"And it was your decision to fire Gigi Beardsley?"

"No. That was a board decision."

"You're on the board?"

"Yes."

Harold shrugged.

Sal said nothing.

Aikins said, "All right."

They both looked at him.

"All right what?" Sal rasped.

"I saw them last night, before Gigi was killed." Sal wished Harold would either say something or shut his mouth. Literally. His bad-cop role had been so well played that Aikins had rolled open like a sardine can. Both detectives were surprised. It was better not to look that way.

Sal figured he'd better take charge here, though he couldn't fault the progress Harold had made.

"You'd better elaborate," he said to Aikins.

"I felt terrible about firing Gigi. She really was an angel. Everybody at Homestead liked her." He stared at the carpet and shook his head again. "This damned business has no heart."

"You mean real estate?" Sal asked.

"Sure. What else would I mean?"

"It was out of your hands," Harold said.

Now he was sympathizing with Aikins, who looked at him in surprise.

Sal looked at him, too. *Toughen up, Harold.*

"Did you and Gigi have something romantic going?" Sal asked, putting this Q and A back on the beam.

"I wish!" Aikins said. Which was not a smart thing to say. Only he wouldn't have admitted it if he were guilty of Gigi's murder, so maybe not a dumb thing to say.

"I knew she spent some time in the neighborhood," Aikins continued. "There was a lounge not far away where she and some of the other Homestead employees spent their time and money."

"Including you?"

"No. Not a good place for a managing director to be."

"Too friendly with the help?"

"You could say that."

"Perfectly understandable," Harold said.

Sal gave him a cautioning look. He was the old Harold again, not the hard-bitten detective out of TV and movie drama.

"I did get lucky enough to catch sight of her," Aikins said. "She was walking on Eighth Avenue, and I sort of figured where she might be going. She still had a master key to the universal lockbox—I forgot to ask her for it, and she forgot to volunteer it. And I knew the Padmont Building unit wasn't far away."

"She might have been going anywhere," Sal said.

"Well, I didn't think so. I wanted to satisfy my curiosity. That's why I followed them."

Sal and Harold exchanged a dead-eyed glance that Aikins wasn't supposed to notice.

"Them?" Harold asked.

"Didn't I say? She was with someone. A man I'd never seen before. That's why I was curious. And, I admit, a little jealous. I had a kind of mild crush on Gigi, but I wasn't the only one."

"Was she the sort that slept around?" Harold asked.

"No. Just the opposite. That's one reason why I was curious."

"What did this man she was with look like?"

Aikins closed his eyes, thinking. Then opened them. "There was nothing unusual about him. I guess *that* was unusual. He was just . . . average."

"You knew the approximate height of Gigi Beards-ley, Mr. Aikins. Using that as a yardstick, was the man short or tall?"

"Tall's relevant. And I don't know what kind of heels Gigi was wearing, or if she had on high heels. I'm tall at six feet one. He seemed slightly shorter than me."

Aikins had looked to Sal to be about five-eleven.

"What else?" he rasped.

"He had on light slacks, a dark blazer."

"Hair?"

"Yeah. A full head of it, like mine. Dark like mine, too. I think. Really, it's hard to say. I didn't dream I might have to describe him, or I'd have paid closer attention." Aikins looked from Harold to Sal. "Do you think he's the one who killed Gigi? The Lady Liberty Killer?"

"Yes," Harold said.

"My God! I could have done *something*. Stopped him."

"You couldn't know," Sal said. "And if you had known, you couldn't have stopped him without killing him."

"Then I—"

"What?" Sal asked.

"Nothing."

"Were the two of them walking okay?" Harold asked.

"You mean, were they drunk?"

"Well, yes."

"Maybe a little. But then, I figured they were coming from the lounge, so I mighta just seen them as being slightly unsteady."

"Were they walking in the direction of the listed apartment where Gigi was murdered?"

"Yeah. Or toward a subway stop that'd get them there."

"What about her own apartment?"

"Not in that direction. Maybe she didn't want him to know where she lived."

"Why would that be?" Harold asked.

"You know. Guys can give a woman—could give her—all kinds of trouble. She maybe . . ."

"What?"

"Just needed temporary comforting."

"Because of what you did to her."

"Easy, Harold," Sal said. "Take it easy."

Sal took out the images of Dred Gant, deciding to spare Aikins the morgue shot of Gigi. He didn't like looking at that one, himself.

He held the copies out for Aikins to see. "This the man you saw?"

Aikins stared, then looked up at Sal. "I can't say. They don't even look like the same man until you study them. And even then . . ."

Sal put the copies away.

"Do you recall what time you saw Gigi and her companion?"

"Nine-fifty."

"How can you be so definite?"

"I always know the time. Automatically check it regularly."

"From being in Human Resources, I guess," Harold said.

"Maybe." Aikins was staring at the carpet again, glum, spent.

Sal and Harold thanked him for his time, and told him he'd be asked later to make a statement.

"So you can see if I contradict myself," Aikins said, head bowed. "Trip myself up."

"Everybody contradicts themselves every day," Sal said.

Though not when they're talking about murder.

"That's sure comforting," Aikins said, still not looking up.

Sal and Harold took their leave.

When they were descending in the elevator, Sal said, "I forgot you could play such a hard-ass."

"Just like on TV, movies, the stage," Harold said.

"Really. You ever been on the stage?"

"A few times in lineups. Does that count?"

"No," Sal said.

62

Jody was on the way back to where Quinn and Pearl were, at Gigi Beardsley's apartment. She was eager to tell Quinn she'd been able to place the killer with the victim near the approximate time of the murder. All Quinn had to do was phone the medical examiner and ascertain whether Gigi had Grey Goose vodka in her stomach at the time of her death. That shouldn't be so difficult.

Then Jody felt a stab of nausea, remembering actually *seeing* Gigi's stomach.

She forced that vivid picture from her mind, or at least to a compartmentalized place where it might lie unnoticed, and assured herself that the police lab could work miracles. Surely they could find traces of vodka, and should be able to identify the brand. Well, the brand, maybe.

The temperature had gained another few degrees, and Jody realized she was walking fast, perspiring.

She stopped, causing several people to pause and stare at her. Telling herself to take her time, she moved into the shadow of an awning over the window of a small bookshop. It struck her that you didn't see very many small independent bookstores these days. The future pecking away.

Best to use part of the tech onslaught to phone Quinn, make sure he and her mother were still at the victim's apartment. Jody fished her iPhone from her purse and was surprised when it buzzed and vibrated in her hand.

She automatically swished her thumb and answered it before she'd fully read the call's origin—Golden Sunset Assisted Living, a New Jersey number.

"Jody?" called her grandmother's voice from the phone. "Are you there, dear?"

Well, no problem here. Her grandmother would surely understand that she was working.

"Hi, Gramma. I can't talk now. I'm—"

"About to hear—and this I don't often say—the *opportunity* of your lifetime. For this, Jody, dear, you find time."

Huh? "I'm helping to apprehend a serial killer, Gramma."

"Killer schmiller. What? Will he disappear like a magician's bunny?"

"Maybe just like that, Gramma. This is really important!"

"I don't have to tell you who you sound like now, dear. This opportunity—"

"Will keep. It will keep, Gramma. Really!"

"Will it, dear? The impetuousness of youth—and I mean this not as an insult—is sometimes unable to pause and open the golden door to the future. Even, I am sad to say, they ignore opportunity's knock. Often it isn't a loud knock, and yet—"

"What is this opportunity, Gramma? Do you want me to buy gold?"

Jody realized she was talking too loud, drawing attention. She moved farther back into the shadows of the doorway, near a tall, leaning display of books about impending climate change. Global warming. *It's here! It's here!* Jody almost said aloud, feeling beads of sweat trickling down the inside of her right arm.

"Not gold—and I assure you I would have no reservations about buying gold at this time, when impending disaster looms, and we mustn't think about that, because what's the use, disasters being what they are? Not gold, dear. Something even more valuable than gold or any of the other precious metals. In so far as any metal is precious when compared to the value of flesh and bone."

Good God! Jody realized she was squeezing the phone. She had observed her mother talking on the phone to her grandmother, seen the signs of stress. At the time, she hadn't understood, and had even been critical of her mother.

Was it time to inform her grandmother that she was "breaking up"?

Jody didn't like the imagery of the remark. Besides, Gramma was never really convinced of this convenient cellular interference, and Jody had been openly disdainful of her mother for blatantly lying to *her* mother. There was no doubt that the old woman wasn't actually deceived.

Right was right. Wasn't that what Quinn preached? Sort of?

Jody drew a deep breath.

"What is this better-than-golden opportunity?" she asked her grandmother.

"It turns out—though to say this in such a trivial manner and without trumpets is to disregard what is, perhaps, meaningful fate—that *Doctor* Milton Kahn has a daughter."

"I'm not looking for new friends right now," Jody said.

"Oh, I'm thinking of more than mere friendship, dear."

A startling thought crossed Jody's mind. "Are you matchmaking?"

"It's an honorable tradition, dear."

Jody was puzzled. "I'm straight, Gramma."

"A daughter who has a *friend,* dear. Which is, in this instance, a man, and is another word for *find*. A recently divorced friend who is a respected chiropractor. His name is Austin Morton."

"Isn't that a British car, Gramma?" She really did feel like breaking the connection but fought the impulse.

"Not in this instance. He is from the Bronx. If you were—and I say this with a grandmother's instinctive knowledge of how personalities might mesh—simply—and *simply* is an understatement as to the momentous importance of the matter—to look at *Doctor* Austin Morton's photograph on Facebook, and read about his considerable, not to say admirable, accomplishments, you would—"

"You're breaking up, Gramma."

And just a fraction of the guilt that her mother felt settled on Jody.

Quinn gave Nift the info—they knew the victim's last hours, the approximate time of her death. And her killer had actually been seen, though identifying him for certain in a courtroom still seemed a long shot.

Most of the Q&A personnel—or human resources— were in the squad-room-like office on West Seventy-ninth. The desks were in two rows, facing each other. There was nothing in between. The place even smelled like a precinct squad room—that unique combination of desperation and perspiration, of misplaced old church pews. There was remorse here without atonement.

Quinn thought the arrangement might keep the heat down, allowing more circulation from the underpowered window-unit air conditioners, than if there were a lot of cubicles. His office was the only actual cubical, and it wasn't permanent. In fact, it usually had only two or three sides in place. It seemed that the hotter the weather, and whatever case they were on, the fewer cubicle walls were up. There was only one of the portable fiberboard panels in use now, propped behind Quinn's desk. Everybody could see anyone, disagree with anyone, and interrupt anyone. This communal arrangement sometimes bred irritation and conflict. And solutions.

Helen, who didn't have a desk, was pacing sockless in her new Nikes. She was wearing a light beige linen suit with a skirt short enough—on her—so the play of muscle in her calves and lower thighs was plainly visible. Quinn supposed that was what everyone was looking at while they listened intently to what she was saying.

"He's nearing the zenith of his career," she said of the killer. "He must sense that. We have his name, we have pictures, we have eye witnesses who saw him with at least one of the victims. His relationship with the media isn't working out as well as he planned. He's being painted as a monster. And we almost had him on Liberty Island. He's still probably breathing hard after that one. They say murder destroys a little bit of the killer each time he or she kills, and they're right. Gant's rationale is being whittled away. His murders aren't supplying the long-lasting relief they used to. His memories of them are tainted now by the fear we instilled in him by breathing down his neck. The latest murder was by far more the work of a mad butcher than a clever and meticulous serial killer."

"Mad butchers we can handle," Sal rasped. "I know one in Brooklyn who's still pissed off over losing this thumb he had that wouldn't behave."

No one said anything, choosing not to hear any more about the Brooklyn butcher and his misbehaving thumb.

"Scales of justice," Harold said, after a while.

"Something else," Helen said.

"About the butcher?" Harold asked.

She ignored him. It was hard to know when Harold was joking.

Helen went to a slim leather portfolio she sometimes carried instead of a purse. She drew out two photo-

graphs that looked as if they'd been printed on ordinary
computer paper.

They were headshots of the same woman, one head-
on, one in profile.

"Mug shots from when Mildred Gant was arrested,"
she explained. "Before she had her hair cut."

The photos were passed around.

"Not an attractive woman," Fedderman said.

"True," Helen said. "But did you notice the facial
bone structure, especially around the eyes, the strong
cheekbones and chin? Isn't it familiar?"

They had all seen it.

"But there's a world of difference in attractiveness,"
Fedderman said.

"That's not what the killer's thinking about," Helen
said. She propped her fists on her hips. "Anybody here
think this woman doesn't—or didn't—resemble Carlie?"

"She resembles Carlie slightly," Jody said.

"Considerably," Sal said.

"Whatever," Helen said. "We can use that resemblance."

Quinn wondered if Renz had prompted Helen about
what tack she should take. He doubted it. Renz was her
boss only up to a point. Helen was, in many ways, her
own woman.

"The killer's still not making mistakes," Quinn said
to her.

"But he doesn't *know* that. He'll start questioning
himself now. He can't be sure of what he's left behind."

"So maybe he'll take a break," Pearl said. "Let
things calm down for a while."

Helen, who had begun pacing again, shook her head

no. Her long, rounded calves flexed, flexed, flexed with every step. "No, no. He's the one who set the tempo for this game, and wanted to play as fast and hard as possible. He needs to take another victim as soon as he can. He needs reassurance as well as relief from his compulsion."

"Like climbing right back up on a horse that's thrown you," Harold said.

They all looked at him.

"That's exactly what it's like," Helen said.

She moved back and forth gracefully, muscles working smoothly in her lanky body. There was about her an equine quality that Quinn hadn't noticed before. Maybe he saw it now because of Harold's *horse* remark.

Quinn's desk phone jangled. He snatched up the receiver and turned his back on the others for partial privacy.

"Nift," the caller said simply, identifying himself.

"It's Quinn."

"You wanted me to call."

"You got something?"

"Yes, and probably."

Quinn knew Nift was talking about Jody's vodka question.

Nift went on. "The victim had a fair amount of alcohol content in her bloodstream, and had ingested some not long before her death. I can't say for sure that she'd recently drunk vodka, but it's certainly possible. As for the brand name, I wouldn't even be able to recognize my favorite drink."

"That'll have to do," Quinn said.

"If I'd gotten to her sooner . . ."

"But you didn't. None of us did."

"Something else," Nift said. "There were traces of dopamine in her blood."

"How much?"

"Again, it's difficult to say. My guess is not very much, but combined with the vodka, or whatever alcoholic drink, it was enough to cause a sudden drop in blood pressure, and then unconsciousness. Dopamine and the alcohol would have made her drowsy and easy to handle. For a while. Then, when she awoke, stripped and bound up like a Thanksgiving turkey, she would have been helpless and well on her way to a memorable experience—for the killer."

"Anything else?" Quinn asked. He didn't like being on the phone with Nift unless useful information was being passed. Pearl was right—there was something repellant about any sort of contact with the little bastard.

"Tell Pearl I said hello."

Was he reading my mind? "I'll do that."

Quinn replaced the receiver more violently than he intended.

"Nift," he explained.

He repeated for them what the nasty little ME had said, though he didn't pass on Nift's personal greeting to Pearl.

"So we've got Gant solid as the man who was with Gigi Beardsley shortly before her murder," Helen said. "What with the vodka and dopamine cocktail, the liquor store identifications are now completely credible."

"It's a case," Jody said, "but not air tight."

"We've got everything but the killer," Pearl said.

"We'll have him soon," Helen said softly. "We've got precisely what he needs now more than ever. What he'll no more be able to stay away from than a junkie from his fix."

No one asked what she meant.

They all knew and were afraid she was right.

"Carlie," Helen said.

63

L et them look for him.
   Urban cops were trying to find him, and he was a
country boy—or could revert to one whenever he
chose. He could feel relatively safe here.

Dred Gant was wearing Levi's, so he didn't mind
boosting himself over the low, time-darkened stone
wall that bordered Central Park along Central Park
West. The country here in the city.

On the park side of the wall, he paused to take in the
scene. The sun was low and the shadows long. There
were people over on a trail. A couple lying next to each
other beneath a tree. A homeless man in tatters, seated
like a lone sentinel on one of the benches.

Was he a sentinel? An undercover cop?

The man didn't seem to be aware even of the pi-
geons pecking away at the ground in front of him. One
of the birds was damn near sitting on his shoe.

Dred trusted no one at this point—*no one*. Even
though his photo and the idiotic police sketch of him
had been shown on TV and printed in the papers, he
thought it unlikely that anyone would recognize him in

his faded jeans, Mets T-shirt, and baseball cap and sunglasses. His jogging shoes gave him a way to run like hell if he so chose, without attracting a great deal of attention. Especially here in the park, where runners were plentiful.

He walked along a path edging the woods, head bowed, kicking at pebbles. knowing that Carlie was radioactive. What really bothered him was that Quinn and company *knew* that he knew.

And they knew he wouldn't, that he *couldn't*, stay away from her. Dred himself knew that.

It was what the game had come down to, and both men understood it. They had both, in their ways, cut angles and blocked avenues so that they were operating in a smaller and smaller universe.

So that *something* had to happen, because the status quo was unbearable.

A squeezable air horn beeped, and a woman in Spandex shorts swerved around him and rode up ahead on a bicycle. She gave him a wave over her shoulder without looking back, letting him know she'd sounded only a friendly message with the horn to alert him she was bearing down on him.

He watched her, following her progress. She was pedaling hard, causing the bike and her hips to dip left, then right, left, right, left, right . . . a rhythm as old as time.

She glanced back, and he knew she'd been aware that he was watching her. All that ass swishing had been for him. *Look at me, look at me . . .*

So he looked. Her long blond hair was in a ponytail that swayed in contra-measure time with her hips.

He couldn't take his eyes off her.

He thought it might be possible to begin jogging, not to catch up with her, but to keep her in sight so he could know when and where she stopped. When the trail curved, he could run straight cross country and more or less maintain the distance between them.

And draw attention if anyone was tailing him.

He'd checked carefully before leaving his apartment in the Village. He was in a defensive, not a predatory, mood. If he were going to stalk Carlie today, he would have waited for her outside her apartment, or latched on to her when she left work.

They didn't know where he lived, so he didn't think they would be on his tail unless he got near Carlie.

To be on the safe side, he'd taken a number-three subway train uptown, lost himself in the crowds of Times Square, then gone to the Port Authority Terminal and ridden another subway before surfacing on Seventy-ninth Street.

Was he going mad? It had been mentioned in the newspapers and on television (the bitch Minnie Miner). How could these people who had never seen him, who had no idea who he was, sagely pronounce him insane?

Part of the game. They want me to think *I might be insane.*

Paranoid?

How can I be paranoid when someone is really after me?

It seemed natural to strike out from the subway stop toward the park. He felt more secure above ground now, walking on the surface of the planet. Dred could usually sense when he was being followed. At least, he liked to think so.

If anyone had been on his tail, he was sure he'd eluded him. Or *her*.

He thought about Pearl Kasner and her daughter, Jody. Nancy Weaver. Helen Iman. The women who were Quinn's allies. His hunting buddies. Dred knew he couldn't underestimate them, but he didn't fear *them*. He saw them more as the potential objects of his game than as worthy opponents.

For Chrissakes! They were only women!

The object he now wanted, needed, *would have*, was Carlie Clark.

It would be dark soon. The sky was clouding up in a mockery of rain. Dred was walking among towering old trees, and shadows were growing along the path. As everyone knew, it was dangerous in the park at night. Killers could lurk in the thick foliage. In the blackness of shadows.

Dred smiled. He might be seen as a possible predator if he didn't get out of the park soon. He'd laid the groundwork for that kind of suspicion, turned the city into a kill zone.

He crossed to a main trail and began moving in the direction of the familiar skyline along Central Park West.

Out of the jungle, into the jungle.

Minnie Miner on TV. *Damn her!* He hated her *now*, the way she was talking about him.

The killer leaned forward in his ruined antique wing chair and turned up the volume with his remote.

"Is it true," Minnie was asking Helen the profiler,

"that the killer's mental affliction has reached an explosively extreme level?"

"The stress on him certainly has," Helen said. "Notice the murders are closer together and more violent and vicious."

Minnie looked interested. "His mind is unraveling?"

"In a sense, yes. A killer like this, who carries the memory weight of such a large number of victims, eventually becomes mentally affected by what he knows are crimes. *Sins*, if you will. He sees himself sometimes for what he is and can't deny. He knows we're in the end game. He *wants* to be stopped, but in some startling, newfound manner."

"He wants fame *and* anonymity," Minnie said. "That must set up quite a conflict."

"His mind is a jumble of conflicts. Not just one. He's a sick man as well as an evil one. At this stage, he's coming apart inside, knows it, and can't prevent it."

"The frustration must be driving him mad."

"Considering that he was mad to begin with, we probably can't imagine his deteriorating state of mind."

"Do you think it's possible that he'll give himself up?" Minnie asked.

"Possible, but I doubt it."

"He'd have all the drama of a trial ahead of him," Minnie pointed out.

"But not his cloak of anonymity."

"But he's a mental case," Minnie said. "A psychopath. How can the police predict any of his moves if he might not know what he's going to do himself?"

What do you mean, mental case? I don't see "doctor" in front of your name.

Gant was on his feet without remembering exactly

how he'd gotten out of his chair. *Why does she refer to me as a psychopath?*

He knew where the program was shot, could go directly to it in the maze of the city.

"He's not that sort of mental case," Helen said. "He's actually quite intelligent and knows exactly what he wants and how he'll go about trying to get it."

"But he's twisted."

"Yes, somewhere along the line he became twisted. And dangerous."

Very good, Dred thought. *Twisted. Another way of saying I'm smarter than you are.*

He sat back down, calmer. Then he stood up and went into the kitchen, got a bottle of sipping bourbon and a glass from the cabinet. He put ice cubes in a glass, then the bourbon with a splash of water.

By the time he'd gone back into the living room there was an attorney's commercial on TV, about various kinds of prescription medicines with horrible side effects that would be the basis for highly profitable lawsuits.

Dred switched it off. Sat in the silence. Drank.

Thought.

It struck him that there were two things wrong with using his mother's money. First: It was *her* money, an undeniable bond between the two of them. Second: He should be thinking about Carlie Clark.

She was bait, of course.

But bait was frequently stolen.

It was time to stop agonizing with the same thoughts over and over again, to stop acting them out in his mind.

It was time he approached Carlie again.

64

R ain.
How dare they predict rain! The people of the city knew better than to fall for another cruel prank.

Yet some of them carried umbrellas, or even wore light raincoats. Hope sprang as eternal as evil in the human breast.

It had thundered distantly all that day. Clouds sailed past like ghostly galleons. Lightning flashed.

All show.

That evening, with the sky still rumbling, Dred stood on the subway platform where Carlie would board a train that would carry her to a stop near her apartment. It would be the first leg of her trip to hell.

He glanced at his watch. Carlie would have left her office in Bold Designs. She should be here in another fifteen or twenty minutes.

He could have simply gone to her apartment, but he knew it was being watched. Quinn had made it quite clear that he and his detectives knew Carlie Clark would be the next Liberty Killer victim. Taunting him.

Daring him. They were using Carlie for bait, and her apartment was a trap.

Dred also wanted to follow Carlie on the subway so he could spot who else might be following her, watching over her. How many angels did she have? He knew by now what they looked like. He wanted to know which of them he had to deal with this evening, so he could plan. Fate would tell him when, and how, to act.

The heat wave and drought might soon break, and the darkening sky foretold rain, giving Dred an excuse to carry an umbrella. Just in case. It wasn't the sort of precaution that would be taken by a man planning to kill a woman that night.

This evening he was Mr. Executive. Mid-level at best. Wearing a plain brown suit, cream-colored shirt, and wildly patterned tie that people would glance at and remember instead of his face. He was also carrying his scuffed brown leather briefcase. In short, he looked like thousands of other career men on their way home from the office.

He casually stood. He sat. He paced the platform. He watched.

Carlie didn't show.

Maybe she'd gone home by cab because of the predicted rain. Or been driven to her apartment by the police or a coworker. She was getting special treatment these days, sometimes without even being aware of it.

Most likely, he decided, she was working late. She did that often. Brownie points. Dred smiled. What a waste of time those were.

The killer waited almost an hour, moving from place to place on the platform and looking for signs that someone might be observing him. Then he went up on to street level and walked up and down the block, pretending to gaze into show windows. All the while, he kept the entrance to the subway in sight.

It was getting late. Thunder still rumbled in the distance. A few drops of rain fell, like miniature artillery shells gauging trajectory. Dred didn't bother opening his umbrella. Instead, he fell in with some other people hurrying to the corner and the steps down to the subway platform, where it was now stifling, noisy, crowded, but dry.

He followed them down, getting his heel stepped on, and slumped on one of the wooden benches along the tiled wall. Ordinarily he would have said something to the man who'd stepped on his heel. Or later, on the subway train, might "accidentally" have ground his heel into the man's foot. Dred knew how to do that in a way that broke some of the small bones.

But this evening promised more important satisfactions than settling petty grudges.

Over the next hour or so, he watched trains come roaring in, disgorge and take on passengers, and then lurch and glide away into the dark tunnel.

He glanced at his watch and frowned. His act was that he might be waiting for someone who hadn't shown up. Which, in its way, was true.

He was about to give up when here she came, down the concrete steps to the platform.

Dressy, dressy. For work. Quite a show of ankle and calf.

The arrival of a subway train coincided with her arrival. The train screeched and squealed to a stop and the doors slid open. Dred joined the press of people waiting to board. Carlie boarded along with a knot of people at the rear of the car. Dred wedged himself in through a different door and moved farther in, toward the center of the car and away from the sliding door. He stood facing away from Carlie, but he could see her reflection in the window, and would be able to see it more clearly when the train entered the dark tunnel and the windows became mirrors.

No doubt someone else was on the train, protecting her, according to plan. The killer had one huge advantage. He knew precisely what Quinn and his minions looked like. He'd stood unnoticed and watched them come and go at the Q&A offices.

It took him only a few minutes to spot the one called Fedderman, tall and lanky but with a potbelly, and a decent enough suit that looked like rags on him because of his disjointed build. There was a flash of white that the killer knew was an unbuttoned shirt cuff.

Fedderman, all right.

It took him longer to spot the one called Sal. He of the short, stocky build and gravelly voice. Might Harold, the other half of the comedy team, be on the train? The killer doubted it. Mr. Mild, Harold—maybe along with some of the others—was probably already up ahead. The detectives could stay in touch with each other via cell phone.

Though she was easy to find, Carlie Clark was certainly well protected. Like an expensive painting on display in a museum. Easy to look at, even up close, but touch it and immediately there would be trouble.

The killer knew that in his business, such paintings were stolen with regularity. A surprisingly large percentage of famous paintings were actually skillfully wrought duplicates. The real paintings, if they could be traced and validated, would be found in the private collections of the very rich.

The train was slowing, about to brake for the stop where Carlie would leave the subway and walk the rest of the way home.

The killer managed to join a group of people standing to leave the car as soon as the train lurched to a stop.

It slowed, coasting now. Then it braked with the scream of steel on steel. The passengers stirred this way and that as momentum ceased, then abruptly reversed to a full stop.

Dred didn't so much as glance at Carlie. He did keep an eye on Fedderman, who left the car via a middle sliding door. Because he was tall he was easy to spot. The detective Sal was nowhere in sight, but Dred didn't doubt he was also getting off at this stop.

The crowd filed through the reversible turnstiles and made for the steps leading to street level.

Halfway up the steps, the killer heard a loud clap of thunder. He stopped, with several other people, just learning that the weather above might be getting serious. He unsnapped the restraining strap on his black folding umbrella, so he could open it in a hurry if he must, then continued climbing the concrete steps leading to the world above.

It was a noisy, messy, darkened world, under a steady light rain. Thunder boomed and roared through the echoing canyons. Cabs swished past without slowing or stopping, all of them with passengers.

The killer raised his umbrella, carrying it low and tilted slightly forward so it would partially block or shadow his face. He strode in the direction of Carlie's apartment and soon saw her up ahead.

Barely visible, half a block ahead of her, Fedderman strode without looking back. He also had a black umbrella. Across the street, almost level with Fedderman, was rasp-voiced Sal.

Fedderman cut away, down a side street. A block over he jogged in the direction Carlie was going, getting out well ahead of her. He gained a lot of ground before stopping, breathing hard from his effort. He'd sloshed through a puddle and his socks were soaked; he could feel it. If they were one of the pair bought by Penny it would be okay. Fedderman's older dark socks turned his feet black when they got wet.

He walked another block south and then used his cell to phone in his position to Quinn.

The rain suddenly became a deluge lit by lightning. Thunder crashed. The leading edge of the storm had arrived. Everything was light and noise.

On the street running parallel with the one Fedderman was on, the detective Sal was facing into the wind, his face set against the driving raindrops. He was trying to open his umbrella without it being turned inside out.

Lightning flashed over and over, like urgent code from a darkened exile.

The killer recognized that Fate was present.

65

As so often happens after a long period of heat and drought, the leading edge of the storm assaulted the city like an invading army. With the suddenness of an artillery barrage, thunder rolled and echoed down the stone canyons. The darkened sky hurled large raindrops earthward, first a few, then thousands. Here was the storm, torrent and thunder.

And momentary distraction.

Fate instructed the killer. He let the short one, Sal, who was tailing Carlie close behind, get slightly more ahead of him on the opposite side of the street. Dred didn't want to be seen in the man's peripheral vision as he closed the space between them.

Rain continued to roar downward, sometimes propelled almost sideways by blasts of wind. Lightning flashed and acted on the city like God's strobe lights.

Holding his umbrella lower now, and partly folded, the killer crossed the street at a sharp angle so that he was almost directly behind Sal. He drew a large folding knife from his pocket and thumbed out the blade, then opened the knife completely and pressed it flat against the side of his leg.

This was happening directly behind Sal, and fast. He saw and heard nothing but lightning and thunder, and didn't so much as glance behind him.

There was no one else on the storm-assaulted street. And if anyone happened to be looking out a window, he or she would see something fragmented by shadow and lightning, so fast it might not have actually occurred.

And if they *did* realize what had happened, if they *did* choose to get involved, if they *did* call nine-eleven, it would be too late to make a difference. Fate would have moved on.

Careful to stay on an approach almost directly behind Sal, slightly to the left because of the way Sal carried his head, the killer rapidly closed the space between them.

Faster.

Squinting against the rain, he shook his head to clear his vision, held the knife low and in close to his body, pointed forward.

He ran into Sal almost hard enough to knock him down, driving the knife into Sal's unprotected side and deep in along the bottom of his rib cage. The blade made a scraping sound on bone.

It took the breath out of Sal and crippled him with pain. He dropped straight down without a sound, aware of a dark form striding over him, continuing the way Sal had been walking—toward Carlie.

Sal struggled to reach his cell phone, but merely

moving his arm brought pain like an electric current down his right side.

Lightning speared the city again.

Thunder cracked. Sal barely heard it.

Time to move fast, before the detective's partner, Harold, would reach the intersection and look east toward where Carlie would be crossing the street. She was only two blocks from her apartment.

Silently, he caught up with Carlie, who was wearing a light, hip-length raincoat. This wasn't the time or place for hesitation. Fate was in charge.

He slipped the knife up under Carlie's coat, under her blouse, and held the cold blade flat against the small of her back. Felt but didn't hear her inhale as she gasped when thunder clapped.

"This way," he said, guiding her with the knife. "Cross the street. We're going back the way we came."

"Who—?"

"Quiet for now," the killer said. "Or you'll be quiet forever."

They walked hurriedly back the way they'd come, then cut down a side street. Shoved along ahead of the killer, Carlie tried to think, to plan, but she couldn't concentrate her thoughts. She kept trying to turn her head so she could see his face.

"Look straight ahead and walk," he said. She'd dropped her umbrella when he'd grabbed her on the sidewalk. He let the wind snap his umbrella all the way open and held it so it kept both of them partially dry. A man and a woman, fond of each other, hurrying to get out of the weather.

"I wouldn't drop anything else," he said.

"I don't understand."

Sure you don't. "You might have a pocketful of bread crumbs."

"It's this way," she said, attempting to turn.

He propelled her straight ahead with the fist that held the knife.

"We're not going to your place," he said. "We're going to take a little walk instead. To my place."

She thought about the Smith and Wesson .38 revolver she had in her purse. The one that Jody had urged her to carry for protection.

If only she could reach it.

But she knew that any attempt to get into her purse, even if she pretended she was reaching for a tissue or some other harmless item, wouldn't be believed as innocent. She might lose the gun, and her only chance to survive.

She needed to choose her time carefully.

After another turn, and another, they were walking south again. Carlie thought so, anyway. They'd done so much maneuvering she was disoriented. She strained to catch an address so she could see which way the numbers ran. Finally she was able to do so. She was right. South.

The killer watched as her head turned this way and that. He knew what she was doing. She was searching for her guardian angels. Like real angels, they weren't there when they were needed.

"There's no one to help you," the killer said. "You're mine."

66

Quinn, sitting in the Lincoln to keep dry, didn't hear his cell phone chime over the noise of the storm. The phone was also vibrating. It slid over the seat cushion and he felt it like something alive on the side of his leg. He snatched it up and saw that the caller was Harold.

Quinn opened the line. "Whaddya got?"

"Sal's down and he's hurt!" Harold said. There was an urgency and pain in his voice that Quinn had never heard. He gave Quinn his precise location, said "Looks like he's been stabbed in the side. That bastard stabbed Sal."

"I'll call nine-eleven," Quinn said.

"I already called." There was a pause. "Quinn, I can't leave Sal. He goes in and out, and he needs somebody with him to stop the bleeding."

"Does the killer have Carlie?"

"Must have her. I cut through to where I was supposed to take over the tail, and the street was empty. Nothing but buckets of goddamn rain! The streets are like rivers. Not even the cabs are moving."

"Stay with Sal till EMS gets there," Quinn said. "I'll get back to you."

"Carlie and the killer," Harold said. "If he does have her and they're still slogging south, they'll be a block away from where Fedderman was supposed to pick up the tail. Not heading toward him, though. A block east. If the rain lets up, or lightning strikes at the right time, Feds might spot them crossing the intersection."

That was possible but a faint hope, in this weather, and with Dred Gant not knowing if there were more where Sal came from.

Fedderman was the last in the chain of angels that included Pearl and was supposed to see Carlie safely inside her apartment.

So where are they going now?

Quinn turned the Lincoln's wipers on at their fastest speed and drove south on Broadway. The storm sewers weren't up to the task, and water sat on the streets. The Lincoln left a wide V wake, like a boat.

Fedderman was wearing the light tan raincoat Penny had bought him. He stood beneath the flapping maroon awning that shielded the door of a closed corner bagel shop. The rain, being from time to time horizontal, had soaked the coat and, gradually, him.

Fedderman wasn't surprised by this violent outburst of nature. That was how these long spells of extreme weather usually ended, with a meteorological attack. As if the Gods of storms used lulls in the weather to build up their arsenals and became anxious to use them.

A sudden gust of wind that built and built fluttered

the awning and made it balloon out. Fedderman wondered if it would hold. Wondered if he was standing in a hurricane.

On an evening like this, he thought, Carlie Clark might have hailed a cab.

But there were no cabs. None that Fedderman could see, anyway. Only occasionally did a car or truck pass. The storm had also created premature darkness, and what few vehicles there were had their headlights glowing.

With one long burst of wind that came spiraling and bouncing down the avenue, half the awning flipped. Fedderman reopened his umbrella and it did what he expected—immediately turned inside out.

He angled it directly into the wind and it reversed itself and looked like an umbrella again. Keeping it tilted that way, he gladly accepted what little good it did.

I'll be dry again someday.

Shadowy movement down the block caught his attention. A man and woman, huddled close together and hurrying to get out of the rain. The man had his arm around the woman's waist, or maybe he was gripping the back of her belt, holding her tight. *So she wouldn't blow away.* They were both leaning into the wind as they crossed the intersection and passed out of sight.

Something seemed not quite right about them, but Fedderman couldn't put his finger on it. Maybe it was because they weren't moving in unconscious synchronization, the way lovers did when walking together. And the woman was slightly in front, braving the brunt of the storm.

Fedderman's iPhone buzzed and vibrated in his

pocket. He pulled it out and, seeing that the caller was
Quinn, ran his thumb across the screen sideways to
take the call. He pressed the phone to the side of his
head and turned his body so that ear was out of the
wind.

Quinn didn't wait for him to say hello.

"Feds?"

"Yeah."

"Listen close."

Harold was out of the game, riding in an ambulance
with the injured Sal.

Quinn contacted the trailing angel, Pearl, made a
slight detour, and picked her up on the way to get Fedderman. She shook herself, almost like a dog, glad to
be in the Lincoln and out of the rain.

"Sal gonna be okay?" she asked, when Quinn had
filled her in.

"Don't know for sure," Quinn said. "Harold will
make certain he gets good treatment."

"What'd he say, knife wound?"

Quinn nodded as he steered through water six
inches deep. "Stab wound in the side." Water from a
puddle like a lake sloshed over the windshield.

"Bastard!" Pearl said.

Quinn glanced over at her. "Were you about to break
for home?"

"No. Not yet. I had a hunch about tonight."

"The storm?"

"Maybe. Or something else."

Quinn knew what she meant. Hunters had a feeling

when the prey was running out of options and might turn on them. He'd read somewhere that tigers would sometimes double back and lie in wait for who or whatever was stalking them.

As soon as the Lincoln turned the corner where Fedderman was waiting, he saw it and rushed toward it. He opened the right back door and threw himself into the car. Shook himself much the way Pearl had.

"Wet," he said, unnecessarily.

Pearl looked over her shoulder at him. "You think?"

"They were walking south," Fedderman said. "Make a left here, and we should be able to catch up with them."

"Unless they went inside someplace," Pearl said.

"You think?"

Quinn braked slightly and pulled the Lincoln to the curb.

"There, up ahead," he said. "Looks like two people walking close together."

Pearl and Fedderman strained to see through the rain-distorted windshield.

"Could be," Fedderman said.

Pearl got close enough to the windshield to lick it and squinted her eyes to narrow her focus. Her nerves were dancing.

"Is," she said.

Quinn switched off the car's lights and drove slowly forward.

67

Running without lights, they followed from a distance in the Lincoln. Pearl continued leaning forward, peering out the windshield during rapid sweeps of the long wiper blades.

"You sure it's them?" Fedderman asked from the backseat, still sounding relieved to be in out of the rain. He was steaming and fogging up the windows.

"Not sure all the way," Quinn said.

"Maybe we should drive up there hard, pile out, and see what we got," Fedderman said.

"If it *is* Dred Gant and Carlie, that might get her killed," Pearl said.

"They're walking like they've got someplace in mind," Fedderman said.

"Not her apartment," Pearl said. "Too far south for that, and they're walking even farther south."

Fedderman looked at her. "His apartment?"

Quinn thought about it. "Maybe. He knows we don't know where it is."

"We sure of that?" Pearl asked.

"We'd have had him a long time ago if we'd known his address," Fedderman said.

"Don't be a smart-ass, Feds." Pearl was the one who'd scoured the Internet social networks and phone directories to see if there was a Dred Gant listed anywhere.

There was one. He was eighty-seven years old and African American.

"If he's got a place to go with her, he must have planned this out," Fedderman said.

"He couldn't have known a storm like this would hit."

"But there was a storm in the forecast."

"This is not the kind of guy who builds a plan around the weather forecast," Pearl said.

No one spoke for a while.

"Let me out so I can tail them on foot," Pearl said.

Quinn didn't answer, thinking.

"I can raise the hood on my raincoat," she said. "They'll never recognize me, never suspect I'd be walking up behind them. I can get close enough to make a positive identification."

"Without them identifying you?" Fedderman asked.

"Yes." She put a hand on Quinn's shoulder and squeezed. "We owe it to this girl, Quinn."

His knuckles were white on the steering wheel.

"That could be Jody," Pearl said.

Quinn didn't brake. He didn't want the red aura of brake lights to be seen. He let the Lincoln coast gradually to the curb, then switched off the interior lights so they wouldn't be noticed when Pearl exited the car.

"Don't lose your cell phone," he said.

Pearl nodded. "My lifeline."

He wished she had put it some other way as he watched her climb out of the car, into the storm. She opened her umbrella, which seemed pathetically inadequate.

They sat and watched her almost disappear into the darkness and swirling rain.

Her cell phone really is her lifeline.

"Whaddya think?" Fedderman asked.

"Gotta be his apartment," Quinn said, and steered the car slowly away from the curb.

It took him a minute or two to find the ideal speed not to gain ground, but to keep in sight what was unfolding in front of them.

Gant continued pushing Carlie along so they maintained a steady pace, even though from time to time she stumbled and almost fell. He had his right hand up the back of her jacket and must be holding a weapon—possibly a knife, since Sal had been stabbed—at the base of her spine. The barely discernible hooded figure behind them, keeping to shadows and building fronts, was only gradually moving closer. Then Pearl was lost to the mist.

The hurrying couple turned a corner. They walked along an avenue lined with four- or six-floor walkup apartments. Some of them had been rehabbed and converted to condos or co-ops. Quinn knew that if Gant was taking Carlie to one of the buildings on the west side of the street, it would back to a block of deserted warehouses and the river. There wouldn't be much escape territory in that direction, unless Gant owned a boat.

Gant and Carlie did turn left, took four stone steps up, and entered a rehabbed six-story building with distressed brick facing. Air conditioners jutted from some of the windows. Flanking the ornate wood door were identical concrete urns with geraniums in them. Lush vines grew up the side of the building the detectives could see. There were lights on in about half the windows.

Quinn steered the Lincoln to the curb and stared at the building, waiting.

A window became illuminated on the second floor, front. Another on the side of the building with the vines. Corner unit.

He backed the Lincoln to where it was less likely to be seen and draw suspicion, and switched off the engine so no exhaust would be visible.

Pearl, who'd been waiting for the car to park, piled into the passenger seat.

"Them," she said.

Quinn nodded. Fedderman continued staring at the building.

"What now?" she asked, checking the mechanism of her nine-millimeter Glock. She thought of it as her cliché gun, the one most fictional detectives favored. Fictional detectives knew their stuff. She was deadly with the Glock.

Her mouth was dry, her heartbeat elevated. She worked a round into the Glock's chamber. The oiled metal slide and click of the action gave her a certain satisfaction.

"I'll call Renz," Quinn said. "We need to do this hard and fast. And right."

68

Dred Gant locked his apartment door behind him. Then he took Carlie's purse and umbrella and tossed them onto the sofa. She watched the revolver come halfway out of her purse.

So much for self-defense.

He led Carlie to the bedroom and forced her to lie down on her stomach on the bed. Within a few seconds he produced a thick roll of duct tape. It was all happening so fast and so smoothly she couldn't gather her thoughts.

She gave a grunt and wheezing sound as he knelt with his knee on her ass and crisscrossed the tape between her wrists to bind her arms behind her. Then he ripped another piece of tape from the roll and fixed it firmly and roughly over her mouth. It crossed her mind that she'd have a hell of a bruise there; then she realized how trivial that was compared to her other problems. He made sure she was breathing freely through her nose, then reinforced the first rectangle of tape with a second, longer piece.

He did not tape her ankles. He wanted her to be able

to move. She felt him remove her shoes, though, and heard them thump on the carpet as he tossed them aside. She would have to be barefoot, if she tried to escape.

Better than in high heels.

Barefoot or not, she knew she wasn't going to tiptoe out of here. She was going to have to run like hell.

She knew she wouldn't get very far.

Carlie remained lying motionless on the bed. She could hear the killer moving around and knew it would be hopeless if she got up and attempted a dash to freedom. That could happen only in her mind, *and he knew that.* Her legs were trembling. Her heart was pounding so rapidly she could feel the vibration running through the mattress.

This is fear.

This is what the others felt.

The killer isn't going to change his mind. Nothing I can do will change it.

None of the others survived.

She saw the killer return to the bed. He was carrying a long black scarf, twirling it so the material became twisted and tubular. She thought he was preparing to strangle her, and she emitted a helpless moan. Her bladder released.

That seemed to amuse the killer. He smiled as if enjoying some interior joke and then put the scarf to use not as a garrote but as a blindfold. He yanked it tight and knotted it at the back of her head, pulling her hair in the process. Her eyes began to tear up behind the twisted material.

There was nothing around her now.

Nothing but blackness the rest of the way.

At least she still had her hearing. Some of it, anyway.

Carlie listened to the killer's footfalls on the old, squeaking floor. The sound was muffled because the scarf blindfold was also over her ears.

"I found the gun," he said, startling her with his closeness. "The one that was in your purse." He was leaning near enough that she could feel his breath on her face. "I appreciate it, but I prefer a knife."

Then he was still. Holding his breath.

He's acting as if something's wrong.

There was more muffled creaking, this time from upstairs. Or outside the apartment, on the stairs.

Something's going on!

Something's happening out there!

Suddenly his hands were beneath her arms, pinching flesh, and she was yanked painfully to her feet.

He half shoved, half dragged her across the floor. She banged a knee painfully on what was probably a door frame. Then they were crossing smooth tile; she could feel the rough grout line between each piece. The kitchen? A door opened. *Yeeowch!* Her toes thumped across a threshold.

Behind her, the door closed.

Cool rain on her face. *Jesus! We're outside!*

Where is he taking me?

And why?

None of the others survived. . . .

The killer shoved her into the maelstrom of wind and rain and lightning flashes. Thunder that made her ears ache.

Somebody please turn down the volume!

She couldn't get her mind around what was happening. Couldn't turn off inane thoughts.

Water trickled down beneath her tunic, like playful cool fingers, despite the warmth of the night.

Carlie decided the killer knew exactly where he was going. He had a destination, wasn't running wild to avoid the law.

He has an escape plan.

It includes me.

She was on a rough concrete walk, then on wet grass that tickled her toes.

Three, four, five, six steps.

Onto a hard surface, with a scattering of gravel on it that stung her bare feet.

She heard a scraping, creaking sound, then what sounded like something small and metallic tinkling on concrete. A few seconds later she was sure she heard a door squealing on its hinges. It must have opened inward, because she bumped her big toe on it as he pushed her inside wherever it was they'd gone,

The door shut behind her with a wooden, rattling sound, and the noise outside abated but didn't cease. She was no longer being rained on.

He led her through darkness, over what felt like a smooth concrete floor. Not a clean floor, though. Now and then something small and sharp hurt her tender soles. For several steps her right heel stamped and re-stamped something sticky.

The NYPD Tactical Unit (the department's version of SWAT) members had entered the killer's apartment building and were as swiftly and silently as possible leading the other occupants down the stairs and outside to safety. The noise of the storm helped to mask what was going on.

The unit was minutes away from using a battering ram and a flash-bang grenade to charge into Dred Gant's apartment and bring under their control whatever was happening inside.

Quinn and Pearl were poised in the building's small foyer, waiting for the bang of the grenade.

The go signal.

Everyone was counting on surprise to help them save Carlie Clark's life.

They were counting on surprise to end Dred Gant's.

There was sudden pressure behind Carlie's knees, and she was saved from collapsing to the floor by strong arms, and then forced to kneel.

It had all been one smooth, practiced motion. Through the twisted scarf material over her ears, she heard the muffled ripping sound she'd come to know was tape being yanked from its roll. Now her ankles were forced close together and taped in the same crisscross manner as her wrists. She would remember that sound for the rest of her life.

Like the other victims.

She was helpless. Her bare knees pressed against the hard concrete felt bruised. They burned with pain. She couldn't move, couldn't see, couldn't make a sound that would be heard ten feet away, couldn't herself hear if someone else made such a sound.

The only sound she *could* hear, like a distant, muffled drumbeat, was the pulsing rush of her blood.

She knelt in darkness.

The last of the building's occupants, an elderly man and woman, both with snow-white hair and poker faces, were led outside rapidly and almost soundlessly by the tactical team.

Quinn wondered if all the armed force was necessary. There was no history of the Lady Liberty Killer using a gun, or even carrying one. Helen the profiler had said he might well choose another way to go, a leap from a high window, or a dash in front of a vehicle or beneath the wheels of a train.

Or he might deliberately draw gunfire.

Suicide by cop? Always possible. Even with this killer.

Better too much force than not enough.

One of the two Tactical Unit guys in the foyer looked sternly at Quinn and motioned that he and his partner were going up the stairs first. That made sense, since they were experts at this and were protected by Kevlar body armor.

Quinn didn't respond.

Probably the Tac Unit guy had been warned that what made sense to other people didn't always make sense to Quinn.

And Pearl?

Who the hell knew what Pearl was going to do?

69

The killer used his knife to pry an old and rusty hasp from rotted wood. Screws and the part of the hasp that held the padlock dropped to the floor.

Gant used his foot to slide aside the lock and what was left of the hasp. He was standing before a row of storage units lining the back wall of a deserted warehouse. The units all had oversized doors that were six feet square, with walls rising eight feet. Both the common walls and the doors of the units were made up of vertical wooden slats. Each slat was about four inches wide, and the spaces between the slats were about an inch.

Carlie's body tensed as she heard the faint sounds of the killer's approach. He hoisted her halfway to her feet and carried her into the storage unit he'd opened. He forced her to kneel again, in a back corner of the unit. When she'd settled down, he moved back to crouch alongside her against the brick wall. Moisture had worked its way between the bricks, and they smelled of damp mortar and the implacable passage of time. Carlie and the killer were in the shadows.

If they were quiet, they might be missed by anyone entering the warehouse.

But if they *were* noticed . . .

He removed from his pocket the revolver that had been in Carrie Clark's purse.

The one she'd been urged to carry for protection.

The Tactical Unit commander, a unibrowed lieutenant named Springer, gave the signal, and two hefty men hoisted the battering ram, swung it backward, forward, and immediately smashed the door open. Hardware flew and the damaged door bounced off the wall.

The tech guy nearest to the opened door tossed the grenade inside and it exploded with an immediate blast that slammed Quinn's eardrums with pain. He saw that most of the Tactical Unit had their mouths open to avoid hearing loss from the concussion.

Thanks for telling us.

All of this within a few seconds, because the Tac guys were on their way inside to take advantage of the approximately five seconds before the apartment's occupants shook off their disorientation and paralysis.

Quinn and Pearl followed them in, and stood listening while the Tac Unit dashed throughout the apartment, yelling as they cleared each room. They were strength and controlled fury in action.

The apartment was unoccupied.

As soon as Quinn realized that, he dashed down the hall to the kitchen and what was a side door to the passageway to the next block. Without a word exchanged, he knew Pearl was following. He could feel her behind him, off his right hip.

Into the wind and rain they went, Pearl on his heels. Quinn figured they were ahead of the Tac team, but not by much.

No sign of Dred Gant or Carlie.

Quinn stood still for a few seconds, as if consulting the maelstrom.

What would he do if he were Gant? If he held a terrified, compliant woman who could be used as a hostage?

He wouldn't want to surrender that final card to play.

Almost directly across the deserted street, what appeared to be an abandoned warehouse loomed.

Quinn jogged toward the sprawling brick building. The Tac Unit leader wouldn't yell for him to stop. This wasn't the time or place to make any kind of noise.

Quinn was braced for a bullet as he approached the warehouse, counting on the killer being addled, unsure of how to cope with his hostage and his rapidly deteriorating situation.

Pearl moved up and was suddenly alongside him, nudging him hard in the ribs.

Quinn looked where she was pointing. One of the series of wide doors to the warehouse was open a few inches. They moved toward it.

On the soaked concrete in front of the door lay a rusty hasp and padlock. The hasp had been yanked from the rotten wood, or possibly pried away with a knife.

To lose momentum was to increase danger. Quinn acted.

He pushed Pearl away with one hand while with the other he slowly opened the old wooden door. The rain provided enough lubricant to keep the hinges from squealing. At the edges of his vision, he was aware of the Tactical Unit taking up positions around the warehouse.

Probably Dred Gant was inside.

Definitely, if he was in there, he was going to leave dead or in police custody.

His old police special at his side, Quinn eased around the partly opened door, into the warehouse.

Into complete darkness.

Then a crash and blink of illumination. There were dirt-marred skylights that provided some clarity when lightning flashed. Breaks and cracks in the roof, and in some of the glass panes, allowed slender trickles of water to reach the floor and puddle with a faint splashing sound.

Quinn got away from the door and moved behind a steel supporting beam. It wouldn't provide much protection from gunfire, but some.

There were few places to hide in the warehouse. The only cover appeared to be a row of slatted storage compartments lined along the back wall. Even during lightning flashes, it was difficult to see what—if anything—was inside them.

Another flash, brilliant and flickering. Quinn knew that the Tac team was moving closer, silently fanning out in the front part of the building. They would soon be inside.

In one of the lockers close to the midpoint of the back wall, the killer checked to make sure Carlie's bonds and gag were firm. Then he settled back in the darkest corner of the wooden structure.

He crouched low, with his hands in a prayer position, holding the revolver as if it were a religious icon, and waited for Quinn.

The situation was, for the moment, a standoff. Quinn, Pearl, and the Tactical Unit didn't know exactly where Gant was—or even if he was actually in the building. With each lightning flash they tried to learn more, but nothing changed between flashes. The rain outside and the heat held by the warehouse caused the vast space to mist up near the skylights. A similar mist began to rise from the damp concrete floor. Soon it would be difficult for the Tac team to see a clear target.

With the life of a hostage in the balance, they couldn't take chances.

After the mad rush through the night to the warehouse, Dred Gant was recovering his perspective.

Now he began to realize his situation wasn't hopeless. He could walk out of here with the revolver's barrel in Carlie's ear. There would be an opportunity to talk to the press, who would no doubt be gathering like vultures anticipating carrion. He could tell them who he was, what he was, what they were.

Then he, and no one else, would mete out life or death.

Flashlights winked on in the thickening mist, no doubt held by cowards hiding behind concrete pillars or steel supporting beams. Trying to draw a shot so they could locate his position. To see if they could take him out with a clear, clean shot that didn't endanger Carlie. Let the fools search. The killer didn't think the feeble beams of light would penetrate the mist and darkness so that they could find him.

He had the whip hand here.

The Tac Unit commander, Springer, used a flash of lightning to imprint his surroundings in his mind. He then made his way over to where Quinn crouched with Pearl behind a rusty steel support.

"Those wooden storage bins," Springer said. "Count nine units over from the left side, and that's probably where he is."

"What makes you think so?"

"One of my guys, watching through his night scope, saw the glitter of an eye."

Quinn glanced over at the barely visible dark form of the man. "You're kidding?"

"No. The glitter of a human eye is quite distinctive."

"But whose eye—"

Quinn's words caught in his throat as he saw movement out ahead of him.

Pearl had straightened up. She was holding a flashlight, moving slowly toward the storage bin the Tac commander had pointed out.

"Where the hell—" Quinn began, but Springer gripped his arm.

"No, no!" he whispered. "Don't do anything to draw attention to her."

"I want to draw attention *away* from her!" Quinn said. "If he shoots—"

"We'll have his position and he'll be dead within seconds." Springer gave a grim smile. "Besides, I think she has something in mind."

"Like getting herself killed?"

"Like exchanging hostages."

"Why would she want to do that?"

"To provide opportunity so we—or she—can take him down."

"And why would she think he'd even let her get close?"

"He knows if he shoots her, he's dead immediately."

"That's what he wants."

"Not that way. And only at the time and place of his own choosing. And something else. Who do you think the killer really wants the most?"

"Pearl," Quinn said through clenched teeth.

"And you," Springer said. "He'd love to have both of you. All he needs is for you to be dumb enough to go after Pearl."

"He's already got Carlie."

"Could be she's already dead," Springer said. "Either way, in the killer's mind, you and Pearl are unfinished business."

"Maybe we're giving the sick asshole too much credit," Quinn said. "You think he's got a plan. Maybe he doesn't even have a gun."

Springer shrugged. "Maybe he's got both."

70

Dred Gant peered out between the vertical wooden slats of the storage compartment's door. The flashlight beams didn't concern him right now. They were too wan and distant for their light to make its way through the mist and reveal his position.

One of the light beams seemed to be moving slowly and directly toward where he crouched. It wasn't very bright, and it played about inaccurately.

But sooner or later it always returned to its course, toward where Dred hid in darkness with his heart pounding out the rhythm of his fear.

This was beginning to *feel* very wrong.

He'd experienced this uneasy feeling before, and it had been right. In that instance he'd been beaten half to death by a truck driver outside of Slidell, Louisiana.

The killer squinted. He could see a form now behind the approaching flashlight beam.

Pearl held her Glock handgun pressed flat against her thigh in one hand. In the other hand, extended out about waist high, was her flashlight. She kept her eyes focused straight ahead. She could barely make out the row of crude wooden storage cubicles. The ninth from the left looked like the others, dark areas above stark vertical slats, with occasional diagonal boards to provide rigidity. She swallowed her terror, made one foot follow the other, and kept walking in the same direction, toward the suspected storage bin, feeling and hearing the gritty concrete floor beneath her leather soles.

Pearl was getting close now. The mist became electric. And there was junk all over the floor. Not large junk, but small cuts of wood, metal pieces, glass shards. The detritus of years.

She continued her slow walk toward what might be her death. She knew Quinn was behind her, and drew comfort from that. The Tactical Unit was supposed to be back there in the dark, sharpshooters who could hit a gnat's eye, looking after her, ready to squeeze the trigger to save her life.

She thought that should give her more comfort than she felt.

A small hard object, maybe a screw or a nail lying on its side, jabbed into the thin sole of her right shoe.

Moving through darkness, except when lightning flashed, was grating on her nerves. She could still back out of this, switch off her flashlight and make her way through the dark to the warehouse door. She could leave Carlie Clark and her dilemma to be solved by someone else. There were ways. Ways to do most anything.

She stubbed her toe on something, lowered the

flashlight beam a few feet, and saw that she'd kicked what looked like a car's old shock absorber.

Her toe still throbbed. She raised the flashlight high, higher, so its beam was aimed at more of a downward angle, spread wider to illuminate the stained and littered concrete floor ahead of her.

The hell with this, Quinn thought.

Immediately after a lightning strike illuminated the warehouse, and darkness closed back in, he moved away from Springer, off to the side in the shadows, nearer to Pearl.

He heard Springer's harsh whisper. Couldn't make out what he'd said. Didn't try.

In the storage locker, his heart hammering, the killer watched the female form approaching through the mist. He forgot everything else and pressed his forehead hard against the wooden door so he could see between the slats. He was a nine-year-old boy in a Missouri outhouse. He could hear the buzz of insects in the night, smell the human excrement, see between the slats. . . .

The woman continued to advance on him in silhouette, yet with ominous substance. Her long raincoat draped her form gracefully. The wind and rain had spiked up her hair. In her hand she held a lamp raised high.

The wretched refuse . . .

His heartbeat was deafening. His rushing blood roared.

I killed her. She's dead. I killed her. She's dead.

I must be hallucinating! But she's so real!

The woman continued her relentless approach. There was no doubt now where she was going.

Toward me!

She has to be killed again!

No one must stop me from doing that! No one!

The killer threw the slat door open and broke from the storage shed. He was screaming, shrieking. The echoing din was startling.

Five feet away from him, still and silent in the darkness, Quinn aimed his police special revolver and squeezed off three rapid rounds. In the flashes of gunfire he could see Pearl's startled pale face.

He could also see Gant, still alive, raising his gun to shoot and kill Pearl.

Quinn had to save Pearl—*now!*

All in a few long seconds: Quinn was in the suspended time of action and danger. He saw Pearl raise her Glock to fire back at Gant. *She must think he's the one who got off the earlier shots.* Quinn fired again at Gant. Pearl was blasting away with the Glock. Gunfire erupted and echoed like grounded thunder.

Gant stood suspended in a brief but violent dance, as if worked like a puppet by the impact of bullets. Bursts of light flashed from gun barrels. There was a terrible beauty to it, almost like a fireworks display.

All in a few long seconds.

Dred Gant saw Lady Liberty, her torch held high, lift her free arm. In her free hand was a gun.

Its muzzle flash was the last thing he saw.

* * *

The Lady Liberty Killer died instantly. He'd been shot twice in the head, once in the throat, and once, with a nine-millimeter Glock, in the heart.

The Tactical Unit had been ordered to aim above waist level. Not a bullet had come within two feet of Carlie Clark, where she was safely bound and low on the concrete floor.

Pearl and a female Tac Unit sniper removed the scarf and tape from Carlie's eyes and mouth, then freed her of her bonds. EMS paramedics covered her with a blanket and wheeled her on a gurney to an ambulance that would take her to a hospital for examination.

Quinn held Pearl tight to him. She was unharmed but trembling violently. She found one of his hands with her own and squeezed.

Gradually, the trembling subsided.

He reluctantly turned her over to one of the paramedics, who assured Quinn she was physically all right but in shock. At the urging of Quinn and the paramedic, Pearl climbed into the back of the ambulance where she might help tend to Carlie. That seemed to comfort both women. It sure as hell comforted Quinn.

When the ambulance had departed, he walked back into the warehouse.

The killer's body lay untended in a pool of blood, pointedly ignored. Quinn saw that Gant had been armed with a revolver. It lay about ten feet from his right hand, but a blood pattern on the floor indicated that it had been kicked there by one of the cops before the killer's death had been established beyond doubt.

Leaving the body where it was, for the police photographer, wasn't taking any kind of risk. In addition to
the shots to his throat and heart, Dred Gant had a bullet
hole in his forehead, and another round had penetrated
his right eye. One of the hollow point bullets had taken
off most of the back of his head. Brain matter was visible on the floor.

As he was leaving, as a matter of formality, Quinn
knelt to make certain the Lady Liberty Killer was
dead.

EPILOGUE

The storm that had so violently ended the heat wave and drought in New York moved on, but another followed. It formed over the western plains, caused major damage in Kansas, then rampaged north by northeast, spawning tornados as it went.

In Bland County, Missouri, its winds banged and splintered the shutters of an old house at the end of a long dirt road and surrounded by a grassless, pitted yard. The wind found its way through the front door, slamming it open and shut, as if an unwanted guest couldn't make up his mind. It gathered beneath the eaves and lifted the roof. Dropped it back down. Lifted it again. Shingles fluttered and flew like startled black-birds into the storm. The back wall swayed and, with a slight break in the wind, fell inward. The rest of the house, without the support of roof or back wall, simply collapsed in on itself.

The storm sorted through the wreckage, hurling it this way and that, as if in a mad selective process.

And then moved on.